SEX

DEATH

DREAM

TALK

Richard Sanders

To Laurie with love.
I'd be dead without you.

We know nothing and can know
nothing
but
the dance, to dance to a measure
contrapuntally,
Satyrically, the tragic foot.

—William Carlos Williams,
Paterson

CHAPTER 1

HELLZAPOPPIN'

Screams Along The Sky

There were no eyewitnesses to the murder, just earwitnesses. The people who lived just north of Dominicus Park all reported the same thing—terrifying, drawn out, phantom-human screams that cut through the pre-midnight stillness of the cold November night. Eleven calls were made to 911 in the first minute alone. No one could see what was happening but they all said the cries were coming from the same place, the part of the park that was walled off from view by a grove of cypresses and pines. And all the callers stressed the horror of the noise. It sounded like a head-back howl, the thunder of pain that comes straight from the rear of the throat, a trapped-animal jungle shriek, the sound of a demon screaming for its eternal life.

Suffolk County police units responded by midnight. There was no doubt about the source of the sound. They found the body of an elderly, large-framed African-American man in the middle of the grove, bathed in so much blood it looked as if the ground itself was bleeding. No ID, no wallet. From the Salvation Army style of his clothes, he could've been homeless. He'd been stabbed multiple times, though the fatal wound had to have been the vicious slash that sliced into his heart after splitting his chest open from nipple to nipple. He was a barrel-chested man, and after he'd fallen on his back, the blood from the gash had flowed back toward his face, so that by the time the police found him his head was a mask of congealed red.

A bad way to go. Still, for those who heard them, it was the death cries that stayed lodged in the spine. They were haunting and profoundly strange, agony wails that spiraled up from the earth and echoed along the sky. *As soon as I heard those screams*, one woman said, *I knew I'd be living that night for the rest of my life.*

I remember reading those words, remember thinking her quote would have to be used in the story. I remember the words because the murdered man turned out not to be some homeless, anonymous victim.
Based on the missing person's report his daughter filed the next day, the police quickly determined that he was Isaiah Robonnet, one of the country's most fabled folk artists.

I didn't know much about him or his work at the time, but as a top editor at *Real Story*, I knew Robonnet was good material. One of 13 kids, raised in and around New Orleans. Confined to institutions for the feeble minded (a term much used back in the day) most of his childhood. Became a self-taught painter later in life, known for his incredible visionary canvases. Emerged as one of the symbols of New Orleans' post-Katrina renaissance.

And now he was dead, catching some nasty and obsessive knifework in the middle of a suburban park in Long Island, N.Y. I assigned reporters to cover the killing; I edited the posts that ran on the website and the larger story that ran in the magazine. Robonnet had been visiting his daughter's house on the north shore of Nassau County that night and he'd gone out for a drive. How and/or why did he end up maybe 50 miles away, slaughtered in a small Suffolk County town where no one knew him? I just wanted to know. I thought it would make a good story and I just wanted to know.

I had no idea where my curiosity was going to lead.

Not that I'd gone all conspiracy-theory crazy about the crime. Nothing like that. It's just that, long after the case had gone cold, after the questions seemed to fade, Robonnet's death stayed in the back of my mind.

An example: The following spring, about a half year after the still unsolved killing, I was visiting friends on the north fork of eastern Long Island. Heading back to the city I hit a very bad patch of traffic on the LIE, a real hell-snarl of delays, and I figured enough with this, I'll find another way to get home. As I was getting off the next exit, ranging for the Northern State, I saw a sign that said *Deer Cross 4 miles*. Why did Deer Cross sound familiar? Right— that's where Dominicus Park was, that's where Isaiah Robonnet had died. I found myself thinking, what's the rush, I'd like to see the place where it happened. I'd like to see where those terrible screams were heard.

The sun was going down by the time I parked the car and located the grove. Just as described—a semicircle of rich-smelling cypress and pine, hidden from the view of any of the nearby houses. Pretty unremarkable, except for the old Hispanic-looking woman who was kneeling on the ground, digging holes in the dirt. She had gray close cropped Gertrude Stein hair and was wearing a dark dress, a dark shawl and a dark pair of Rockports. She was working the ground with a gardener's hand spade, and whatever she was digging up, she was dropping it in one of those green reusable Stop & Shop bags.

She looked worried when she saw me approaching and she started to make a few preparatory getting-up moves. I raised my right hand shoulder high, fingers extended, open palm facing her. The *abhaya mudra*. But you don't have to be Buddhist to recognize the universal symbol for *no fear*.

She stopped moving but stayed wary.

I asked what she was doing.

Her English was as rough as my Spanish. *Los dedos*, she said.

Fingers? Toes? I didn't get it.

Los dedos de la mano.

Fingers. The digits of the hand. But I still didn't know what she was talking about.

Seeing the confusion on my face, she showed me the inside of her bag. It was filled with pieces of some kind of root—gnarled and grubby and covered with prickly dirt-caked hair. Yes, they looked just like chopped-off fingers.

They were instantly creepy, instantly dreamlike and weird. I asked what they were for. What was growing in this once blood-soaked dirt? Just looking at the stuff inside the bag made me feel that the ground beneath us was rising and falling with breaths.

The old woman wasn't going to give me any

more answers. Either she didn't know how or she didn't want to. I was guessing mostly the latter, because she was getting more nervous the longer I stood there. A few seconds later she tossed the spade in the bag,
stood herself up, gave me an under-the-brow stare and took off.

My chest went tight as I watched her walk away. It was like the ground could breathe but I couldn't. There was just something so strange about the whole scene—I think that's why my lungs started seizing up. It was like the silent echo of some sorrowful cry had worked its way inside my chest that day, and what I didn't realize at the time was that it would stay steeped inside me for a long, long time to come.

The Flat Earth Theory

But a year and half would go by before the murder
jumped back into the front of my mind. People
stopped talking about Robonnet in the meantime. The
circumstances of his death were never explained, the
killer was never caught. Other stories came along and
took me away. My memory of the park, the strange
old lady with her bag of handy roots—it all dropped
into the background. Life and its headlines went on.

Then one June night I ended up going to a
charity benefit at Milk Studios with one of my
coworkers, a miracle-working reporter named
Kumiko Davis. She dragged me along because we
used to go out together, although our relationship has
since evolved into friendship. Kumiko, in fact, is
married now, and whatever her husband's vices and
virtues, he doesn't share her passion for art. So the
idea of going to see something called *The Flat Earth
Theory, Part Six*, a piece of performance art put on by
a group called HIPS (Hidden In Plain Sight), didn't
rate all that high with him. Me neither, but I went
along anyway. Maybe I'd meet somebody.

Kumiko and I grabbed a cab from the *Real Story*
offices to West 15th, took the freight elevator up and
found out that the large loft-like spaces of Milk
Studios had been taken over by dozens of artistes in
feathered devil masks and black dance sweats who
were singing and shouting and swinging multicolored

hula hoops around their waists. A few hundred other people were also on hand—the innocent bystanders who served as spectators—but all attention went to the performers. They were roaming through the rooms in some kind of hellzapoppin' frenzy, telling stories that seemed to be about some apocalyptic class warfare that had broken out in the United States and accompanying themselves with a grab bag of kazoos, slide whistles, New Year's noisemakers, tambourines, triangles and tin drums.

Didn't care much for the story, but I liked the music part of it. Ditto for the feathered devil masks and the synchronized swing of the hula hoops. Kumiko told me HIPS was known for both—aside from Hidden In Plain Sight, the group's name was meant to be associated with the hoops.

I'm no expert, but it looked to me like HIPS was straddling that perfect point between bullshit and beauty.

Waiters were serving amber-colored cocktails in stemless martini glasses. Kumiko took one. I got a Diet Coke at the bar. We checked out the crowd together—lots of stiletto heels, limited edition sneakers. They were mostly the kind of people you never see on the streets during the day so you have to rightfully assume they get Airbussed in from Europe every night just to go to parties like this.

Kumiko saw an art critic she wanted to talk to and went off. I took the opposite direction, looking for love or at least a reasonable facsimile of it. Have to say I was getting less impressed with *The Flat Earth Theory, Part Six* as I made the rounds. At one point the performers were screaming something about a showdown at a hospital ER where *the soulful wounded and the street urchins were severely maimed.* What kind of talk was this? Who uses words like *street urchins* any more? And *maimed*? Who the fuck gets *maimed* these days?

As I walked into another room the HIPSters suddenly broke into a full-throated song with aria-like language. I thought it was Italian. But it could've been Spanish.

I asked an attractive, dark-eyed woman standing next to me.

She smiled. Yes, she said, it was most definitely Italian.

Do you speak it?

Over the next five minutes or so, I found out that not only did she speak Italian, but:

1) She hated the language. She thought it was a completely useless, fruity, overrated, consonant– ridden way of speaking.

2) She hated the country. She thought Italy was one of the most backward, corrupt, washed-up and smelly pieces of inhabitable land you could possibly find.

3) She hated Italian food.

4) She hated Italian people.

Her name, by the way, was Gina Madaloni.

It takes a special gift, I think, to meet someone like that.

I was moving away from her at a pretty good clip and had just made it back into another room when I saw Kumiko. She was talking with a striking black woman with a big frizzed-out halo of an Afro and unusually wide turquoise blue eyes. Kumiko waved at me and waved me over. It was like she's been looking for me.

I worked my way through the crowd—which as becoming more and more glazed with a coating of willed indifference—and gave a wide berth to the hula hoopers. Tough going, but it was easy to keep

Kumiko and her friend in sight. Everything about the stranger stood out, her eyes, her hair, her Persian blue caftan, her jade and aquamarine necklace.

I got to Kumiko. She made the intros.

"Quinn McShane," she said, "Genesis Robonnet."

Kumiko looked at me looking at her, all the questions in my eyes.

"That's right," she said. "Isaiah Robonnet's daughter."

>>>>>>

Because You Killed A Man

It made sense. Kumiko had been the lead reporter on
the murder story and she'd done a long sit-down
interview with Genesis. They both recognized each
other tonight as soon as they saw each other.

"I was telling her about you," said Kumiko.
"She wanted to meet you."

Nice.

The three of us talked about the exhibit or the
show or whatever it was that was unfolding around us
while I did my best to stare at her without looking like
I was staring. She was hands-down beautiful. Her
skin had the deep, burnished color of an antique
copper coin, and she showed an attitude of assurance
and easy confidence that was a total turn-on for me.
And while the caftan flowed loosely around her body,
its thin, silky material gave me the distinct impression
that she wasn't wearing a whole lot of anything else
underneath.

Her eyes, though, her eyes were something else.
The contrast between their turquoise and her brown
skin was amazing, really, but they were too wide. Her
eyes had too much size for her face. They looked like
they might've been naturally wide at one time, but
something—too much work, maybe—had stretched
them even wider.

Another thing about her eyes—there was a kind
of distance to them, a kind of diamond chill. You

wouldn't pick up on it from the way she was talking or acting, but if you looked into her eyes long enough, like I was, you'd catch the hint of the freeze. You'd get the feeling that under the right circumstances, or the wrong ones, this woman could put out a fire with a single stare.

We all talked for about 10 minutes, hitting it off, when Kumiko saw someone else she just had to say hello to and she excused herself. "You two can carry on, can't you?"

I'm thinking, is Kumiko trying to hook us up?

Genesis was also drinking one of those amber-juiced cocktails. She sipped at it now, looking at me, waiting.

Get right into it. Go straight for the heart.

"I'm sorry about your father," I said. "I'm sorry it's gone so long without any answers."

Her face never moved. I remember. She lowered the glass and kept looking at me and her face never moved at all.

"Kumiko was telling me about your background," she finally said. "I wanted to hear more."

"You mean your father's story? I was in charge?"

"Before that. Well before that. You used to work as an investigator?"

Oh that. "Before I got into the journalism racket, yeah, I had a license."

"What kind of work?"

"Everything. Insurance fraud, identity theft. Any kind of cheating, sexual, financial, whatever. Recovering stolen property. But mostly finding missing children. That was my specialty."

Another amber sip. "Were you good?"

"Most times."

"But it ended."

"It ended."

"Because you killed a man." Just like that.

"That's what happened."

"Kumiko told me. You don't have to talk about it."

"Nothing to hide. I went on a long booze and meth rampage and I ended up with a manslaughter conviction. I used the time to get straight."

She nodded and finished her drink, then held the glass raised in the air like she expected someone to abruptly materialize and take it from her.

And someone did. A waiter appeared out of nowhere, placed the glass on his tray and disappeared into the wait-staff ether.

Genesis glanced at the HIPS performers, who were still hula hooping away while shouting something about the blood running from the Thanksgiving turkey.

"This working for you yet?" she said.

I shrugged. "Still half good, half-assed."

"Do you understand it?"

"I don't know much about art. I don't even know what I *don't* like. It keeps changing."

She smiled, I remember that. She smiled and then she did something odd with her body. She kind of bicycled her shoulders up and down under her caftan. I couldn't tell if the gesture was meant to be seductive, or of her arms were just getting tired and she was trying to get the circulation going.

"Plans for tonight?" she said. "Anything special?"

"Not really."

"Why don't you come with me?" She took a phone out. "I have a car waiting."

Just like that.

"Why not? Just let me tell Kumiko."

"What it is," she said, "I'd like to talk to you. I'd like to talk some more."

Strange thing was, she sounded almost apologetic about it. It was like she'd been going around for months telling herself she *didn't* want to talk to me, even though she didn't know me, and now she'd decided she was wrong.

Making My Bones

She had a car waiting all right—a two-tone Rolls-Royce Corniche, navy blue on top and silver on the bottom. I don't know what year it was but it was vintage, and so was the driver who came complete with an undertaker's black suit. Yes, I was impressed.

We got in the backseat, sliding our fannies over soft bull-hide leather. With no crowd around now, I could smell her perfume. I liked it, though it was one strong and even aggressive scent.

She pressed a button. The smoked glass of a privacy panel rose to block us from the driver's view. "Tell me more about the investigation work," she said.

I told her. I talked about studying journalism at NYU but eventually switching to criminal justice at John Jay, getting a job at an agency on Long Island, setting out to make my bones. I was just going into my marriage and the birth of my daughter when I saw the horizontal stream of lights outside. The Rolls' side windows were tinted but I could pick out the yellow lamps stringing the inside of the Midtown Tunnel. Like my story, we were heading for Long Island.

I was an ambitious guy, I told her, anxious to top-dog the agency and give my family the best. I pushed myself hard, taking on every case I possibly could and then what the hell even a few more. I never said no.

Course, there was a bit of a price to pay. I started to do a lot of leaning on meth to keep up with my own demand. I'd been tasting crystal since I was a teen but now I was racking up heavy usage points, shooting at least a couple of spoons a day toward the end and naturally downing gallons of booze at night to bring myself back to earth. I was a mess, and I was absolutely the last to know it.

Like I was telling Genesis, I specialized in locating missing kids. My final case, I was hired to track down this numbnuts junkie shithead who'd been beating up on his girlfriend and then snatched her year-old baby to blackmail her into staying with him. I found the guy. He pulled a gun on me and I got it away from him and I could've ended things right then and there in a peaceful and reasonable manner, but I didn't. I shot him. The meth and alcohol madness had steamrolled to such a point that I hated him almost as much as I hated myself and I wanted to do some kind of fatal damage to one of us if not both of us, so I selected a spot just between his need-a-trim eyebrows and put a bullet in his brain.

For a long time after I honestly believed that I'd gotten the worst of it. The guy, sure, he was dead, but I was still around and I *knew* how much I'd destroyed. I couldn't use death as an excuse—I *knew* what I'd lost. I'd lost my wife and my daughter, my license and my job. I'd killed off that whole part of my life.

It wasn't until I was sitting in a cell upstate, subsisting on a daily diet of bile and self-pity, that I realized what a break I'd been given. I could've been tried for murder. Tried and I think easily convicted. But I wasn't. The woman who'd hired me lied and testified that I'd shot the guy in self-defense. Instead of getting put away for murder, I did a much shorter ride on manslaughter. It was almost a reprieve.

That's when I decided to turn my shit around and turn my life over. I started going to AA, and from there I got involved in Buddhist meditation. I might've been in prison, but I could try to be delivered into the freedom of God.

"Toward the end of my time," I said, "a reporter from *Real Story* got in touch with me. They were doing a story on meditation and prisoner rehabilitation and they wanted to talk. I told the reporter okay, but could I write my own story? Her name was Kumiko Davis, and eventually she got me a job at the magazine. Which is how I eventually became an editor. Which I guess is how I ended up in the backseat of your car."

Genesis was nodding again. That was the only reaction she showed to my story. Nodding, absorbing, processing.

"Can I ask a question?" she said.

"Like I told you, nothing to hide."

"When you were an investigator, was everything done on the up-and-up?"

"The up-and-up?"

"Was everything done within the letter of the law?"

I broke out laughing. "Are you kidding?"

No, she wasn't. She was wintertime serious. My laughter, in fact, seemed to be pissing her off.

Need a comeback.

"I know why you're asking," I said. "I think I know what these questions are about?"

"Do you?"

"You want me to look into your father's death. You want me to find out who killed him, and if I have to bend a few laws to do it, that's okay."

She smiled but didn't say anything. She smiled and looked off in the distance, or in as much distance as you could find in the backseat of a Rolls-Royce Corniche. No nodding this time, but she was definitely thinking of something.

Then she suddenly leaned into me and slid her hand over my crotch, giving me the fastest, smoothest erection I ever had. A moment later her jade and aquamarine necklace was draped over my legs and she was sliding her tongue along the line of nerves on the underside of my cock.

This was *not* what I expected.

She took me in her mouth and she kept me there for the next five, 10, 147 minutes, I don't know, all I know was that it was happening against all odds somewhere in the middle of the LIE. She never let me get carried away, but I seriously have to say that the angels of sex were hitting some pretty powerful high C's on their trumpets.

Then she lifted her head, examined the light streaks outside the car's tinted windows, and promptly sat up.

"We're home," she said.

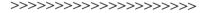

CHAPTER 2

THE SECRET HISTORY WILL BE TOLD

Signs And Revelations

We had to be deep in the center of Great Gatsbyland.
The car was pulling into the cobblestoned, half-
circular driveway of an ancient Colonial, a sweeping,
three-story house that could've been built as a
museum for dreams.

A dark-suited weightlifter met Genesis at the
door and led us inside a gigantic foyer. This entryway
was decorated with black marble and white spider
lilies and its walls were so tall it could've easily
hosted a handball tournament.

Other staffers quickly showed up, checking in
with Genesis and reporting that all was well. They
were all men, all polite and officious, all bone-crusher
big. And they were all packing guns—I could see the
bulges under their mortician-perfect suits.

I noticed a few other things as well: The
security cameras outside. The NASA quality keypad
just inside the door. The tiny motion detector disks
embedded in
the marble.

Wild guess: Genesis Robonnet was kinda
serious about her possessions.

I was trying to be cool about it, just taking it all
in. I didn't pay attention to the guys' bulges, and they
didn't pay attention to mine.

Yes, it was still there. Considering what had
been going on in the car, how could it not be?

And frankly, after what had happened in the backseat, I was thinking Genesis would be taking me to a bedroom without too much delay. But she seemed to have something else in mind.

"I want to show you something," she said in an all business tone, grabbing my hand and leading me into the great room of the house.

I could barely see the other side. The room was a looming ocean of oriental carpets, bronze lamps, alabaster busts, Nepalese silk, Genoan velvet, a grand staircase made of Carrara marble and enough fresh flowers to stock a billionaire's wake.

She took me around the staircase to a door behind the steps, an elevator built into the carriage. The door opened at the push of a button. Dark oak paneling, soft concealed lights, another military grade keypad. She pressed a combination and the door closed.

We're taking the express up? Well, no, because the elevator only traveled two levels, this one and one below.

We started the slow drop, Genesis not saying a thing, the whole situation giving off a kind of sepulchral vibe. Not so pleasant.

Ten seconds later the ride stopped. Nothing happened until Genesis typed a different combination into the keypad. Then the door slid open, and I got hit by a tidal wave.

I'd seen Robonnet's paintings before, but only in reproductions. I'd never stood in front of them in the flesh—I had no way to prepare for the rush of clotted delirium that swept over me when I stepped out of the elevator. I was in a room filled with canvases that were dense and dazzling and ghostly all at the same time, paintings that were crazy and color-lush and as crowded with words and images as Times Square on the world's final New Year's Eve.

We were in a subterranean gallery, long white walls with a row of backless sofas in the middle, where maybe a few dozen people could sit and look at the art. Not me. I couldn't even stand still. I had to keep moving and looking. I was lost in the forest of the paintings, melting in a drug buzz trance.

I had to keep looking at the titles, the names painted on the canvases:

Did We Know When We Lived In Paradise?
The Old Ones Said The Dead Will A-Wake
Dream Song Of a Thousand Suns
King Oliver is Taken Down From The Cross
Signs And Revelations Dream Talk
This Man Also Was With Jesus

I had to keep looking at the textured paint, colors mixed with metal flakes, coffee grinds, cellophane strips, egg shells, Wheaties and pieces of aluminum foil. The 3D paint was used to create kaleidoscopes of images, from serpents to butterflies to pagodas, from Tibetan temples to Egyptian priestesses to Christian saints. The faces were all painted in crude, medieval-flat cartoon style but they were all recognizable: Elvis Presley riding a streaking comet. Adam and Eve picking fish off the Tree of Knowledge. Louis Armstrong with flowers blooming out of his trumpet. Jesus strapped to an electric chair. Vishnu using all four arms to braid his hair in Rastafarian dreads. Winged nuns hovering over the Garden of Eden. A huge bat tied to an operating table with Franklin Delano Roosevelt wielding a scalpel. The Buddha squatting in the belly of a whale while Fats Domino plays the piano next to him.

And blended in with all this were words and
numbers and voodoo symbols and ceremonial signs,
all of it coming out of backgrounds that looked like
close ups of blood cells under nuclear microscopes or
Hubble photos of quasars burning on the other side of
the universe. I was stunned, I was staggered. They
were like scenes from a world that was just about to
be created, just about to be named.

"My father believed in divine inspiration," said
Genesis. "He believed he was moved by the grace of
God. He considered it a privilege to use his hand for
God's work."

"I can see that."

I could see it in the words, in the stream of
consciousness thought-bursts that appeared
throughout the paintings like scrolls in tapestries.

The Journey commences at this point,
At 14788, at 93124,
At the heeliotropic of 001644,
At the point where the Ancient Ones sang of the
Holy Mounten,
Where They knew that a separate person does
not exist behind the eyes,
Where They knew that the Secret History would
be told.

Behold, it is spoken,
The stone has been rolled away,
And the Voyce comes from within
Speaking the sacred words,

Saying do not stagnate in the pool of the self,
Saying His wounds will bleed where He was
peerced,
Saying the demons can be called by Name,
Saying die to yourself and be reborn.

The Old Ones sang their dreams.
The Old Ones, the True Ones
Knew that they were not creating their Minds.
They knew that their Minds
Were creating Them.
So They sang their dreams
To the mountens
And to the rivers
And to all the creachures of the Earth.
This is how They cured their Madness.

I was gone. I was transported by the words, carried away. They were like things I'd swear I'd heard before but couldn't remember until now.

"His work," said Genesis, "can have quite an effect on people."

Was she kidding? Was she that big on understatement? I turned to look at her, and it was only then I saw that she wasn't wearing anything except the necklace. She'd taken off the caftan and let it fall on
 the floor.

Her bruise-purple nipples were swelling with blood. The hair between her legs was honey colored with wet. The flesh just below her navel, where the green and gold tattoo of a macaw took wing, was going flush with heat.

She was smiling, almost laughing. "Are you feeling it? Are you feeling the effect?"

I could feel my cock coming alive, I could feel my
whole body coming alive. She was as beautiful as the open heavens on Revelation Day, and I was all ready to answer the call.

>>>>>>

The Southern Gates Of Hell

I woke up in her bedroom around 4 a.m., surrounded by brocaded curtains and tassel draped bordello lamps, the lemon taste of her pussy still in my mouth. We'd made love twice, once in the gallery and then here on the
second floor. Both times were the same—fierce, manic, beast-feast sex, her screaming and digging her fingers into my skin.

No surprise, I asked myself a few questions as she slept next to me. Like, what the hell was this all about? Why is this attractive, self-possessed woman jumping all over my bones right from the go? I mean, as much as I might like to think I'm the answer to every maiden's prayer, I know I'm not and I know this sudden seduction was an extreme reaction if there ever was one. I had to assume she wanted something out of me. But what?

A secondary question: What kind of person gets *that* turned on in front of her own father's paintings?

I'm not complaining, just asking.

She was awake. I felt her hand on my head, stroking my hair.

"Do you feel like taking a little walk?" she said.

"Walk? Where?"

"Just next door. I have to show you something."

Next door was a library the size of a modest bowling alley. Walls of warm birch shelving.

Thousands of books and monographs on art and artists. Tables piled with auction house catalogues.

It was all very archival and leather bound, except for the huge flat-screen monitor mounted on one wall.

Genesis gave a tighter wrap to her robe and began typing on a laptop. Me wearing nothing but my pants, I watched as the screen came to light. Its image went from a gray ionized TV void to some official looking Isaiah Robonnet website. Genesis scrolled and clicked and moments later the monitor was taken over by a life-size Robonnet painting.

And just by looking at it I felt like I was being turned inside out.

It was definitely a Robonnet, but not like the others. This thing was darker and claustrophobic and infinitely more demented. This thing was a night-terror orgy of violence and violent sex, each image standing out with meaning like the hieroglyphics of a death obsessed language.

A goat-headed man was shoving spikes through the bodies of cockroaches.

A procession of lepers was peeing on the Dalai Lama.

Corpses were levitating out of coffins.

Angels were pulling the eyes out of beggars' sockets.

A mongrel dog was eating the body of a baby.

A nun in one corner of the canvas was giving birth.

A nun in another corner was giving head.

A tropical bird was being torn apart by a lice ridden goat.

An Inquisition priest was castrating Carl Jung's mushroom penis.

A nun sat with her legs spread open while a beggar bent down to eat the filthy communion wafer stuck in her vagina.

In the background, the night sky was burning with blood.

There words were different too. The words matched the clotted madness of the pictures.

Do you think I do not know?
Do you think I could not heer
The words whispered
On the cancerous breaths
Of those who no longer know,
Of those who have forgotten
You are not who you think you are?
Do you think I could not heer
The echo of the words
In the fatal rooms and liquid chambers
Of the Secret Pyramids,
Where serpents were summoned and snakes were called,
Where powders were com-pounded of
Wormwood and myrrh and
Black balsam and bloodsalts
And mixed with the substance of Night and Time?

The Souls in Tor-ment
At the Southern Gate of hell
Number 900,413,777,262
And there is no release for them.
They suffer fever and sleep
But they will never be released.
I cry to Yahweh
And to Ra and Baal 14-%-A
But They will not let me go.
I heer howling beneath the Golgotha moon.

The angels from hell are here,
Exu and his snarling dogs are here,
Those who have hidden their hearts are here
And they will not let me go.
The Dead aren't coming back.
They don't want to.

What the hell was *this*? It was like some nightmare matrix of a painting that somehow seemed to contain all the other paintings and yet still stood dangerously on its own.

It had some power to it, no denying that. It had some visceral, body-shaking power. I could feel it. It was like an 18-wheeler had come barreling through the cobblestone driveway right in front of the house and the rumbling was running up my legs.

"It's called *Sex Death Dream Talk*," she said. "It was his last painting. He finished it just before he was killed."

"I've never seen anything like it."

She nodded. "It's his most controversial canvas, easily. Some also say it's his most beautiful. But there's a problem with it."

"Too disturbing?"

"The problem is that I can't show you the original, I can only show you a digital copy. The problem is that it's gone."

"Gone as in stolen?"

"Exactly. Exactly as in stolen. It's been taken from me." She took two drifting steps to the wall and stood in front of the monitor, gazing into the screen. "My father was taken from me, and now this. His most beautiful work has been taken away from me. I've had *enough*."

>>>>>>

The theft had taken place nearly a month ago, at the warehouse her brother maintained in New Orleans. God-obsessed Robonnet had worked at an almost assembly line pace and hundreds of his paintings were included in the inventory, but only *Sex Death Dream Talk* had been stolen. Genesis didn't think the timing or the selection was coincidental. Months before, she and her brother had quietly floated the sale of the painting on the private market. Negotiations had been ongoing with several established Robonnet collectors, old and trusted friends of the family.

I asked how much it was worth. I'm a journalist—I have almost no sense of shame.

Even though we were sitting around one of the library tables, her answer was stand-up fast. No hesitation, no bullshit.

The market-rate range was $45-50 million, she said. Being a final painting gave the title significant value. The bloody and erotic subject matter didn't hurt either.

"We've done very well by the paintings, my brother and I," Genesis said. "But it wasn't always that way. Things my father had to sell for $50 in the beginning go for millions now and we see nothing out of it. Our price for this is more than justified."

"Do the police agree with the money?"

Another stand-up response. "The police don't know it's been stolen."

My reply, I think, was just as upfront. "Are you shitting me?'

She shook her head. "Building up private negotiations is a delicate process—it requires even greater degrees of patience and understanding than public discussions do. Once private talks are derailed, it's very difficult to get them going again. Too much trust has been lost."

I probably looked stupid-stunned but I didn't care. "Are you saying you're still negotiating?"

"Yes."

"You're trying to sell something you don't have?"

"We're hoping to resolve this without going to the police."

"Even in the art world, is that legal?"

She gave me an impatient look. "There are other reasons for avoiding the police. Any reported theft would raise our insurance rates, and it would cost us future bargaining power. Besides, my family's from New Orleans. We have an inborn distrust of authority."

Well, there *was* that.

"Is there anybody you suspect?"

She got up, went to another table and came back with a sheet of paper. Five names had been written out.

Julia Pervez
Bobby Hucknail
Orfa Collins
H-L Lincoln
Abdul Bazzi

They were all *nuovo Robonnisti*, relatively new Robonnet buyers, and they were all people who were hungry, maybe even point-of-pride desperate, to boost the value of their collections. None of them had been included in the negotiations—too inexperienced, too reckless—and they'd each expressed their displeasure in highly vehement ways.

"How did they even know about the talks?"

"There's an underground," she said. "Word gets around."

"And they'd actually *steal* the painting for bragging rights?"

"You have no idea."

"But you have no proof."

She sat down again next to me. "Here's what I know. I may have lost my father, but I will *not* lose this. It is *absolutely* out of the question."

"I can understand that." I went to hand the list back.

"Keep it."

"Why?"

"I want you to get me the painting."

Just like that.

Plus Expenses

I laughed. Once again she didn't. We really didn't have the same sense of humor.

"Sorry?"

Her voice was completely calm. "I want you to get the painting. I'm asking you to get the painting back."

"And how am I supposed to do that? *Steal* it?"

"Not steal. Reacquire. Repossess."

"*Steal* it."

"Steal it *back*."

This was some conversation to be having with nothing but a pair of pants on.

"What makes you think I'd even *think* about it?"

"The talk I had with your friend, with Kumiko. She mentioned that you'd assigned the story on my father. Then she began talking about you, about your, shall we call it, your previous life. That's what got my interest. Now…now I think I know you."

So that's what this was all about. The invitation, the sex, this whole twilight zone production.

"I'm flattered, I guess, but I don't think you've thought this out."

"Believe me, I have. I've looked at other ways of retrieving the painting. Nothing's working out."

"I think I'd rethink the police."

"They can't even find my father's killer—I wouldn't waste any high hopes on this. Now on the *other* end of the spectrum, yes, there are people who specialize in illegal art procurement. Of course there are, but I can't afford to deal with them. How could I trust such people?"

"So that leaves me?"

"You're just what I've been looking for. You've worked as an investigator, you've recovered stolen property. You come with the qualifications, plus I know what you do, I know where you are. I know I can trust you."

She's known me a few hours and she can trust me? I took a look at her, this beautiful but pretty fucking crazy woman, sitting in the glow of library light at three or four in the morning.

I think she knew what I was thinking. She leaned into me and started to say something, but there was too much throat in her words. She had to stop and clear her voice.

"I want you to understand something," she said. "There's nothing I can do to bring my father back— I've come to accept that. I can't get him back, but I *can* get this back. It's the one thing I *can* do. I'm asking you to help."

I counter-leaned into her. "As much as I might want to help you, why would I do something like steal a painting?"

"Because I'll pay you a million dollars to do it."

Man, that room was quiet.

This was an historic first. I can unequivocally say that since the dawn of time no one has ever sat in front of me and offered to dump a million dollars in my lap in one swell foop. Just never happened before. And don't get me wrong, I could use the money. I have a daughter, for starters—I could *surely* use the money. But I didn't say yes to it. I'm not sure why. Maybe it was the size of it, the abstraction of it, the round numberness of it, the ease with which it was offered, but it just didn't feel real. It had no meaning for me.

"A million dollars," she said, trying to drive it home. "We have a private foundation, a 501C3— we'll pay you out of that. Cashier's check— watermarks, security threads, color shifting inks, everything. A million dollars, plus expenses."

Wait a minute. Plus expenses? Why did that make a difference to me? I don't know, but it did. The million dollars at the moment was doing nothing for me. But *plus expenses*? That was different. There was just something about it. A sense of freedom, maybe? A promise of no limits?

I looked at the painting in the monitor again, at the hypnotic torment of colors and faces. I looked at the words again.

The Dead aren't coming back.
They don't want to.

This was insane. This was truly, dangerously off the wall. Money, expenses—what difference did it make? This was one cockamamie, tipping-the-scales situation and I knew that the best thing I could do was get up, get the rest of my clothes and get the hell out of there.

"Of course I mean all *reasonable* expenses," said Genesis, "and I would need to approve them. But I promise you that any job related expenditures that you incur will be reimbursed to the fu—"

"I'll do it. I'll do the job."

And there it was. There were the words coming out of my mouth, still waters suddenly a stream. I hadn't thought about saying that. I hadn't weighed it or deliberated it. I don't even know if I meant to say it. I just took a breath and opened my mouth and out came the words.

Just like that.

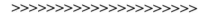

CHAPTER 3

THE BORED
AND PISSED OFF
CRAZY LOVE THEORY

Why did I say yes? It was a weird choice, I'll admit that, but I have to point out that I'm using the word *weird* the way Shakespeare uses it in *Macbeth*. Weird in this case means fate or destiny, so when Shakespeare calls the witches the Weird Sisters, he's describing them as the Sisters of Fate. The word comes from the Old English *Wyrd*, a concept related to growing into something, becoming something. Your Fate, your Wyrd, is a destination that turns out to be right, even though you might not realize it at the time. It's a lot, I think, like me agreeing to the offer. Your head might be telling you to go in one direction, but your legs end up taking you to where you're supposed to be.

But that's a looking back answer. It doesn't really explain why I said yes that night. I've done a good amount of thinking about it since, and I have to say I'm not laying this one on Shakespeare—there's no blaming the Bard here. The only reasonable way I can account for what happened that night is by invoking what's technically known as the Bored & Pissed Off Crazy Love Theory.

The Bored Part Of It

I have a good job, no denying that. I'm not suggesting anything otherwise. But once they have you hauling too much management and administration weight around, gotta say the excitement tends to drain off. There's a good story out there, hey, my heart is pumping. But sitting in an office all day, my butt is numbing.

The day I met Genesis I'd sat in a meeting with the edit finance people going over spreadsheets on bureau cost analyses—overtime, stringers, itemps, T&E, whatever—and during the course of this fascinating colloquy we spent exactly 53 minutes, I counted, debating how to cut back on the amount of paper used for the reporters' printers in LA. I understand how finance types can get quite passionate about cost cutting and I admit that they occasionally reached the heights of eloquence when talking about bulk buying and lighter-weight bonds and recycling the backs of old copies. But really, 53 fucking minutes? From 2:43 to 3:36 peefuckingem?

So can you understand why I felt I needed a break, why I felt I had to get away, why I felt that my entire working life at that point consisted of dealing with the same crap over and over and just flushing it down different toilets?

The truth, I was seriously thinking of taking a leave even before that night. Lots of people at *Real Story* do. They use the time to write a book or get to know their families or pursue some special project.

And if this wasn't a special project, then what the hell is?

The Pissed Off Part Of It

The week before I ran into Genesis I'd been out in Scottsdale, visiting my daughter, Millie, and my ex. I make the trip every few months, birthdays, holidays, the like. Remote parenting sucks but it beats nothing by a long shot.

Last time out, though, I don't know, it all went pretty bad. Millie all of a sudden wanted nothing to do with me. Didn't want to spend time with me, didn't want to go anywhere or do anything with me.

Just standing there in that goddamn living room with the Pueblo prints, her arms folded, saying, *I don't like you.*

My daughter had turned into someone else.

She's 10, her mother said. *That's what the attitude is like.* My ex, Gabriel, who's going out with somebody named Tommy or Timmy, I can't keep it straight, she's telling me, *That's what 10 is like. Believe me, I get it everyday.*

But see, that's the thing. She gets it everyday. I don't. I'm not used to it cause I'm not there. I phone her, I email her, I text her, I tweet her, but I'm not actually there. So walking into it cold was a rock-hard shock. What happened to my baby girl? All the little understandings I'd had with her, all the little games we'd played when she was younger, all that was gone now and no history or memory of them was left. It was like they'd never existed.

Oh yes I was angry. Another part of my life was gone—better believe I was angry. I couldn't blame my daughter from growing up but that didn't stop me from feeling this kind of floating and rootless rage. I'd been carrying it around ever since I'd gotten back to New York, this anger that could've gone anywhere because it didn't feel connected to any one thing.

I should've tried to deal with it. I should've faced it and meditated on it, but I didn't. I was too angry to handle my anger—you know how it goes. Instead I tried to leech it off on something else, I tried to bleed it away. By the time I ran into Genesis Robonnet, face it, I was looking for something crazy to get involved in, and motherfucker I found it.

>>>>>>

The Crazy Love Part Of It

Like I told Genesis, I'd tried to put my prison time to
good use by getting into AA and Buddhism. They
might sound like two separate things, but I found a
deep connection running between them. What AA
basically says is, get over yourself. To which
Buddhism adds, good idea, because what you think of
as yourself doesn't really exist. For me, they're both
good ways to learn how to surrender your mind to the
mystery of God. They're both good ways to find
answers to questions like who am I, why am I here,
what's it all supposed to mean. They're good ways to
deal with the questions we've been asking ourselves
ever since we were able to throw words back at
ourselves.

Of course, when I call myself a Buddhist, I
should point out that I'm not a particularly *good* one.
There's too much anger, too much boredom (see
above). There's not enough of that Om shanti peace,
that God's Love We Deliver. But I'm trying. I'm
trying to get there.

Now as a lapsed Irish alcoholic addicted
Catholic, I believe that all roads lead to God, and
while I'm not saying that Robonnet was a Buddhist, I
recognized that he was walking down a similar path. I
could see in the paintings that he was a fellow
traveler, could see it in the way the images burrowed
beneath the surface of thinking and tapped into the
substance of the mind. And I could hear it in the
words, definitely in the words. In things like:

you are not who you think you are
die to yourself and be reborn
do not stagnate in the pool of the self
The Ancient Ones, he said,
knew that a separate person does not exist
behind the eyes

And the Old Ones, the True Ones
Knew that they were not creating their Minds.
They knew that their Minds
Were creating Them
And there were other words. I found them at that Robonnet website, like these from a painting called *Resurrection and Wakening Death Song*:
Under the tree with 14,000 branches,
Each branch with 282 leaves,
The Forgotten Profet will come to us
As had been promised.
He will sing the songs of freedom.
Saying,
When it is exactly nothing,
Then it is exactly everything.
Saying,
The storey is everywhere
Hidden only to those
Who do not see.
Saying,
If they believe the mind resides
Inside the borders of the skull
They will never understand.
They will perish of con-founding madness
With the taste of nightshaded opium
Upon their dying lips.
They were like the words you'd discover in a zen dream. And hearing them, hearing them was like listening to the spaces between words, the emptiness between syllables.

Again, I'm not saying Robonnet was any kind of Buddhist—zen is just one way to get there. But he'd plainly sailed into the mystic on a very similar craft. He seemed to know that the mind doesn't exist just inside your head with no connection to the outside world. He seemed to grasp the interiority complex.

He seemed to understand that what we call our selves are just stories that we tell ourselves, narratives that we build as we go along, and that we shouldn't confuse fiction with reality. You aren't what you think you are because what you think you are is just a thought, and the totality of what you are is more than just a thought. What you are is more than can be named, more than can be known.

That's why I felt a bond with him and his paintings. Looking at his work left me intensely conscious of consciousness, like my mind was folding in on itself. It was like the air I was breathing was breathing itself.

I felt an affinity with him, a kinship. That's why I wanted to help his daughter, his family. I wanted to find justice for them. I wanted to find out who'd taken his final painting and I wanted to get it back.

And most of all, for my own sake, I wanted to find out who'd sliced his chest open in one long horizontal slash and robbed him of his life.

CHAPTER 4

PHANTASMAGORIAS

Thy Will Be Done 10 Days From Now

I didn't tell Kumiko exactly why I was taking a leave from work, but I let her know it had something to do with Robonnet. I wanted to go to school on the guy, I told her, especially on the way his work was sold, so where should I start? She directed me to the Whitmore Primitive Museum on the north shore of Long Island, in Sea Cliff, just a few miles away from where Genesis lived. The Whitmore, Kumiko said, not only held the world's largest number of Robonnets in its permanent collection, it also served as a cynosure for sales of his paintings.

According to the official Whitmore website, the museum was the worldly legacy of one Harold Whitmore, an industrialist (semiconductors, piston rings, plastic plumbing fixtures) invested with a passion for spiritual art. He was a man committed to the belief that he could inspire his workers—and thus improve efficiency and increase productivity—by hanging the works of visionary outsider artists like Robonnet on the walls of his factories. Bit of a lunatic? Probably, but a successful one. When he died he left a sizeable estate to his family plus a separate $30 million endowment for a privately owned museum devoted to the art that most touched his heart. The Whitmore Primitive Museum now housed about 3,000 works under its roof and had increased the endowment to approximately $90 million. Said so right on the site.

Clearly the museum took a certain interest in money. Good to know.

Though it was equally obvious, upon pulling up, that not much of the capital had gone into the architecture of the joint. The Whitmore was a large, white, utilitarian, pedestrian, resolutely undistinguished single-story sprawl of a place, a building with absolutely no sense of humor. It had a reflecting pool and a cavern of shade trees out front, but they didn't help. Except for a few details here and there, it was impossible to tell the museum apart from just another suburban supermarket.

Same deal inside. All-white walls, big chunks of space divided into different sections. Only instead of pushing your cart through Meat or Produce or Frozen Foods, you'd find yourself strolling through Tropical Flowers (galleries for Caribbean artists), Pioneer Trails (19th Century Americans) or Angels Of Death (serial killers who'd come to God in prison).

Anyone I know?

The museum was supermarket-crowded as well. Under a pyramidal skylight the lobby was filled with art students carrying sketch pads and tour groups of people who seemed to be from Kansas and were all wearing red baseball caps and matching T-shirts. Plenty of Japanese tourists too, mostly heading for the serial killer section.

Two entire galleries were dedicated just to Robonnet. I went there first, taking in those dense and clotted panoramas. The titles alone were making me high.

The Book Said We Would All Be One
Thy Will be Done Starting 10 Days From Now
Water Talk At Lake Pontchartrain

The Neville Bros Receive Their Auras
This Light Once Came From God's Mouth
I was walking though some antediluvian forest, hearing the cries of animals that hadn't been named yet.

Security cameras, I noticed, were everywhere.

I went back to the info desk in the lobby and identified myself: David Brannigan, vice president of Sheridan Financial Services. I'd printed out a few business cards, just in case. I said I had an appointment with Joy Cheng, the museum's Public Affairs Administrator. As I'd told her on the phone, I was representing a client who was thinking about investing in primitive art.

Joy Cheng turned out to be a striking woman with a blue pinstriped suit, tortoiseshell glasses and a shaved head. And as I'd guessed, given the museum's institutional fascination with dollar amounts, she was more than willing to provide advice.

"Of all the creative sectors you could look at," she assured me, "growth potential in the primitive field is the most wonderful."

She took me to a gallery called Heavenly Visitations, showing artists who'd been inspired by alien and/or UFO encounters. I know everybody's a critic, but most of this stuff looked to me like stills from old *X-Files* episodes tinted over in lollipop colors.

Still, I suppose it was a good backdrop for her spiel. Primitive art, she said, went by various names—outsider art, folk art, visionary art, intuitive art. But it all came down to the same thing: Art that had been produced with no formal training, art that defied accepted aesthetic norms. The form was first designated as such in the early 20th Century by psychiatrists trying to categorize the art produced in mental asylums. The painter Jean Dubuffet called it Art Brut—Raw Art, art that hadn't been cooked by the influence of culture. Good call, because the people who produced it tended to be loners and eccentrics, people whose isolation and intense drive resulted in work that was completely unique.

"That's what makes it valuable," said Joy, "the singular voice, the individualistic style. As the world becomes more mediacentric, individuality becomes a real rarity. Look at the internet. An hour on the internet, you'll see thousands of images from all around the world. That means untainted eyes are getting harder to find. That's why primitive art will only increase in market worth."

Interesting stuff. She walked me through a few other galleries and we were getting along fine. No problems. The only *slight* area of friction between us was Robonnet. Joy didn't seem terribly anxious to talk about the man. I'd bring his name up every once in a while—you mean like Isaiah Robonnet? Would Robonnet fall into that category? Things like that. But every time I'd mention him, she'd just nod and gloss it over and keep on talking about something else.

After about 20 minutes of this I decided to bring things to a head. I came right out and said it: "My client has expressed a real interest in Robonnet. In fact, she's *only* interested in Robonnet."

I think if I'd farted blood in front of her I couldn't have gotten a more negative reaction.

Joy's expression was exactly halfway between sour and surprised. It was like I'd asked if she sold porn.

"You're quite sure about that?" she said. "You're *absolutely* sure?"

"I'm sure."

"Only in Robonnet?"

"Only."

She frowned. She passed a hand over her bare skull, thinking. She gave up. "I don't think I can help you."

"Why not?"

"You really should be talking to someone else about this." Her tone had gone pretty cold by now. "We have someone who specializes in Robonnet, an associate curator. I really think you should talk to her."

"Fine, but I'm happy talking to you."

"I'll see if I can get you an appointment."

What's the sound of ice forming?

She took me out to the lobby, positioned me by the info desk and stepped away to use her phone. I'm running this through my head: The Whitmore has two whole galleries full of Robonnets, it has the world's largest collection of his stuff, so exactly *which* taboo had I broken?

Joy came back. The associate curator's name was Shannon Kubliak and she could only come in at 5:30 today. No, nothing earlier—5:30. Which was curious, because according to the signs in the lobby, the museum closed at 6 p.m. That didn't seem to leave much time for a free and open exchange of ideas. Was I getting squeezed?

"Tell me something," I said, "what did I do again?"

"Sorry, nothing, I'm simply not permitted to…" Then she said something else, almost whispering it before walking away. "Committee rules."

Whatever *that* meant.

I Could Remember
Who I Was Going To Be

So what was I supposed to do, go all the way back to the city just to make a 5:30 return trip? Huge waste. Instead I drove into downtown Sea Cliff, found a Starbucks that was only moderately mobbed and started going through the Robonnet biofiles that Kumiko had sent me. Yes, I'd edited a story on him, but now I wanted a better understanding of who Isaiah Robonnet was.

Details of his early life were as solid as marsh fog. He appears to have been born near Barataria, a small swamp town in the Jefferson Parish bayous just south of New Orleans. The place held one pre-Robonnet claim to history: Jean and Pierre Lafitte built a smugglers' market there in the early 1800s to sell their pirated merchandise.

By various accounts, Isaiah was either the seventh, eighth or ninth of 13 children in the Robonnet clan. His father was a much-traveled farm worker and occasional shrimper on the Gulf boats. His mother picked up a little extra cash as a medicine woman. In later years Robonnet would remember going with his mother to the woods, where she'd pick out the herbs and plants needed to cure illnesses and influence the spirits. (Reading this, yes, I thought about the woman pulling root-fingers out of the ground where he'd been killed.)

The big family moved around the south Louisiana area quite a bit before settling in New Orleans. In interviews Robonnet would describe a blurred succession of cramped houses and downright shacks where everyone slept in one room, the children on the floor.

Maybe this all had something to do with the boy's unusual personality. Isaiah was a muscular bruiser of a kid but very shy, very withdrawn. Whole months would go by without him saying a word. Eventually, when the family was living in New Orleans, he was diagnosed as an idiot. This despite a ravenous passion for reading. He consumed books, newspapers, flyers he'd find in the street with an autodidact's fever. Didn't matter—the boy didn't talk. He was labeled feeble-minded and retarded and placed in a number of institutions throughout the years.

At some point in his 30s he was working as a handyman at a Catholic charity in the city and living on the premises. Somewhere around that time one of his older sisters, Ginnia, passed away. He'd been very close to her and the loss dropped him into a depression that lasted for weeks. He became convinced, he later said, that he was also about to die.

One night in his room the fear grew so intense that he realized, as he said, *I had to take everything out of my mind and throw it all away. I had to forget everything. That was the only way I could remember who I was going to be.*

The moment he did that, he felt what he called *a bolt of electricity start from the base of my spine, run up my back and blow out the top of my head.* He was experiencing what's known in yoga as *kundalini,* a surge of energy moving up through the nerve centers along the axis of the body. This sometimes happens to people who meditate (me, in prison) and the result is usually a soft explosion of overwhelming love. Everything in the world, even a miserable little shit like yourself, suddenly feels touched by divine all-belonging love.

In Robonnet's case, though, he began hearing voices. God's angels, he believed, were speaking to him, describing scenes to him and giving him words of wisdom. He had to get it all down. He'd had no art training and no previous desire to paint, but now he felt compelled to record what he was hearing on canvas.

He started working in his room, transcribing the voices nonstop. Nothing got in the way of his obsession. He had no easel, so he propped the canvases up on his pine dresser and leaned them against the wall. He had little money for supplies, so he made his paint go further by mixing it with things like molasses, sorghum, muddy water, brick dust, crushed coal, burnt matches, boiled jimson weed, broken glass, cornflakes, Cheerios and the cracked-up shells of colored Easter eggs.

Combining these textured pigments with a text-image style he'd invented himself, he turned out hundreds of what he called his *tapestries* or *phantasmagorias*. God, he said, *had stepped in and saved my life. All I'm doing is returning the favor.*

But few people knew about it. Robonnet worked in obscurity during the first few years, showing his paintings informally in the lobby of the charity or occasionally selling them on the streets. As Genesis mentioned, this was the time when his canvases were going for $50 per.

Then he was discovered by a local dealer, Danielle Patout. She recognized the power of his originality and she began arranging exhibitions for him and finding him buyers. Apparently she liked what she was seeing at both ends of the brush, because within a year of meeting they were married. Under her tutelage, Robonnet's popularity and reputation grew over the decades until he was widely seen as one of the country's most important outsider artists.

After Danielle's death, the family marketing tradition was taken over by the couple's two children, Genesis and her younger brother, Leviticus—better known as Slim. Genesis moved to New York to spread the word among northern Robonnistas while Slim stayed in New Orleans to cultivate the home roots.

Their father remained downhome as well until Katrina hit. In the months after the storm he lived on Long Island with Genesis, then he began dividing his time between here and there once the rebuilding efforts slowly struggled to life. With his liberal use of New Orleans content—everything from local musicians to voodoo symbols—Robonnet had long been identified with the city. Now he became one of the campaigners for its rebirth, often holding fundraisers at the Whitmore Primitive Museum (where the size of the Robonnet collection steadily grew).

By the time of his death he'd turned himself into something of a folk hero—a down to earth visionary, a loveable madman, a big bear of a man as unselfconscious as a child. I watched a video link to a TV interview with a reporter who, trying to dig for what he called a "thinky question," asked the artist where he found the keys to happiness. Robonnet shrugged and scratched his head before drawling out an answer. *I guess I have to ask where you CAN'T find the keys. Cause they're everywhere, man— there's no lack of keys in this life. You know how to look, you're gonna find 'em somewhere.*

I Am Ready To Go With You

I don't know what I was expecting in an associate curator. Some tweedy, curdled-up, academic type maybe? Whatever, the woman I met when I went back to the Whitmore at 5:30 was something else altogether. Shannon Kubliak was one of the most beautiful women I'd ever seen. She had a low voice and sly eyes and skin that looked as smooth as white Thassos marble. She mixed curly black hair with blue eyes that had some kind of slow glow to them, and her eyes made me think that if moonlight ever turned blue Jesus Christ it would look just like this.

I kept wishing this was somewhere else, because if we were anywhere besides a hush-mouth museum all I'd be thinking about was fucking her full of babies. That's how lotus-flower beautiful she was. But we *were* in a museum so I tried not to think along those lines and concentrated on listening to her instead.

Which turned out to be not that hard because she had plenty to say. For starters, she thought Robonnet was an outstanding investment choice. His style, which she called largely figurative but with semi-abstract elements, was truly transforming and achieved through incredibly dynamic composition. Sounded good to me.

"He reaches an apocalypticism," she said, "that sometimes just takes me away. Sometimes I think I'm looking at illuminated manuscripts from medieval monks. Really, it just transports me."

Whatever Joy Cheng's problem had been, it left no lingering effects. Shannon Kubliak was completely open about Robonnet, completely amicable. Things were going splendidly.

She took me to the Robonnet galleries and told me more about his work. In color, composition and symmetrical formalism, she said, she saw parallels not only with medieval art but Australian aborigines, Hindu traditions, Islamic patterning, Aztec and Tibetan calendars, pagan mystery cults, the Cabala and the Catholic Church.

"He was *very* Catholic," said Shannon. "Actually I think his Catholicism, his early exposure to it as a child, is one of the portals you have to enter to understand him. The world he created, it's not rational and ordered. It's sacramental rather than logical. It's open to everything. It's a world where everything was shot through with the mystery of God."

I liked her.

We were standing in front of a painting called *I Am Ready To Go With You*. Near the middle of the canvas, a few dozen gargoyle-faced members of a steel drum band were getting sucked into a giant hole in the ground, screaming in agony as they started the drop into the pit below. But they weren't falling into the fires of hell. They were landing, unexpectedly, in a paradise of flowers and fruit and exotic trees. They were falling into heaven.

"When people first come across him," she said, "sometimes they only focus on the deficiencies. He draws his figures in a very simplistic manner, for example, very undeveloped. He pays no attention to perspective or scale."

"I can see that."

"But see, that's the genius of it—that's what makes it all work. By totally disregarding representational conventions, he's giving his figures an almost mythical status. Again, medieval. It's like the medieval monks painting the lives of saints. He's turning everyone into legends."

I was looking at the words painted alongside the steel drummers as they took their tumble:

A Masonic carriage of 64 horses
Carryed us to a celestial Temple
Measuring 119, 350 leegues to the very top,
Where an ancient man named Exu
Stood on the steppes and said
Which of you will help Christ carry the cross
I saw an opening.

The name *Exu*—I'd seen it before, on the monitor in Genesis' library. Something like *all the electromagnetic vegetation you see belongs to Exu.*

I saw a way in.

"A question?" I said. "What's with this word?" I pointed

She looked. "Exu?"

"I've come across it before in Robonnet. In a painting called *Sex Death Dream Talk.*"

A couple of heartbeats went by. Shannon didn't say a thing, just kept staring at the canvas. Then she raised a hand and rubbed her neck like she was having one long day.

"It's Brazilian," she said. "Exu is one of the spirits of macumba, from Brazilian voodoo. There's quite a bit of voodoo in Robonnet—macumba, candomble, local Louisiana juju. I think it helps create the dreaming effect. He borrowed words and symbols from voodoo, possibly even numbers. All the numbers he paints? Lots of people believe they're sacred numbers and can be used for gambling. A lot of people try to decode the paintings to play the numbers. In fact, there's a whole cottage industry that's sprung—"

She was talking too much about this. It almost felt like misdirection.

"That painting I mentioned?" I said. "*Sex Death Dream Talk*? I've never actually seen it, only copies, but I understand it's very famous."

And there you go—it happened again. Somehow I'd tripped over another taboo and shattered it. There was some definite tension in the ozone now, just like there'd been with Joy Cheng.

Shannon never moved her eyes away from the painting in front of us. "So you're interested in *Sex Death Dream Talk*."

She could've used the same voice to say, *So you have an infected penis.*

"I'm just saying, I hear it's famous."

She nodded. "There's a good deal of controversy attached to it, if that's what you mean."

"Controversy?"

"Its content. His mental state when he painted it. Questions like that."

"Is getting stolen part of its controversy?"

Now she turned to me, a little too slowly. "I know nothing about that."

"You don't follow Robonnet news?"

"That hasn't been in the news."

"Underground?"

She went back to her contemplation of *I Am Ready To Go With You.* "What have you heard?"

"It was stolen from the Robonnet family. Taken out of their warehouse."

"If that's what you heard, you should probably ask them."

"Possibly stolen by a potential buyer."

"Again, if that's what you heard, go to the family."

"You're an expert, I thought you might have something."

"These are questions that I'm—"

She was interrupted by a voice over our heads, a canned public address voice. *Attention, please, may I have your attention. The museum is about to close. I repeat, the museum is about to close.*

She looked at me. "I'm sorry, I don't know what to tell you. What else can I say?"

Shannon Kubliak suddenly seemed tired. Or no, not just tired. She suddenly seemed drop-to-the-floor *drained*. Clearly I was doing something wrong here, pressing some bad buttons, and the effort to put up with me was just wearing her *out*.

Hard Currency

Still, she was onto something when she said *go to the family*. Genesis, of course, was already accounted and spoken for, but how about the *rest* of the family? That felt like the right next step for me. Go to New Orleans and talk with Leviticus, aka Slim Robonnet. Examine the warehouse, examine the place where the theft had taken place.

Made sense to me, so why was Genesis so noncommittal when I laid it out to her that night? She was listening to me as I talked but her mind was in some other room of the house. I didn't know why. Had she been bullshitting about the all expenses paid? Did she not want me talking to her brother? Was it me?

It was only when she crawled on top of me and begged me/ordered me to put my finger up her ass and ram her body down on my cock that she said yes. As she was coming she finally agreed that I should go.

I was beginning to understand her. Some people do things for love, some people do things for money. Where I was concerned, the only hard currency that counted for her was sex.

CHAPTER 5

THE DEAD AREN'T COMING BACK. THEY DON'T WANT TO

Now I See What The Old Ones Saw

Funny thing about not drinking or drugging anymore—none of the places I used to hang at look the same. The bars, for example, are all smaller now than I remembered, darker, dirtier, sadder. The only exception to this odd, dawning-of-reality rule is New Orleans. I still feel like I'm on a five-day no-sleep booze-and-meth binge. The aftereffects of what the locals simply call The Storm hasn't made any difference. The streets still feel like they're rippling under my feet. The walls are still breathing with swollen humidity. Every piece of metal in the city is still rusty and hallucinatorily mossy and if you look close enough you can see the whole place going ripe as you watch.

I flew down with no problem. Aside from the ride to the hotel with a cab driver who was probably crashing from coke and who seemed completely bewildered by the presence of other cars on the road, the trip was made without incident.

In fact, the driver told me I'd come down at just the right time because the roads were finally frog-free. Unusually heavy rains, he explained, had flushed thousand of frogs out of the sewers and the swamps, resulting in traffic jams and dangerous driving conditions (his own, presumably, not included). Lucky for me, we wouldn't be running into any slime hoards.

I was staying at the Vieux Royale on Canal, just off the Quarter. I'd been there before for *Real Story*—my name was in the system. People at the desk pretended to know me. *Welcome back, Mr. McShane.* Oh yes, there was a Fedex package waiting for me.

I'd sent it to myself the day before. It contained the Glock 9 millimeter that I'd carried when I was investigator. I'd found it in my possessions when my time was up. Through some species of bureaucratic fuck up, the gun had never been confiscated. I'd shipped it down here as a precaution. *Sex Death Dream Talk* had been stolen here. Things could get a little serious. Somehow, they always do in New Orleans.

I had an appointment to meet Slim Robonnet at his art and antiques gallery on Toulouse. The place offered a mixed bag—high-ended collectibles for the cashed-up crowd, porcelain Mardi Gras masks for the tourists along with packets of gris-gris powder and other voodoo charms. Two Robonnets were hanging on the walls: *The Lord Calls For Adam And Eve* and *He's Got The Whole World In His Hands But Be Careful He Doesn't Throw It All Away.*

Slim, of course, had plenty of pounds on him. He was a tall, extravagantly overweight man with short arms and long dreads and rings on almost every finger. Facially, he looked a lot like his sister, except he had brown eyes instead of her caffeinated blue ones. Another difference: That kind of glass-wall distance I could see in her eyes was absent from his.

Slim left the customers to his staff and led me to his back office. Much dark brown leather Smoking Club furniture, ceiling fans slowly rotating overhead. Very South.

He took two bottles of some creamy lime green concoction out of the refrigerator: Punch's Florida Smoothie. His father's favorite refreshment, he said. Robonnet believed the drink to be of divine origin— he was convinced that God had personally whispered the recipe to the Punch's people and had given them instructions for marketing and distribution.

Slim opened one bottle and offered me the other. "It's non-alcoholic," he said. "My sister told me you don't indulge."

The stuff looked like an invitation to instant diabetes. I politely passed.

As we settled in, Slim thanked me for helping out. He told me the same story about the theft that Genesis had given me, gave me the same theory about jilted buyers.

"Here's the great, awful irony of it all," he said. "Everything about this comes down to money." His father, he said, had not the slightest interest in gathering stores of wealth. Robonnet had been a shy and humble person who betrayed no concern for material possessions of any sort. True enough, he'd enjoyed the recognition that had come his way in the later years of life, but only because it opened people's eyes to the glory of God. Money never worried him.

Except once. Only one time did his father show any perturbance over financial justice. It centered around a painting called *Is It Nothing To You, All Who Pass By?* Did I know it? Well, it was one of his earlier titles and he'd sold it for a pittance of $70. Many, many years later, the original owner sold it for a flat $9 million. Pretty nice profit.

Slim and his sister believed Robonnet deserved a modest cut of the windfall. After all that time, they argued, he should be given some compensatory remuneration, and they urged their father to ask for one percent of the sale price. Maybe they shouldn't have, Slim admitted, but they did. One friggin' percent—$90,000 out of $9 million. The original owner refused.

"My father fell into a real bad way," said Slim. "I'd never seen him in such a state as that. He was hurt, he was brooding on it, he could just not let the thing go. Couple days later, he started painting *Sex Death Dream Talk*. That's how that debaucherous thing came about, and my sister and I, we do bear some responsibility for it. I know that for sure. We bear some responsibility for that dark night of the soul."

Bear some responsibility. I came to one conclusion right then and there. In terms of personality, Slim wasn't much like his sister at all.

I wanted to see the warehouse where the crime had taken place. Slim said he'd drive me, but did I first want to see a portion of what people called the Visitors' Circuit? The still damaged areas of the city? Most everyone from out of town did

If you believe you've gotta take the good with the bad, even though it's mostly bad, here was your perfect opportunity. We traveled past a number of good houses, structures that had been levitated on pilings at least eight feet above the base flood marker. They looked like fairytale colored mini Babels, trying to stretch up to the safety of heaven.

But for every good house, we passed too many bad ones—rotting ruins with padlocked doors, vacant foundations, weeded lots, ancient FEMA trailers, boarded-up box homes where plywood was the dominant design motif.

"We can't get nothing," Slim said as he drove. "Can't get contractors, can't get supplies, can't get shit. Even my father's house—we ripped out the carpets, three layers of linoleum, tore the walls back to the studs, took out tons of debris. And that's it. Still standing there, still waiting for the restoration to come through. He was hoping to move back in all that time. Now we'll give it over to the Robonnet tour they got running down here, if it ever *does* get rebuilt."

"He was still living there when Katrina came?"

"He loved that place. We grew up there, me and my sister. He went to live with Genesis right after The Storm. Then he was staying with me and with her, but that was just temporary. His plan all along was to go back to the house. He was going to get the house together again and move back in, just like before. But then…"

Yeah, but then… I looked over at Slim, noticed his heavy hand on the steering wheel. I guess because of all the rings on his fingers I hadn't seen it before, but he had a tattoo of an angel on his right hand. It showed a winged creature in amber and red, her features flattened and symbolic like a Byzantine icon. Or a Robonnet painting.

"That was a terrible way to die," I said.

He nodded and kept on driving. "I've replayed it so many times in my head, the police report of it. I still don't know how it happened. I still can't believe nobody else does either."

"That painting you were telling me about, the original owner wouldn't pay the one percent. Did the police investigate that?"

"His named was Cedric Grady and he alibied out. He was in a hospital down here at the time, dead now. I never thought it could be him. My father was hurt by the rejection, but he never threatened Grady. He wasn't that kind of man."

"When was the last time you saw him?"

"Right before his last trip up."

"Was he worried about any other kind of trouble?"

Slim smiled. "Here's another one of the ironies for you. Doctor had just told him he had to watch his heart, had to take more care of himself. I was talking to him about it and he said he wasn't worried. Said *I'm not afraid of dying. Going back to the Lord is okay by me. I just hope I get all my work done on time.* Those were among the last words I heard him say."

"Good words to have."

"Yeah, but I wish I had more. I wish I knew what the hell happened in that park that night. It kills me that nobody knows."

Interesting to hear. Genesis had said she'd given up trying to find out the truth about her father's death. Good to know that *somebody* in the family seemed to care.

The warehouse was on Poydras Street, a few blocks from the Superdome. Not much to look at—8,000 square feet of industrial floor tiles and fluorescent light, presided over by video surveillance, a security system, an armed guard and the slight whiff of ammonia.

Slim went through the story again—three masked and armed men disabled the alarms, jumped the guard on duty that night, tied him up, knocked the video out and made off with the painting. Quick 'n dirty.

"Had to be a stolen-to-order job," Slim insisted as today's guard took us around. "They didn't touch anything else."

And there was plenty to touch. The warehouse was jammed with hundreds of canvases, each stored in its own custom crate and labeled with a brass strip on the side. Slim unlocked one of them, something called *Time & Space Died On Thursday*. I saw a horse-drawn carriage leading a funeral procession across the middle of the painting, priestly jazz musicians marching through a crowd of ectoplasmic faces, colors and shapes. It was like looking at the world from underwater.

Words ran in a banner over the parade.
Now I see what the Old Ones saw.
Now I knew, in another time,
That flitter will flatter and glitter will glatter
That the Prophet will die thrice in 666333222
That Veenus will disappear for 90 magus-measured days.

I took a breath.

"When you heard the painting was gone," I said, "what's the first thing you thought of?"

"The first thing?"

"The first person. Soon as you heard, who was the first person you suspected? Any of those buyers on your sister's list?"

"Not really, no."

"Who?"

Slim turned to the guard, signaled that he should get himself some coffee.

"There *is* one guy," he said. "Pimpish kind of person, Dewey Tarantonio. A grifter-slash-antiques dealer. His face came right to me that night."

"Why?"

"Cause he'd been sniffing around just before that, few weeks before. He'd been asking people questions about the paintings, and that's not like him. That's not his game."

"What is?"

"Stealing from the dead."

No joke. As the world saw when the levees broke under Katrina, New Orleans sits below sea level. Because of that, the dead are buried above ground to stay dry, often in mausoleums that are so elaborately decorated they look like miniature mansions. There's a big black market in those decorations—marble Madonnas, granite cherubs, the like. Pukemongers like Dewey Tarantonio feed it, said Slim, by prying ornaments off the tombs and selling them to collectors.

"They already got him under indictment," he said. "What do they call it? *Habitual* possession of stolen property, conspiracy to traffic in the same. I think he was looking to branch out since the cemeteries were a pardon the expression dead end for him."

"You mention this to the cops?"

"Absolutely. They say he was out of town that night. Which could very well be—I'm not saying he actually did it, but he fuck-all knows who did. I know he knows. I bone-feel know that he knows it."

"You know where he's at?"

Slim wiped his brow. He was getting worked up. "Yeah but, as I said, cops already talked to him."

"I know they did. I just speak a different language."

>>>>>>

The Backchannel

Dewey Tarantonio lived deep in the Garden District, where every shade tree looks like it's at least 200 years old. I took a cab out, keeping the Glock tucked in the back of my pants and covered with a hoodie. The hoodie was lightweight, a cotton and linen blend, but it didn't help at all against the heat and humidity.

Dewey's house was an ancient Greek Revival in much need of the latter. The pitched roof was coming apart and the white clapboard walls were mottled with rust. The Spanish moss was showing root rot and the dead grass should've been cut back a month ago at least.

The place, much like its owner, was in a state of perfect decay.

Not to generalize or anything, but Dewey Tarantonio was a vastly peculiar man. He answered the door and let me in not just with an ass-kissing deference, but with an almost coolie subservience. He might've been a good-looking hustler not too long ago, but he was starting to betray the wear—a meatless, boyish blond going fast to wrinkle and gray. If his goal was to be the most dissipated felon In Orleans Parish, he was getting there in record time.

For reasons unknown, he gave off a trace odor of rye bread.

I repeated what I'd told him on the phone. I was repping a party who had an interest in the stolen

Robonnet painting. I wasn't a cop, I wasn't seeking payback, I wasn't looking to get him into any more trouble than he was already in. I was simply looking for information and I was willing to make it worth somebody's while.

Dewey just kept shaking his head, the wonder of it all.

"Why do people suspect me of these things?" he asked, not without a little rhetoric. "Thievery, malfeasance, desecratin' graves—a terrible litany, and why is it directed at me? Cause a gossip is why. Gossip is an art form down here and it can get pretty thick in the practice. Am I plunderer? No. Am I marauder? I am not. I'm just an inconsequential element in the entire process."

The inside of his house had seen as many better days as the outside. Long, stained curtains waved at scattered pieces of musty and tattered furniture. A full-size bronze harp stood in the living room, testifying to some former glory. A wine-colored carpet showed every particle of the room's dust. Only the silence of the place was immaculate.

Dewey conceded he was under indictment for the cemetery art but he said it was all a stunning misunderstanding.

"I have a well-trained eye," he said as he poured iced tea from a tarnished silver service. "Occasionally I'm asked to take a look at certain pieces of bric-a-brac—that's all there is to it. So much of what comes on the market these days has so little artistic merit."

Sex Death Dream Talk, though, that was a different story. He wasn't a Robonnet expert. He wasn't even what he called *expertish*. When he was growing up in the area, he said, they used to sell blotter acid with Robonnet's face on it. That was the only thing he really knew about the painter.

Had Slim Robonnet, he asked, put me up to this? He knew Slim had been making allegations against him.

"That boy is a study," Dewey said. "There's nothing worse than fat people with suspicions."

We played a back-and-forth game for the next few minutes. The exchanges consisted of him basically saying, *You think I know something.* Then me saying, *I KNOW you know something.* Then him saying, *You THINK you think I know something.*

I've always believed that given enough patience, understanding and faith, we can all end up communicating with each other. If you're in a hurry, though, nothing beats money. I laid five of Genesis' $100s on the chipped marble table between us. I held five more in my hand, spread out like a fan.

Dewey looked at the bills, then leaned back in his chair and thoroughly investigated the space in front of his eyes.

"What's my life become?" he ruminated. "A piss-poor sorry thing, beset by false accusations and mounting legal bills. Otherwise, I hope you know, I wouldn't be entertaining your offer."

"I know."

"Now as regards to this painting, the painting in question, did I engineer its removal? I did not. I most emphatically did not. That's just a bunch of hooey."

"Understood."

"But if the question is, did I play some small part, more or less, in the *backchanneling* of it? Well, then, yes, perhaps I did. Perhaps I did. I won't waste your time with the whole involved story of it, if it's all the same to you, but yes, perhaps I did."

"I don't need the whole story. I'm just looking for the present whereabouts."

"So the question becomes, can I help you with that? Yes, I believe I can. I believe I know a little something about the purchase."

"Okay…"

Dewey didn't say anything. I gave myself a little $500 breeze-off with the bills in my hand.

"I'm led to believe," he said, "that the person who bought the painting is from up your way. He's from New York, from what I understand."

"Okay."

"I also believe he's something of an eccentric. From what I hear, he lives in some sort of *castle* or something."

"A castle."

"A castle."

"In New York."

"On Long Island, I believe?"

Getting weird.

"What's his name?"

"I don't quite recall it. I was never in a position to come into direct contact with the individual."

"That's too bad."

"I *do* remember, though, that it seemed to be a rather odd name."

"Odd?"

Dewey strained on it. He looked like a psychic trying to focus on a vision. "The first name. The first name was just initials."

"That's not so odd."

"But there was something about it. If I rightly recall from seeing it, the letters were separated by a dash, not by periods."

"A dash."

"Yeah, it wasn't *H-dot, L-dot*. It was *H-dash-L*."

I remembered Genesis' list. *H-L Lincoln.*

"What was his last name?"

He tried. "It's not coming to me. Just not. There was something presidential about it, but it's just not coming to me."

"Washington?"

He shook his head. Didn't sound right. "Lincoln. More like Lincoln. Like H-L Lincoln."

I laid the money on the table. Considering my luck in the market, this was probably the best investment I'd ever made.

Dewey picked the pile up and sat fingering all 10 $100s. He wasn't counting them—it was more like he was stroking them. The masturbatory flavor of it all was more than creepy.

Four slow seconds went by. I went to get up, but he put me on pause.

"I was wondering," he said. "Any more of these?"

"Why?"

"Might you be looking for some additional information?"

"Additional information's usually a good thing. Why're you asking?"

He shifted his skinny ass in the chair. "It occurs to me, what if I could get you a little closer to the deed itself?"

"To the theft?"

"The theft. What if I could get you in touch with someone like that? Might there be another taste in it for me?"

Any job-related expenses that you incur. That's what Genesis had said.

This qualified. Knowing H-L Lincoln's name was one thing—knowing where he'd stashed the painting was something else. More information could help me get there.

"There might be."

"How much?"

"Depends on how close I can get."

He closed his eyes and nodded. He seemed to be having trouble breathing. "Where can I get you?"

"I'll give you my cell."

He went on nodding like a junkie who'd just gotten off, then he opened his eyes and started picking at the lint of his worn-out chair.

"Please don't think I enjoy doing this. I don't. Believe me, I don't. But I'm sorry to say that my future at the moment only exists in shades of black. What I'm trying to do, I'm trying to *buy* me some light."

Why Do You Want To Die Here?

I took a cab back. The sky was turning dark, November gray in the middle of June, but it didn't bring me off my high mood. I was making some progress here. I'd gotten a name, and maybe I'd be able to get me an *in* on H-L Lincoln.

The only roadblock I could see on the path was the traffic on Canal. It was terrible—we'd moved maybe 50 feet in the last five minutes. Frogs? The driver didn't think so. Accident somewhere up ahead, he thought.

I decided to pay up and walk the rest of the way back to the hotel. Which didn't seem like such a wonderful idea at first because I stepped out into the kind of heat that turns your legs to lead in 3.2 seconds. But I caught a break. A nice rain started falling a minute into my walk. I left my hood down. I could use the cool-off, the refreshment.

I thought about Dewey as I made my way. Sad case, for sure, and now we were about to take our relationship to a whole new level. Were we ready to make that step? How far could I trust him? For that matter, how far would he trust me?

I'd been thinking along those lines for a few minutes when it came to me that something about this street didn't feel right. Something about this street— about me on this street—definitely didn't feel right. Some bad electricity was running through the wet air.

One of those old New Orleans flashbacks?
Could be, but there was something specific to this
sensation. It almost felt like I was being followed. It
almost felt like somebody had been following me for
a couple of minutes.

I glanced over my shoulder, trying to pick
something out of the umbrellas, people ducking for
cover in the storefronts. One guy stood out—tall dude
wearing a rose-colored Saints sweatshirt, a fringe of
long, tangled hair outlining his otherwise bald head.
Why him? I don't know. Because he was a tall guy
with a lot of bounce in his step, only he kept his body
completely rigid, so that he looked like a walking
telephone pole? Because he was strolling along open
to the rain, like me? I don't know.

Maybe it was just paranoia, but why take a
chance? I stayed on Canal for one more block, then
made a turn on Bourbon. Typical late afternoon
Bourbon Street crowd. Throngs of tourists drinking
from the walk-up sidewalk bars, undeterred by the
downpour. A man and a woman, staggering on their
feet, were having a loud screaming argument about
whether today was Friday or Saturday. In fact, it was
Tuesday.

I took the first right on Bienville then went left
on Chartres, starting to smell the river. Less people
here. I carefully switched the Glock to the front of my
pants and zipped the hoodie up a few inches.

Chartres took me to the corner of Toulouse.
Head for Slim's gallery? Not wise—if anything really
was happening, keep it away from him.

Time for a quick look-back. Son of a bitch—a
truck had pulled up between Conti and St. Louis and a
bunch of guys were unloading something on the
street. It looked like there were at least a couple of

pedestrians behind them, but I couldn't tell if walking phone pole was included. Keep moving.

I turned on St. Pete, corner of Jackson Square. A group of street musicians wearing gold headbands were still playing their brass in the rain. Kids were running in and out of the crowd's raised umbrellas, laughing their little asses off. I kept looking behind me and I didn't see anything, but just for
 good measure I zigzagged around the Square, taking Royal all the way over to St. Philip before ending up back on Bourbon again.

In 1816, Pierre Lafitte bought a house on the corner of Bourbon and St. Philip, and historians have noted that the intersection was bad even then. Bourbon was just a little too deserted here, a little too far away from the action further up the street. A homeless guy slept in the doorway of a rickety building, his head protected by the trash bag of his belongings. Just him and me.

I started walking toward the bars, the drenched tourists. A few blocks up I passed a guy who was yelling into his cell. "Don't say that to me. Don't cut me off." Home safe.

I was still listening to the guy and walking past a building fronted by scaffolding, checking out the crowd ahead of me, and who the fuck do I see bopping along Bourbon? The walking phone pole, coming my way. No coincidence. He was looking right at me, like he'd anticipated all my moves and was just waiting here for me to show.

It was so New Orleans. You're walking down the street and suddenly anything can happen.

He came right up to me. I stood by the scaffolding, got a closer look at the fringed hair and the rosy Saints shirt. Dark eyes, demented gaze. I caught the mental flash of a dog howling underneath the moon.

"Why do you want to die here?" he said, first thing out of his mouth.

Not with the Chamber of Commerce, I'm guessing.

"Ex*cuse* me?"

"Why do you want to die here? You don't think we have enough?"

I had a feeling he wasn't really asking my opinion about local mortality rates, and that feeling was reinforced when he pulled a knife out from under his sweatshirt.

I thought, for a moment, about Robonnet in Dominicus Park.

Strangest thing: Guy's standing with a knife in his hand—and I'd have to say we were talking about seven inches here—and he's doing it in front of all these people, on a street jammed with tourists and whatnot, and nobody's paying any attention.

"This might be news to you," I said, "but I have no idea what you're talking about."

"If you want to die," was his answer, "why don't you stay at home and do it? Why don't you stay back in New York, back with Robonnet's daughter, to get it done?"

So now I knew—there was nothing random about this. Even my strong sense of addict's denial couldn't buy a way out of this one. He knew exactly who I was.

He took a step closer. I unzipped the hoodie, let him see the Glock. I wasn't gonna pull the piece, not with all these people around, no matter how oblivious they might be, but at least I could show it.

He stared at the handle. "It's people like you," he said, "makes everybody nervous."

I wasn't exactly sure what that meant, but I didn't think it was a compliment.

Anyway, there we were, he's looking at the Glock, I'm looking at the blade, and I never saw his leg shoot up until it was way too late. He gave good kick, karate fast and with a lot of power to it. His foot caught me square in the solar plexus and sent me bouncing off the scaffolding like he was flinging a bag of shit into monkeybars.

My hand went to the Glock and he hesitated, waiting to see if I'd pull. I didn't. I was too busy thinking that if I got very very lucky, in about an hour from now I'd be able to breathe again.

He came at me with the knife. I had just enough strength left to jump to my right and drive a hook into his kidney. I'm sorry to say it didn't have much effect, but it slowed him down enough for me to grab both his hands.

Unfortunately, he was stronger. I've got his wrists and he's pushing me back toward the scaffolding with not an extraordinary amount of strain. Now a few of the tourists are watching us but with no reaction—it's just part of the street entertainment.

The bolts protruding from the scaffolding were digging into my spine. I shoved him back—one last effort. He let me do it because he was getting ready for one massive push. That's when I decided not to resist. As he came into me with all he had I just held onto his hands and let him attack. I just sidestepped him and used his momentum to slam him into the scaffolding.

And then nothing happened. He just stood there flat up against the metal bars, not moving. I let his hands go and thought about hitting him but I didn't have to. His fingers opened and he let the knife clatter to the ground.

"*Fuck*," he said. "You *fuck*!"

He pushed himself off the scaffolding. One of the bolts was dripping with blood. So was the hole that had ripped open just above his hip.

"Look at what you fucking did to me," he said, about as hurt as he was surprised.

He took a limping step away from me, rain bouncing off his bald head, blood streaming out of the wound.

"Who the fuck are you?" I said.

He kept backing off and he wasn't happy about it. "You *fuck*! You think you're in New York? You think you're back in New York? New York's a long ways away."

What could I say? It *was* a long ways away.

The Man Who Lost His Head

I put Genesis and Slim on conference call back at the hotel. They both agreed that I'd been right to let him go—any further confrontation probably would've attracted police attention, and in light of what we were planning, none of us needed to get the police involved. So that left one large question, how did the tall wingnut know who I was? One obvious answer was that Dewey had tipped him off, but I couldn't see Dewey blowing his chance at money. Alternative explanations: Somebody had been watching Dewey, and I'd been followed from his house. Or somebody had been watching Slim, and I'd been followed since meeting him. Or—the real brain blower—I'd been followed even earlier than that.

Either way, I wanted to stay at least one more day to see if Dewey called. Slim didn't like it—he was worried about the attack and he thought I should get out now. Genesis disagreed and reminded him how valuable Dewey's information could be. Two to one. I was here for another 24.

Dewey didn't get in touch that night. Not as far as I know. Around 4 a.m. I dreamt that my cell was going off, and by the time I realized I wasn't dreaming the ringing had stopped. The missed calls showed a 504 number, New Orleans. It wasn't Dewey's house. It wasn't Slim. I tried it back. No answer.

>>>>>>

My room at the Vieux Royale was littered with tourist brochures. One of them, I noticed out of boredom, was for the Authorized Isaiah Robonnet Bus Tour, an excursion that took you to all the important sites in the painter's life. Good way to kill the morning, I thought.

The tour office was down off Jackson Square. I walked there—carefully—and found a pleasant woman wearing what smelled like English Leather on duty behind the counter. With much enthusiasm, she listed some of the stops on the itinerary. Like the Sisters of the Sacred Heart Charity, where he'd mopped floors and did carpentry work and fixed the plumbing. The little upstairs room where he'd lived and started painting, complete with the original pine dresser and spartan hardwood floors. A house where he'd stayed as a child with his 12 siblings, though the building had been torn down years before and was now a public parking lot. Some of the institutions where he'd spent most of his childhood. The gravesite where he'd been buried after his unfortunate passing.

The only spot no longer on the tour, the woman said, was the memorial fountain his children had built. Because of a drainage problem, people kept slipping in mud and getting hurt. The site had been shut down until the city could make repairs.

That omission aside, she said, the tour was extremely popular, and not only because of his artistic reputation.

"Lots of folks," she explained, "think he also brings them luck. There are stories about him, when he was alive? You could bring him a lottery ticket, he'd just touch the thing and turn it into a winner."

Not for nothing was he into voodoo

The first tour wasn't due to take off for another hour. Did I want to reserve a ticket? I didn't feel like waiting, so I bought one of the maps she had for sale. It gave directions to his grave in St. Louis Cemetery No. 1, on the corner of Basin and St. Louis. Not far away.

Most cemeteries in most places are subdued affairs—they all pretty much look the same and they're all hidden away, out of sight. Not in New Orleans. They *revel* in their cemeteries here. What I saw in Old No. 1 was, pardon the expression, drop-dead incredible. It was acres of everything—luxurious shrines and modest brick tombs, formal gardens and jungles of ferns, marble, granite and patinated steel, all watched over by angels and Mothers Of God, all erected above the ground to avoid the rising water-level tide, all—pardon again—laid out in narrow twisting Holy Land lanes lined with muscadine vines. It was like walking into a dream of death.

What a way to go. And frankly, not a bad way to start the day. The temps were still cool, the air as filled with soft morning haze and the smell of sweet olive, and I was alone in the city of the dead.

Or, actually, not alone. Two minutes inside, I'd stopped to check the map again and I noticed some movement off to my side. Someone was taking a path maybe half a football field away. No big deal. It was a public place. Visitors come here all the time. Why shouldn't somebody else be out for an early mausoleum stroll?

But after another minute or so of walking, that somebody was still off to my side. And still about 50 yards away. I was getting that being-followed feeling again.

I moved a few more feet and stopped at a monument built to resemble a Victorian gingerbread house. A peripheral glance showed a thin, slight figure in the distance, an aging, ruined beachboy. Dewey Tarantonio.

The fuck was he up to? Was he *tailing* me—although he didn't seem to be looking my way. Or was he trolling for new mortuary booty and his presence here was just a coincidence?

Forget the map. I headed off in a different direction, a lane winding off in the opposite direction. I gave it 30 seconds before I looked back. Dewey was gone. All I could see was the skyline of tombs. He wasn't tracking me. It was a true coincidence.

I started working my way back in the direction of Robonnet's grave. If Dewey wasn't following me, maybe I should be following him. But I'd gone, I don't know, no more than 20 seconds when I heard a strange far cry. It sounded at first like a bird, maybe a crow. Then I heard it again and I wasn't so sure. Not so sure at all. I reached behind and put my hand on the Glock.

Just about five seconds later I heard another sound. A long, drawn out sound, almost a moan. It was like the air around me was moaning.

I remembered standing in Genesis' library looking at the painting and feeling like the floor was rumbling. Same thing was happening now—the ground seemed to be vibrating with the *hum*.

But this time it was fear.

The sound faded. I pulled the Glock and started running in its direction.

I found Dewey next to a low stone wall. His body was lying on its back, forming the delta for a large red lake. A few bloody feet away was his head.

He'd been cleanly decapitated. Somebody who knew how to use a knife had separated his brain from his spine in one quick cut.

I backed off, I moved away. There was nobody else around, not a sound in the whole cemetery. Blood was still flowing out of the skinny stump of his neck. Somehow his body still seemed to be groaning in pain. And for a reason I guess I might never know, I thought about a phrase I'd seen in the painting:

The Dead aren't coming back.
They don't want to.

This time Slim and Genesis both agreed—time for me to get the hell out of town. No need to wait for Dewey to call anymore. It was time to street it.

Slim felt bad about Dewey. He was never a huge fan of the man, but still. Maybe he never should've mentioned his name.

Genesis had no sympathy for the hustler's fate. But she wondered about the motive for his murder. None of us knew why he'd been killed—a person like that, she pointed out, could've made any number of enemies and probably did. But if Dewey had been dispatched because he was trying to sell us information, did that tell us anything about H-L Lincoln and the people who stole the painting for him?

"Besides that they're fucking *serious*?" I said.

There could be a meaning to it, said Slim. *There could be a meaning to the way he died.*

What do you mean a meaning? his sister asked on the third end of the conference call.

Like a message. It might be meant as a message.

"And what's the message?" I said.

You mess around with this thing, you're gonna lose your head.

CHAPTER 6

THE DELIVERABLES

My Hands, Stained With Blood

The first thing I did when I got back to New York was call DeMarcus Boyd, a Nassau County police lieutenant who's an old friend. Or maybe friend isn't exactly the right description, since we first met when he was arresting me for killing that child snatcher. But we've formed a bond over the years, doing each other professional favors. Like the one I was asking now. If he had any contacts with the New Orleans cops, I said, could he use them to keep an eye on the homicide of a low level felon named Dewey Tarantonio? No, don't ask. Just, if anything breaks in the case, let me know.

The next thing I did was to call Kumiko and ask her for any background she could get on a burgeoning art collector named H-L Lincoln. He was wealthy, eccentric and reportedly lived in a castle. All I knew.

And then I called another professional acquaintance from my past, the Rev. Dook, pastor of the Pentecostal Cease Suffering Center and Covenant Church.

The storefront church was located in the grim heart of Hempstead, Long Island, bordered on either side by Moonglow Liquors and the New Wave Laundromat. Nothing much to look at it, outside or in—rows of stiff-backed chairs facing a bare altar, banks of fluorescent lights glaring off white paint. The walls were empty except for a bulletin board by the door. Notices offering help for child care, job searches, rent payment or INS difficulties were pinned to the cork. So were photos of the congregation members with the best attendance records, their faces mostly Salvadoran, Guatemalan and Honduran.

Place was roomy, though. About three decades earlier, it had been the site of one of the town's biggest all-wood furniture stores, although its main business at the time was laundering drug money. In a great irony that Slim Robonnet might appreciate, the store had also been owned by Rev. Dook, just like it was now. But he wasn't a man of the cloth back then.

His real name was Nuon Mok, and he was known on Long Island during that period as the leader of a stunningly vicious Cambodian-American gang. Nicknamed Dook, he was personally responsible for record levels of violence and torture and occasionally murder. Much of this activity was done to protect his heroin trade—he was said to be particularly concerned about maintaining the quality of his product—but some of it, especially the torture, was done just for the hell of it.

Eventually Dook got popped on various RICO conspiracy charges and did a decent amount of time in federal pen. His operation broke apart and dissolved, gradually giving way to groups like MS-13. But as Dook took up residence with the government, he saw the wickedness of his ways—you know how it goes—and gave himself up to God. Discovering what the prophet Ezekiel called *another heart and a new spirit*, he became a Pentecostal minister. Now he was back in Hempstead, spreading the Word among the poor and disenfranchised, some of them his former customers.

These days, Rev. Dook looked less like a killer fiend than a quiet, retiring Cambodian grandfather who against his better judgment had agreed to a game of Twister with his grandkids. He was sitting in one of the chairs in the front row, patiently talking to a mean looking Latino boy who was maybe 8 years old. The rev saw me and signaled to wait.

The only other person in the church was a middle-age guy with Downs Syndrome, long blond hair and a cowboy hat. He was sitting at a card table, rubber stamping the church's address on a pile of pre-printed pamphlets.

Rev. Dook was counseling the kid. Or trying to. "You understand what I say? You see me, how I spend the later half of my life, I try to undo what I did in the first. You understand?"

The kid was *so* bored. "Yeah."

"I did terrible things to people."

"I heard."

"My hands, stained with blood."

"I heard."

"It brought no pleasure. Opposite, in fact. Now I hope to serve people, hope to serve God. Satisfaction is much higher."

The kid couldn't give one flying shit.

The old man spoke to him for another minute before giving up and letting him go. He watched the boy run out the door. "The ones like that," he said to me, "they're hard talking to. Families, even worse. All is me, me, me. What can you say to people so in love with themselves?"

"I don't know. Tell 'em their bar is too low?"

Rev. Dook shrugged and got up, checked on the Downs cowboy and walked with his stoop-shouldered shuffle to the closet he called an office. Small desk, two hard chairs—that was it. Robonnet would've felt right at home.

I asked how things were going. Well, he said. The soup kitchen he'd opened last year was coming along. He was about to lease space for an after school program and after that he was hoping to raise funds for a day care center.

"I think I can help you out some," I said.

I'd been doing business of one kind or another with him for a long time, starting when I was an investigator and then as a journalist. He'd feed me insight and advice and I'd pay him for it. But he wasn't selling spiritual tips. I don't mean to cast any aspersions on him or suggest that he wasn't the real thing. He was. He did a lot for his community. But to keep his church going—a church otherwise supported by a poverty level congregation—Rev. Dook dabbled once in a while in fencing stolen goods. He didn't make a lot of money, but it was enough to afford things like soup kitchens and after school programs.

To serve that purpose, he kept his ears on the grapevines that ran through various sorts of criminal activity, and I'd go to him with an open wallet to get the fruits of his hearing.

This time, though, it was a little different.

I gave him the basics. I'd met a family who'd lost a valuable painting to thieves. They'd hired me to make a recovery. I believed I'd found the current possessor, but now what do I do?

"Is like military," he said, "like special ops. You, you're civilian contractor. You need to hire specialists."

Specifically, he said I needed a picker and a rapper. I didn't get it. Why was he suddenly talking about music? I needed a guitar player and a hip hop singer?

No, a *wrapper*. With a W. A wrapper, he explained, was crucial to any art extrication. It meant someone who knew to remove a canvas from its original premises without hurting it and who knew how to take care of thereafter. It meant someone who knew how to *wrap* a canvas.

A picker, on the other hand, wasn't necessarily an art expert. Old days, it was someone who knew how to pick locks. These days, it was someone who knew how to pick a way through locks, motion detectors, infrared activation or any other security system a latter day thief might face.

Rev. Dook said he'd make some calls, get some names. Odd career choice for me, he remarked, but he supposed I had my reasons. We negotiated his finder's fee after that with no problem—I'd just expense it.

"None of my business," he said, "but for my own mind. What's the get?"

"Ever hear of Isaiah Robonnet?"

"I know of him, yes."

"One of his. *Sex Death Dream Talk*."

He just stared at me. "Whatever happened," he said, "to starting small?"

The Wrapper

His name was Nick Manetto, though everybody called him Nick the Five. That's what he told me himself. I asked why. Cause of his hands, he said. He had great hands—he had *fantastic* hands. His brains, he admitted, maybe not so much, but he could do anything with his hands. If it's the hands, I said, just breaking the ice, shouldn't it be Nick the Ten? He had no idea what I was talking about.

He lived downtown on Allen Street, which was cool. Allen has always been one of my favorites. Almost a highway-size street divided by a center strip, with benches and pedestrian walkways on the meridian, it doesn't look like it's part of Manhattan. You're in another city, another place.

Nick the Five owned a condo over a Chinese realtor. We met in the doorway between the agency and a bodega. He said did I want to go for coffee at a bar down the street. Early in the day for a bar, he knew, but he avoided the Starbucks around the corner because it was always crowded with gentrification snobs and Hasidim. He couldn't quite come up with that last word.

"You know," he said, "what do they call 'em, orthopedic Jews."

"Orthodox Jews. It's orthopedic *shoes*."

"Shoes, right. I'm not, you know, professionally smart."

He was a mook was what he was. I could see him standing on any street corner, a muscular, reliable, eager to please guy talking up the girls all day, a streak of orange dye running front to back through his black, shaggy, early Beatles hair. I could see him hanging out, but I couldn't see myself working with him. He might be well built, but he did most of his thinking in the lightweight division.

He seemed to know his business, though. As we walked along Delancey, dodging skateboarders and stepping over bits of lettuce that had been spilled during deliveries, he told me that wrapping was more important than it might sound. It involved knowing how to get a canvas out of its frame, knowing how to do it fast and usually on the spot. It involved knowing how to roll the canvas up without damaging it and how to wrap it for safe transport. It involved knowing how to put a canvas *back* into another frame.

I'd be surprised, Nick the Five said, by how much money had been lost on jobs because somebody put the wrong painting in the wrong frame the wrong way.

The bar was called Smooch's, on Delancey. The wallpaper seemed to sag like the postures of the four other people scattered inside. We ordered at the bar and sat at a table off by ourselves. The coffee was incredible—a rich, mud-dense brew that went right to the follicles on your head.

Nick the Five asked how I liked it. That's good, he said, but did I want a drink instead? He apologized for not offering sooner.

I told him I don't drink anymore.

"Program?" he said.

"That's it."

"Me too. Trying. Got a year clean almost."

"Hard work—good for you. What was on your menu?"

"Vikes, perks, general booze. Nothing fancy." He glanced around, tuned his voice even lower. "That's what I'm saying, about this thing, what Rev. Dook said? If you're looking to use somebody, it would help my sobriety."

That stopped me. "Not sure I heard you right."

He bore down on it. "It's like some people steal to get high? I steal to stay sober. I'm doing a job, I'm thinking about it, it keeps me in the moment, it keeps me in the *now*. I'm not wrapping, shit, I'm afraid of a slip."

"Okay, now I *know* I've never heard anything like that."

"What I got, I got a disease, an illness. That's the price I gotta pay. It's like, if you get what you pay for, shouldn't you pay for what you get?"

Maybe it was the coffee, but that made perfect sense to me. I was starting to like this guy.

We came to terms. I said I'd be in touch and I took Delancey to Bowery, turning north for the subway on Houston. The skyline offered an almost totally unobstructed look at the Empire State Building far uptown. You couldn't get that kind of isolated view when you were standing closer to it in midtown. Hovering by itself against a gray sky, the building seemed to shimmer in the distance, like its grids had been transformed from steel to glass. It seemed to be shivering like a mirage.

Could be an omen, I decided in my caffeinated state of mind. Question was, good or bad?

The Picker

Rev. Dook had strong feelings about this guy Bernard
Harrison. *The finest*, he'd said. *Finest of the fine.*
He'd given me an address in North Southern Point, a
small Westchester village a few miles outside White
Plains. The neighborhood was well-manicured middle
class, the house an economic cut or two above that.

A sour faced African-American woman
answered the door, the corners of her mouth drooping
like wet cement. She was wearing a pink robe and a
blond wig and said she was Bernard's mother, Mrs.
Harrison.

Well, not exactly.

"It's not BerNARD," she corrected me. "It's
Be'Nad. Lots of people, they hear it, they say
Bernard. No. Bee-ee-apostrophe-en-ay-dee. Be'Nad."

I was led through an upscale living room into a
kitchen outfitted with all new appliances. Mrs.
Harrison sat me down and poured me an iced tea—
not asking if I wanted one—from a pitcher that had to
be filled with maybe 100 cut up lemons. She said she
knew Rev. Dook had sent me and she was grateful for
that, the reverend being so high on her boy,

"Is Be'Nad home?"

"He's here. Out in the garage."

"Can you let him know I'm here?"

Hearty laugh. "Oh, he knows, he knows. If he
doesn't, there's no point of you—"

"*Mother...*"

A bone-thin black guy was standing in the side door. His expression was serious and self-conscious, somber almost to the point of agony. You could be dead and still be happier than that.

"My son's a genius, Mr. McShane. Plain genius. And you know why? Did Rev. Dook tell you why?"

"Mother…"

"It's his *ears*. His *hearing*. He's got the most sensitive hearing you ever heard. He can hear a thunderstorm 75, hundred miles away. He can hear a watch tick other side of the house. If he concentrates on it, filters out the extraneous, he can hear a fly land in the next room."

Be'Nad took a seat at the table—and also got an unasked for glass of tea. "I understand," he said quietly, "you're looking for a picker."

"And *that's* what makes him an outstanding picker," said his mother. "He can hear the inner workings just about any security device you got. Don't matter what it is. Mechanical, he can hear the tumblers. Electrical, digital, he can hear the *algorithms*."

"Mother…"

Embarrassed as he was, Be'Nad was way too soft spoken to mount much protest.

Mrs. Harrison sat and gave herself a glass. Her son, she said, had always been very special. Even his name was special. No doubt I was curious about his name. Originally she was going to call him Bernard. But while she was carrying him, this was in the seventh month, she had a dream where she'd found a child sleeping in a field and she couldn't wake him up. She kept calling *Bernard! Bernard!* but he just wouldn't stir. But then, in her panic, she began

yelling *Be'Nad! Be'Nad!* That's when the child came
to life, opened his eyes and said, *Mommy?*

Be'Nad was squirming. "Maybe," he ventured,
"you can tell me something about the job."

"We'll need to know a number of things," said
Mom. "The money, of course—we have our ask all
ready. And the goals of the job—the deliverables, if
you will. We'll need to know all that."

"Happy to tell you."

"And just as important, Mr. McShane, just as
important is the company he keeps. Be'Nad is very
fastidious and prone to nerves—he can't be associated
with people who are unsavory or unkempt. Or
untrustworthy. I don't want him working with any
pack of thieving Mormons."

"No Mormons."

Be'Nad was in great psychic pain. "Why don't
we discuss the money?"

"Let's do," said Mrs. Harrison. "You know why
the money's important, Mr. McShane?"

"Sure."

"I'll tell you. You know what Be'Nad's going to
do for me with the next score?"

"Mother…"

She got up and went to the fridge. "He's going
to build me a pool in the backyard. And I'm going to
have this installed in the cement."

"*Mother…*"

She took a plastic bag out of the freezer. I could
see bloody meat beneath deep layers of frost.

"It's Be'Nad's placenta. I'm going to have it
installed in the Jacuzzi."

"You kept it all this time?"

"Sure, it was easy. I just keep putting these
labels on it. See? Capital letters. DO NOT EAT."

Noted.

>>>>>>

Genesis didn't even want to talk about the new costs until after we'd made love. So it was only when my body was covered with bites and the sheets were soaked with sex waters that I mentioned the numbers again. She just lay there next to me, staring high up to her ceiling. She was hesitating again, and I didn't know why. What as going through her mind? Maybe the painting's not worth it?

"Once I say yes," she said, "there's no going back, is there?"

"No."

"Once we pass this point, there's only one way to go."

"This is it."

And it was.

CHAPTER 7

LEFKOWITZ CASTLE

You Saved My Fucking Life!

Yes, H-L Lincoln *did* live in a castle, a place described on its website as an *authentic replica* of a European castle, built during the Gatsby era on the shining edge of the Long Island Sound. It was called Lefkowitz Castle, and if the name doesn't exactly conjure up visions of mystery and romance, well, that sort of speaks to its origins. It was designed as a giant Fuck You.

Herschel Lefkowitz was an industrialist who chose to celebrate the end of World War I and the return of peace and prosperity by taking up golf. The only thing that interfered with his love for the sport, besides a pathetic short game, was being denied admission to the Upper Aborville Country Club. Despite Lefkowitz's millions, and he had a lot of them, the club was determined to remain restricted— no Jews.

Well pissed off, Lefkowitz bought a few farms in the Upper Aborville area, tore up the land and built his own private course. And by private he meant *private*. He was the only one who used the course— him and such select friends as the Gershwins, the Marx Brothers, W.C. Fields, Al Jolson, Kaufman and Hart.

He really enjoyed playing his own 18 holes. He enjoyed it so much, in fact, that he eventually asked himself why do I have to travel out here from the city all the time? Why don't I *live* here?

Part of the land bordering the course included a high bluff overlooking the Sound. Lefkowitz snapped it up, overpaying by only half a million, a proceeded to erect an authentic replica of what actually wasn't a European castle but an amalgam of four castles he remembered fondly from his European travels.

But neither Lefkowitz's bitterness nor his money survived his death. His heirs, assimilated but poorer, were forced to divide the property and sell it off after World War II. The golf course became a membership club. The castle became a prep school, then a psychiatric hospital and finally a refuge for squatters until it was bought by H-L Lincoln.

So who is this H-L Lincoln and how did he become king of Lefkowitz Castle? According to Kumiko's information, he was a bile-spewing, name-calling, dirty-fighting queen—emphatically, broadly gay, completely uncloseted—who'd forged a reputation in the mortgage banking trade for ruthless, though wildly successful deals and colorful, often outlandish clothing choices. Story was he'd started out as a freshman in high school, offering 12 percent loans to fellow students in the cafeteria. I had to applaud his industry. I wasn't doing stuff like that when I was 14. When I was 14 I was alone in my basement contemplating suicide like any other normal American kid.

In any case, after surviving the various downturns in his profession, H-L decided to invest a good chunk of his money in Lefkowitz Castle and turn it into a profit center. He restored the ground floor—its ballrooms, salons and formal dining rooms—to its former glory and rented it out for weddings, parties, fundraisers, conferences, bas and bar mitzvahs and any other affairs you might have. Meanwhile, he lived on the upper two floors, rabidly building his art collection and often dressing as if he was about to take his place at King Arthur's table.

My guess: The painting was in the castle.

Be'Nad, Nick the Five and I had it in sight right now—three layers of imposing gray stone lifting off a clifftop at the water's edge, set against a clear sky that went on for miles. We were approaching the place from the 14th fairway, wearing the pastel shirts and pants I'd just bought. I'd also rented three golf bags and three sets of clubs—I had the Glock in my bag—and I'd found a sneak-through opening to the course from the road. I'm not sure how much we looked like golfers, though Be'Nad's agonized expression certainly helped.

What we were actually doing, of course, was scoping out a way to eventually get inside. We started by looking for perimeter detection systems around the grounds of the castle—looking for an electronic moat, as it were. Once we'd mapped that out and figured how to get past it, we'd think about the interior alarm systems. One step at a time. And when we were finished, we'd go back and plan for what Be'Nad called a *spatial interlineation*. I.e., a break in.

Not even pretending to play the hole—Be'Nad wasn't terribly keen on the idea anyway—we just lugged our bags along the fairway, edging closer to the castle. This gave my colleagues a chance to get to know each other.

Nick the Five was suitably impressed. "Be'Nad Harrison? I'm totally turned around. This is legend, man."

Be'Nad just nodded. He was as fidgety as he'd been in his mother's kitchen.

"Shit," said Nick the Five, "you did Allegheny, right? The Allegheny job, few years ago?"

Be'Nad nodded, shrugged—no big deal.

"*Piece* of work that was. Seriously—I'm serious."

"I wasn't completely happy with it, not from a stylistic standpoint." Somehow, Be'Nad could still wax reflective while trembling with anxiety. "It was all right at the time, but I look back on it and see a certain underdeveloped aesthetic I don't care for. Some of my more recent work, I think, reflects a different vision."

"Whatever, it was a real breakthrough at the time."

"I'm in a different space now. I'd take a more fully realized approach today."

Nick the Five gave him a chummy slap on the shoulder. "Don't have to tell me. There's plenty do-overs I'd like to be doing."

Be'Nad nodded with a vast Confucian reserve.

We worked our way over to the long barrier of trees and bushes that separated the course from the castle grounds. I took out a five iron, dropped a ball on the rough and pretended I was contemplating the lie. Be'Nad and Nick the Five stood nearby like they were offering advice. The morning sun was starting to bake down.

I looked hard around me, trying to memorize the landscape. I could see small cameras on the turret tips of the castle. They'd capture anything that happened on the grounds, but they'd have to be monitored by people. They weren't automatic alarms. Something else had to be working here.

"Gotta be sensors somewhere," I said, "but I'm not seeing a thing."

"Wait," said Be'Nad.

His eyes were half shut and his face was set in total concentration. He looked, frankly, like he was taking a dump in his pants.

"I'm getting noise," he said. "I'm getting electronic noise." He looked up in the trees. "*There*. There's... No, wait. *Wait*."

He started moving along the line of trees, still looking leafward. We followed.

"They're *there*," he said. "Look at these trees, each one of them. Look 10 to 12 feet up. Each of them has a short, stubby branch with no leaves. See? Those are the sensors. They're motion sensors, attached to the trunks and camouflaged as dead branches."

Every word his mother said about him was spot fucking on.

"Did I call it or what?" Nick the Five said. "He's the best. He's the one true. He's the—"

"Wait." Be'Nad held up a silencing hand. "Wait, I'm getting... Cries. Crying."

Nick the Five was puzzled. "Electronic crying?"

"Human. Crying. Or grunting. Angry grunting. Somewhere... Somewhere over there."

He led us along the barrier of trees and bushes. Twenty seconds later, just as I was starting to pick up the sounds, we came to their source. Peeking through the branches, we could see two men in a clump of high shrubs on the castle side of the trees, out of the sensors' range. One was a big cold slab of a man with a suit and tie and a face that looked like a pock marked ham. He was holding a gun on the second man, and the sight of the other guy was something I have to admit I'd never seen before and I hope to God I never do again.

The second guy was a short, frog-eyed person, about as tall as Napoleon, with a gag in his mouth and his hands tied behind his back with a plasticuff. Except for a red velvet jester's cap and a pair of orange renaissance slippers with the curled up toes, he was completely naked.

Not to judge a book by its cover, or lack thereof, but I knew I was looking at H-L Lincoln.

"That's vile," Be'Nad whispered. "That's disgusting."

"Some kind of S&M thing?" Nick the Five wondered.

"It doesn't sound consensual. Not at all." Be'Nad didn't look well.

I put the five iron in my bag. "Wait here."

Before I had a chance to think myself out of it, I started snaking into the trees. Doing a soft walk, still carrying the bag. Halfway through I could hear the ham-faced suit making some kind of threats. H-L's face was a nice heart-stopped white. A pile of red and orange silk had been tossed on the ground. H-L's clothes.

I began acting drunk as I moved in. I've studied the phenomenon—method actors got nothing on me. A little stagger in the step, a little slosh in the face, a little slur in the mouth. But not too much.

By the time I came out on the other side of the trees, I was crocked.

"You seen my ball?"

Both men looked around sharp.

"The fuck you want?" said the suit.

I stepped closer, spoke louder. "You seen a ball? I sliced it over here."

"Get the fuck out of here."

I blinked at him over the next few steps, attempting to focus. "Dude, the fuck're you *doing*?"

H-L started making this mix of shouts and screams through his gag. The suit brought the gun to H-L's eye level.

"There's no ball here, you fucking drunk. Get out."

But I had my mouth agape and I was too stunned to stop. "What're you doing? You robbing him or *fucking* him?"

"This is none of your private concerns."

I was close to them now. "Holy shit, are you guys homosessuals?"

"I'm telling you, get the fuck—"

He went to swing the gun to me, warn me off. But the moment he moved his arm away from H-L, I grabbed his tie, jerked him toward me and tried to put 10 years of pain into one punch.

I got about seven—the golf bag got in my way. Still, his hand went limp enough to let the gun go and his eyeballs jumped up and down for a moment like fruit in a slot machine. I thought he was going to cash it in.

But no payout. He rocked on his feet but stayed steady, and then, jumping on it so fast it was almost funny except for how much it hurt, he threw an NFL-quality shoulder into me and sent me rolling in the dirt. I heard him running off as I lurched back on my feet, but by the time I fished the Glock out of the golf bag's divided club compartments he'd disappeared in the trees.

I took H-L's gag off. The spittle immediately went flying.

"That fucking son of a bitch! He *jumped* me! Pulled a gun and fucking *jumped* me!"

"You all right?"

"Fucking son of a bitch!"

Avoiding the spray, I undid his cuffs. "What did he want?"

"Trying to get inside. Trying to *steal* from me, fucking son of a bitch."

H-L quickly put his clothes back on—purple silk underwear, a matching pair of shirt and pants in the loudest pattern of red and orange checks I'd ever seen.

Be'Nad was right—vile.

"Thank God you showed," H-L said. "All I got to say—thank God you showed. You saved my life."

"Well, I don't know how far—"

"You hear me arguing with you? I don't hear me arguing with you. YOU SAVED MY FUCKING LIFE! Son of a bitch pulled a *gun* on me, you came along and who the fuck are *they*?"

He was referring at this point to Be'Nad and Nick the Five, who were stumbling through the trees with their golf bags and running up to us.

"We have to go," Be'Nad said, shaking. "We've all violated the perimeter system. People are coming."

"Hold on, hold on," said H-L, looking at me. "You're not really drunk, are you?"

"I'm not drunk."

"You were just *pretending* to be drunk, to save my fucking life?"

"We have to *go*," Be'Nad insisted. "People with walkie-talkies are coming."

"Wait, hold on. Hold on a fucking minute."

Be'Nad's face collapsed. "They're *here*."

They were. Radio static was everywhere all of a sudden. A few seconds later a half dozen security types in navy blazers and beige pants swarmed through the shrubbery, guns out and walkie-talkies crackling.

"Where the hell've you been?" H-L greeted them. "I was almost dead out here."

The guards saw my Glock and turned their guns on me.

"Not him," H-L corrected. "Not them. Another guy. Cheap suit. He went in there."

All but one of the guards took off through the trees. The stay-behind wore a nametag on his lapel: *Barry Bendini*. He had a third grader's part in his hair and a lifetime of suffering in his face.

H-L began jabbing stubby fingers in his direction. "Guy was trying to get upstairs. He was out to *take* something. Where the fuck were you?"

"How did I know you were out here?" said Barry, picking up the suit's dropped gun. "How was I supposed to know?"

"You call yourself head of security? You're supposed to fucking *protect* me!"

Barry summoned as much patience as he could. "Just tell me what happened."

It was like this, said H-L. The guy was supposed to be a security consultant, or so he said. H-L had been thinking about bringing him in to do an operational review of the system-wide security set up, a remark that left Barry bristling.

In any event, when the guy showed up for his appointment, he told H-L that just walking in the front entrance he could see there was an exposure problem with the perimeter protection. C'mon, I'll show you. Then, once they get in the bushes, the guy's suddenly Mr. Hot 'N Horny. He comes on to H-L, makes a proposition, and H-L drops his drawers in complete and honest expectation of some nature fun and games. Instead, the guy whips out the gun and the gag and the cuffs and he's demanding the keys and codes to the upper floors.

Barry asked if he knew what the guy was after. H-L said they never got that far. I thought I might be able to take a guess.

Barry's sigh was deep and penetrating. "I keep telling you, you don't need an outside consultant."

H-L begged to differ. "I want this whole thing checked out."

"The systems here are fine."

"If the systems here are so fucking fine, then why did I need a total fucking stranger [he gestured to me] to save my fucking ass? By the way," he said, looking at my Glock, "you always play golf with that thing?"

Well, there it was, served up on a big fat plate.

"Actually, I do," I said. "I'm a security consultant."

"You're a *what*?"

"A security consultant."

"You're shitting me."

"I'm not. David Brannigan." Yeah, the same name I'd used at the Whitmore Museum. It was the first thing that came to mind.

"You're not shitting me."

"I'm not. And these are my associates. We we're just playing a round when…"

"You're really a security consultant."

"I am."

"Well *that's* ironic."

"It is."

H-L took a step closer. His face had the look of a high school teacher who was about to hand out a test. "So tell me, Mr. David Brannigan, how good a security consultant are you?"

"I think I'm very good."

"Do you?"

"I do."

"Are you as good as you *think* you are?"
"I am."
"How do you know?"
"I saved your life."
"Sorry, you *what?*"
"I SAVED YOUR FUCKING LIFE."

So that's how it happened. That's how H-L came to give us what he called *one sweet-ass deal*. He wanted to hire us to give things a thorough checking out and see if everything's working the way it's supposed to be working. Security, he said, was at a premium.

Barry Bendini protested. H-L said fine, he was thinking maybe he should fire Barry and get himself a new security chief. Then he asked me how long we'd need to do a review. I thought back to my investigation days, when I'd done similar jobs. Ten to 12 hours, I thought. Good, H-L said—why not start now? We could spend the night as his guests and finish up in the morning. He'd even give us a tour of the castle, personally.

I glanced at Be'Nad and Nick the Five. They both looked like they'd just been slobber-knocked in the head. They weren't used to getting a guided tour of the place they were trying to rob.

Follow Your Own Damn Dream

In H-L's modest opinion, if you didn't like Lefkowitz
Castle, you needed to move to another universe. Hard
to argue with him. We started with the formal
gardens, H-L and Barry taking us past fountains and
gazebos and landscaped terraces and reflecting pools.
It was like walking through heaven. You couldn't
even see the parking lots from here. Barry was just
pointing out the spot where Al Jolson had danced
with Ruby Keeler all night when the walkie-talkie in
his hip holster blared up: His people hadn't been able
to find the guy in the suit. He'd gotten away. H-L
cursed without interruption for 38 seconds but even
that couldn't detract from the beauty of the place.

The inside of the castle was pure Camelot. You
stepped into a world of swords and shields, suits of
amour and coats of arms, iron grillwork and gray
stone columns, copper goblets and brass candelabra.
H-L's jester's cap and curled-toe slippers suddenly
seemed only slightly bizarre.

No early parties or events had been booked for
today, so we had an unobstructed look at the ground
floor. Our guides showed us ballrooms and grand
ballrooms, loggias and libraries, two-ton chandeliers,
acres of waxed wood floors, the great lawn where
Toscanini once conducted an orchestra in full view of
the Sound.

Curious thing, while H-L was happy to brag on the restoration work, Barry was supplying all the history. Franklin Roosevelt had eaten in this room, Carole Lombard in that one. W.C. Fields had juggled knives over here, John Barrymore had passed out over there.

We were heading to the marble staircase that swept up to the second floor when H-L's cell went off. As he stepped away, I tried making amends with Barry. I said I was sorry about the way this was happening. He waved it off—he'd taken so much shit from H-L he'd lost count.

"Only reason I stay," he said, "I get to be here. I tell myself I'm not working for him, I'm working for the castle."

"You know a lot about it."

"I've always loved it, ever since memory serves. I've been collecting the memorabilia all my life. Someday I'm hoping I can write a history of the place."

"Does H-L know?"

"I mentioned it once. He said *follow your own damn dream.*"

The second floor was a little more sarcophagal—long, dim-lit corridors, stone-chilled air. But it wasn't quiet. Staffers kept coming and going—housekeepers, assistants, security, maintenance crews. We saw the guest bedrooms, all big-ass and beautiful. Barry noted where Douglas Fairbanks had slept, the Duke and Duchess of Windsor. H-L's own suite of rooms was fairly impressive—stick it in Versailles and no would've noticed any difference.

I was really enjoying the tour, especially when I could spot sensors on the windows and doors, or miniature cameras concealed in ceiling beams and flower arrangements. One corridor alone must've held $18,000 in security equipment.

H-L herded us toward an elevator. The top floor, he said, was where he entertained. We *had* to see that, he said. He had an aquarium up there, an aviary, a specially built sun porch with a fantastic view of the water. And oh yeah, we *had* to see his collection.

Be'Nad and Nick the Five managed to slip me looks. None of us could believe this. We couldn't believe the break we were getting.

The third floor gave us more staffers, more darkish corridors. We saw the aquarium, we saw the aviary—they were really quite something, had to give him that. Then we came to an unmarked door in the middle of a corridor, its lock secured by a military-grade keypad. H-L punched in numbers and led us into a kind of antechamber or outer office. It was as silent as a convent, with stained glass windows and a woman with black ringleted hair bent over a laptop at a desk. She looked up as we came in.

My eyes felt like they'd been set on fire.

It was Shannon Kubliak, the Robonnet expert from the Whitmore. Sitting right there.

H-L made the introductions, presenting her as his personal curator. And this is David Brannigan... And I'm thinking this is it. I'm busted. She's going to blow the cover.

But it didn't happen. She showed no sign of recognizing me. Then H-L explained that she was tending to his collection, advising him on what to buy, verifying authenticity, etc., and she started looking at me, looking...

But then he launched into an explanation of why we three were here, going over every self-obsessed detail about his encounter with the man in the suit.

Shannon looked bored. She dropped her eyes back to the laptop and didn't glance at me again.

Didn't do much for my ego, but a lot for my peace of mind.

And how did *she* end up working here? I remembered that the museum had to contact her to make an appointment, meaning she wasn't on staff. She probably freelanced for them, freelanced for H-L, freelanced for who knows who else.

There was another door in the office with another mungo-size keypad. H-L entered more numbers.

"Gonna give 'em a look," he said to Shannon.

She got up and followed us into a tomb of a room—no windows, climate controlled to a chill. About two dozen paintings were hanging on the walls, a good half of them Robonnets. I could see the titles of the two closest to me.

Dip Your Hands Into The Waters
One Heaven Versus 17 Hells

The others were too far away to read, but it didn't matter. None of them was *Sex Death Dream Talk*.

"I'm really getting into this guy his name is Isaiah Robonnet," said H-L. "I love this stuff. It really captures a mood of... Well, I don't know what it captures, but it's the mood of something."

I'm getting the cold thought that maybe H-L *doesn't* have the canvas. But wait—since the painting is hot, couldn't he be keeping it on ice somewhere else around here?

"Problem with Robonnet, though," H-L said, "I'm a newbie to the game. Lot of the old time dealers look down on me, they try to shut me out of the action. They think I'm just some foul mouthed faggot."

"Which is not fair," said Shannon.

"It's not, no. It might be *true*, but it's not fair. So that's why I brought Shannon in. You got your own curator, shit, it's proof *positive* that you're serious.

But enough with this. He wanted to show us the sun porch. *Had* to see it. Our tour group left the paintings and Shannon went back to doing whatever a curator does.

H-L took us into a long, empty corridor that stretched for a few hundred feet but felt more like a mile. It just went *on* is what I'm saying, and it ended up there in the distance in some sort of light-splashed room. That was the sun porch ahead, he said. Spectacular views, panoramic. Great for parties.

But what a schlep to get there. And what a weird piece of architecture this corridor was, nothing in it but a chair and a small table crouched against a wall at the middle mark.

H-L was going on about some of the parties he'd hosted on the porch when we passed the little setting. Upholstered armchair. Tiny bit of table. Ornamental mirror hanging on one of the wall panels. Really no big deal.

It wasn't until we'd walked another 15 feet or so that I realized—wait, why would anyone plop such stuff in the middle of nowhere? I'm no decorator God knows, but it seemed like an odd aesthetic choice. What possible purpose did it serve?

Well, maybe I could make an educated guess.

>>>>>>

Bodies Rising

By 12:38 a.m., guests at the night's two events—a Sweet 16 party and a 50th wedding anniversary—had come and gone. The castle was creepily quiet. I paid a visit to the control center, right next to Barry Bendini's office, both of them located in a windowless space on the ground floor. The control center looked like a TV director's booth, banks of monitors showing the video feeds from all the security cameras. When we hadn't been roaming the premises, Be'Nad, Nick the Five and I had spent a good bit of time here during the day, familiarizing ourselves with the systems and putting a lot of our focus on that corridor leading to the sun porch.

Two guards were on duty in here now, blazers off, sleeves rolled up, taking it easy but still alert. Four other guards were on patrol throughout the castle. I told the pair in the control room I couldn't sleep. No, the room H-L had given me was fine—no complaints. But did they mind if I watched the screens with them a
little while?

At exactly 12:41 I pointed to a group of monitors to the left. They showed the exterior views of the north side of the castle, the side facing the water. That was one area, I said, that seemed a little under protected. I wasn't totally bullshitting. If I really had been looking for holes in the security, I'd wonder about somebody approaching the castle by boat.

The guards scoffed at me. Look at what you'd be facing, they said. Look at that cliff. You come by boat, you'd have to scale a huge wall of rock that drops almost straight down into the Sound. Be one tough climb, one ballbuster-from-hell of a climb, they agreed.

While they were talking, corner of my eye, I was peeking at a monitor off to the right, the one showing the sun porch corridor. For a moment I saw what looked like a young thin black man reach up with a Handi-Wipe and unscrew a bulb in one of the wall sconces. The cameras in that part of the third floor, we knew, were all Xytel 600s, good camera but sometimes a little contrasty. A second later the corridor looked the same, though the area around the furniture setting was just a bit darker than it had been.

I talked to the guards for another minute, telling them that, Jesus, yeah, they seemed to know what they were talking about, then I said I'd head back and try to get some sleep. Before I left, though, I pointed out the corridor monitor. "Looks like a bulb burnt out."

"They're always going," said one of the guards. "Fucking H-L. He spends all this money on equipment, he buys the cheapest bulbs. I'll make a note, get maintenance on it in the morning."

I took the service stairs to the third floor. Nick the Five was waiting in a corner near the elevator. We knew the corner was a blind spot, a nonessential area the cameras didn't bother covering. I took a quick look—yes, our new belt pack was secure around his waist.

The three of us had only left the castle once during the day, telling H-L and Barry we were going to get some of our own equipment. Not a total lie. We'd gone to a few specialty electronics shops and bought a couple of things, all stored in the belt pack.

Now we moved slowly down the corridor to where Be'Nad was waiting, backs flat against the wall. Any quick action would be picked up by the cameras.

Nick the Five and I ducked on either side of the upholstered armchair. Be'Nad stood by in the shadows and watched. A pessimist, he was still dubious about finding anything behind the wall panel.

"It's just a interior design trick," he whispered. "Break up the monotony of a long hallway with a furniture setting like this."

"You know much about interior design?" I said.

"Some."

"How?"

"I don't know. My mother, I suppose."

On our knees, Nick the Five and I started moving the table and chair away from the panel. The idea was to shift the furniture down the corridor, toward the camera. With the bulb out, it should look like the stuff was in the same place.

"Your mother's an interesting woman," I said as we worked.

"Yes," Be'Nad conceded. "She is."

"She doesn't seem to mind what you do for a living."

"She's been around. She used to work in casinos. Pit boss, then manager."

Nick the Five was intrigued. "Foxwoods? A.C.?"

"Local. White Plains, Yonkers, the Bronx."

Nick the Five didn't get it.

"After-hours places," Be'Nad explained. "Illegal casinos. Rough crowds. She can handle herself."

"I don't doubt it," I said. "She talks a strong game."

"Yes, she can talk. She's very talkative. It's embarrassing at times, always was. But I have to realize I've inherited my liveliness from her."

Nick the Five and I looked at each other. *Liveliness*?

We were done moving. The mirror we left hanging—no telling what it's hooked up to. Be'Nad took a Handi-Wipe out of his pocket, tore the packet open and began scrubbing an area on the panel.

"What're you doing?" said Nick the Five.

"I don't know who's been touching this, where their hands have been.

He cleaned the spot exactly 12 times. I didn't say anything about the time he was taking. According to the patrol patterns, we had 18 minutes before a guard showed up here.

Be'Nad pressed his ear against the clean wood. I could see him concentrating, his breath slowing down, everything slowing down. Nothing around us but cool silence.

"Damn," said Be'Nad.

"What?" I said. "Nothing?"

"No, something. Damn I think you might be right."

Another Handi-Wipe, 12 more precise scrubs. He listened to another part of the panel.

"I'm getting something," he said. "A hum. An electron hum."

More wiping and more listening on the other side of the panel and he was done.

"It's wired," he said. "This thing opens. It's got eight sensors—three along each side, one each on the top and bottom."

"You know where the gaps are?"

"Try this." He pointed to a spot on the right side of the panel, about a foot up from the floor.

Nick the Five took a pair of goggles and a thin cable out of the belt pack and handed them to me. I felt the spot—there was like 1/32 of an inch space between this panel and the one next to it. Good enough.

"Careful," said Be'Nad. "There are probably more sensors inside."

"I'm betting there are."

I began threading the wire-thin cable through the space. When I got maybe 15 inches of it inside, I plugged the other end into the goggles and put the goggles on my head. What I was using here was basically a tiny light and a camera attached to a length of flexible cable—it was like performing a colonoscopy on the wall.

I pushed another few inches through. When I had two feet to work with, I turned on the light. The camera showed the inside of a small room, about the size of a walk in closet. All I saw was more paneling on the wall across from me, but turning the lens I caught sight of picture frames on the left wall. Two paintings were hung there—neither of them Robonnets. Some other purloined art that H-L didn't want seen by stray guests? Man has a bad habit I was thinking as I checked the rest of the wall with no results, and I'd just turned the camera to the right wall when I saw something that didn't belong to any place on earth.

I saw bodies rising out of coffins. I saw gargoyle faces and voodoo signs and visions of purgatory. I saw a nun with a communion host straddled in her vagina.

I moved the camera, finding text messages I hadn't noticed before.

I have known this in another time.
Twelve were the flocks who came to the well.
Two were the butchers who slaughtered them.
I will listen no more.
I have been cast down from the mounten.
At ½ 9 o'clock I have been cast down.
The profit was right, Joel 2:31.
The sun is dark, the moon is blood.

I remembered Dewey Tarantonio telling me they used to sell blotter acid with Robonnet's face printed on the sheets. I understood—realized that's how looking at the painting made me feel, like I was getting off on the first virgin glow of drugs, like somebody was talking to me in a dream.

And now I felt something else—like some tiny Satan was lighting firecrackers in my head.

We'd hit the payday, I told them. We'd made our approach and were cleared for landing. I took off the goggles and handed them to Be'Nad, asking him to take a look and see what other alarms were in there. Nick the Five would look next and examine the framing. We still had a shitload of shit to do. Tomorrow, we'd tell H-L the job was bigger than we'd thought and we'd need one more night to get it right. Then Be'Nad and Nick the Five would go back and get their respective retrieval tools. By tomorrow night, we'd be ready to go.

Be'Nad was still looking through the wall when Nick the Five took a small photo camera out of the pack. It was designed to attach to the goggles and he'd said he'd need it to remember how the painting was framed. He offered it to Be'Nad. "You want photos for yourself?"

Be'Nad turned to him and shook his head. "I never rely on photos. No photos, no drawings, no blueprints. Once I see it, I retain it."

Nick the Five couldn't buy this. "Serious? All those little doodads in there? You can remember what—"

"Wait." Be'Nad was listening again, but his ear wasn't against the wall. "Wait."

"For what?" Nick the Five's head was swiveling in all directions.

"Someone's coming."

I looked at my watch. "Guard's not due for another nine minutes."

"Someone's on the floor... Steps are getting louder. They're coming this way."

Shit. We pulled the cable out of the wall and stuffed everything in the pack. Fuck the furniture for now. We'd move it back later.

We started edging our way back down the corridor. My mouth, I noticed, was suddenly tasting like paste. As we got closer to the elevator I said to Be'Nad, "How soon?"

He was going so limp I thought he was about to pass out. "Right about now."

But there was nobody by the elevator. Nobody by the service stairs. Nothing around but shadows

"You still hear steps?" I whispered.

"No." Be'Nad gestured to the blind spot across the way, the dark area where Nick the Five had waited for me. "Just a heartbeat."

A woman's heartbeat, as it turned out. She took a half step into the dim light, the illumination just catching her curly hair. Shannon fucking Kubliak.

She hadn't changed since our meeting earlier in the day, except now she had a gun in her hand. A .25 caliber Raven automatic. A small but very effective weapon at this range.

Shit, shit, shit.

"I'm going to ask what you're doing here," she said. Flat voice, no fear.

"We're doing night surveillance," I said. "Just checking things out."

"Really, Mr. Brannigan. I thought you might be checking out an investment for your clients."

I'll say it again—shit, shit, shit.

"Okay, that," I said. "That thing at the museum, that was just... I really am a security consultant. All of us—we really are."

"And you're just doing surveillance."

"That's right."

Her non-gun hand pointed to Nick the Five's belt pack. "And if I look in that bag, what will I find? Surveillance equipment? Or something more...*invasive*?"

"We really are security consultants."

She ordered Be'Nad and Nick the Five to move to a corner a few feet away. Another blind spot. Interesting how she knew where the cameras didn't cover.

"I'd call this quite a coincidence," she said. "You come to the museum asking about *Sex Death Dream Talk*. And now you're here."

I played dumb—not a stretch. "How's that a coincidence?"

She pointed the Raven below my belt. "Tell me

who you are and why you're here or I'll blow your balls off."

It's worth repeating—shit, shit, shit.

Others might disagree, but faced with permanent castration or telling the truth, I've often found that honesty is the best policy. "My name is Quinn McShane."

She shoved the gun into my crotch and it hurt. "*REAL* name!"

"That *IS* my real name! My name's Quinn McShane and I'm an editor with *Real Story* but I used to be an investigator and I got hired to get the painting."

"Get? You mean steal."

"Matter of interpretation."

"Who hired you?"

"The Robonnets. The family."

"There's only his children."

"Right. One of them."

"Which one?"

"His daughter. Genesis."

It wasn't that Shannon looked surprise, though she did. It was more like I'd just said something that ruined her whole damn life. "What are you talking about?"

"You asked who hired me. *That's* who hired me."

"Genesis Robonnet hired you?"

"She hired me to get the painting back."

"I don't believe you."

"Why would I lie at this point?"

"Because it's impossible."

"It might sound improbable, I'll give you that, but it's not impossible."

"No, it's impossible."

"Why so?"
"Because she hired *me* to get the painting back."

-18 Degrees Fahrenheit

I suppose you could say it was very hospitable of
Genesis to invite us into her home at something close
to 3 o'clock in the morning. On the other hand, since
she was directly responsible for this entire
unbelievable fuck up of a mess, did she really have
much of a choice? Shannon and I had called from the
castle and said, uh, little problem has come up here—
we need to talk. Be'Nad and Nick the Five were still
back there in their rooms, waiting for this muddle to
get straightened out. It seemed highly unorthodox,
highly suspect, to both of them.

Genesis had us brought up to the big library
next to her bedroom, the place of course where I'd
first seen *Sex Death Dream Talk*. The wide flat
monitor—a construction clearing among the buildings
of a few thousand books—was blank now. Shannon
and I sat at one of the catalogue-piled tables. Genesis
paced in another of her loose fitting robes, her eyes
following a strict scorched-earth policy. She wasn't
happy.

I guess it was somehow right that we were
meeting in the library. It was the same place at almost
the same time of night that we'd originally sealed our
deal. It was also the same place, on the same night,
where she'd hinted that I hadn't quite been her first
choice. Her exact words, as I recall: *I've looked at*

other ways of retrieving the painting. Nothing's working out.

Turns out she was talking about Shannon.

Yes, Shannon Kubliak was a curator, a Robonnet expert—nothing bogus about that. It's just that, to pay the bills, she occasionally dabbled in thievery. She usually worked it from the inside. She'd approach collectors, sometimes those she'd met through the museum, warn them about fakes, and then gain their trust with her extensive Robonnet expertise. That's how she'd been playing H-L.

What happened was, Shannon had known Genesis from the Whitmore, and right after she heard a rumor about the painting being stolen, she'd gotten in touch. She'd told Genesis that just between us she knew a few things about the black art market, and for an appropriate amount of reward money she'd look into the theft and try to get the painting back.

"So I hired her," said Genesis. "Why not? What other options did I have at the time? She was an expert, she said she might know something and at least she'd know if it was the real thing. It *is* the real thing, isn't it?"

Shannon nodded. "It's the original. I verified it."

Genesis stood still with her hands on her hips. The look she gave Shannon had to be registering at -18 degrees Fahrenheit.

"And that was how long ago? A month and a half? *More*? I never heard from you."

"I told you I'd let you know when I had it. I'm very careful. I don't make unnecessary contact."

"And how was I supposed to know you'd made *any* progress? I didn't even know you were at the castle. As far as I was concerned you were lost in the weeds. That's why I went after Quinn when I met him. I didn't know where else to go."

"I told you to trust me."

"Trust you to do *what*? What've you been doing all this time?"

Shannon was patient. "First I had to determine who had possession. Then it took me time to get inside."

"That took you what, *weeks*?"

"Yes."

"Quinn got inside in a *day*."

It wasn't warm in here by any means but the air felt like it was crackling.

Shannon was still bristling from the last remark but she wasn't budging. "How could you do something like this? We had an agreement. One million for the return."

Genesis shrugged—so what? "I made the same arrangement with him, same money."

"Plus expenses?" I said.

They both ignored me.

"Now he's a day away from getting the painting," said Genesis, "and *you*? What do you have to show? Do you even *know* where the painting is?"

"I know it's somewhere on the third floor," said Shannon. "I was allowed to examine it twice, but I was blindfolded both times. H-L and his head of security took me to a small room each time and I know we'd never left the third floor."

"And what did they say?" said Genesis. "Did they explain all that secrecy?"

"No need. Discretion is a priority in certain circles. So's *trust*. It's *understood*."

Genesis looked tired now, like the night was finally landing on her. She sat at the table closest to us, pulling her robe around her. For once she had nothing to say.

I spoke. "So what're we going to do?"

"I know what's going to happen," said Shannon, insistent, defiant. "You're going to make a choice. You *have* to—you have to choose between us, and it won't be me. I know that. I know you won't choose me. No one ever does."

Genesis looked her over with weary curiosity. "Once again, you've made a mistake. You or him? That's the choice? Here's what you're missing. Let's say I cut one of you loose—goodbye. How do I stop you or him from going to H-L and making some money by telling him everything?"

Shannon saw the point. "Outside of killing one of us, nothing."

"Exactly. So here's what I propose." She sat forward in the chair, her face, her eyes, completely still. "Same arrangement as before—one million to *each* of you. But you have to work together. You have to partner up."

This didn't go over well.

"I don't know who she is," I protested.

"I don't know who *he* is. I don't know his bona fides."

Genesis cut us off. "Let me ask you something. How did you get here tonight?"

"My car," I said.

"Isn't that interesting. You came in one car. And when you called, it was one call. I didn't get two separate calls, two separate visits. You came together. I'm impressed."

"We came together," I said, "because we both felt you fucked us over."

"So you share something. Good basis for a partnership, good foundation for teamwork."

"I already have a team, you know that.

"Now she's part of it. She's with you and you're each making a lot of money. What's the problem here?"

"It's not just the money," said Shannon. "There's all the—"

"I *want* the painting!" Her eyes were the blue now of a high desert sky. "I think I've made that very clear to both of you. I want the painting and I want you to both help me get it back. I'm paying for it, it's the only way I can trust the two of you, but it's the way I want
it *done*."

Nothing more was said. No need. Her words were as resounding and final as the first shovelful of dirt on a pine coffin.

The Clues In The Code

Driving back at 4:30 a.m., I found it hard to make conversation. There was the resentment, there was the shock, there was the ground-brain exhaustion of a long, strange day that had started innocently or maybe not so innocently enough on the 14th hole of a friggin' golf course. I didn't feel like talking.

Neither did she. Any possibility of chit chat seemed several continents away. Then I muttered something about the painting and she muttered something about the painting and then she said something about Robonnet in general and then something else and something else and something else and by the time we hit the expressway she was off. Clearly Robonnet was her passion.

She was talking about the textures he used in his paint, and not just the homemade ingredients. Not just the matches and coffee grinds and the various breakfast cereals. There were other techniques he used. Did I remember what the background of *Sex Death Dream Talk* looked like? I did. Night sky on fire, the colors of burning blood.

"Okay," said Shannon, "did you notice how *crusted* that red paint is? Like you can see through it to four or five layers underneath? The way he did that, he mixed oil and tempera *and* a transparent watercolor. *Nobody* does that. You're taught *not* to—

but that's how he got that incredible granulated surface."

We had the windows down, clean, sharp air coming in. The sky was starting to sliver with the blue sedimentary streaks of dawn.

"Know what's ironic about this?" I said.

"Lots of things."

"I mean right now. I'm listening to you, I'm thinking—I never would've had any appreciation of Robonnet, never would've cared, if he hadn't been murdered."

"That's how life works sometimes."

"And death."

I told Shannon how I'd jumped all over the story of the stabbing in Dominicus Park, how interested I was in the mystery of the killing.

"Well," she said, "then you're after the right painting."

"Why's that?"

"There's been some speculation about messages hidden in the painting. Supposedly, his voices were warning him he was going to be killed—or he knew he was getting himself into some kind of trouble. Either way, he allegedly encoded the warnings in his work. You don't know about this?"

"News to me."

"There are a few critics and Robonnet scholars who've developed the theory. It's one way of explaining why the tone is so dark. They believe the painting holds clues to the murder."

Suddenly I felt like Hamlet—I'd gotten so caught up in the logistics of the take-back I'd pushed his death to the back of my mind.

"How's it work?"

"There's a whole schematic they've come up with, a whole methodology. It's based on misspellings, numbers, repeated words and images. There's one part, I'm trying to remember. There's a part where he's talking about maps that lead to invisible lands, something like that, and he says

The betrayer will seek to punish
The proclamation has been written in hell.
The betrayer is fated to punish me
Like Joshua nearing Gericho.

But it's Gericho with a G. Why? He'd spelled it the right way many other times. So why not here?"

"It means something."

"If you buy into the clue theory, then yes. The misspelling is a signifier, a cryptogram. It's leading you to something else. So you go to Joshua in the Bible and what do you see? *When Joshua was near Jericho, he raised his eyes and saw a man standing before him, grasping a naked sword.* The interpretation: He's saying the betrayer will punish him with a blade."

I felt like 2,000 volts of electricity were passing through my body.

I mean, sure, the clue could just be coincidence. This could be nothing more than wishfully misread random bull. Still, it felt like the electrodes had already been attached to my body and the first surge of voltage was starting to flow.

But I wasn't going to leap head first into what she'd said. I was going to keep myself steady. I wasn't taking any plunge. I did, however, make one concession: I had to admit that Shannon Kubliak wasn't half bad. Not only was she one of the most beautiful woman I'd ever met, she wasn't anywhere near as big a pain in the ass as I'd thought.

>>>>>>

The dawn gods were just starting to drag their butts out of bed when we approached the castle parking lots. She was still talking about Robonnet, how certain obfuscated critics were always debating about whether a person with aural hallucinations could really be a unique artist or was he simply a madman. And she was just saying why couldn't he have been both, are the two things mutually exclusive, when we got a view of the castle.

Something wasn't right. It wasn't even 5 o'clock yet, so why were all the ground floor lights on? And lights on the *third* floor? What were they doing on?

We pulled into the main lot. Cars with flashing lights were parked by the castle entrance. Security guards—many more than the six on night duty—were running in and out of the door. This couldn't be good.

The ground floor lobby was mass chaos. Guards in a panic, walkie-talkies chattering, lights on everywhere you looked. Be'Nad and Nick the Five were wandering through it all, bewildered.

"Something's wrong," Nick the Five confided.

I nodded. "Yeah, I'm getting that impression."

"We have to get out of here," said Be'Nad.

The whole scene was watery and unreal.

Barry Bendini appeared. Christ on the cross wasn't suffering *this* bad.

"I'm fucked!" he said. "I'm *so* fucking fucked!"

"What's going on?" I said.

His words came out choked. "One of his paintings—gone. Stolen."

"Which one?" said Shannon.

"The one you saw. You know, *that* one."

"*Sex Death Dream Talk?*"

Barry nodded, too overcome for words.

I glanced at Shannon, Be'Nad, Nick the Five. We looked like all our mothers had just died.

Somehow I managed to discover the presence of a tongue in my mouth. "How did it happen?"

"By boat," Barry said. "They did it by boat. They got in through the boat tunnel."

"Through the *what*???"

To his credit, Barry was apologetic. "H-L had a boat tunnel built back when he bought the place. Had it built in the cliff rock on the Sound, in case he ever had to escape. You know how he is with security."

"I wish you'd fucking told us. Would've been nice."

"No one's supposed to know. Not even the guards."

"Why the hell not?"

"In case one of his old mortgage clients really came after him, he wanted a foolproof way out."

Jesus H. Christ. A boat tunnel? I knew something was off about the castle's north side. I should've paid more attention to that cliff face. But I'd let myself get too obsessed about the third floor.

Barry looked like his head was about to be used for a bowling ball. His walkie was alive in the holster, voices telling him *pick up pick up pick up.* He was just going to answer when a live voice cut through the rest.

"What have you fucking *DONE* to me?" The words bounced and echoed between the stone columns.

Yes, H-L was joining us, performing a short-step march down the marble staircase. He was wearing a brown ankle-length monk's robe with a rope around the waist. Thank God—I couldn't take any color combinations right now.

"How could you let this happen?" he said, confining his remarks to Barry. "How could you *fucking* let this happen? Why weren't your people watching the tunnel?"

Barry was purely astonished. "Because you wouldn't *let* me. Remember? You wouldn't let me *let* them."

"Then you should've fucking talked me *into* it!"

"But you told me—"

H-L suddenly raised his arms and gripped his own head. "You see what I'm doing? You see these hands on my head? You know why they're there? They're the only things stopped my fucking *brains* from blowing apart!"

Shannon stepped in, trying to mediate. "H-L, it's not really his—"

"*No*! It's *gone*! You understand? The painting!

The painting! It's gone because this dicklick can't do his fucking job."

He pivoted to the dicklick in question. "Barry, you wanted time to do a book? You got it. Get your ass out of here cause you're fucking *fired*."

Back to Shannon. "And *you*. You're fired too. The painting's gone—I don't care anymore. The fuck I need you for *now*?

"And *you*." This was me. "You and your friends—you're all fucking fired. Supposed to be security consultants? What the fuck good are you?"

"You could've told us about the tunnel," I said.

"If you were any fucking good, you would've *found* it!"

Gotta say, he had a point.

CHAPTER 8

A FLOWER THAT GROWS FROM THE SOULS OF THE DEAD

Not An Easy Line Of Work, Is It?

The Pentecostal Cease Suffering and Covenant Church had a flat roof, so I don't know what kind of rafters were holding it up, but whatever they were they had to be shaking. The former storefront was now a showcase for a booming, bopping Caribbean cocktail of salsa and reggaeton turned out by a group of take-you-higher musicians. Their rhythms were being picked up by every person in this big roomful of congregants. And there were no shorts or flip-flops here, like you see at other churches. This was all shirts and ties and best dresses—well-groomed people going religiously crazy with screaming prayers and shuttering tambourines.

I'm betting Rev. Dook never partied like this in the past, not even when he was dealing.

He was standing off to the side of the altar, Bible in his hand, gentle rock to his body. The centerstage of the altar was occupied by a younger man of the cloth, a Hispanic guy with a bruise-purple birthmark and a helmet of tightly trimmed curls copied from Tom Jones circa 1975. I could catch some of the Spanish he was shouting to the crowd. Something like *a dark time* and *contamination* and *death dawning unaware.*

Downbeat, definitely, but it wasn't stopping his listeners from whooping and stomping and dervish dancing. This is why they're called *los aleluyas.*

Rev. Dook looked up from his Bible and saw me in the back of the room. I'd called earlier and told him what happened—he knew I was coming. He left his spot, no hurry, and made a casual curve around the side of the crowd, acting like there was nothing more pressing on his mind than a trip to the men's room.

"Sorry to interrupt," I said.

"It's okay."

I referred to the preacher with the disco curls.

"Who's he?"

"My assistant. I have no energy for services anymore."

"Looks like he's doing a good job."

Rev. Dook shrugged. "Too much negativity, but he'll learn."

He took me by the bulletin board, closer to the front door.

"Anything?" I said.

"Nothing. Silence. Not a word."

"Shit—excuse me."

He waved it off—or gave me absolution.

Back on the floor, all attention was going to a short, fat woman with a small head. Between her size and the way she was hunching her shoulders, her tiny head looked like the turret of a tank. Her eyes were closed and while she swayed like the tank was about to topple over she was shouting *Alashalaba! Oltanaganana!* She was speaking in tongues, taken over body and soul by the Holy Spirit, just like the disciples in an upper room in Jerusalem on the first Pentecost.

"She's all right," I said, "right?"

"Never better."

I showed him the list Genesis had given me that first night, the names of the starter collectors who hadn't been allowed to negotiate for *Sex Death Dream Talk.*

> *Julia Pervez*
> *Bobby Hucknail*
> *Orfa Collins*
> *H-L Lincoln*
> *Abdul Bazzi*

Did he know anything about them?

The answer was yes, not really and no.

"Bobby Hucknail, this Julia Pervez, I know something of them. They've bought dirt in the past."

"Bought dirt. Dirty art?"

"Black market, yes, but in the past only. Lately, nothing. Not for long time, in fact. These others..."

"H-L we know about."

"Yes, but these others. Orfa Collins, Abdul Bazzi—never heard of them. No bells." He handed me the list back. "Basically, come right down to it, I have nothing to say but sorry."

We checked on the woman. She was still glory-shouting and head-rolling and swaying so much like a gyroscope gone amuck that people had to hold onto her arms to keep her from pitching over.

"What do I do now?"

Rev. Dook gave me a been-there nod. "Not an easy line of work, is it?"

Genesis wasn't quite so understanding. She yelled, she screamed, she sounded a lot like H-L, as a matter of fact. How could this happen? You had it right in front of you! You nearly had your goddamn *hands* on it!

I'd let her know as soon as we'd gotten booted out of the castle. Shannon suggested I make the call. She likes you better.

Didn't help.

Genesis said she'd done everything she could. She'd stuck a long arm under the mattress and come up with the cash whenever it was needed. And what did she get in return? She expected better. She demanded better. *Much* better.

And you tell *her* that.

Now I was getting in touch post-Rev. Dook. She wasn't in any better spirits. It has to be *somewhere*, she said. It hasn't just *disappeared*. It hasn't *vaporized*.

This was all by phone, of course. She hadn't asked me over. No sex—that was my punishment.

Wherever it is, you *get* it, she said. I don't care if it's in the buckle of Orion's belt, just *get* it.

I almost wish it was in Orion's belt—at least I'd know where to look. As it stood, though, there were no leads. Be'Nad and Nick the Five had asked around—nothing on the streets. Shannon had made calls and asked oblique questions—nothing, nothing, nothing.

I was even starting to wonder about Rev. Dook. Could he have sold me out? Be'Nad and Nick the Five said no way. The reverend had a long established reputation and he wouldn't be changing it up at this stage of his game. Too much to lose. He wouldn't do anything to hurt his church.

"We just have to wait," said Nick the Five. "Some jobs, you do it, you sit on the cashbox for a while. Maybe this is too soon. Maybe this is all just fantastically too soon."

One thing I did know: This job was turning out to be a lot more complicated than I'd thought.

I Recognized The One
Who Would Sacrifice Me

Shannon called—she had something. No, not about
the location of the painting. She'd been looking into
all these clues-to-the-killing theories. There was more
to them than she'd suspected. Much more. She really
thought there might be something here.

We met at a diner in the West 100s, near her
apartment, just a few stops up from my place in Hell's
Kitchen. We took a booth but sat on the same side so
we could look at her laptop at the same time. The skin
of her throat was patched with red, flushed with
heat—she was excited about something.

She called the painting up on that Robonnet site
and pointed to a small set of images near one of the
corners. It showed Jesus standing before an authority
figure dressed in a red Roman tunic—Pontius Pilate,
presiding over the trial.

"Usually when you see this scene," said
Shannon, "you see Jesus surrounded by the Sanhedrin
who accused him. But look what we have here."

Three men were standing around Jesus and they
all appeared exactly the same: obese and flesh-
rippling naked, black hoods covering their heads.
They seemed more like deviant executioners than
upright Jewish judges.

"The theory says that whenever Robonnet repeats a motif," she said, "it has significance. Whenever he repeats numbers or words or images. He's doing it here with these men."

True, the three S&M porkers not only looked alike, they were all painted in an identical way—identical postures, identical positions.

"You have to ask, is he just getting lazy?" she said. "Or is there a reason for the repetition. You see their right arms, how they're trying to hide something behind their backs?"

"Yeah."

"You see what they're holding?"

"Too small."

She blew the image up a few percentage points. Now I got it. They were each holding a knife.

"Why is that?" she said. "Same thing he was killed with—why? No one ever tried to stab Jesus in the Gospels, so why knives?"

"Sort of interesting."

"More so if you look to the right."

A short scroll of words had been painted next to the images.

I looked into the darkness,

I saw what had been prophesized, what had been planned.

I heard the black words that are spoken everywhere,

But always in disguise.

I recognized the one who would sacrifice me,

Like a flower that grows from the souls of the dead.

The text ended at a picture of a solar eclipse, the moon concealing so much of the sun that only one ray of light was able to spill over the umbra.

"Here," said Shannon, "is the real killer, so to speak."

I followed the line of sunlight as it traced a path across the canvas, moving over a crumbling obelisk, a medieval sundial, a man on top of a woman in the missionary position, his back gashed with bloody flagellant slashes.

The light ray began to stutter like a lightning bolt before it stopped at the image of a ruined temple. One word had been engraved on the face of the stone: *Esagila*.

"What is that?"

She'd researched it. "The early Hebrews worshipped at the temple of Esagila, and once a year, during the New Year's observations, they recreated the mythological battle that led to the creation of the world. The battle took place between Tiamat, the dragon creature who ruled the primal ocean, and Marduk, the warrior god. Marduk won. He stabbed Tiamat with a lightning bolt and split the creature in half, right along the line of its chest. One half became heaven, the other earth."

The shiver I felt zigzagged up my spine just like that lightning bolt.

"That's a lot of symmetry," she said. "I don't think it's coincidental. I think it's intentional. I think the theories are right."

"He knew. He knew what was going to happen."

"Either he knew or he was experiencing some kind of premonitory vision. Either way, I think if you want to know who killed him [she nodded at the screen], the answer is somewhere in here."

It felt like something was buried inside me,

waiting, clawing at me. Something was hidden inside but it was too deep to bring to the surface, too deep to put into words.

Yet.

The Stone Has Been Rolled Away

Barry Bendini lived in a crowded but tidy apartment in Douglaston, Queens. I went out to see him, check on how he was holding up. I still knew a few people from the investigation days that maybe he could call for security work.

He looked like a man with a seriously crushed heart. I gave him my contacts; he thanked me. He thought he'd be able to find another job—he thought he could put a good resume together—but it wouldn't be at the place he loved.

"Just walking through there everyday," he said. "All the history to it…"

Did I want to see some of his memorabilia? He'd been collecting Lefkotwitz Castle stuff since childhood.

"Some people think I'm kook crazy with this," he said, "but I don't give one good goddamn."

Barry brought cartons of the goods out of his bedroom. Just a fraction of the total, he assured me. Soon his living room was spread to capacity with photos, souvenir programs, promotional brochures, thank-you letters, menus, napkins, matchbooks, newspaper and magazine clippings, video and 16 millimeter of the biggest weddings and parties, at least one story behind each event.

He had everything. Posters and postcards from the castle's glory days. Yearbooks and banners from its prep school years. Parking permits and involuntary admission forms from its use as a psychiatric hospital. Production notes from the movies shot on location at the castle during the 1930s and 1940s.

He even had the original plans for the boat tunnel. A sore subject, sure, but I was still interested in taking a look—just sorry I hadn't seen the thing myself. Barry explained that when H-L purchased the property, his engineers discovered a grotto—a natural cave—in the stony cliff facing the Sound. The grotto extended roughly 200 feet into the rock formation under the castle, and H-L realized that if he excavated 60 more feet, he'd have himself the means to sneak away if needed.

It was all here—memos, proposals, contracts, blueprints. Barry unfolded the master blueprint on his carpet, showed me where the work was done. I slowly deciphered the diagrams in diazo blue and white, gradually saw the umbilical shaped passage that led out to the water.

And maybe, maybe I was still thinking about the painting. Maybe I was still thinking about looking at the painting with Shannon—I don't know—but I let my eyes drift down to the block of words in one corner of the blueprint. It listed the contractor's name and then, beneath it, the names of the subcontractors who worked on the project.

My eyes just grazed over the thing—why was I even bothering with this?—but they stopped at one of the subcontractors' names. Michael Hucknail.

Hucknail. As in Bobby Hucknail?

I didn't know *exactly* why, but at that moment I thought about one of the Robonnets in his daughter's underground gallery. I thought about the words I'd seen.

Behold, it is spoken,

The stone has been rolled away.
Hucknail? Michael Hucknail? How common a name can Hucknail be?

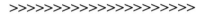

CHAPTER 9

I WILL TEAR THE NAME OUT OF THE SECRET NIGHT

Diaper Rash

Not very, as it turns out. Bobby Hucknail did indeed have a brother named Michael, and Michael ran a construction company that had done work in Manhattan, New Jersey and Long Island. So the brother of one fanatical Robonnet collector knew how to get inside the home of another fanatic Robonnet collector. How cozy is that?

And who was Bobby Hucknail? Kumiko helped me out with that. She reminded me that he'd once been featured in *Real Story*. Remember? No. The Shiney

Hiney guy?

Of *course*. His name meant nothing to me, but who could forget Shiney Hiney? If you couldn't remember Shiney Hiney—the ointment that people rubbed on their babies' butts, their own butts, their lips, their shoulders, their elbows and just about every other body part known to humanity—then you couldn't remember shit.

It all began years ago at a drugstore in a small town in central New Jersey. The store was called Fischer's pharmacy, and old man Fischer helped make ends meet by mixing up his own diaper rash cream in the back room. It was just a local product and it didn't even have an official name outside of Fischer's Diaper Rash Cream, but every mother in town swore by it. Any chaffing or irritation on baby's bottom would disappear in days, if not less, with only a few applications. There was nothing exotic in the stuff, zinc oxide, boric acid, mineral oil, castor oil—and possibly a so-called mystery ingredient, a balsam imported from Peru or Bolivia or somewhere in that same neighborhood. Whatever, it worked.

In those days, all the drugstores in central Jersey and I guess most of America were mom-and-pop operations, independently owned. As time went on, though, the indies folded in the face of Walgreens, CVS and the corporate chains. Fischer's was the last holdout in the town, and when its doors finally closed, old man Fischer sold the formula for his diaper rash cream to this local guy, Bobby Hucknail.

Up until then, Hucknail had been engaged in a variety of entrepreneurial enterprises, which meant he wasn't doing shit. Once he got hold of the formula, though, it was a different story. Maybe he was inspired by the balsam. In any case, he gave the cream a riper but spelling-skewed name, Shiney Hiney, set up an internet distribution system and began hawking the product at trade shows, something old Mr. Fischer had never bothered to do. In just a few years—the stuff, remember, was *good*; it actually worked—Shiney Hiney was being carried by a few hundred Wal-Mart stores across the country. Hucknail was making decent money.

But then he hit upon a truly genius scheme. He started marketing different versions of Shiney Hiney—one for chafed adult skin, one for dry hands, one for chapped lips, one for jock itch, one for irritated pets, one for acne, one for poison ivy, one for chill blains for all I know. There were at present time about a dozen variations of Shiney Hiney available in all the thousands of Wal-Marts in America. The basic formula for the ointment was the same, only the packaging was different, which meant that with no development costs, millions of dollars from Shiney Hiney sales were falling directly to Hucknail's bottom line.

He was sick rich.

So That's A No?

That's how he could afford to live in the village of
Brighton Manor, a serene mecca of big money set in
Morris County, N.J., only about an hour west of the
city. Specifically, Hucknail lived in a luxury condo
called The Carlton Arms, a glass and blue-quartz
concrete building with absolutely no sense of humor.
Bobby owned a large apartment of the top floor,
which meant the fifth floor, the limit allowed by the
village's ultraconservative zoning codes.

One of the many advertised attractions of The
Carlton Arms was its walking distance to New Jersey
Transit. No lie. Its entrance was only a block away
from the Brighton Manor railroad station, a quiet little
structure marred only by posters for a local theater
group's annual production of *Ah, Wilderness*.

The station's landscaped parking lot, in fact,
directly faced Hucknail's apartment. And that's
exactly where we sat ourselves one morning, we
being Be'Nad, Nick the Five, Shannon and myself.
I'd scouted the site the day before, and with a little
rudimentary photo-shopping I'd been able to forge a
parking permit for the van we'd rented.

Again, all kudos to Kumiko, who not only told
me who Bobby was but who also tracked down a few
Hucknail contacts. I'd spent part of yesterday and part
of Genesis' money talking to two former Shiney

Hiney employees. Now I was sharing my notes with the rest of the crew.

The most important thing to know about Hucknail was that while he made his fortune by focusing on the final stage of the digestive tract, his primary passion was its opening act. He was obsessed with food, he was crazy on food. He was consumed by what he consumed.

And man did it show. Bobby stood about 5'6" but his weight ranged from 350-400 pounds. He not only never missed a meal, he never missed any of his in-between snacks. One of the people I talked to said she once saw Bobby in a brown suit standing next to a UPS truck and it had taken at least a second to figure out which was which.

Now it's true that his appetite for art couldn't compare to his lust for eating, but it still wasn't small potatoes. The ex-employees said that his apartment, which doubled as his administrative office, was dripping with art. Shannon's research showed that Bobby owned a number of Robonnets, and it was possible that a few of them had been purchased in less than legitimate ways. She now knew too that Bobby had been shunned by many of the other Robonnistas because of his weight and his means of livelihood.

He was a perfect candidate for the painting, which was why we were sitting in a van staring at his fifth floor apartment.

That was the good news. The bad news was that Bobby rarely dragged his gigantic butt out of said apartment. He almost qualified as a hermit these days in that he did all his work from the condo, hardly ever had visitors and maintained contact with the outside world mostly through IM chatting, email and cell phone. True, he had a full time staff come in during the day and he had two live-in bodyguards, which—

technically—most hermits don't. But otherwise he was a stay-at-home kind of guy. The only times he went out was to go to a good restaurant for dinner. And once in a great while, when he felt the need, he'd take off for a fat farm.

Be'Nad sniffed with great emotion. "Somewhat of a *pagan* reputation, isn't it?"

We agreed that Bobby was a freak. Shannon thought Diane Arbus would be training her camera on him if she were still with us. The question was, how do we find a way in? How do we get a window on this big boy?

Nick the Five suggested that since he does a lot of IMing and emailing, we try to hack his systems. But without knowing what kind of protection he had in place, that could get backfire-tricky.

"Okay," said Nick the Five, "he's on the phone all the time, right?"

"From what I heard."

"Okay, why didn't I think of this? We listen in on his phone talk. We listen in on the cell phone conversations. We can do that, right?"

Be'Nad was eating a bag of pomegranate seeds and he kept popping the round red berries in his mouth while he stared out the van window. It took a while for him to realize we were all staring his direction.

"What are you looking at me for?" he said. "I can't do that. I can't pick out a single wireless conversation."

For Nick the Five this was a near impossibility. "You can hear *anything*."

"With all the wireless noise going through the air right now, even as we speak, you expect me to isolate a single conversation? At this distance?

Through the soundproofing of cement walls? You ask too much."

Nick the Five refused to accept this. "You can't be saying you *can't*."

"There are limits to everything. Obviously."

"So that's a no?"

Be'Nad went back to his berries. So much for that. We sat in silence for a minute. There was still some early summer haze in the distance. It was like looking at the sun through cotton.

Shannon seemed to have something on her mind and it was giving her the struggles. I looked at her and she looked at me looking at her and she looked away. Seven seconds later she looked at me again.

"I like the idea of the conversations," she said.

"Well, yeah."

"I think it would really help to hear the phone conversations."

"Sure it would."

"I think I might know how to get it done. But it'll cost. You think Genesis would pay?"

Depends. Targeting Bobby Hucknail had taken some of the sting out of the painting's loss.

"She might."

Shannon nodded quickly but spoke slowly. "Then I think I might know somebody. I think I might know someone who can help."

Confetti Out The Ass

The someone she knew, a woman, lived in Lincoln
Towers, a few minutes from my place. Shannon
called and when the woman said yeah she was
available, I suggested we all go back to my apartment
and meet her there. We waited in the living room,
everybody seemingly comfortable, while Shannon
explained to me that her associate was a wireless
specialist, a person known in the trade as a sucker.
The term wasn't derogatory—it referred to the ability
to vacuum digital data out of the air.

Be'Nad wasn't opposed. "Some of them," he
conceded, "can be quite good."

The woman showed a little after 2 p.m., and for
sure no one would ever confuse her with the more
traditional kind of sucker. She was hard-bitten Latina
with lots of weather in her face and a scar on her chin.
Her name was Randi Gutierrez and she spoke with a
husky, gravelly voice that maybe had been worn
down by whatever left all those lines in her face.

Her favorite colors were red and white. I only
say that because her pants and blouse were patterned
in red and white and she was carrying a large red bag
with a small white fluffy Maltese dog inside. Her
pocketbook was a vivid red and white and so was the
backpack strapped to her shoulders.

She looked like Mrs. Santa Claus. After six
years in Sing Sing.

Shannon made the introductions, saying she'd worked once before with Randi and she was brilliant at what she did, and it was right about then when I noticed that Randi was staring hard at Nick the Five. Why? The orange dye streak running through his hair wasn't *that* unusual.

I looked at him. He was staring at her with utter surprise. If he'd seen confetti blowing out of his own asshole he couldn't be more surprised.

Awkward. Nobody spoke for a few seconds. Just stare, stare, stare.

"Just guessing," I said. "You know each other?"

They both nodded.

"Is there history between you?"

"Yes," said Nick the Five.

And that's all he said. No explanation.

"Whatever it is, is it gonna interfere?"

"No," said Randi, and she said it with complete finality. "No way."

With the question asked, answered and dismissed, she put the dog down and began showing us the contents of her backpack. Which, aside from a variety of peripherals, came down to a laptop and a flat, rectangular piece of metal that could've passed for a cheese grater. Randi tried to explain that there was no outstanding mystery to what she did. Once any form of cell message was in transmission phase, it wasn't sound or text anymore. It was simply a string of digital bits arranged in coherent numbers. And all she did, really, was identify the patterning of those numbers using algorithms that…

That's exactly when Nick the Five stood up, said, "this is *bullshit*," and walked out the room. Randi just watched him go, profoundly unmoved either by his outburst or the way he stomped into my kitchen.

Guy's pretty sensitive about algorithms.

I found him leaning his head over the sink. He was solidly shaken up.

"What's going on?"

No answer—staring straight into the drain.

"Talk?

He turned to me, then gazed back at the living room.

"Out here."

Many years ago, when the building went condo, the sponsors combined two railroad flats into this one big apartment. As a result, my place has two entrances, one in the living room and one in the kitchen. I released the keypad on this door and we stepped into the privacy of the outside hall.

"Tell me."

He brooded on it for several seconds. "She's my ex."

"Your ex. Ex-girlfriend?"

"Ex-*wife*."

Jesus. I felt like I was driving a bus and every passenger I picked up was crazier than the last.

"How long were you married?"

"Little over two years."

"When was this?"

"We broke up, it was 16 months ago."

"How bad?"

Nick the Five shook his head. Too much for words. "I haven't seen her in nine months. Though it feels like…well, I guess about nine months."

I took a step back and a long breath. "So what can we do about this? What's it gonna be?

"I don't know. You're the shot caller here—you think you need her, you need her."

"What if I need you both? Then what?"

"I don't know. I mean, I'm not saying I want to be included out or anything. It's just, she walks in, I'm not ready for this."

"Let me ask. Is she good at what she does."

"Oh yeah, she's fucking superior."

"And do *you* think we need her?"

"I guess."

"So what do you think? Can you make the adjustments? Can we make this work?"

Nick the Five did a lot of staring at the hallway carpet. "I guess. I guess so. A lot of what this is, I guess, it's a self-inflicted womb."

"There you go."

>>>>>>

We went back to the living room. Things weren't good. Everybody was on their feet and their voices had risen proportionally.

Randi had the little Maltese out of the bag and was holding it in her arms. "Well I'm sorry it's such a big deal to you," she was rasping at Be'Nad, "but you know what? I don't give two shits. This is how I work. This is how do things."

Be'Nad wheeled to me and I didn't like the way he looked, not at all. "Did you know about this?" he demanded.

"About *what*?

Now Randi wheeled on me. "You don't mind if I bring Hillary, do you? I don't work without her. It's a stipulation. Shannon knows."

"It's all right," said Shannon. "The dog is fine."

I was confused. "You're saying you need the dog—Hillary, is it?—on the job?"

"That's right."

"Why?"

Randi hesitated, but only for about 5/8 of a second. "She speaks to me."

Be'Nad clarified. "She claims the dog communicates with the dead."

Shannon qualified. "But only by whimpering. She never barks. She's very quiet."

I looked at Nick the Five. "Did you know about this?"

"I would've remembered."

"Look, look, look," said Randi, "I can understand why certain people might have a problem with this, but Shannon has no problem with it, and I obviously have no problem with it, so if other people have a problem with it, then it's *their* fucking problem."

Be'Nad was seething. "I can't *stand* circular logic." Then to me. "Can I have a word?"

So it was back in the kitchen, turn off the alarm, out in the hall again.

Be'Nad was breathing heavily, trying to calm himself down. "I'm not happy about this."

"Yeah, I can see."

"I won't do it. I won't be locked in a van with that animal."

"Okay, why, exactly?"

"Where's it *been*? Is it *clean*?"

"What if we make sure it is?"

"Has it had it shots?"

"What if we make sure it has?"

"I *still* don't like it!"

"Be'Nad, listen, I have to ask. You're sure it's the dog?"

"What's that mean?"

"You're sure it's not professional jealousy?"

"*Jealousy*?"

"Randi can hear something you can't?"

"Please. If I were going to be jealous, it would be of the *dog*."

Maybe we could use a pause here. I took one. Three seconds, four...

"Well," I said, "I appreciate your telling me."

"I appreciate your listening. And I appreciate your calling me in on this job. It's just that..."

"The job, yeah. A question about that. Your opinion. Would you agree the phone conversations are important?"

"I would agree with that."

"And that we need to hear them?"

"Of course."

"And that Randi is the only one who can do it?"

"Yes."

"So?"

"So?"

"Can you get this right in your mind?"

Be'Nad gave it considerable eyes-on-the-carpet thought. "Just make sure that dog's not diseased."

Crisis over. We went back to the living room. Time to get down to business.

Or maybe not. Shannon was standing in the middle of the room, arms folded. "We need to talk."

With the door from the kitchen opening and closing so much, this was starting to look like a French farce.

In the hallway, Shannon went right to apology.

"I feel bad about all this," she said. "I just want you to know. Randi, I know, she can be a little disruptive. That's why I hesitated about bringing her in."

"She's got a way about her."

"And I had *no* idea about Nick the Five—none. I didn't know she was married to him. I knew she had an ex in the business, but she never said who."

This was getting exhausting. I leaned against the wall. "Well, here we are with the two of them. How big a problem are we looking at?"

"I don't know. I know nothing about her with him. What I *do* know is that she's good. She's very good."

"You vouch for her?"

"I'm vouching."

"Good enough. Let's do it."

"You're sure?"

"Let's use her. With the dog."

Shannon tried to be reassuring. "I know things aren't supposed to work this way. But I also know that this is how things work."

Right. As we went back inside, I was thinking I'd worked with some lunatics before, especially at *Real Story*, but a bigger collection of misfits than the people in this apartment would be hard to find.

Myself included.

The Trinity Site

Shannon stayed behind for a few minutes after the others left. There was something she'd noticed in the painting last night that she wanted me to see. She called the image up on my computer, saying she'd been looking at a fragment of text that had always baffled her. Never could figure it out. But looking at it in light of the killing, she thought it was suddenly making sense.

She pointed out the area on the screen:
I have told you, I have promised,
I will secretly tell this story
716194552945
I recognized the face in the darkness,
I will secretly speak the name
716194552945
The number of my fate is 716194552945
The number of my phantoms is 716194552945
I will tear the name out of the secret night.

She said it was very unusual for him to repeat numbers and she never knew why he was doing it here. But thinking about it last night, thinking about his death, she believed she had an answer.

716194552945—what did it mean? She didn't know until she happened to focus on the 1945 near the middle of the sequence. Could it refer to a year? Could the number signify a date? She broke it down—that gave her July 16, 1945, but it still left five numbers hanging.

So what happened on July 16, 1945? She looked it up. The world's first atomic bomb was tested that day at the Trinity Site in White Sands, New Mexico. It occurred that morning, at 5:29 and 45 seconds.

716194552945

The text, she said, was a prediction of a violent, catastrophic end. It was a prediction of his death. *The number of my fate is 716194552945.*

And to reinforce her interpretation, she pointed to a small image painted just below the last line. It was a half closed eye surrounded by eight arms. It was the symbol, she said, of Ollin, one of the carvings on the Aztec Calendar Stone. Ollin meant movement, sky shaking transformation, change that comes with the force of an earthquake.

"He's foreseeing his own murder," she said. "Not only that, he's telling us who did it. He's telling us that whoever did it is named somewhere in the painting. *I will secretly tell this story. I will secretly speak the name.* God, it's so *obvious* now."

"It's *something*, I'll give you that."

"Something else. I thought of something else last night, another motive for stealing the painting."

"Besides what it's worth?"

She nodded. "If whoever killed him is named in the painting, wouldn't that person want to keep the painting hidden?"

"Why bother? You want clues, you do what we're doing. Go to the digital version."

"But what if there are details in the original that we can't see in the digital? This looks like hi-res, sure, but who knows? Who knows what we're missing? You see what I'm saying?"

I did but at this point it didn't really matter. We could talk about hidden clues and missing details for the next five hours, 29 minutes and 45 seconds, but it all came down to the same thing: We needed to get our hands on the painting.

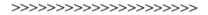

CHAPTER 10

NIETZSCHE, LIVER DUMPLINGS AND ONE TOO MANY WIVES

9:15 am

Things at the Brighton Manor train station were quiet now that the rush hour crowd had taken off for Manhattan. All five of us—six if you count Hillary the dog—were sitting in the van, watching the sun glint off the brass *Please Curb Your Pet* signs strategically placed along the Carlton Arms' front lawn. Randi, dressed in a different red and white outfit today, was setting her equipment up and explaining how it worked. The thing that looked like a cheese grater, for example, was a unidirectional antennae with an intercept field of 1,200 feet. The laptop held the scanning software she'd designed. Specifically, it was pattern-capture software that used the algorithms she'd mentioned yesterday to decode, analyze and build a database for any wireless communication she was able to skim. All she had to do, really, was plug the antennae in the computer and aim the thing at Bobby's apartment.

Actually, it wasn't quite that easy. Bursts of static and other forms of electronic gibberish were followed by long stretches of silence. But Randi kept making her adjustments, and within 20 minutes we were listening to a man with a fast mouth and labored breathing making call from that apartment.

...you talking about? You're serious? The langoustines? You sure? He can't do that—he can't take the langoustines off the menu. God fucking

forbid. I'll call him—I'll call him right now. I'll say
you lose the langoustines, you lose me as a
customer...

Within moments, however, the conversation
shifted to a related topic.

...don't ask. A tragedy. My weight is a tragedy.
When did we talk?... Okay, four days ago I put on a
pound and a half. Two days ago I dropped the half.
Yesterday, up three. Today, forget it. I won't even talk
about it. I won't even go there... Of course there is.
What do you think? I take that padlock off the
refrigerator, I'm dead... No. No, you're wrong. Food
is not my problem. Eating it is.

A minute later Bobby was calling someone else.
If we were compiling a list of his compulsions, we'd
have to add talking.

...no, it's my knee. The fucking knee. Bad today,
killing me... Yeah, well, I'm seeing the doctor
tomorrow, but fuck it, if she can't do anything, I'm off
to the farm. I gotta lose some weight... I don't know
which one. Fuck does it matter? Farms are all the
same. I've just gotta—wait! WAIT! Did you get to
Choo-Choo's last night? Did you go? You went?
So?... Yes, yes, the liver dumplings. Tremendous.
Fucking superb... Pasta chiturra? Okay, that's good,
that's good. Everything at Choo-Choo's is very
passable. Except the baby spotted sardines... No, no,
I had the baby spotteds couple months ago. Next day,
worst farts I ever had. History making farts.
NIGHTMARE farts.

"He's a vile man," said Be'Nad. "He's an
obscene man."

No one disputed the assertion.

And he hadn't given us anything we could use
yet. Still, Randi was recording every word. You can

never tell when some random piece of bloviation might later prove handy.

Interesting intravan development: It looked like Be'Nad had gotten over his aversion to Randi. I couldn't speak for the dog, but he was definitely impressed by Randi and her technology. At one point he asked how the pattern-capture software worked. Bobby had taken a break for whatever reason— working, visiting the bathroom, snacking—and he'd stopped talking. So Randi had much opportunity to explain how the algorithms were able to locate proportional wavelength contours and convert them into nodal identification points.

Be'Nad followed along. "As a rule," he said, "I usually don't pay much attention to automated eavesdropping. But this, this is interesting."

"Well," said Randi, "as a rule I usually don't reveal this much of my process. But you asking, it's a different story."

"Why me?"

Randi laughed. "The legendary Be'Nad Harrison? I'm surprised you don't know all this already. They say you can hear people talking to themselves, hear what they're thinking."

"That's a *bit* of an exaggeration."

"Well, Allegheny, that was no exaggeration. The Allegheny job was phenomenal."

"Oh, he's beyond that now," said Nick the Five, suddenly butting in. "He's in a different space, *completely* different space." This was a good amount of mocking in his voice and it wasn't exactly good natured. "He's striving for a more mature vision."

"I'm trying to operate on a somewhat different aesthetic," Be'Nad quietly explained.

Nick the Five laughed out loud. There was no reason to laugh, but he did.

Shannon and I exchanged looks. What the hell was *that* about?

11:30 am

You had to wait on these things, be patient. You just had to sit there and let Bobby Hucknail's jackhammer mouth gradually give you a picture of who he was and what his daily routine was like. So far, we'd gotten a good grasp on the range of his conversational themes.

•There was more of what we'd heard before. Weight gain, weight loss, what he ate, what he'd like to eat—each word off his tongue shot through with obsession.

•There were soul-searching debates over which restaurant to go to tonight. Most of these struggles went on for 10 minutes and none had yielded a decision as of yet.

•There were discussions about marketing Shiney Hiney. Bobby, evidently, was trying to develop a new branding campaign. The product, he argued, should speak to people about more than just sore butts and other afflicted body parts. Shiney Hiney should connect with issues of well being and good health. Shiney Hiney should be all about the quality of *life*.

•There were complaints about someone named Mitzusuka who'd apparently fucked him over a business deal.

...can't get over what the old bastard did. I just can't get over it. My feelings are hurt. My feelings are very, very hurt... Well who does he think he is, walking around like he's God's gift to the pharmaceutical retail community... No, he doesn't listen is what it is. He just doesn't listen. He should

*take his AARP discount and buy some fucking Q-Tips
with it is what he should do...*

Bobby was still bemoaning his fate when Randi
noticed a van pulling away from the Carlton Arms.
Cars and trucks had been coming and going all
morning, but this one got her eye. Azuma
Extermination.

"That's funny," she said. "I know the guy who
owns that. Azuma. Could be interesting."

"Why so?" I said.

"He might be, what's the word, sympathetic.
He's got a little history to him."

"What kind?"

"Attempted carjacking. It was years ago."

"Attempted?

"He couldn't drive stick. But I'm just saying, you
know, for a price, he could be useful."

"We'd need to know more about Bobby before
we go there."

"I know, I'm just saying."

"How do you know this guy?" Nick the Five
wanted to know. "This carjacking exterminator?"

Randi ignored him. "I'm just saying, could be
interesting."

"I asked you," said Nick the Five, "how the hell
you know this guy?"

"None of your damn business is how I know
him."

"I asked you a fucking question!"

"Bite my fucking ass!"

And there they went, full-lung screaming at each
other, Randi cutting loose with Spanish explosions
that were too fast and rich for me to understand but I
knew they were curses because of all the *fuck you's*
and *fuck this's* Nick the Five was giving back to her.

Nietzsche said man is a bridge, but the tolls these two were collecting were unfuckingreal.

11:50 am

Randi said she had to go potty. She told Shannon to keep the antennae in position and the thing would work by itself, keep an eye on the dog, and she stormed out of the van.

A minute of silence went by, and pretty strained silence at that. Be'Nad seemed sick with upset. Nick the Five, I didn't even look at. Shannon's expression was telling me that maybe this wasn't such a great idea.

I said I was getting out to stretch my legs.

I met Randi on her way back.

"Let me guess," she said, "you want to talk about him. Well so do I. What's his problem?"

"You tell me. Tell me what we're dealing with here."

"We're not dealing with anything, so far as I'm concerned."

"I know we're dealing with *something*—I just don't know what it is. I asked him yesterday, all he said was it ended bad."

I could see the artery pulsing in Randi's neck.

"I guess you could say that," she said. "I guess any time you go off and marry another woman, you can call that a bad end."

"Another woman. You mean after?"

"No, before. *Before* the after."

"Before the after?"

"*During.*"

"You're saying he married another woman *while* he was married to you?"

"That's exactly what I'm saying."

Nick the Five was turning out to be complicated in some radically unexpected ways.

She told me how the hell it all happened. "Short version, we met at work. Remember *Metamorphic Red Rites*, that job?"

"I don't follow the trade."

"Nice painting, nicely done. We grabbed it together—we were part of the team. We got along, we got married, everything seemed fine. About a year into it, he starts acting strange. We're both working different jobs, didn't see much of each other. I ask what's wrong. Oh nothing, nothing, nothing. Few days later he shows up with this tattoo on his chest. R.G., my initials. He says look, see, this is how much I love you. But I'm thinking this is weird. How come just my initials? Why not Randi? Or R.M., Randi Manetto, my married name?

"A week later, my cell's not working, I go to use his. Pick it up, I happen to notice he's got this name programmed, Roberta Gundersen, lots of calls to and from. Roberta Gundersen—R.G. I call the number. Are you Roberta Gundersen? Yeah, who's this? I say I'm Nick the Five's wife. I'm expecting her to say I didn't know he *HAD* a wife. Instead she says, no, *I'M* his wife.

"I put it to his face. He starts crying, he's all weepy and sorry. I made a mistake, I made a mistake. They met a few months before, got married in some quickie ceremony. He says he'll leave her, he'll cut it off. He says he loves me, I'm the only one. He's begging please please trust me. You know what I tell him? I'll never trust you again, and I walk out. And that's *it*. That right there, that was *it.*"

I nodded in sympathy. "That was enough."

"So now he's here? Means nothing to me. BFD."

"Big fucking deal?"

"Let's just proceed. He's got trouble with it, tough. I can handle his shit."

For a moment it looked like she'd get a chance to prove it. Nick the Five was out of the van and approaching us. But he wasn't looking to start something. He had news: Bobby had made up his mind and picked a restaurant for tonight. Shannon wanted us to know.

"Place called The Tango Grill," Nick the Five said as we walked to the van. "He wants the corn-fed tilapia at The Tango Grill."

"Corn-fed tilapia?" I said. "Can't be."

"Something like that."

"They feed corn to fish?"

"Tilapia's a fish?"

Turned out to be cornbread-crusted tilapia, but yes it was going to be served at The Tango Grill. Shannon googled the location. Salisbury, N.J., an easy half-hour's drive from Brighton Manor each way. This was big. Bobby was going to be gone for a while tonight. We had an opportunity. Now we had to find a way to use it.

3 pm

Life in the van seemed to go smoother after that. Knowing we might make some large progress tonight soothed everybody down. We discussed various scenarios, various ways we could try to get a closer look inside. Meanwhile, we kept listening to Bobby as he kept hashing over the same topics. Food, weight, his knee, his bouts with various forms of gastrointestinal malfeasance. The guy Mitzusuka came up again—*they say he's got vision? His vision matches the size of his dick.* Then it was back to oral consumption. Couple of months ago, he told one person, he'd eaten so much he'd ended up hemorrhaging. Again.

Man had one powerful addiction.

But even that seemed to help us relax. Feeling was, after a rough start to the day, we were finally settling into a groove. Now we could just sit and listen and plan, watch the world outside go ripe in the afternoon light.

Then Hillary spoke up.

The tiny Maltese had laid dormant throughout the day, but a little after 3 o'clock she started whimpering. Randi gave her careful attention, like a patient listening to a doctor's instructions, and came to the conclusion that her late mother was speaking to her through the dog.

This naturally aroused some interest. Be'Nad, in particular, was percolating with curiosity. By contrast, Nick the Five was just a teensy bit skeptical.

"Maybe it means she's hungry," he suggested. "Or she's gotta go."

"No," Randi insisted, "those're different sounds."

She said she *knew* this dog. She'd bought Hillary right after the marriage ended and had spent considerable time with her and if there was one thing she knew for certain the dog was channeling her mother at this very moment.

Her remarks prompted Nick the Five to remember the Christmas day they'd spent with her mother. He'd turned the TV on to the Channel 11 Yule Log and her mother told him to turn it off because it was getting too goddamn hot in here.

Randi conceded her mother had been getting a little senile at the end, but said she was fine now and claimed her mother talked to her just like she did when Randi was a little girl.

Nick the Five said she was full of shit.

Randi just looked at him, completely calm. "That's all right," she said. "Your mother talks to me too sometimes."

That got a rise out of him. "*My* mother?" he said. "You're shitting me, right? *My* mother?"

"Your mother."

"Saying what?"

"She doesn't like where she's resting. She doesn't like where you put her. She says where she's buried, all she's looking at is a transmission shop. It's unsightly."

"I didn't pick that place. *She* did."

"She picked the cemetery, but you let them lay her in that plot. It's all she talks about. You should show more respect for her feelings, her view."

"She's right," Be'Nad agreed. "You have to respect your mother."

Shannon, I noticed, was squirming mightily at all this—but not as much as Nick the Five

"I *do* respect my mother. Who says I don't?"

"Then don't leave her in that shithole," said Randi.

"You need to get her out," Be'Nad advised.

"*Do* I?" he shouted at Be'Nad. "Fucking business is it of yours?" Without waiting for an answer, he rocked out of the van.

Nothing like a little drama.

I caught up with him as he was pacing the parking lot. He was walking around like every blood cell was pumping with attitude. How much of this fucking guff, he wanted to know, did he have to put up with? I told him when it came to guff he was giving way more than he got. He wasn't pushing the emotion pedal—he was mashing it all the way to the floor.

He blamed it all on her. She was goading him, digging into him. Her intentions were less than honorable. Well, I said, I can understand why she'd be pissed. She told me about your other wife.

He turned somber. "That was a bad time," he admitted. "It was a...it was a fucked up situation, I guess you could say, for lack of a better word."

"No, I think that about covers it."

"Two wives, let me tell you, it wore my ass out to shreds."

"How did it happen?"

"How did it happen? I don't know. I mean, how it happened, it happened cause I was crazy high back then. I was high all the time. That's why I stopped. Randi left me, I didn't want to lose her. I lost it, I broke down, ended up in the hospital. That's when I stopped."

He was looking straight ahead at absolutely nothing. Whether he was staring into a gray past or a gray future I didn't know, though sometimes it's possible to do both.

I asked him to remember what he'd said about doing jobs, how they helped keep him straight. You know, we've got a job here, so you should be keeping all your mind on that. He nodded, agreeing. He wasn't arguing the point.

All this anger, I said, all this jealousy, what do you think? You catch it from a public toilet? It comes from your own fucking head. When this shit with Randi comes up, you gotta turn it over, you gotta pray it away.

He said he'd try. He said he'd sincerely try to make a 365-degree change.

We started walking back. He stopped.

"One thing," he said.

"What?"

"Be'Nad. I think I'm clueing to something about Be'Nad."

"To what?"

"Is he cracking on Randi?"

I fought the crack of a smile with everything I had. "Be'Nad? No. Not at all."

"You sure? You sure he's not making a move on her?"

"Believe me, it's not gonna happen. And you know something, that kind of suspicion? You're still thinking in the past."

"You're right, you're right." He started walking. "What the fuck, no use crying over water under the bridge."

3:45 pm

The climate was tense back in the van, still quivering from the aftershocks of the argument. I was thinking what I needed to do was meditate, get my mind clear again. Hard to pull off, though, with Bobby coming in loud and clear.

...killing me! I'm telling you, my God, it's fucking killing me! I can hardly stand, this goddamn fucking knee... I'm going, yeah, I'm going tomorrow. I'm seeing the doctor tomorrow. Got an 11:45, but fuck it. You know what I'm saying? You KNOW? I'm sitting here, there's a plane flying right over my head, I'm thinking maybe that's where I should be, flying off to the fat farm...

I looked out the van. Yeah, there was the plane. Probably coming out of Newark or JFK, flying from east to west over the other side of the building.

...know what it's like? Just like that time, remember the time I ate the whole wheel of brie? The whole fucking wheel? How sick I was? You remember how sick I was?...

I kept listening to Bobby, but something was bothering me. Something about the plane. I'd seen it go over the apartment, but...

I took another look at The Carlton Arms. Bobby had a big wide apartment, mostly southern exposure but with a few windows on the east and west. The plane, though, the plane had flown on the *north* side of the building. It had flown *behind* his apartment. He couldn't have seen it from any of his windows.

I called one of the ex Shiney Hiney staffers. A follow up question: Did Bobby have a skylight on the roof? Not exactly. He had *skylights*. The apartment was loaded with skylights. Every major room in the place had at least one skylight.

I studied the building, its grounds, its fifth floor, thinking about something I hadn't done in some time.

"You know how to climb?" I asked Be'Nad.

"I've only done it," he sniffed, "oh I don't know, 16 or 17 times, so yes I know how."

"How about tonight?"

Be'Nad sighed like an old man who'd been resting comfortably for hours and had just been told to move. "I suppose, if I must."

9:30 pm

Walk though the grounds of The Carlton Arms at night and you feel like you're walking through some gigantic illuminated map. Little lotus-shaped light fixtures dot the path around the artificial lake in back of the building and line the walkways leading to the gym, the spa and the enclosed pool. It's like teams of landscape designers went crazy stringing amber pearls everywhere they could.

For all the glow, though, you'd find dark pockets here and there along the walls of the building. Be'Nad and I were crouched in one of them at the moment, taking the equipment out of our backpacks. I was assembling the tube of a climbing gun, an expensive piece of toolery that resembled a wide-mouth bazooka. Be'Nad was tying a rope to a closed metal claw.
When he was done, he dropped the claw in the barrel of my gun.

Okay, here we go. One more look around—clear. I took aim at a point just above the roof and pulled the gun pin. A soft *poofff* went off as the claw rose, arced and landed five stories up. Be'Nad produced a remote and pointed it at the roof, hoping he was making the claw—a collapsible grappling hook—unclasp its fingers.

I pulled on the rope. It gave a few feet, then yanked to a stop. I tugged—it held. The grappling hook was open and had caught the lip of the wall.

"It's good?" he whispered.

"It's good."

We stepped into our leg and waist harnesses and made sure once more that our phones were shut off. Then we double-laced the harness webbing to make it secure and started tying figure-8 loops in the rope. Be'Nad was going to go up first. He went flush to the wall and put a foot on a slab of blue quartz concrete.

"Ready?" I said.

"Yeah." He gripped the rope. "No. Wait. There's something I need to ask."

"What?"

"Is something wrong with Nick the Five?"

"Like what?"

"Does he think I'm interested in his ex?"

This was a hell of a thing to be whispering about under the circumstances, but what can you do?

"He might be."

Be'Nad nodded with great gravity. "I'm getting that impression."

"He's a little jealous."

"You have to do something for me. You have to tell him I don't get involved in things like that. You have to tell him it's not true."

"I already have."

"I'm just not a relationship person."

"I understand."

"I can't let anything get in the way of my work."

"You ready now?"

Up he went. I followed. We took it very slow, very easy, testing each foothold, each new hoist on the rope. No rush, no noise. In patience lies safety.

I could feel the heat building up inside me as I passed the third floor. Been a long time. Eyes burning with sweat, salt taste in my mouth, hands getting wet and slippery. Don't think about it. Don't think about how far you could fall or how much further you have to go. Just move step by step, pull by pull, breath by breath. Zen and the art of breaking and entering.

The roof—at fucking last. We rested for a minute, getting our muscles back and getting used to the smell of tar paper. Be'Nad had a towel with him, using it not to wipe but to slap the sweat off him like he was swatting at flies. I looked at the dots of light on the ground below. There's a certain magic in altitude, even when it's only five stories up.

Ready. We stepped lightly to the closest skylight. It showed us the kitchen—a room, obviously, that had to see a lot of action. A serial steroid abuser was sitting at the table, drinking a beer and watching TV. He had to be one of Bobby's bodyguards, an awkward heap of molded muscle with an Adam's apple that even from up here looked as big as a fist.

The other bodyguard, presumably, was sitting in The Tango Grill at the moment, watching his boss stuff his face. Bobby's business staff was gone for the day. The guy beneath us was supposed to be alone, and he looked it.

Be'Nad took out a Handi-Wipe and gave the corner of the skylight 12 internally counted strokes. He bent in, put his ear to the sanitized glass and listened. After 20 seconds went by, he shifted to another corner and repeated the process.

"He's got four sensors on this thing. Diebolts."

"You'll be able to shut 'em?"

"Take me about five minutes for the lot."

We went to the next skylight. This one gave us a view of the living room. The place was thick with Old World style—armoires and credenzas, ottomans and tapestries, floral prints and overstuffed upholstery.

"French Provincial," said Be'Nad.

Not what you'd expect from the Shiney Hiney king. Or maybe you would.

After a minute or so of looking down, we realized we were seeing only part of the living room. We switched to a skylight 15 feet away that promised the rest of the view. The first thing I saw was an artificial fireplace, complete with andirons and a mantel. Then, crouching down at the skylight, I could see the space over the mantel.

And there it was. No more than 10 feet below me—there it was. Not a digital image, not a pixelized imitation. The real thing, separated only by the glass panes of a skylight. I was looking right at it, looking at the nun spreading her legs, the scrolling lines of coded words, the bloody background sky on fire. It was *here*. It was right fucking *here*.

He had the painting hanging right over the fireplace, right out in the open. That took balls. Though maybe a man who rarely had visitors could afford to get away with it.

Be'Nad cleaned a spot on the skylight and listened to the glass. "Same thing here. Four Diebolts. Five minutes to get in."

"Good. That's good." I kept looking at *Sex Death Dream Talk.*

Be'Nad leaned in again, concentrating. "Thing is, once we get past this, what other systems does he have? I don't know—I can't get a read. I don't know what else he's got down there."

"Yeah, okay, we'll find out. We'll find a way to find out."

Not the greatest answer, I know—it lacked a little something in precision and detail—but my head was scattered. I couldn't turn away from the painting. Just looking at it, I could hear strange animal cries, I could hear birds beating their wings in overgrown trees, I could hear the sounds of a jungle that existed 30,000 years ago.

If I had any doubt before, I had none now—this thing could put a spell on you.

As soon as we got back in the van I turned my phone on and made two calls. The first was to Genesis.

Good news—Bobby Hucknail did indeed have possession. It was hanging in his apartment. I'd just seen the thing myself.

She took the news even closer to heart than I'd expected. Leviticus—aka her brother Slim—had just been hospitalized in New Orleans. Dizziness, shortness of breath. The large man had a complicated coronary history.

"Good news," she said, "is exactly what I needed to hear today."

The second call was to Randi. I asked her to go through the recordings and doublecheck. What time was Bobby's appointment with his doctor? He said 11:45, right?

Oh yeah and one more thing. That friend of yours at Azuma Exterminating? Can you give him a call?

CHAPTER 11

THE LABORS
OF OUR FRUIT

A Match To Gunpowder

At 11:30 the next morning, Be'Nad and I were standing in front of Bobby's apartment door. We were wearing plastic mesh basketball caps and sea-blue uniforms with *Azuma Exterminating* patches over our hearts. Be'Nad was carrying a canister of cypermethrin insecticide with a long spray nozzle. I was carrying a Sharpie and a metal clipboard. During the night we'd come to an arrangement with Randi's friend, promising him that we were just going in to look and wouldn't do anything to sully his name. In exchange, he got a nice chunk of Genesis' cash.

The bodyguard we'd seen last night, the one with the nuclear Adam's apple, answered the doorbell. He was even bigger at eye level. I felt like I was staring at the entire state of Kansas.

No Glock today. Unless you were dealing with some *really* big roaches, an exterminator wouldn't be carrying a piece.

The bodyguard's treble-heavy voice asked what we wanted.

"The building's sending us around," I said. "The apartment just below you, they've reported an infestation. We just want to make sure it hasn't reached you."

"Infestation?"

"Right."

"Of what?"

"Cockroaches."

He blinked at us. "Cockroaches can climb? They can go up a floor?"

"They can go anywhere, sir. Up, down, around."

"Height is no impediment," added Be'Nad.

"Shit. Come on in."

He led us into as foyer that was as big as the Brighton Manor railroad station itself. More French Provincial furniture, of course. And a skylight. We had a glimpse of the living room off in the distance. Corridors running to the left and right of the foyer led to other rooms. The sound of clacking keyboards was coming from the right side. Must be Bobby's staff, meeting the Shiney Hiney demand. As for Bobby himself, we were guessing he was gone, off for his 11:45.

"Might as well start here," I said.

We slowly orbited the foyer, checking the baseboards and looking behind the furniture. I made a couple of notes on the clipboard. Be'Nad, meanwhile, had this quizzical, far away look on his face, like he was listening for hidden music.

"I got to tell you," said the bodyguard, "I never seen any kind of roach here. Not one."

"You don't want to start, do you?"

"Guess not."

We'd nearly completed our tour of the area when Be'Nad began squinting and fidgeting, looking up and around. Whatever security system was in place, he was getting something.

The bodyguard blinked at him. "Why're you looking at the ceiling? Wouldn't bugs be on the floor?"

"He's a little unorthodox," I explained. "He can *sense* infestation."

The bodyguard swallowed. His bobbing Adam's apple looked like something they'd toss in the shot put. "Jesus, creepy. That's—that right here is kind of…"

Regrettably, further description was cut off by the sound of an argument blaring from the left side of the foyer.

"Will you come on?" someone was saying. "We're running late."

"I *am* coming on. Look at me. Do I look like I'm doing anything *but* coming on? I'm moving as fast as I can."

No mistaking that second voice. Bobby was still here.

"I'm just saying, we're gonna be late."

"I fucking *know* we're gonna be late!"

A moment later, as the floorboards bent beneath us, we were looking at Bobby in the flesh. And what a lot of flesh there was. He was a baby faced fat man with tiny hands and feet and he was wearing a white suit that I swear had to be visible from Mars.

He slowly hobbled into the foyer with a bad limp (that nasty knee) and what had to be the second bodyguard. The latter was another slice of hired meat, a fugly guy wearing a wildly colored Hawaiian nightmare of a shirt.

Bobby regarded us—slightly. "Who're they?"

"There's roaches in the apartment below," the first bodyguard said. "They're checking it out."

Bobby shook his head sadly. "Those people downstairs are pigs. I don't know how they let them in the building."

"We gotta go," the Hawaiian shirt guy said.

"Okay, okay." Bobby moved to the front door and glanced at the first bodyguard. "You know the drill."

Our guy nodded, walked out of the foyer and stepped in to the corridor on the right.

Bobby gave us another look. "Make sure they check the kitchen," he yelled.

"I will," our guy yelled back.

The following things happened next:

•The second bodyguard opened the door.

•He and Bobby walked out.

•The first bodyguard rejoined us in the foyer.

Simple. And yet something was up with Be'Nad. He suddenly seemed baffled, troubled. He was looking at the air and he wasn't happy. Something had changed in the last few moments. Something was different.

The front door closed, got locked.

"I better show you where the kitchen is," the bodyguard said.

We followed him to the left. Be'Nad caught my eye, shook his head. I didn't know what had just happened with the security system, but I knew it was causing him grief.

The kitchen walls were made of cubes of milky green glass. We spread out, opening cabinets, looking under the sink, peeking behind the refrigerator.

"If you're gonna spray," the bodyguard said, "I can still eat, right?"

"Be our guest." I made a *yech* note on the clipboard.

"Gonna have me a snack."

I saw the bodyguard reach for a bowl of fruit on the counter and pick up a peach. I'm still not sure what happened next, but it happened fast. I was looking under the table, going through the motions, when I heard Be'Nad say, "What are you *doing*?"

It wasn't a casual question. He was asking with fear.

My head went to the bodyguard. All he was doing was taking a bite out of the peach.

I looked over at Be'Nad. He was going all jittery and spastic. He was staring at the bodyguard and saying it again. "What are you *DOING*?"

The bodyguard blinked at him. "I'm eating myself a peach."

No good. Be'Nad was getting hysterical. "What the *fuck* are you *DOING*?"

The bodyguard turned to me. "What's wrong with him?"

"I don't know. I've only been working with him a few days." Which was true.

Now Be'Nad's whole body was shaking. The spray can fell out of his hands and thumped to the floor. "Put it *down*," he said to the bodyguard. He had tears in his eyes.

"I think he's having a fit," the bodyguard said.

"Talk to me," I said. "Tell me what's wrong."

But Be'Nad wasn't looking at me. "Put it *DOWN*!" he said, trembling like he was peaking with fever.

"Get a hold yourself!" the bodyguard urged.

Be'Nad didn't. In fact, he began to tilt to one side and look like he was about to pass out. But he grabbed the ledge of the sink and was able to steady himself, keep himself from toppling, and for a moment he seemed almost okay. Then he suddenly doubled over and puked on the floor.

This brought some hard blinks from the bodyguard. "You can't *do* that. You can't be *DOING* that."

Be'Nad responded with a fresh stream of vomit.

"*Stop* that! Look at the *mess* you're making!"

Be'Nad wasn't looking at anything. He was too busy with another gut heave.

"I'm telling you to *stop* it!" The bodyguard stepped closer to Be'Nad. "You slimy fuck! I want you to stop it right *NOW*!"

The kitchen seemed to flash with white light at that point, like someone had put a match to gunpowder. The bodyguard lunged for Be'Nad and put him in a choke hold, trying to stop the spew of vomit.

Not on my watch. I jumped up behind the guy and wrapped my arms around his neck, locking my hands and squeezing them against that cannonball he called an Adam's apple. Didn't have much effect. Still holding Be'Nad, the bodyguard jabbed a humungous elbow into my ribs and sent me crashing into the cabinets with my ass on the floor.

As I gazed around and tried to remember when, and if, I was born, I noticed a half dozen frightened faces just outside the kitchen. The Shiney Hiney staff. They'd heard the ruckus but they were keeping their distance. They weren't going anywhere near this shit.

Meanwhile, the bodyguard was really giving it to Be'Nad. He was going dog wild, putting such a tight clamp on Be'Nad's throat that it knocked the Azuma cap off his head.

I got to my feet, and before I could think myself out of it I picked up the metal clipboard. It wasn't much of a weapon but it had a nice solid edge. Which is what I rammed straight in to the back base of the bodyguard's neck.

Thing worked. As he turned his head around you could see it mostly in his eyes. You could see the electrodes in his brain going on and off and on and off and then shutting down as his big body collapsed to the floor.

I scooped Be'Nad up—and his cap and his can— and hustled him out of the kitchen. Bobby's staffers were still standing there. I felt they deserved some explanation.

"Some people just don't like exterminators," I said.

I dragged Be'Nad to the front door and a moment later, as we were stumbling down the outside hallway, I was thinking, that guy who owns Azuma? Randi's friend? We were gonna have to throw some more cash his way after this.

We Have Ourselves A Plan

It was the peach that set him off. Be'Nad's mother
had no doubt on that score. "One thing I knew early
on," Mrs. Harrison was saying, "he couldn't take the
sight of peaches. Never could, not a chance. He'd lay
an eye on a peach, he'd get as nervous as Ezekiel. All
the shaking and the upchucking and the passing out.
Even as a child, a tot, no, no, no, he could never abide
a peach."

Be'Nad had insisted I take him back to
Westchester. He could barely breathe in the van, let
alone talk, and he was showing a bad, bad case of the
all-over shivers. So home it was.

His mother wasn't surprised. He had a very
sensitive constitution, she said. Anything overly
elaborate—Hebrew silverware was one of the
examples she mentioned—could upset him terribly.
But nothing, for whatever reason, could compare to
peaches.

"You see I don't keep no peaches around here,"
she was saying. "No peach motifs, either. Take a
look—dishes, napkins, wallpaper. No peaches in
any form."

"Mother."

We were sitting in her kitchen again, drinking
more of her lemon-clotted ice tea. Be'Nad had
calmed some since the episode, but he was still worse
for wear.

"He's got his peculiar ways," said Mrs. Harrison, still wearing that pink robe and blond wig of hers. "There's no dancing around that. He was a child
once, he tried to levitate himself. You tell Quinn about that one?"

"No."

"He got it into his head that if he hyperventilated fast enough, he'd turn lighter than air. He'd just float away like a piece of I don't know what. Cottonweed or something."

"I was a crazy kid," Be'Nad allowed.

"Even had an old umbrella with him as a parachute. Funniest thing. Course all he managed to do was pass out and keel over. Poor little fella."

"*MO-ther...*"

Mrs. Harrison devoted another couple of minutes to explaining how her son's oddities, no matter how bent, were probably the price he had to pay for his exceptional gift. She then decided that as soon as we were done talking he was going to need some rest, so she went upstairs to turn down his covers and fluff his pillows. Her departure gave Be'Nad a chance to finally talk without interruption and answer the two prime questions before us: (a) What about the security system? (b) Why was he perturbed even before the peach eating incident?

Identifying the system had been no problem, he said. It was one of the Pro-test 2000 series, a solid, acceptable program, fairly conventional. It had been operating when we walked in, and Be'Nad hadn't foreseen any difficulty disabling the thing when required. But then, just before Bobby left, the entire system amped up beyond belief. When Bobby said *you know the drill* and the peachophiliac bodyguard went off to the right, he must've made an adjustment to the alarms.

"The system just took off on me," said Be'Nad. "It just overwhelmed me—I'm sorry."

"Not your fault."

"The signals, they just got away from me. It's not good. Not good at all."

"It's something you can't override?"

"They've obviously built a booster into the program. I can't jam something like that, not at those levels. No way. Sorry."

I poured him another glass of ice tea.

"But it was fine when we got there."

"Perfectly workable," he said.

"Then Bobby leaves and the system gets upped."

"Way."

"And he said *you know the drill,* so it's part of a routine."

"Correct."

I called the ex Shiney Hiney employee I'd talked to yesterday. Hey, does Bobby ratchet the security up when he goes out? Unequivocal answer: *All* the time. Man *never* walks out without turning the alarms on full. He always leaves one of his bruisers to watch the apartment, but he doesn't think they're totally competent, so he tightens the security to the top notch. Which makes it a real pain in the ass if you're trying to work. You have to be careful not to touch the windows. There are certain walls you can't go near. It's like a fucking prison.

I got an earful, yes, but it was worth it. We'd just made a big leap in our knowledge. We now had two things settled for sure: (a) We had to do the job when Bobby was home so that Be'Nad could negotiate the alarm system. (b) We had to do it at night, when it was dark enough for us to get up on the roof.

I called the others, including Genesis, and we all agreed: We had ourselves a plan. In fact, what the hell, if things broke our way, we could probably pull it off tomorrow night. All we had to do was make sure we knew when Bobby was on the premises. A guy that size, how hard could that be?

The Sign Of The Four

I talked to Shannon while I was driving back from
Westchester. She was excited, all the way—she was
ready for it. Oh and something else, as long as she
had me. She'd been going over the painting again,
thinking about it all day. *The more I look at it, the
more I see.*

Uh-huh.

Something else had been red-flagging her—a
large, backward number 4 in one of the left-hand
quadrants of the canvas. Did I remember it offhand?
No, well, it has lines of text wrapping around it, and
listen to this, listen to what the words say:

I will chart a map on the darkness,
A map that will lead you to the unseen lands.
I will tell you the secret history,
*The unknown storee of the day he went to the
Temple*
*And drove out the merchants and the money
changers,*
The buyers and the cellars
Who then began to plot against his life.
I will point my finger at one of their Number,
Here is the one who has done the deed.
I will tell those who fill their purses
With the fruit of my life
That greed is like fire.
The more it is fed

The hungrier it gets.

I was honest—I told her I really didn't know what all that was supposed to mean. She said it might help if I knew something about the symbol, the backward number 4. This was known as the Sign of Four and also as the Mystical Sign of Four. It developed from an early Christian symbol, the Chi Rho, in which the first two letters in the Greek spelling of Christ, the X and the P, were laid over each other. As time went on the outlines of the sign had become abstracted and simplified, and by medieval usage it had come to resemble a reversed 4.

It was around then that a newly powerful class of people, the merchants, began adapting the symbol for their own purposes. In one of history's earliest efforts at branding, merchants combined the Sign of Four with their own names or initials. The practice became so prevalent that the symbol was eventually known as the Merchant's Mark.

Okay, so…

It all fits, she said. It's all part of the whole gestalt, the whole anti-money, anti-merchant theme in this part of the painting. He's talking about Jesus driving the merchants and money changers out of the temple. He mentions greed, he paints the words around the Merchant's Mark. And where does it lead? What happens after the buyers and sellers are tossed from the temple? They begin to plot against his life. I will point my finger—here is the one who has done the deed. I could see all that, couldn't I?

Sure. Seemed like a legitimate piece of text messaging.

Now take it another step, she said. Make the next connection. What merchants could he be talking about? What other merchants could be more important to his life than the people who collect his paintings? Right? They're all merchants of one sort or another—they're all selling something to make their money. Those who fill their purses with the fruit of my life? What else could he mean? He's talking about the collectors. He's pointing to one of them. You follow the symbolic progression, this is where it goes. He's saying that one of the collectors will take his life.

I could see all the lines closing in on one central point, I could see them about to intersect. I just couldn't really believe it.

"Like Bobby Hucknail?" I said.

I could hear her weighing her words. I could hear her putting her words on a scale and checking to see if they had enough mass to hold a balance with reality.

"Like Bobby Hucknail," she said.

CHAPTER 12

A POINT-BLANK
SHOTGUN BLAST

Cobras

The mood in the van was way up today. We were getting close on this, we were making the right moves. Be'Nad, he was fully recovered from yesterday's trauma. He was, as he put it, *back to my ultraplus, number one self.* Yes, his choice of words caused a few eyes to roll in the van, but it was good to hear.

Bobby was also in fine form this morning, very talkative, and it didn't take long for his conversational topics to emerge. There were four:

1) He'd made it to the doctor's yesterday and she'd told him in no uncertain terms re his knee that he had to drop weight *NOW*. Bobby's response was *tell me something I don't fucking know*, but he admitted that even by his own gut-busting standards the pounds were really piling on. Catching his body in the mirror this morning, he said, made him realize that the heart is truly an amazing organ.

2) He wasn't at all happy, in his phrasing, *with what's coming out of my asshole.* His most recent bowel movement was unusually, disturbingly long and thin. *It looked like a fucking squid.* Bon appetite.

3) Whoever this Mitzusuka was, he was still incurring the Hucknail wrath. *What do you expect from the Japanese? They have no staying power. Two little atomic bombs and they're all ooh, we give up.*

4) In what we handily regarded as his most important decision of the day, he announced that he was having dinner with friends at Angelina's On Bank. Eight o'clock tonight.

I knew the place—on Bank Street, downtown Manhattan. I'd been there, I'd met the owner through *Real Story*. Say what you want about Bobby, man knew where to eat.

We had a lot to talk about in the van. We knew he wasn't traveling, he wasn't taking off for a fat farm. If he was definitely going to be home tonight, then we were definitely on.

But Be'Nad wanted assurances. He wanted to be absolutely certain tonight that Bobby was back in the apartment. In fact, he suggested that someone should tail him to the restaurant, know exactly when he was done and alert the rest of us when he was leaving so everything would be ready.

Made sense. And I thought it made even more sense to follow him inside the restaurant and keep a close eye on him. Fine, but who goes? Nick the Five thought it should be a couple and he volunteered Randi and himself. Randi said no—they weren't believable as a couple. Before Nick the Five could work up a full head of pissy steam I proposed a different solution.

That's how Shannon and I ended up going to dinner together.

Although Angelina's On Bank was built on the ground floor of an old brownstone, it wasn't anywhere near as cramped as it might sound. There was plenty of room for a large, ample dining space and even for a closed off bar area on the side opposite

the entrance. Bobby had taken one of the bigger
tables in the middle of the dining space, white napkin
draped over his chest like a bib. He was sitting with
four friends, three men and a woman. His other
bodyguard, wearing a different but equally eye-
mauling Hawaiian shirt tonight, sat off by himself at
the far end of the table.

I'd made an 8:15 reservation and mentioned that
I knew the owner, Jeffrey Finkelstein (Angelina was
just a made up shiksa-fantasy name). This way, we
could see where Bobby was seated when we got there
and we could ask for a table that kept him in our
sightline. I wasn't too worried about him or the
bodyguard seeing me. Neither had paid an undue
amount of attention to the exterminators yesterday.
Besides, Shannon and I had a good table, nestled up
against the back wall and its shadows.

We'd met out front after we'd each gone home
and gotten dressed. I'd shown up in a suit and a dress
shirt, nothing extremely fancy. Shannon, though, God
help me, she was wearing a skirt, a jacket and a sheer,
see-through blouse that let the entire universe know
she wasn't wearing a bra. It was one of those outfits
where the only things keeping her nipples from full
exposure were two pieces of double-sided tape on the
inside of her jacket.

"That's some set of clothes," I'd said.

"We're supposed to be on a date, right? All I'm
doing is trying to sell it."

Sold.

So there we were, sitting in that lovey-dovey,
side-by-side position against the wall, carefully
watching Bobby. The place was packed, but every
once in a while the heavy breathing Hucknail voice
would rise above the noise.

"Oh Jesus *yes. YES!* You've *got* to try the
baccala. You've *GOT* to!"

His waiter came over. We heard Bobby ordering
appetizers. The baccala, a bowl of ciuppin, the
chicken liver crostini.

No, that wasn't for the table. That was just
for him.

"You know why I think he eats like that?"
Shannon said. "It's to hide. He's hiding behind all
that fat. He uses the fat so no one can see who he
really is. Basically, it's a disguise is what it is. That's
what all his fat is, a disguise."

Interesting that we were talking about disguises,
since we were sitting here disguised as people on a
date. Come to think of it, didn't we both get by
sometimes pretending to be something we weren't?
And what was Bobby over there camouflaging?
Could he really have killed a man?

We ordered drinks; they came. Diet Coke for
me. She was working on a Cobra, vodka with coconut
and pineapple juice and blue Curacao. She asked me
why I didn't drink, which I thought was unusual
because
most people who are drinking don't want to know
why you aren't.

"Long story," I said.

She looked at Bobby digging into his starters. "I
think we have time."

So I told her. Same story I'd told Genesis. I told
her about a woman named Olivia Sullivan who'd
hired me to help her. I told her about the record-
setting amounts of crystal meth and booze it was
taking me just to get through one day. I told her about
getting so fucked up that when I finally tracked down
the guy who'd been beating Olivia up and who'd
snatched her child, I killed him. I didn't have to. I'd

already put a bullet in his leg and sufficiently fucked him up to the point where he wouldn't be a problem anymore. I didn't have to shoot him again. But I did. I aimed

the gun at his head, pulled the trigger and watched him die.

Shannon nodded. "You're right," she said. "You shouldn't drink."

Talking about food was a point of loud-voiced pride with Bobby. We easily heard him order his next course. He wanted the salt-roasted steak with sides of Sardinian gnocchi and fried radicchio.

We ordered our food. I asked about her past. It quickly ended up being about Robonnet, the first time she ever saw his work, the pure hypnotics of it all, the first time she ever saw *Sex Death Dream Talk*, how her life had never been the same after. Then we talked about the clues and the codes, the hidden meanings. Time was passing at a nice pace.

We were coming up on 10 o'clock when we heard Bobby cry for dessert. Panettone filled with mascarpone cream. Double espresso. Oh and a couple of those marzipan lambs. A few of those.

I called the van, Be'Nad's cell. "It's about to happen. It's *just* about to happen."

And so it seemed. By 10:25 Bobby had consumed everything on the table and was making signs like he was about to ask for the check. But that's when a party of four spilled out of the bar area on the side and started stumbling through the dining room. They saw Bobby. He saw them. They knew him. He knew them. Lots of hello's, how are you's, I didn't know you were here's. By 10:29 the two seats near the bodyguard were filled and two more chairs had been pulled up to the table.

Bobby was in fine spirits. We could tell because at precisely 10:37 he began ordering more food. And not a few more desserts, some more coffee—that would've been understandable. No, Bobby was ordering more *appetizers*. A frittata with salami. A platter of carne cruda. Another serving of baccala.

"You know me," we heard him say. "I'm a martyr to the baccala."

I called Be'Nad back. "There's been a slight delay. Hang in there for a while."

Stealing a painting isn't as easy as people might think.

The restaurant was starting to feel like the place boring goes for advanced lessons. Even the bodyguard was struggling to stay awake. Shannon and I made small talk while we waited for Bobby to wrap it up and our talk only got smaller. Eventually we were sitting in silence. I went through a review of the day in my head, realizing that this massive slow down could bring a sorry end to what had been a pretty good 24 hours. Really, the only downer of the day had come in the
van, when Hillary the dog began channeling Randi's mother again.

It's all gone, she said, according to Randi. *All forgotten. Everything that meant something in my life, everything that was important to me, it's gone and forgotten. There's nothing left.*

Which made me think about my daughter Millie, how she had no memory of the little things we used to do together. All gone, all forgotten. It had

given me a sad moment that afternoon. It was doing the same
thing now.

Bobby was barking again. Time to go? Shit, no. He was ordering more entrees. The beef fillet with truffles and apples. The squid ink risotto. A scallop polenta. Whole new definitions of hog heaven danced before my eyes.

I called Be'Nad, gave him the latest.

I'm getting tired, he said. *My concentration won't hold forever.*

"Don't worry. He can't eat all night."

Though I wasn't so sure about that.

Shannon got another Cobra. She seemed to be feeling it. Her eyes, somehow, were turning bluer and I don't think it was a reflection from the Curacao.

Meanwhile, Bobby kept packing it away. He should order food by the gallon—probably cheaper that way. Plates came, plates went. Midnight approached.

The bar area was doing good business, but the dining room was growing sparse. Not such a good thing. Too much visibility. I asked the waiter to lower the lights in the back near our table. Shannon and I held hands in the demi-shadows, giving it the romantic touch, doing anything not to get noticed. Her hand was a little damp. Probably the vodka.

It finally ended at 1:12. At exactly 1:12 a.m. and not a fucking second before Bobby gave up the good fight and called for the check. I called Be'Nad.

I think it's too late, he said. *I'm spent. Randi's asleep. Nick the Five's nodding out. I can barely keep my eyes open, let alone my ears.*

"So, what, we try again tomorrow?"

You're the boss here. You're the roadman. Say the word

There was no reason not to wait. Unless, of course, Bobby got some sense in his lard head and took off for a fat farm. In which case, we were screwed.

"We'll try tomorrow."

It would be difficult, I think, for me to stay bouncy right now. Goodnight.

A Vote For Insanity

Outside of Jeffrey Finkelstein, who'd probably met a
month's worth of overhead just on Bobby's bill, no
one would argue that this wasn't a wasted night. No
one would have the temerity to say that this hadn't
been one lost fucking cause. Still, it was pretty nice
outside. Except for some light traffic and the busboys
dragging trash bags to the curb, the night was quiet.
The street lights felt soft and silvery. Shannon and I
stood down the block a bit, letting the cool dark
breeze soak in.

"Unbelievable night," she said.
"A night to end all nights."
"I've never seen anyone eat like that."
"I never want to again."
"He can really put it away."
"He can. That he can."
"The baccala, Jesus."
"The baccala, lots of baccala. He likes his
baccala."

We started walking, keeping an eye out for cabs.
She seemed a little tipsy to me. I kept catching a wet
light in her eyes. It was like it had just rained, but
only in her eyes.

"You'll be okay going home?"
She looked at me, suspicious. "What does that
mean?"
"You'll be okay by yourself?"

Now she wasn't suspicious. She was mad. "I had two Cobras all night long. Are you kidding me?"

"Just asking."

"You think I'm drunk, is that what you're asking?"

"You were drinking—I'm asking."

"And next it's what, I'll take you home? Let's share a cab?"

"We're both West Side."

"Fucking AA types. Fucking AA-Buddhist types. You think I don't know? You're just trying to get into
my pants."

"I'm not. And you're wearing a skirt."

"Bullshit. You've been giving me that eye all night long."

She wasn't holding a gun on me this time, but I still decided to be honest. "You're a beautiful woman, I'll admit that. Any other circumstances, sure. But not now."

"Why not?"

"We've already got enough trouble with Randi and Nick the Five. Then there's the whole Genesis thing. It would make everything more complicated."

"I guess it would."

"That's why you and I can't have anything going. It would be insanity."

Shannon took a breath and seemed to get a hold of herself. "You've got a point. I'll give you that, you've got a point."

I had nothing else to say on the subject. Neither did she. We just stood there.

Then the breeze picked up. It didn't feel that strong, but it was evidently blowing hard enough to force one piece of the tape inside her jacket to come unstuck from her see-through blouse and to flip that half of her jacket open. And keep it open.

I was still standing there, staring at her breast. She was still standing there, staring at me and making no effort to close the jacket.

I made my move so fast it surprised even me. It couldn't have been more than 3/10 of a second later that our lips were locked together and my tongue was sliding down her wet warm mouth.

Then we broke it off and were whispering into each other's necks.

"We shouldn't do this," I said.

"We shouldn't," she agreed.

We did.

Arguing With Potatoes

One of the things I liked about Robonnet was the feeling that the world in his paintings was just about to be created, or just had been. I got that right from the first look—these paintings could have been made in the first light that anyone had ever seen.

And that's exactly how I felt the next morning, like I was waking up in one of those first dawns. Seeing Shannon sleeping on my arm, watching her opening her eyes and smiling at me, it was like waking up somewhere in one of those first dawns.

It'd been a long time for me.

Maybe that's also why, for a good part of the day, the world smelled like it had just rained. Everywhere I went, everything I did, I caught the smell of wet earth on a rainy day.

Which made it hard to be cool about things in the van. We tried—we tried to keep the glow out of our faces—but it wasn't easy. Randi I think picked up on it because every once in a while I'd spot some small conspiratorial smile on her face. Be'Nad and Nick the Five, fortunately, were oblivious.

And Bobby? Bobby wasn't feeling so good. He was calling people all day long, telling them he'd been, as he put it, *overserved* last night. *I can't do that again. Oh Jesus no—I can't let that happen. Do you know what I'm saying? I mean the cost to me, the cost to my body. The fucking COST.*

He'd gained three pounds from his extended stay at Angelina's On Bank. Which in itself was something—I would've put 30 pounds on from a pig-out orgy like that.

He was so subdued today, so out of it, that several of his usual themes went unaddressed. Still, no day of Bobby's could pass without at least one mention of defecatory matters. *I don't know why this is,* he confided to one friend, *and it's weird, it's totally weird, but my farts are almost sweet today. There's a sweetness to them I'm finding very odd. Even, I got to tell you, even kind of troubling.*

Nevertheless, by 1 p.m. he'd picked a destination for dinner—Twizzle's, a pan-Asian place in Ticksdale, a few miles north of Brighton Manor.

We were set. Shannon and I were a go again for tonight—no one seemed to question that. We kept monitoring the calls, but otherwise we got ourselves ready.

Nick the Five began doing maintenance on what looked like a power drill attached to a water thermos. What it was, actually, was a rotary compression staple remover. Basically, the thing used a vacuum pump to pull staples out of a painting with minimal damage to the frame and especially to the canvas.

"It's all got to be fast," Nick the Five said. "You go in, you got to look at the back of a painting and one-instant figure out how the canvas was put on the frame. You got to see how the canvas was stretched, how it was tacked. You got to see the pattern and then go in the opposite direction. You go exactly backwards, start at the last staple in and work your way back to the first. You don't, you can warp the canvas, distort the painting. Or you can rip the canvas, in which case it's worthless."

"It can't ever be fixed?" I said.

"It's *worthless*. I had this job once—toughest
job I ever had. It was *Traffic, Broome Street*, by that
asshole photorealist Fletcher White. You remember,"
he said to Randi. "I told you about it."

She shrugged. "You told me."

"We get in there, I don't knew who stretched
this canvas but they must've been schizophrenic.
Most times, you do one side of the frame first, you're
stapling from the center to the corners. Then, duh,
you do the other side. This way you're giving the
canvas balance, equilibrium. But this nutjob, whoever
it was, he put a staple here, then a staple there, then
one in the middle of the motherfucking crossbars. No
methodology. Totally, totally fucked."

"It was a real challenge," said Randi, supremely
bored, "but it was no Allegheny."

Jesus save us—did she *have* to say that?

Nick the Five turned square around to her,
looking—hoping—for some back-off. "What does
that mean?"

"You know what it means. "It was no Allegheny
job. It means what it means."

"Which means?"

"Which means what it fucking *means*."

And off they went.

I'm just glad Randi's mother wasn't tuning in during
the next 15 minutes because I think even the dead
would've been rocked by the massively blown out
piss-off that subsequently took place. He'd given her
a chance to soften it up but she'd kept things hard and
now they were dense in battle. Shannon and I stayed
out of it. Hillary too. Be'Nad, unwittingly put on a

pedestal for the Allegheny job, looked nervous and uncomfortable throughout.

What Randi did, in summary, was call Nick the Five a brick-dumb genetic loser who couldn't hold an argument with a potato and who wouldn't know shit if he found it on his shoe. He said she was a dipshit bitch and suggested that the strain of being right all the time was finally getting to her. She said she was glad to see he still wasn't letting himself be mislead by reality and then she said she wasn't going to say anything else to him because after all this time they had nothing left to say to each other, although that didn't stop her from spinning out long strings of Spanish invective for another solid minute or so.

It didn't end until Nick the Five let loose with one of those strange, out-of-nowhere laughs and announced, "I'm a take me a pee." He got out but didn't even bother with the pretense of going to the train station restroom. He just wandered between the parked cars in the lot, aggravated beyond reproach. Shall I compare thee, Shakespeare might've asked, to a winter's day?

I caught up with him a minute later. No question she can be a pain, I said, but you're *choosing* to let it get to you. He knew, he knew, he knew. At least he knew it in his head, he said. In his heart it was all *fuck* her.

Most times, he said, he could work the program by working on a job. Wasn't happening here. I said you know how addiction is a progressive disease? Gets worse over time? Well sobriety is a progressive cure. Gets better over time. But it takes time.

We kept talking and he finally managed to dial his feelings down to the point of mere bitterness. Eventually he got back in the van, but he had me thinking, all these personnel problems? I might as well have stayed at work.

Tipping Close To The Edge

What had been a pretty decent day turned weird on me after that. Just sitting in the van was a painful affair. The small talk was washed out now, closer to last gasps than conversation.

Genesis called around 4. That was strange because I'd already talked to her twice today. I'd called in the morning, told her how nothing had gone down because Bobby had stayed too late at the trough. Then I'd phoned after we found out about Twizzle's. Unless Bobby pulled another all-nighter, I said, we were good.

Now she was calling me, wanting to know how things were progressing, was everything still okay. And Shannon? Was she holding up?

Odd question. I said she was.

She's an attractive woman, don't you think?

"Yes she is."

But have you ever seen her in direct sunlight?

Okay, I take it back. *THAT* was the odd question, hands down. That was a question you could only ask out of jealousy. That was a question Genesis might ask if she knew that Shannon and I had slept together last night. But how could she know? How was that possible?

I never actually answered the sunlight question because it didn't matter, Genesis wasn't banking on a reply and she hung up a few moments later. But man she had me shook.

Ten minutes later Shannon sat next to me, wanted to show me something. She had the painting on her laptop screen. Between Bobby's chatter and Genesis' call and the general mood of the day, I had a hard time concentrating on what she was saying, but it had something to do with Jesus being nailed to the cross. Robonnet kept using the words *nayles* and *nayled*, deliberate misspellings that in her opinion had to point to clues. And they were connected somehow to the number 4211519, which worked out in her calculation to April 21, 1519, the day Hernan Cortes landed in Mexico and began the invasion that ended with the slaughter of the Aztec seers and priests. *And*, very important, notice how the words flow around the painted stalk of a single reed, and remember that 1519 is the year of Ce Acatl in the Aztec calendar, the year of One Reed.

Like I said, I couldn't follow her thought patterns, but in sum she was seeing even stronger signs of accusation and guilt. *Nayles*, nails, Hucknail, slaughter, murder, Robonnet's death. The symbols, she said, were falling hard in Bobby's favor.

I didn't know whether to agree or disagree. I couldn't tell. I was focused more on the larger sense of strangeness that had settled over us. It made me feel that everything was tipping close to the edge, and that very soon, maybe any second now, something was going to crack.

Bobby Goes Down

Twizzle's, which boasted enough red velvet for several high kitsch Bangkok bordellos, was crowded that night, but not terribly. The hostess told us there'd only be a short wait. We stood at the bar, Shannon ordering a Cobra again. She picked one of the dollar bills off the change pile and pointed to the eagle on the back. Did I realize that in addition to the 13 stars over its head and the 13 stripes on its chest, the eagle was holding 13 olive leaves and 13 arrows? Which is interesting, she said, because 13 is the number of Acatl—reed—in the Aztec calendar. Yet another Robonnet connection between money and murder, and it made her wonder whether 13 played a role in the part of the painting she'd examined earlier. Maybe there were references she'd missed, clues that needed another look to discover.

I was too nerve-wired to really get into it. I nodded my way through the monologue, steadying myself with a Diet Coke and a bowl of mixed nuts.

Fifteen minutes later we got a table. Bobby was sitting on the opposite side of the room, out of earshot but not eye. Again he was with friends—three women and a guy—and one bodyguard at the lonely end of the table. Only this bodyguard was my juice-pumped friend with the enlarged Adam's apple, the one who wouldn't be giving out endorsements for Azuma Exterminating any time soon.

I sat with my back to their table—I thought that might be wise. Shannon did both analysis and color commentary, telling me what was going on.

"All right, those look like appetizers. Yes, they're getting their appetizers. He's getting... I think that's the Crab Rangoon." She consulted the menu. "I'll bet that's what it is, the Crab Rangoon... *And* an order of the firecracker wings. Those are definitely the firecracker wings."

"Just two appetizers?"

"Just the two."

"That's an improvement."

We were running behind them so we skipped the appetizers and just ordered entrees. I got the Japanese teriyaki salmon. She got the Singapore chili shrimp.

She looked incredibly beautiful tonight—again. I said so. She wondered about us. Was there a chance for something between us? And what about Genesis? Just business, I said, not going into detail. So we talked about us. Maybe this wasn't so insane after all. Maybe we could pull it off.

She stopped to describe the arrival of Bobby's entrees. "I'm guessing those are those, what was it, the sago balls? Some kind of sago balls?"

"Pork-filled sago balls?"

"That's it, that's what it looks like. And that—I think that's the fish head curry. Oh yeah, *definitely* the fish head curry."

"That's it? Still only two things?"

"He's really behaving himself."

"Gandhi's got nothing on him."

She continued watching the table. "He's really loving that curry. He's already had— Wait, the bodyguard's getting up."

I tensed. "Coming this way?"

"I don't… No. No, he's going out. He's going toward the restrooms."

She periscoped back to the table. "God, will you look at him? Eat, talk, eat, talk. No one else can get a word in."

"He's in his own heaven."

She nodded, bringing her eyes back to me. "Anyway, I was… What was I saying? What were we talking about?"

"Us."

"Right, us. I was thinking, I don't know, it occurred to me that…something's wrong."

"I don't know if I'd call it *wrong* exactly."

"No." She chin-pointed to the table. "Something's *wrong*."

It was Bobby. He was on his feet, teetering, and it wasn't just his bad knee. There was a blue tint in his face and especially his lips. He looked like a fish with malfunctioning gills.

As he was starting to stagger away from the table, his friends were jumping out of their seats, frightened. One of the women went to grab him but no go. He made a weird little gesture with his hands, did half a pivot and collapsed on his back with a 4.5 on the Richter scale.

His friends screamed. Other customers got up and screamed. Six waiters rushed over and stood there staring at him. There was a lot of screaming and standing and staring and nobody was doing a thing.

What was it about this job? Anything could happen and it usually did.

I ran across the room, asking what was going on. All his friends were talking and it sounded like they were all speaking in tongues. Group approach—not working.

I asked the woman who tried to grab him what

was wrong.

"It's happened before," she said. "He eats too fast and he passes out."

"What do you do for him?"

"One of his bodyguards gives him CPR."

Obviously, none of these people was or had been a serious drug user. Except I guess me. I'd seen ODs. I knew some CPR.

I knelt down next to him and ripped his shirt open. His eyes were dull and still and slipping back in his head. He looked like a dead cow. I put my hands between his nipples—he was totally cold. I started the compressions, pumping fast, more than once a second, feeling the ripples waving across his chest fat.

It wasn't working. Should I try old school CPR? Lace in some mouth-to-mouth? I wasn't ready for this. But shit, I couldn't let anything happen to him. There was too much at stake.

I bent over him, titled his head back, pinched his nose and went down on his mouth. The taste of the fish head curry made me want to vomit but I kept blowing. A strange little sound came out of his throat, half cry, half moan, and a second later his chest was rising by itself, billowing up like a bedsheet in the wind.

His eyes popped open. He was breathing on his own. He was all right.

Some guy—he might've been the manager— bent over him. "I've called an ambulance. It's on its way."

"The fuck I need an ambulance for?" Bobby graciously replied. "I don't need an ambulance. Just get me to my feet."

Fortunately, the bodyguard, probably the only person who could comply with Bobby's wishes, returned from the crapper just then. After getting a brief explanation of what had transpired, he muscled Bobby into a standing position. Guy really was strong.

"I'm fine," Bobby assured the manager. "This wasn't the first time. I eat too fast, the blood rushes to my stomach and away from my brain. Fairly common medical phenomenon, from what I've been told."

One of Bobby's friends pointed me out, saying I'd brought him back to consciousness.

Bobby looked at me. No recognition whatsoever. "You did that?"

"Least I could do."

"I owe you a meal."

"Quite all right."

The manager interrupted. "You're sure about the ambulance?"

"I'm not getting in any ambulance. I'm not going to any hospital. You see all that fish head curry? You think I'm letting *that* go to waste?"

Bobby proceeded back to his seat at the table. The bodyguard helped him, but the guy kept looking back at me, staring.

Like the gospel song says, you gotta move.

I went back to Shannon. "I think the bodyguard might be clueing to me. I'm going outside. Anybody asks, I needed some air."

Shannon understood. "I'll get the check in a couple of minutes. Meet you out there."

"We can wait in the car."

"Got it." She noticed I wasn't moving. "What?"

"Just one thing. You have any breath mints?"

>>>>>>

A Death In The Living Room

By 1:43 we were on the roof. Me, Be'Nad, Nick the Five. This had been a tougher, slower climb since we were backpacking our equipment. Nick the Five was carrying his rotary compression staple remover, plus a long, insulated cylindrical container for the painting and the thick cloth he'd layer inside the canvas when he rolled it up. Be'Nad had what looked like the black box from a jet. I had my stuff. We rested for a moment, letting the heat sweat itself away. Everything was going good. Shannon and I had waited outside the restaurant, saw Bobby and the bodyguard leave, no problem. The last lights in the apartment had gone off 20 minutes ago. Things had finally fallen into place.

We did our check-offs, making sure once more that our phones were shut off and that we had everything we needed. Then we put on our gloves, crouched around the target skylight and turned our hooded flashlights on. Yes, thank you God, the painting was still there, hanging over the artificial fireplace.

Nick the Five trained his light over the rest of the living room. "Nice stuff," he whispered. "Very cherry." An unsuspected fan of French Provincial.

Be'Nad set up his black box, which was a portable ultrasonic processor. Thing used blasts of ultrasound to disable security sensors, much in the way that swiping a magnetic card opens an electronic lock. He did his 12-stroke Handi Wipe thing, attached electrodes to one of the skylight's sensors, checked the meter on his processor and let the sonic juice flow. The process was repeated three more times, each requiring 12 rubs with a fresh Handi Wipe. Any other circumstances, he'd be driving me crazy, but at the end he leaned over the skylight and listened carefully.

"It's clear," he announced.

I took four suction cups out of my backpack and stuck them on one of the glass panels. While Be'Nad and Nick the Five held the cups, I cut the panel with a glass cutter. One of the skills left over from my distant past. No force, no pressure, just four quick, clean lines. When I was done, I gave the glass a slight tap with a rubber mallet. Be'Nad and Nick the Five lifted the panel off.

"Fucking fantastic," Nick the Five whispered. He could barely contain himself.

Be'Nad took the electrodes off the processor and replaced them by screwing on two small metal tubes. He then lowered the tubes through the opening in the skylight, adjusted his controls and sent 433-MHz sound waves pulsing through the apartment. Two minutes and a couple of Handi Wipes later, he had his head suspended over the opening. "We're good," he said.

We used the same grappling hook that got us up here to lower ourselves down through the skylight and into the living room. We did it slow, no hurry, but with a nice rhythm, like a piece of well planned choreography.

Except for the hum of air conditioning, the apartment was silent. The flashlights showed other paintings in the big room. At least one of them was another Robonnet. Might've been *The Wild Magnolias Receive Their Blessings*—I know that was one of Bobby's legitimate buys. In any case, from where we were standing, we had a clear path to the fireplace.

"This is good," Nick the Five whispered. "This is A-fucking good."

He was right—the thing was working. I felt like we were on top of it. It almost felt like I could ease up and just let the thing happen.

We moved through the living room with care, taking each moment as it came, each breath, each step.

Especially each step, since Be'Nad was counting them off under his breath. Three. Four. Five. His OCD was really kicking in.

We got to within six feet of the fireplace. I stopped and put my light up to the painting, caught sight of that dense jungle panorama, a fragment of the words.

If you believe that the Mind
Only exists inside the Body,
You will never Understand.

This was the first time I was seeing it head on, not through a skylight or a camera lens or on a screen. It was like a point-blank shotgun blast. It put me right there, standing on the border of some wild and trembling new world.

Be'Nad and Nick the Five had also stopped for a moment of contemplation. Now Nick the Five, not even putting his equipment down, stepped in and made an eager reach for the painting.

Be'Nad yanked his arm back. "The fuck you *doing*?" he hissed.

"What do you mean what the fuck? I'm taking it down."

"Not *now*."

"How'm I gonna check the tacking?"

"How do you know it isn't wired? Got to check *THAT* first."

Uh-oh.

Nick the Five stopped. He just realized he'd made an over-enthused mistake and he wasn't happy about it. Especially since he'd made it in front of Be'Nad.

He jerked his arm away. "Don't touch me."

"Sorry," said Be'Nad. "I'm just saying, you don't know if there's an alarm hooked—"

"I *know* what you're just saying. I'm just saying don't ever touch me like that."

"Hey, there's no problem with you."

"Then there's no need to keep bragging on it."

"I'm not *bragging* on it, I'm just—"

I got between them. Their whispers were getting *loud.* "Guys, we gonna steal this thing or not?"

Be'Nad responded by taking a knife out of his pocket. No, not for that. He went to the painting, slipped the blade just under the back and lifted the frame no more than 1/16 of an inch off the wall. "Let's take a look."

I gave him the mini camera and goggles from my pack, and once he'd threaded the cable behind the painting, I switched the camera light on.

Be'Nad looked and nodded. "It's hot. Hanging on a weighted hook. Move the painting, you change the tension on the hook—the alarm goes off."

"So what do you do?"

"I can handle it."

"Zap it?"

"No, it's mechanical, not electrical."

Be'Nad took the goggles off and pulled a plug of copper wire out of his pack. Then he gave a long look at the wall above the painting.

"I'm going to put a screw up there," he stated, "and wrap some of this wire around it. I'll have to stand on something, one of the chairs. I'll drop the wire down behind the painting and loop it around the hook. When the painting comes off, I'll tighten the wire around the screw."

"That'll do it?"

"The tension on the hook'll stay the same." He glanced at Nick the Five. "Believe me, the alarm won't go off."

"The alarm won't go off." Nick the Five repeated the words in a mincing, scoffing tone. "Fine."

"It won't."

"Right. I know Randi'll be impressed."

"Randi?"

"Next time you're cracking on her, tell her all about it."

Be'Nad spun to me. "Will you tell him, please? Will you *tell* him I have no interest in his ex?"

"Guys," I said, "is this really the fucking time for this?"

"He's after her," Nick the Five insisted.

"He's not."

"I'm not."

"I don't know, *Bernard*. I think you're fulla shit."

Be'Nad couldn't believe it. "What did you call me?"

"You heard what I called you."

"That's it," I said. "That's enough."

"What did you call me?"

"You heard it. You fucking *heard* what I fucking called you. I fucking called you—"

Nick the Five put a sudden brake on his shit, and it was all because of Be'Nad's face. Because of the frightened look of wide eyed shock on Be'Nad's face. But Be'Nad wasn't looking at him. He was looking past him, into the rest of the living room.

"We're not alone," said Be'Nad.

I spun around with my hand on the Glock. There was nothing to see in the darkness until my eyes adjusted and I picked up the lump of body on the floor. I pointed my light. It was Bobby, face down in front of an overstuffed sofa with nailhead trim.

"How long's he been there?" I said.

"I just noticed him," said Be'Nad, bending his head forward, listening. "He's dead."

"How do you know?"

"At this distance? How come I don't hear him breathe? How come I don't hear his heart beat?"

"Oh my fucking God," said Nick the Five. "Fucking tell me what happened."

"I *never* heard him," said Be'Nad. "He's been dead since we got here."

I went further into the living room. Bobby had one cheek flat on the carpet, one open eye facing up. I felt for his carotid, but just by looking at the eye— glazed, almost gummy—I knew this was death.

Back at the fireplace, Be'Nad was so agitated I thought he was going to throw up again. "You see what's happening?" he said. "You see what this means?"

"It means he's dead," I said.

"No, the *larger* picture. Do you know what the *larger* picture means?"

"What?"

"It's a *curse*. Do you understand? This painting is *cursed*."

"What the fuck?" Nick the Five wanted to know.

"I agree. What the fuck?"

Be'Nad pointed to the canvas. "*Look* at it. Look at these terrible things, these...*mutilations*. These...*CARNALITIES. That's* what killed him."

"I don't know what killed him," I said, "but he passed out in the restaurant. That might have something to do with it."

"No," Be'Nad insisted, "it's the painting. I didn't want to say anything before, but *look* at it. Look at what that homeless man is doing to that nun." He was referring to the act of, shall we say, communilingus near the center of the canvas. "It's blasphemy. It's *sacrilege*. It's a fucking *curse*."

"Take it down a notch," I urged. "Take a deep breath."

"*Fuck* my breath! It's a *curse*. I know this. I believe this. This thing, this painting, is *CURSED*."

He was getting so crazed on this that the last word came out as an hysterical, full-lung *hiss*.

CHAPTER 13

THE NAME THAT CAN BE NAMED IS NOT THE TRUE NAME

I'm Sorry, I Have Issues With Death

I don't believe in curses. I believe you make your own lousy luck and you don't need outside agencies to do the job for you. And I certainly didn't believe that *Sex Death Dream Talk* was cursed. True, Bobby was dead, but aside from that we had very little trouble lifting the painting. Be'Nad continued going ape shit for another minute or so and he was refusing to lay a hand on the canvas, but once I pointed out the obvious—no painting, you don't get paid—he settled down. So did Nick the Five. They forgot their differences, and Be'Nad was able to put the corpse laying a few feet away out of his mind. He got the screw in the wall, dropped the wire behind the painting and successfully bypassed the alarm. Nick the Five analyzed the tacking patterns, removed the staples from the frame and carefully rolled the canvas inside the tube. We got back to the roof, down to the ground and into the van in what would have been record time if they kept records for these things.

Be'Nad was still shaken, telling Shannon and Randi (and of course Hillary the dog) all about Bobby as soon as he climbed inside. Hey, let him freak all he wants. Didn't matter. The job was done, it was over. We'd pulled it off.

I shot out of the train station parking lot, took out my cell and turned it on.

And that's when I started thinking, you know, maybe there *is* something to this curse crap after all.

I had one missed message, clocked in at 2:02. It was from Genesis. *Don't make a move tonight*—first thing she'd said. *Not tonight.* Her brother, she said, had suffered a heart attack while he was in the hospital. Slim's weight and blood sugar had finally caught up with him. She was booking a flight down to New Orleans right away, private charter. She'd try to get back as soon as she could, but until then, just stay still.

My first thought: If this isn't a fucking curse, if this isn't a motherfucking the-turd-has-landed curse, it'll have to do until the real thing comes along.

Then I'm thinking, okay, okay, this is a bizarre turn, but it's not evidence of a *curse* per se. It's just a temporary setback. So I'll sit on the painting for a ittle while—what's the big deal? First of all, what choice do I have? Second, really, what the hell could go wrong?

I have to say, Shannon did *not* help the situation at all. Neither did Hillary, for that matter. In fact, it was Hillary who started it. We'd all gone back to my place for what I hoped would be a modest celebration and calm-down session. With the exception of Be'Nad, everyone wanted to take a long, lingering look at our prize, so Nick the Five undid the painting and taped it to my living room wall. Be'Nad's objections were noted.

We're standing there, looking at this shimmering hurricane of faces and symbols and words, and Hillary starts to whimper. She was facing the canvas like the rest of us and she started making these little lost cries. Randi didn't know what the dog was up to—it sounded like she was channeling someone but Randi didn't know who.

Be'Nad, naturally, had a ready explanation. Obviously, the art's possessed. It's cursed.

He'd been maintaining up until then. He'd managed to contain himself on the trip back. I'd put food out and he was eating, he had a good appetite—although he had to wipe his mouth 12 times after each bite. And then he'd need a fresh napkin for the next bite. After the fifth bite I just gave him a roll of paper towels. But he was relatively okay up to that point.

Then Hillary whined and he mentioned the curse again and that's when Shannon starts in with, well, funny you should be talking about that because there's all this urban mythology attached to Robonnet, all these stories about his supposed voodoo and macumba and candomble powers. The numbers in his paintings, for example, were said to bring good lottery luck.

"There's even a story," she said, "if you brought a lottery ticket to him, all he had to do was touch it and it would turn into a winner." She laughed—unbelievable what people will believe. "There are all kinds of stories like that. You could bring him broken dishes, shattered crystal. Just one touch from him and, zap, it's restored."

Be'Nad had stopped eating by now. By now he was on his feet and pacing, his legs doing maybe a mile an hour but his body and face looking like he was doing 160 inside.

I was trying to catch Shannon's eye and wave her off the subject, but you know her. Once she starts talking about Robonnet it's like all the brake linings have been stripped.

She proceeded to tell tales about terrible things that have happened to Robonnet dealers and brokers and collectors. Involved in bizarre accidents, dying strange deaths. All coincidence of course, she noted, but *still*.

Be'Nad saw the light. *That's* what killed Bobby, he said. That's *exactly* what killed Bobby. I said, well how about him refusing to go to the hospital after he collapsed? No, said Be'Nad, it was the curse—that's why he was dead. And if we didn't believe him, then what about Robonnet? What about his grisly murder? What else but a curse could explain his unsolved death?

"I'm sorry," he said, "but I have issues with death." Be'Nad then went into a full nuclear meltdown, pointing to parts of the painting where he could plainly see evidence of satanic love and horned paganism, fertility worship and excessive vegetation, unutterable perversions and other things that his mother, he assured us, would invariable describe as being forged in hell. Within minutes he was so overcome with emotion his speech gave way to a series of wordless grunts and groans that might easily be mistaken, if you didn't know better, for the sound of someone doing a pretty passable imitation of Ella Fitzgerald singing scat.

I needed a break. When I saw Randi and Nick the Five slip inside the kitchen to get more food, I decided they needed my help. Turns out they didn't. Nick the Five was telling Randi about the pre-death events in Bobby's apartment, how he'd nearly tripped the alarm and blown the job. Maybe he was thinking, better from his lips than Be'Nad's.

But if that's what he was thinking, he was wrong. Randi decided it was time to get him told about a few things and apparently it didn't matter if I was there or not. She ripped him too many new assholes to count, characterizing him, in general terms, as someone who had to be holding a blackbelt in blatant ignorance, a doctorate in higher stupidity.

She left to bring more food to Be'Nad. Maybe it would pacify him.

"You okay?" I asked when we were alone.

"Yeah."

But he wasn't looking at me when he said it. He was looking at his hands for some reason, looking at them like they were distant relatives he didn't particularly care for.

"Lot of people," he said, "lot of people pay a lot of attention to Be'Nad."

"How about this curse? You buy it? You think it's true?"

He gave it a few moments. "It's one of those things. I know it's not true. But I also know it is true."

"Okay, so what does that—"

"Forget it—it's nothing." He started moving away. "I'm heading out. Long day."

"Okay."

"What about the painting? You want me to wrap it up?"

"No, leave it. I could use a longer look."

"Maybe I'll come back in the morning, do it then."

"Sure."

He took a few steps toward the living room before he stopped. "The curse, what I mean. No, I don't believe in it. But that doesn't mean it isn't true."

What a crew.

>>>>>>

Three Is The Number Of My Betrayal

Forty minutes later Shannon and I were finally alone
with the painting. Be'Nad was okay enough to make
it back to Westchester. Randi and Hillary caught a
cab to Lincoln Towers. I'd call when Genesis came
back and we'd all go collect our money. For now,
though, Shannon and I had the canvas to ourselves.
We could just stand there in front of it, up close and
unrushed, letting ourselves get lost in its forest.

Shannon had been right about seeing *Sex Death
Dream Talk* in the flesh. It was more vivid and
detailed than the digital version, more immediate, if a
painting can be that. I was seeing things here I hadn't
noticed on the screen. Bats, serpents and dragons,
lotus flowers and kaleidoscopic vines, piles of bones
and skulls, Jelly Roll Morton leading a steel drum
band. And Jesus, the paint itself. The translucent
blues glowing like tourmaline. The reds so thick they
could've been made with Christ's blood.

There were new words too, texts I hadn't picked
up before.

I have known this in another time.
I have found this on 12047 maps.
Do you remember who you are?
If not, let this be written
Like Jeramaya on your hearts:
The name that can be named
Is not the true name.

It felt like the world was breathing, like the air was breathing itself.

The painting was dream talking to me.

It was speaking to her as well. To say that Shannon was excited would be like saying kids tend to get a bit animated on Christmas morning. She was completely fever-spike hyper, pointing out how patterns kept mirroring each other throughout the canvas. Did I see these swirls in the angel's wing, how they're moving downward? Follow their direction and look—they lead to the snarling dog down here. The hairs on the dog repeat the same pattern, only these are swirling to the right. Now follow *their* direction and your eyes go to this coffin—same patterns on the lid of the coffin. That's how he keeps the rhythm going. That's how he keeps the whole design connected, he ties in all these...

She suddenly shivered, like she'd gotten touched by a chill.

"Wait a minute," she said, stepping closer to the wall. "Wait one fucking minute. I didn't see this before. Why didn't I see this before?"

"What?"

She pointed to a tiny number 3 painted on the side of the coffin, then to the words floating next to it. "I don't remember seeing this before."

"Because you never saw it live before?"

"Look at it. It's more code. It's more clues."

"Moot point. With Bobby gone, we'll never prove—"

"It's not Bobby. Look at it."

She was in full senses-tingling revelation mode.

The letters were small but readable.

Three is the number of my betrayal.

Sun, Moon and Earth.

Beginning, Middle and End.

Father, Mother and Chyld.
Three times did Yahweh bless Creation.
Three times did Balaam bless Israel.
Three are the Judges of Death.
Three is the number of the one who left me on
 the shore.
Father, Mother and Chyld.
Three times did Peter deny Him.
Three were the crosses of Golgotha.
Three was the hour in which He Died.
Three is the number of the one who betrayed
me.
Father, Mother and Chyld.

"It's one of them," she said. "Can you see it? It's one of his children. It's one of his kids."

"Come off it."

"*Look* at it. The repeated misspelling? The repeated phrase? It just flashed on me. He's pointing to one of his children."

"Pretty convenient. Now that Bobby's dead, you're seeing another suspect?"

"But look how *direct* it is. How explicit. It's the most explicit clue we've found."

"It is?"

"I think I was wrong. I think I've been misreading the code. He's accusing one of his own children."

I was too tired for this—physically, emotionally, spiritually. I was tired of all her theories and twisted constructions. So why was I starting to believe her? Because I was wondering while I stood there why Genesis had never been particularly curious about knowing who killed her father. Slim, he'd shown some interest, but in the conversations I'd had with Genesis, the subject of the murder had always been a kind of blind spot.

Something else, too—why didn't either one of them ever report the theft to the police? I'd believed Genesis when she told me about the private negotiations. She didn't want to do anything to interfere with the sale of the painting. But maybe they had another reason to keep things hidden.

I was tired of all these tortured decodings and crypto connections. But why was I starting to think this one could be real?

What Happens Next?

We made love right in front of the painting, right there on the living room floor. As worn out as I was, I turned and looked at her and it felt like my chest and cock had just caught on fire. I had to have her.

Had to.

I kissed her full on the mouth—a full, deep, long-gone kiss—and I could feel her heart beating into my chest. And within what felt like three seconds she was on the floor and I was rolling her panties down past her black pussy hair. It was all going so fast I felt like I was under the influence.

It happened right there, under the painting, though it felt like we were in the shade of some leafy place, on the edge of an unnamed sea. I closed my eyes when I was inside her and when I did I could see words on the interior darkness. His words, but not from the painting above us. They were from a canvas I'd seen in the New Orleans warehouse.

Now I see what the Old Ones saw
Now I knew, in another time.

Great sex? Put it this way. On my deathbed, I swear, I'll remember making love to Shannon Kulbiak that night on my living room floor.

We woke in the peachfuzz light of early morning, the sun just starting to fill the living room, tiny white flares of planes skimming over the horizon. She propped herself up on an elbow, facing me. I'd pulled a couple of pillows off the couch for us to sleep on. Her head had been pressed so hard into her pillow the fabric looked like a scallop shell

Of all the things she could've said, of all the things people say to each other after a night like that, she said:

"So what happens now?"

I was blinking the sleep out of my eyes. "What happens?"

"What happens next?"

I still wasn't with her. "I'm not sure what—"

"When she gets back, what happens?" No need to define *she*. "We'll have the money—we'll each have our money. But then what, with us? What happens?"

I nodded, which of course meant I had no idea.

"We've been together 24 hours. I don't have an answer for that."

She shrugged. "I believe in getting it down."

"I guess I'm more used to a day at a time."

"I'm not in the program."

"How I meant it was, I want to be with you now. That's what I know for sure. I know I want to be with you."

"That's now. What about later?"

"Being honest, everything that's happening, I haven't had time to think about it. Shouldn't we be giving ourselves some time?"

She didn't answer at first. She just stared at the window, out the window, never blinking her eyes.

"You won't choose me," she said. "I know that. It won't be me." Her voice was completely calm and unmoved. It was like she was reading a set of instructions. "I know it won't be me."

Then she got up and went to the bathroom, just like that.

You won't choose me. Another word-driven flashback. That's what she'd said that night at Genesis', when we'd gone there to confront her about hiring us both. We were all standing in that fate-heavy library and she said that if Genesis had to decide between us, she knew she'd lose out. *I know you won't choose me. No one ever does.*

What the hell was that all about?

It occurred to me, stealing art might not be the best way to meet women.

CHAPTER 14

DEAD ZONE

You Have No Idea

Bobby Hucknail's sudden demise was all over the news that morning. It wasn't the top story by any means, but *Shiney Hiney King Meets Mysterious End* (or heds to that effect) ran within the first five minutes on the newscasts and got high posting on the news sites. Pending an autopsy, the cause of death remained unknown, though Bobby's famous fat was prominently mentioned.

Once Shannon went home I jumped all over the reports, trying to find something new. The only niblet I uncovered was on FoxNews.com, which cited an unofficial police theory involving a possible robbery. The way it went, Bobby might have been surprised by thieves and had a heart attack—though exactly what had been stolen, if anything, seemed to be a source of confusion.

Good luck on that one.

Nick the Five called around noon. Was this a good time? As good as any. Who knew when Genesis would come back? Best to have the painting hand-over ready.

He showed up a half-hour later, a little quiet and withdrawn. Still suffering an emotional hangover from last night. Hard to blame him.

He took the canvas off the wall, brought it into the kitchen, spread it out on the table and placed a roll of thick cloth at one end. I stood and watched.

"I can still leave it up for a while," he volunteered.

"That's okay. I guess this is the last look."

He began unrolling the cloth and covering the canvas. The painting was disappearing vertically, one foot at a time. When he was done, he worked another layer of cloth underneath the canvas, then started rolling the whole thing up. A pediatric nurse diapering a preemie couldn't have been more gentle.

My cell rang as he was opening the top of his cylindrical canister. It was Kumiko Davis. *Real Story*, of course, was doing a story on Bobby's death. What did I know? She'd sent me all that background on Bobby—I must know something.

I left the kitchen. No—no, I didn't know anything. I never had a chance to follow up on Hucknail, I told her. I never got around to chasing him down.

I hated lying to Kumiko but I didn't see another way out.

She asked me how I was and, not getting much of an answer, started filling me in on the office gossip. I let her talk all she wanted. The Robonnet thing would be over soon and I'd be heading back to work. I'd need to be up on all this.

I drifted through the apartment while she went on, wandered around the living room and into the bedroom while Nick the Five worked in the kitchen and Kumiko told me about Derrick Russell, one of the art directors, who'd just left his wife and was going out with Kareen Allen, one of the photo editors. Which was fine, except that Lee St. John, another photo editor and one of Kareen's best friends, had also been interested in Derrick and now she was pissed at Kareen and putting the whole photo department in an uproar.

Kumiko was just telling me how the photo editors were splitting into two warring camps when Nick the Five knocked on the bedroom doorframe and mouthed *all done*. I put Kumiko on pause and walked him out to the front door, telling him to take it easy, don't get down on yourself, I'll get in touch as soon as I hear.

Back to Kumiko. She finished up the Derrick-Kareen-Lee controversy and moved on to other interoffice scandals, none quite as juicy but still stuff I should know. I sat on the couch. After a good 10 minutes or so my mind started sliding to other things. I caught myself staring at the blank space on the wall where the painting had hung. Maybe I should've left it up longer. Did I get my fill? No. Would I ever?

I stood up, strolled out of the living room, still listening, and walked into the kitchen.

And everything went dry. My mouth, my throat, the whole kitchen went crackling and dry. The canister, the insulated container, it wasn't there.

"Let me get back to you," I said.

Sure, but she kept talking.

Did he hide it somewhere, keep it out of harm's way? I looked in the cabinets, under the sink. Nothing.

"Let me get back to you."

Sure. But more talking.

I ran into the living room, searched under the couch and chairs. This is insane. The fuck is it?

Nick the Five wasn't carrying anything when he left. It had to be somewhere in the kitchen, and I'd just gone back there when I saw the security keypad on the second entrance. I hadn't used this door since the day we'd met Randi and everyone was arguing. I hadn't even looked over here before but now I could see that the keypad had been torn off the wall, disabled.

"I really have to get back to you."

Okay. I want to know how the easy life's going.

"You have no idea."

This time I punched the call dead. Then I opened

the door and looked in the hallway. Empty. Back inside, the whole apartment seemed to be strobing with unreal, desert-dry light.

I got Nick the Five on his cell. He sputtered with shock when I gave him the news.

It JUST happened?

"Did you see anybody?"

Not me.

"When you left, anybody in the hall? Hanging around the building?"

Not that I saw.

"Shit."

It JUST happened?

"Just."

Like minutes ago?

Patience. "Yes."

All right, all right, so it's... Quinn, I have an idea. I'm having an idea here.

"Like what?"

No, let me look into it. Let me look into it for you.

"Why don't you just—"

I'll take care of it. Trust me, I can handle this one.

He hung up.

I'm having an idea here?

This was so fucked.

I circled the kitchen and ended back at the door.

Who knew the painting was here? Only five people—Be'Nad, Nick the Five, Shannon, Randi and me. I opened the door and stepped into the hall again. So who could've busted in here? I felt a flush of paranoia as I bent to look at the outside lock. Shannon? Shannon angry and trying to cut me out of…

No, wait—look at this. Will you look at this shit. The lock, the keyhole, even the door handle—no marks, no scratches. Everything was clean. There was no forced entry. Nobody had come in from the outside

I went back in the kitchen and looked at the keypad again. It was an abortion, all torn to shit. Every wire in the thing had been ripped out. Which was bizarre—why go to all that trouble? Unless you didn't know what the fuck you were doing. Unless you knew next to nothing about taking a security system apart.

I can handle this one?

That's when I knew. I was Nick the fucking Five.

Next Brain Cell 5 Miles

I like to slice things with Occam's razor, go for the simplest explanation on the principle that it's usually the one that's right. In this case, it worked: Nick the Five messed with the keypad while I was on the phone. He took off, goodbye, and as soon as he hit the hall he slipped in the kitchen door and took the painting.

I called him back. My voice was calm. All I said was, "Talk to me."

What?

"Talk to me."

About what?

"You know about what."

Quinn, I'm sorry, I just…

"Go to your apartment."

He sounded alarmed. *What're you talking about?*

"I'm talking about wherever you are, go to your apartment. I'll meet you there. We'll talk about this."

Quinn, it's just, I didn't come into this thing to get baby sat.

"Nobody's baby sitting you. I don't even know what that means."

It's just, I'd like a little gratitude, you know? Just a ta. Just a little.

The call ended right there. I don't think it was because he'd suddenly entered a dead zone.

1) One of his old friends had experienced a disturbing dream last night. Jackie Robinson's widow, in his opinion, had no right to go around saying his wife was a lesbian.

2) When you let coffee warm in the pot for too long, as we discovered at another old pal's apartment, it can start to smell like rusty pork.

3) None of the people we talked to had seen or heard from Nick the Five since he checked into rehab. He was just a distant memory.

The man had truly gone to ground because he wasn't answering his cell even when Randi tried calling. This left her frustrated. He had an elfin brain, she said, with the emotional maturity of a fruit fly, and she was all ready, as she put it, to murder his beige ass.

"Why did he have to get so goddamn greedy?" she said at one point.

"You think that's what it is?"

"I think he wants the whole thing. I think he wants the whole slam-damn for himself."

"I don't know. I think it might have something to do with you."

"Don't say that, even as a joke don't say that."

"I think he still wants you."

She sat quietly in the car while I drove. "Sometimes," she said, "I wish he'd die so I could miss him."

>>>>>>

That Old Black Magic

I don't know how it happened. One moment we were in the middle of a bright and shiny day. Next thing lights were coming on, outbound traffic was getting heavy and stores were rolling down their metal grates. Suddenly it was night. Even time was out of order.

We went back to Allen Street and found a nearby place to park. I tried Rev. Dook again as we walked. Still a total nothing. Nobody was catching word of the painting or Nick the Five.

Pedestrian presence was light on Allen as we stood in front of the building's door, Randi carrying Hillary, me taking out my old set of lock picks.

"This is super shitty," said Randi. She was looking pretty ragged by now and her voice was even more ground down than usual.

Fortunately, the lock wasn't terribly sophisticated—even I could handle it. The lobby was quiet inside, all hard fluorescents and recycled wood pulp paneling. The floor tiles had recently been scrubbed with ammonia.

We walked to the elevator and I'd just pushed the up button when Hillary began fussing and whining. Excellent timing.

"No, it was *Unchained Melody*," Randi firmly whispered to her. "I'm telling you, *Unchained Melody*."

Years ago, Randi explained as we rode to the seventh floor, she'd thrown an anniversary party for her folks and she'd gone to great lengths—*great* lengths—to have their wedding song played. Which, she'd been told since she was a little girl, was *Unchained Melody*. But when the big moment came her folks were sitting at the table completely blank. Randi says what's the matter with you—this is your song. Her mother says no, that's not it. It was *That Old Black Magic*. Randi says bullshit—you always said *Unchained Melody*. Where do you get *That Old Black Magic* from? They fought about it all that day and they'd been fighting about it ever since.

Like the one downstairs, the lock to 714 wasn't particularly high grade. It took no more than a minute of work—the smell of bacon floating from one of the neighbors—to get past it. Ditto for the alarm system. I was able to shut it down *without* tearing the shit out of it.

I let the ladies in and turned my hooded flashlight on to guide the way. Every step I took now I could swear I was walking on plasma.

We were in the living room. Your basic Ikea-catalogue furniture, except for the framed, autographed photo of Ronald Reagan over the couch. *Dear Bill*, it was signed. *Warmest Wishes.* Randi said he'd had it forever and she didn't see anything amiss here. Nothing seemed out of place.

One of the doors led to the bedroom. He'd left his bed unmade. A half dozen crucifixes formed a halo around the headboard. Nick the Five was a never ending source of surprise. But we went through his closets and dresser and all his clothes appeared present and accounted for. There were no signs that he'd taken off or been planning to go anywhere.

We crossed the living room and went into the kitchen. Check the fridge first. Fully stocked—the man expected to be home. My light picked out a pile of papers on the counter. Mostly bills, waiting to be paid.

I was just reaching the bottom of the pile when I caught something at the edge of the light. A smear on the wall. Dozens of Post-it notes were stuck to the plaster and one of them was smudged with a dark stain. I spotlit it. A bloody palm print.

There were other blood patches further down the wall, and then, over in the corner, a knocked-over chair, a small table tilted against the windowsill and three distinct pools of blood on the floor.

"Oh my God what has he done?" said Randi. "What has he done now?"

My bones felt like they were made out of electrified rubber.

I went back to the Post-it notes. My name and cell was written on one of them. But the note with the smear was further away. All it said was:

WALTER ZUBROWSKI

With a 718 phone number.

"You know this guy?"

"It's kind of familiar," said Randi. "I think I heard him mention it once. I think it's, what's that AA thing? His mentor?"

"His sponsor?"

"That's it."

I remembered how worried Nick the Five sounded when I said I'd meet him at his apartment, like he was expecting somebody else to be here. So what happened? Something insane was going on and somebody accidentally put a bloody hand on the wall? Or something insane was going on and Nick the Five was trying to call his sponsor?

"What the hell is he up to?" I said.

"I've tried to figure him out." I didn't need the light to know Randi was crying. "You can try and try, and then and even then, you wouldn't know.

It felt like we were trance-walking when we reached the street. I crumpled the Post-it note with my name, stuck it in my pocket and tried Walter Zubrowski. No answer. Not even voice mail. I didn't know what to do. I was thinking the 718 number was probably a home phone and I could use it to find his address when my cell went off in my hand.

Of all the calls I didn't want to get, here it was.

Genesis had just landed. Her brother had been released from the hospital—no need for her to stay in New Orleans any more. Now what about the painting?

What Does She Know?

She didn't say a thing. Not one damn thing. I told her everything—except the part about sleeping with Shannon, or what Shannon was thinking about the murder. But I told her everything else and she didn't say a thing. Outside of *I want to see you. Now.*

I dropped Randi and Hillary off, Randi saying let me know what's happening—I'll do anything I can. All the way out to Long Island I'm thinking Genesis' security corps are gonna work me over so hard I'll be spritzing piss out of my nose for years to come.

But no.

The library again. Just the two of us again. Her walking back and forth, me standing still. She looking a little jet lagged but as cold as ever. Put a match to her skin, you'll see fire turn to ice.

She said she knew I'd never done a job on this scale before. She knew I wasn't a professional, she could make certain allowances. But now I had to get it back. I had to do everything I can to get it back. I said, yes, I would, I'd definitely get it back. Do that, she said. You do that.

This went on for minutes. The whole time I'm thinking, does she know who killed her father? Has she known all along?

She asked me again about this Nick Manetto, this Nick the Five—tell me everything you know about him. I told her again.

"You're sure Shannon Kubliak has nothing to do with this?"

"I don't see any evidence that she does."

She mulled it over a few minutes, not saying a thing. Then she came over to where I was standing, pulled the top of her caftan down until I could see her breasts and knelt in front of me. There was nothing really erotic about it. In a very workmanlike manner she unzipped my pants and took my cock in her mouth.

It was the most interesting take on motivational management theory I've ever seen.

Minutes later, as she was rubbing my semen on her breasts, she started saying get it back, get it back, just saying it over and over.

On my deathbed, I swear, I'll still be trying to understand what Genesis Robonnet was all about.

An Angel On The Hand

Driving back to the city I tried Walter Zubrowski one more time. Nothing. It was about 2 a.m., getting late. I was weighing the pros and cons of tracing his address or grabbing some sleep when Shannon called. She wanted to know what had happened. I told her everything—except the part about Genesis kneeling in front of me.

She said she knew it was a bad time but she'd found something—she'd found something big, something important. She needed my help.

You're sure Shannon Kubliak has nothing to do with this?

I said I'm on my way.

Shannon lived in a pre-war brownstone with high ceilings and arched windows, but I didn't get much chance to examine the architecture closely. She let me in her door, immediately cupped my face with both hands and slid her tongue between my lips. Not a word about choosing or not choosing her. As our tongues met she let go of my face and began unbuttoning my shirt. I'm thinking, Jesus save me, I'm sleeping with two women. I'm having sex with two separate women on the same night. I'm just like Nick the Five.

Of course I hadn't *married* either one, but the night was still young.

>>>>>>

More workmanlike sex, very perfunctory. Some people might say well at least she punched your ticket, but that's exactly what it felt like. As soon as she was finished she jumped out of bed and came back with
the laptop. It was already on, the painting already on the screen.

She'd centered her attention this time on a spot near the top left of the canvas, a spot we hadn't much looked at. She pointed to a procession of gargoyle-faced pilgrims marching beneath a comet. The comet had an unusual tail, made of hundreds of hand-stippled, rainbow-colored dots.

Right next to the tail were fine lines of tiny text.
I looked into the darkness,
I saw my body covered in blood.
This will come to pass.
My blood will flow everywhere,
My face will be bathed in my own blood.
"Isn't that how they found his body?" she said. "Isn't that exactly what happened?"

She was sitting right beside me but it felt like her voice was reaching me in a dream. Yes, that's how it happened. He'd fallen on his back and the blood had flowed over his face.

This was one eerie piece of prophesy.

Her finger moved further up the screen to another comet with a rainbow-dotted tail. She was making a pattern connection, like the swirls she'd shown me before. This tail was the same, a densely detailed clot that must've taken hours to paint, only it was much shorter, abruptly fading into a shadow.

Only two lines of words were touching it.

The one who will sacrifice me
Walks with an angel on the right hand.

"That's where I'm stuck," she said. "*Walks with an angel on the right hand.* I've searched the hell out of that line. There're dozens of references to *angel on the right hand*. Biblical refs, Hebrews 1:13—there're probably hundreds. But I can't find any context that has meaning."

I could. I remembered. I remembered that day. Slim driving, his ringed fingers on the wheel. He had so much jewelry, I remembered, it took me a while to notice the tattoo. An angel in amber and red ink. On his right hand.

I told her. I told her what I'd seen. And as soon as I heard the words coming out of my mouth I had a sensation, just for a moment, that I was standing outside myself, watching myself from a distance. I saw myself in a bedroom in the West 100's, watching myself watch myself.

This was getting too confusing. Everything about this painting was getting way too much to handle. I couldn't believe it was Slim. I couldn't believe my own testimony. I liked Slim—how could it be him? I remembered him talking about the death. *I've replayed it so many times in my head, the police report of it.* He was the one who cared.

I told Shannon she was wrong—we were going in the wrong direction. What about her other theories, the money-driven theories? I thought it was all about money.

It could still be about money, she said. It could still be about Slim *and* money.

I disagreed. Right before Robonnet painted *Sex Death Dream Talk*, he'd been angry at other people over money. I repeated the story Slim told me, about an early work that had just sold for $9 million. Robonnet had asked for one percent of the sale price, and when he was turned down he poured his venom into *Sex Death Dream Talk*.

Shannon looked like she was suddenly queasy. "That's a famous story," she said. "What he told you, it's a well known Robonnet story. The painting was *Is It Nothing To You*. The title comes from Lamentations."

"That's it, that's right. *Is It Nothing To You*."

"But it happened years ago. It didn't happen just before *Sex Death Dream Talk*. It has nothing to do with *Sex Death Dream Talk*. The dispute over the one percent happened years before that."

"You can prove it?"

"I'll show you right now." She turned to me full face. "I know maybe you can't take this, but it's true. Slim lied to you."

Mixed Nuts

Bad night. Bad, bad night. Almost no sleep. All my
open-eye thoughts stuck on the same damn things. No
painting, no Nick the Five, no trace of either. Why did
Slim bullshit me? I woke up with a thousand
miniature hummingbirds fluttering in my head.

I said goodbye and got back to my place at let's
say 6 a.m. Heavy rain to top it all off. Three cups of
coffee got me through the backtrack on Walter
Zubrowski's number. He lived in the Port Richmond
part of Staten Island.

The puddles around Lincoln Towers where
getting deep when I picked the girls up. Randi was a
crock-eyed wreck. "I know he's fresh out of idiot
school," she said, "but I prayed for him all night."

Zubrowski also lived in a prewar building—pre-
Civil War. I don't want to say the place looked
unkempt, but I'll bet the rats were big enough to carry
their own Social Security cards. His name was on one
of the outside buzzers, but after five minutes of
pushing he wasn't buzzing back.

We walked around to the back of the building,
looking for the super. We found stairs leading to a
basement apartment, a hand drawn sign on the door
saying *Mind The Step*. Not *Watch Your Step*. *Mind
The Step*. The super's probably Irish. If so, having
a name like Quinn McShane could finally be an
asset. Putting a little brogue in my voice might help
even more.

The door was opened by a stubbly gray elf of a man who smelled strongly of bleach. I could see why. He was working a wad of cotton between his gums and teeth. He was bleaching his teeth with Clorox.

Yes, he was the super, yes, he was from the old sod, and yes, we established a sort of mick-to-mick rapport. I told him it was vitally important—earth-shaking *critical*—that we talk to Walter Zubrowski.

The super made a face. "I don't know where the fookhead is. But you can probably try him over at Julius'."

Which way was that?

"There's only one way to go around here—there and back."

The fucking Irish.

Nice teeth, though.

A maze of soaked streets took us to Julius'. A crunchy, crappy dive of a bar. A *Hot Dog Buffet* was advertised in the window, *4-7*.

Not a good place for somebody's AA sponsor to be at almost 10 in the morning.

I'd never been here before, but I had. A good size but moody crowd was on hand despite the hour. One guy sat at the bar with bare feet. Another kept smelling his fingers. They still had a coin operated pool table in the back, a true antique.

The air in the place, I noticed, was actually blue.

We walked up to the bar. I put 20 of Genesis' dollars down and asked the bartender if Walter Zubrowski was around. He turned away from CNBC and pointed to a guy in one of the booths—a hefty, sweaty, virtually mouthless man. They must've been rationing lips when they were making his face. He was sitting by himself in the booth, half a beer and an empty shot glass in front of him.

Not even 10 a.m. and he was full on fried.

We slid in across from him. He didn't seem
pleased to see two strangers and a dog invading his
booth. In fact, he seemed downright belligerent.

I asked if he was Walter. He grunted in a thick,
heavy voice. He sounded like a brontosaurus with a
cold. When a guy like this is your only lead, you've
hit investigative bottom.

Our subsequent conversation proceeded neither
smoothly nor coherently. But it can be divided into
four separate stages.

What the fuck

I asked if he knew Nick the Five. No response.
Did he know where Nick the Five was or that he was
in trouble? No response and no response. When I
asked, just to be sure, if he really was his sponsor,
Walter came to angry life.

"I know him," he blurted. "Why're you saying I
don't?"

"I'm not saying that."

"Then what the fuck're you saying?" He was
quite agitated. "You're saying I don't know him?"

"No."

"Then why're you saying I don't know him?"

"Is that what I said?"

"I don't know *what* the fuck you're saying."

"He's saying you *do*," said Randi. "He's saying
you *do* know him."

"Of *course* I know him!" Walter suddenly stood
in the booth and leaned across the table, hovering two
feet from Randi's face. "Fucking *A* I know him!"

She was hardly fazed. "What, is it against your
religion to take a breath mint?"

A sour piece

Walter reacted by sinking back in his side of
the table and staring at her. He stared at her for a
long time.

It came to him. "You're the ex. One of 'em, at
least. You *have* to be the ex."

Randi asked why's that? Because, Walter said, I
know all about you. Nick the Five talks a lot about
you. I know what you are.

"You're one sour piece of pussy, aren't you?"

"That's about what I expect from you," she said.
"That's just what I expect from a red-assed, squirt-
dick fuck-butt like you."

Their remarks became a bit disparaging after
that.

Cancun

I tried to get things back on point by saying that
Nick the Five was in trouble, in case anybody's
interested.

Walter thoughtfully finished his beer. "He's got
a problem. You probably know this."

Well, this was what we were trying to find out. I
asked exactly what problem he meant.

He pointed a finger at Randi like she was a
block away. He still loves her, he said. He can't get
past her. I know cause I listen to him. He can't bring
himself to let her go, even if she looks and sounds
like a Cancun whore. "That's his problem. That's
why he won't make it. Cause of that right there."

Randi tore into him like her mortgage depended
on it. "*He* won't make it? You should fucking talk.
Sitting here shit faced this early in the day."

"Cockafuckingdoodle doo," said Walter.

Foom

I thought Randi was on to something. Maybe talking to Walter about his very obvious slip would get us somewhere. When did it start? I asked. When did you go back to the bottle?

"It all happens fast," he said. "One minute you're sitting in the living room wondering how it all went wrong. Next minute—*foom*—you're sitting here."

We talked for a while, quieter now. Walter ended up with his head on the table, crying like a lost child. As for Nick the Five, he hadn't heard from him in almost two weeks. Their last conversation, we realized, had taken place just before Randi met us all at my apartment.

Walter calmed down enough to tell us the name of *his* sponsor. I called—the guy said give him 40 minutes, he'd be right there. Yes, he knew where Julius' was. We stayed with Walter while we waited, Randi complaining that we were nowhere, this whole effort was just one big bowl of dick-suck. The bartended switched from CNBC to the local news. The usual. Massive traffic tie up. Brooklyn politician arrested. Family protests suspect's shooting. New developments in the Shiney Hiney death.

That got my blood going. Even Randi stopped talking.

Yesterday, according to the story, New Jersey cops had spent an hour at a restaurant called Twizzle's, questioning the staff about Bobby Hucknail's last meal. They wanted to know whether Bobby had eaten anything containing peanuts or peanut-based products or anything prepared in the proximity of peanuts. There was no official word from the cops, but one police source was saying that, going by preliminary autopsy results, Bobby's death was the tragic consequence of a peanut allergy.

The owner of Twizzle's was on camera. I recognized him from that night. He'd called the media on the story. Directly or indirectly, he insisted, Bobby had consumed no peanuts on his premises. Nothing he was served contained the legume. Moreover, the restaurant prided itself on the nut-free portion of its menu and went to extraordinary lengths to maintain the integrity of all its dishes. Bobby, in short, couldn't have been contaminated by anything he'd eaten here.

That sounded right. I remembered what he'd ordered—Crab Rangoon, firecracker wings, pork-filled sago balls, that fish-head curry.

Then I remembered what I'd eaten. Not the teriyaki salmon—no, I wasn't thinking about that. I was thinking about what I'd eaten in the bar while Shannon and I were waiting for a table. Mixed nuts. A bowl of cashews, walnuts, smoked pecans. And peanuts. Definitely peanuts.

I'd killed Bobby.

The Twizzle's owner wasn't mentioning Bobby's collapse—probably not the greatest publicity. But Bobby had passed out and I'd brought him back with mouth-to-mouth. I'd killed him. Trying to help him, I'd killed him.

It was still raining. I could hear traffic sloshing on the street outside. I could hear all that. And I knew I'd killed Bobby.

"You all right?" said Randi. "Can I get you anything?"

What I wanted was a drink.

I didn't know about the allergy. I didn't know anything about that. I was trying to save him—save him to rob him, true—but still I was trying to save him. It wasn't my fault, and yet telling myself that didn't help one fucking bit. I was trying to save his life and I ended up taking his life.

Was I dreaming this shit?

That's what it felt like. Sitting there in that booth, smell of bad booze all around me, it felt like dream talk. Like death dream talk. It felt like suddenly I was in the painting, caught inside the frame.

The angels from hell are here,
Exu and his snarling dogs are here,
Those who have hidden their hearts are here,
And they will not let me go.

A Connection

We got out of there as soon as Walter's sponsor showed his face. Walking to the car, headlights skimming over wet streets, I felt completely rootless. What I needed to do was get a quiet moment and pray. I needed a good dose of God.

Randi wanted to know what was what. You're acting miserable. You'd make the grim reaper look like he just got laid.

So I told her. I told her about Bobby. She said are you fucking kidding me? It was a terrible thing, yes, but did you *mean* to do it? You can't take total blame for an accident like that.

Things were starting to feel a little lighter when my cell went off. The name-flash surprised me. DeMarcus Boyd, my Nassau County cop friend, the one who'd busted me. I answered. First thing he says he wants to talk about the murder.

My throat went methedrine dry. The paranoia was that instant. He's calling Bobby's death a murder? He already knows I killed him? How is this his jurisdiction?

"Murder?"

DeMarcus waxed impatient. *The one you told me to look into? New Orleans?*

Jesus fuck me—he was talking about Dewey Tarantonio, the sketchy antiques dealer whose headless body I'd found in St. Louis Cemetery No. 1.

They'd made an arrest, NOPD had, DeMarcus
said, guy named Lyle Davies. He'd been picked up
for stolen mortuary sculpture, but once the
investigation got rolling he ended up getting charged
with Dewey's decap. DeMarcus gave me a
description. Lyle Davies was a tall, stiff-bodied
individual given to wearing New Orleans Saints
paraphernalia, and he compensated for his baldness
with a fringe of stringy hair. *Ecce homo*—he was the
dude. He was the one who'd followed me back from
Dewey's house, the one who'd pulled a knife on me
near the scaffolding on Bourbon Street.

There's also a local connection, said DeMarcus,
*it's maybe somebody you know. This Lyle was
working the stolen art with a guy from up here,
arrested with him. Manhattan guy, a Michael
Tamburello? You know him?*

"New to me."

*Or Mikey Tamburello? He goes I believe by
Mikey Tamburello.*

"Never heard of Mikey Tamburello either."

We talked for a few more seconds, I thanked
DeMarcus for getting back and I killed the call.

Randi was staring at me like I was in the middle
of exposing myself.

"Did you say Mikey Tamburello?" she said.

"You know him?"

"I know the name. Nick the Five did some
business with him once. This was before we met, but
I remember the name."

This was kinda interesting. Lay it out:

1) Dewey Tarantonio knew something about the
painting.

2) He'd been offed, literally, by Lyle Davies
after talking to me.

3) Lyle had an association with Mikey Tamburello.

4) Tamburello had a prior association with Nick the Five.

Hell, it was *something*.

I called Rev. Dook. Yes, he knew Mikey Tamburello and didn't particularly like him. Was glad, in fact, to hear he was currently incarcerated in a Louisiana jail.

I put my speculation to him: There was a loose link between Nick the Five and Mikey Tamburello, and a loose link between Tamburello and the painting. If I wanted maybe to tighten those links, what would I do?

There's a person he runs with, said Rev. Dook. *Almost like his partner. Izzy Edwards. I don't like him either, God forgive me. Very skeevy sort. I'd look at him. Operates out of a warehouse in the West 50s. I can get you the address.*

Very skeevy sort? This was sounding hopeful. For the first time in 24 hours, we had something that could almost qualify as a decent lead.

It's true what they say. It really *does* depend on who you know.

Spotting The Tell

It sure wasn't much to look at. Izzy Edwards'
warehouse sat rotting in the industrial section a few
blocks away from my apartment, the one area of the
neighborhood that had been spared gentrification so
far. The building's windows were covered with metal
grills, glass gone from half of them, replaced by
plywood. Ancient garbage was piled against the sides
of the dumpsters, or had been blown there. Rebar was
showing through the cement walls like Wheat Chex at
the bottom of a bowl of milk.

A worn out sign over the truck bays said *United
Marketing*, about as nondescript a name as it gets.
Trucks were pulling in and out of other warehouses
and small factories near the river. Here, there wasn't
one car in the parking spaces alongside the bay doors.
And the bays themselves were covered with
scaffolding, which besides giving me a New Orleans
flashback, gave the impression the building was under
renovation and nobody was around.

"You're sure this is the right place?" Be'Nad
said as we sat across the street in my car.

"From what I hear."

"It could be a mistake, very possibly a mistake.
I'm almost willing to bet it's a mistake."

"Why's that?"

I had to ask. Because of what he'd been talking
about, he said. Because something is *wrong* with this

job. Because no matter what the sweating pigs of progress tell us, the world is still filled with omens and curses and energies unseen.

I told him what happened with Bobby. It wasn't the result of a curse—it was the result of me. He wasn't swayed. Bobby's fate was just proof that the curse had infected us all, me and him. In fact it was keeping him up at night. Twenty minutes of solid sleep and he was tossing all night.

"I'm tired," he said, "of not sleeping."

When you're staking a place out, sometimes it takes a while for your eyes to settle and let the details stick out. Like the windows that hadn't been boarded with plywood. They were all broken, but after a few minutes you notice that they all look the same, like rows of jagged upper teeth. They've all been shattered in the same way, from the bottom, leaving the top shards of glass to hang down like icicles. Pretty remarkable coincidence if the windows have been accidentally broken. But what if somebody's intentionally trying to make the place look empty?

Or take those pieces of cardboard in one of the sidewalk dumpsters. Even though they're wet from rain, you can still see that they've been carefully folded and flattened by hand. Somebody made a very neat job out of it, and not too long ago.

And what about the door at the main entrance? It's an old rusted and stained piece of crap, sure, but look long enough and you realize it's been drilled with a shiny new industrial lock.

"Question," I said, pointing. "If this building's so abandoned, what's it doing with hardware like that?"

Be'nad knew what I meant. He pointed to the truck bays. "See the wiring along the edges of the doors? Fiber optics. Someone's outfitted an empty warehouse with a lot of security."

If we were playing poker, we'd just spotted a tell.

Now it was onto the next step: Determining what security system was in place. Assuming it was something Be'Nad could work with, we'd come back after dark.

Be'Nad sat looking at the building. "I should just walk over there?"

"Get close enough to listen—that's the idea."

"Wait. People are coming."

True. A skateboarder gliding through the drizzle turned around the corner and wheeled past the warehouse. Moments later an Orthodox Jew walked past smoking a hand-cupped joint.

Be'Nad still wasn't moving. "So I go over there and do what? What's my cover?"

"Your *what*?"

"Won't that look odd, I'm just standing there?"

"Take a pee behind that dumpster. That should get you close enough."

"You want me to *urinate* in public!"

"*Pretend.*"

From the way he crossed the street, I could tell he was counting his steps. His OCD was getting *bad*.

After 45 seconds of elaborately mimed piss-taking, Be'nad came back looking concerned.

"Can you handle it?"

"I know the system. I can get in."

"So?"

"I thought I heard something. Inside the building."

"What?"

"I think someone's in there. I think I heard someone whose heart is beating *really* fast."

We had some time to wait. Be'Nad went home to pick up his equipment and get himself ready. I called Genesis, told her about the progress. She said she wanted to hear the details in person—report in. Only as soon as I'm shown into the library she's nibbling and biting on me. Like I had nothing else on my mind, nothing else to do.

The weirdest thing: She cried out at the end, letting her lungs loose in a drawn out and almost painful wail. And what did it remind me of? What her father must've sounded like that night in Dominicus Park. I remembered the descriptions, the spiraling trapped-demon shrieks. It was like I was hearing an echo of her father's death screams.

Back in the city I called Randi and Shannon to let them know about the warehouse. Shannon said she wanted to see me. Just for a minute, I said. But she opened her door wearing nothing but a babydoll negligee. This was turning into a long day. She started giving me the closed eyes and the open mouth, but then she held back and gave me a funny look.

"If you're sleeping with her," she said, "I hope you're using protection." Then it was a dirty look. "Like a hazmat suit."

>>>>>>

Nearer, My Glock, To Thee

The rain had picked up again and by 10 that night it was coming down so hard it felt like the ocean was falling. Sounded like it too. Standing right next to the warehouse door to work the gleaming new lock, Be'Nad couldn't hear inside anymore. Any sounds of rapid heartbeats or anything else couldn't make it past the heavy weather.

I stood beside him, holding the hooded flashlight on the lock. Despite the considerable precipitation, Be'Nad was still washing everything down with Handi-Wipes before he touched it, only the number of times he'd clean anything was past counting. He'd gone far beyond his usual anti-dirty dozen strokes.

"One thing," he said as he checked his processor. "I'm not going in. I'll get you inside, but I'm not following."

"Why not?"

"Whatever's in there, it's not my purview."

"Your *purview*?"

"I only steal things—I know my limits. I'm sticking with my comfort zone."

"So what? You wait in the car?"

He straightened up. "I'll be frank. I feel like something is going to happen in there. And when I feel like that, like something's going to happen, it usually does."

"Wait in the car."

"The door's open."

The interior was studded with faint nightlights but they didn't show much. All I could see at first was a maze of walls and shadows. There didn't seem to be any big open space, just what was looking like a ramshackle series of rooms and spaces, all rigged together by shells of plywood and corrugated metal. It was like a demented shantytown.

I edged into one dark spot and waited, listening for anything. Nothing came, but at least one of my senses was activated. The warehouse smelled like all hell. It was filled with some black stink, some vomitocious odor mixed with traces of sour detergent. The place was as aromatic as a meth house.

The hooded flashlight gave me a single straight beam to follow. I whispered through doors, walled-off spaces, heading for the middle of the warehouse, moving past sorry piles of junk, the oxidized purples and blues of flaking paint. The whole place looked like it was about to fall down. I shifted the gun from the back of my waistband to the front.

Nearer, my Glock, to thee.

The rain outside stopped. It suddenly faded and disappeared, 10 seconds tops. So fast it was scary. Nothing but silence. The smell, though, was getting stronger as I moved. I could identify the main ingredient now. It was shit. *Shit* shit—feces. Actually, it was more specific than that. It was a kind of tomatoey diarrhea.

The floor started to tremble under my legs. It was rippling, turning liquid, just like being in New Orleans, just like I was walking in New Orleans. It was fear. My legs were going wobbly and weightless with fear.

God, I don't know what I'm getting into, but please make sure I get out.

Half a minute later, the corridor I was taking led me in to an area where the makeshift walls dropped away. Finally, a large, open space, sitting in what seemed to be the middle of the building. The nightlights only showed an army of tall, cylindrical shapes. The flashlight: Hundreds of large metal tanks were lining the walls.

I moved my light. All it picked up was corroded, tubular metal. Then it caught something near the center of the room. A sudden orange zag on a field of black. A streak of orange dyed Beatle-cut hair.

Nick the Five was ass-down on the floor, his arms bent backwards and duct taped around a pole. Tape covered his mouth and was wrapped around his legs. He was alive, blinking in the light. His eyes looked terrible and the rest of him was no better off. Face battered, splotched with dried blood. I don't know how many times he'd shit and peed in his pants, but somebody had tried to clean the mess up with the mop and the bottle of generic cleaner nearby.

I ripped the tape off his mouth. I know it hurt, but I still thought a thank you might be in order. What I got instead was:

"Just shoot me. Just shoot me right now. Put a bullet in my head and get it over."

"I'm not shooting you until I get the painting. Where is it?"

Even in the weak light I could see his face flush.

"You're not gonna like it," he warned. "You're not gonna like it a lot."

"I'm already there. Where is it?"

A confessional sigh. "All right. I took it."

"I fucking *know* you took it. Now where is it?"

"I don't know. I don't know where it is. All I know is I got fucked over. I got beaten to shit and I got fucked over, all because of I took it."

"So start with why you took it. Were you stoned and I didn't see it?"

"You know you don't have to be stoned to be stupid. It was just, Quinn, I couldn't think. I just couldn't think. It was like…"

He stopped. We both heard it—a noise coming from the other side of the building.

"The fuck is that?"

"There's this guy," he said. "He, uh…he…"

"Stay quiet."

I turned off the flashlight and moved back to the shadows by the wall. Once I'd slipped between a couple of the tanks, I took out the Glock.

Moments later, somebody stomped in from the opposite entrance. The dim nightlights showed a kid—he was maybe 19 or 20—a kid with a strenuous, lumbering gait. He walked like he was trying to squash cockroaches with every step.

He looked around, squinted at Nick the Five, moved closer to him. At first I thought he was wearing a loud green and white checked jacket. But then I saw the faces of Grant, Hamilton and Franklin on the material. It was a money jacket, made with blow ups of various denominations, everything from Washingtons and Lincolns to Grover Alexanders.

Guess where *his* heart's at.

He got a good look at Nick the Five and he didn't like what he saw. "Who took that tape off you?"

"It fell."

"The *fuck* it fell. Who took…"

Now another sound could be heard, but this time from my end of the warehouse. Feet slapping flat on the ground, somebody running this way.

The guy retreated into the shadows on his side of the room.

Ten seconds passed. Be'Nad appeared in the door, breathing hard, stopping as he came to the open space.

"Quinn?" he said in a stage whisper. "You there? Quinn?"

I whispered back at him, at a much lower volume. "Get out of here."

"I heard someone. There's someone else in here."

"Just *leave*."

"The rain let up—that's when I heard it. There are two people in here. Or four, counting you and—"

And that's when the firing started. Five wild rounds came blasting out of the dark where the guy had vanished. They twanged and vibrated off the tanks near Be'Nad. I shot back. All it produced was more metallic twangs, followed by echoes on both side of the room.

Be'Nad, foolishly helpful, was still somewhere near the entrance. "Nick," he called, "are you there? I think I hear you."

"You hear me."

"Watch out for yourself."

"How the fuck'm I gonna do that? I'm tied to this—"

The guy's gunfire ripped across the open space, hitting more tanks and chewing cement out of the wall.

"Be'Nad!" I yelled. "Get the fuck out!"

I was rewarded for my concern with a volley of shots aimed in the direction of my voice. Bullets slammed into the canisters around me. I shot back and jumped away, getting off just enough fire to shut the guy up.

We waited. Six motherfucking seconds passed. "Be'Nad!" I yelled. "*Go!*"

This time I moved *before* the bullets started punching dents in metal. Moments later, as I wedged between a new set of tanks, I could hear Be'Nad's footsteps. They were falling fast and they were fading.

So now there were two of us. Or three, counting Nick the Five, caught out there in the middle with all the long term prospects of an Aztec virgin.

I didn't know exactly where the kid was and he didn't know exactly where I was, but he was determined to find out. The next explosion of his gunfire was all over the place, strafing side to side and up and down as the gun searched for a target. The bullets gouged into metal and kicked up dust and even when I wasn't in the direct line of the spray I could feel the jolt of the shots. I ducked deeper between the canisters and squeezed a few rounds back—firing at his fire, shooting at shadows.

He went quiet again. The echoing this time ran soul deep. The wounded tanks were ringing like a hundred Buddhist gongs, like a thousand Tibetan monks had gone mallet-mad and run amok.

It didn't last. The gunfire just *poured* out of that dark womb on the other side of the room. It came at me like floodwaters, the guy letting loose with a frustrated, pent-up shitstorm of bullets. They blew chunks of cement out of the wall behind me and smashed into my tanks with a hellbent force that sent a rattle through me from my throat to my balls.

Yes, I was scared. I was fucking *terrified*. On top of it all Nick the Five started screaming out there. Was he hit?

It couldn't go on like this.

The kid let up. I didn't shoot back. I just stayed down and didn't do a thing, wondering what would happen if I waited him out.

A few moments later he opened up again. The gunfire tore into the metal around me with impact tremors that felt like they were running from the center of the earth to the top of my head. But I stayed still. Praying my ass off, yeah, but I stayed still. I wanted to see how much patience this guy had.

Not enough, it turns out.

The shooting stopped. This time the pause lasted for more than a few moments. Almost 15 seconds went by with nothing happening, nothing moving. Then I saw something across the way—a green and white shape separating from the shadows. The guy stepped slowly, carefully, creeping out just far enough to be outlined in one of the nightlights.

I aimed at one of the presidents' faces and fired twice.

The kid yelped with surprised pain, like a puppy getting hit by a truck. His legs danced for a second, then he fell on his back. There was no resistance, no effort to stay standing. He just flat gave away.

I waited. Then still waited, watching as the layers of gunsmoke played in the nightlights and rose to the ceiling.

Nick the Five wasn't hit. He couldn't say anything as I walked past—too rattled to talk—but he wasn't hit. There was, however, a fresh puddle by his pants.

The kid, he had two holes in Grover Cleveland's face, two holes in the $1,000 blow up over his heart.

Blood had spilled from his chest and his mouth and had been pulled by gravity down his neck and around his ears. Despite the mess, he had a peaceful look on his face.

Yes, he was dead. Double-tapped in the chest and dead. Let's see, what does that come to? Oh, right—two. Two people. In the space of only a few days I'd killed two people doing this fucking job and it wasn't over yet.

I didn't like the way this thing was trending.

No One Is More Surprised Than You

When my hands finally stopped shaking I cut Nick the Five loose. "We should talk."

He stayed on the floor, as exhausted as he was filthy. "I don't know what to say."

"Try telling me what happened."

"What happened, most of it, is I'm a fucking idiot."

"Maybe a little more detail?"

"What happened was, I lost my *why*. You know? I lost my reason for doing anything. I lost my fucking *why*."

"Tell me."

It was pathetic. He'd boosted the painting to impress Randi. The whole sad thing came down to that. He'd set off on this little adventure to get her attention and respect. It wasn't premeditated. He got the idea while he was rewrapping the painting in my apartment. He'd snatch the thing, turn it over to somebody else, then tell us he'd gotten a tip on its whereabouts, play the lead role in getting it back and reap a hero's reward in recognition. Finally he'd make himself look better than Be'Nad.

Only the guy he turned it over to, Izzy Edwards, wasn't so cooperative. Izzy and his crew, they turned on him in his apartment. They not only took possession of the painting, they took possession of him. He was going to betray them and they ended up betraying him. And that's what it was, simple fact, a betrayal.

(And don't tell me I haven't been hearing enough of that word lately.)

"They were going to kill me," he said. "They were gonna sell the thing, I don't know to who, but they were gonna move it tonight and when the deal was done they were going to *kill* me."

"I can understand the feeling."

"Quinn, I'm *serious.*"

"I'm not? Why did you pick Izzy?"

"I dealt with him before. I know he's got some interest in art."

"Did you know he'd had some interest in the painting before?"

"*This* painting? The same one?"

"He probably had a hand in taking it from New Orleans and passing it on to H-L Lincoln. And what happens? Hello, you walk in with it under your arm."

Nick the Five shook his head with grave sorrow. "This turned out to be a bad idea."

"No one is more surprised than you."

"I didn't know what to do. I was like, *trapped,* you know? I just wanted Randi to stop hating on me."

I believed him. I believed his story. It was so meat-dumb, so utterly fucked up, I completely believed it.

"Let's get you cleaned up and get out of here."

We found a bathroom where he could wash off. I gave him the dead kid's pants and stood outside the door, letting him have some privacy. I heard water running, him starting to hum (man was unbelievable) as he scrubbed, then his voice.

"Hey Quinn?"

"What?"

"You know, I'm standing here looking in the mirror?"

"It happens."

"You know what I do sometimes at home? I stand in front of the mirror, I don 't see anything. I see a big hole where I'm supposed to be, a big nothing. There's just nobody there. I can't stand it."

Dear fucking God.

We talked. We talked about what it was like to wake up everyday with the terror. We talked about the dull and dangerous gray days of depression. We talked, as he was wiping his ass, about finding the mystery that was bigger and deeper than yourself, about reaching that last ledge where you either die or become a believer.

As we were talking I could see the words from the painting in my head.

Do you think I do not know?
Do you think I could not heer
The words whispered
On the cancerous breaths
Of those who no longer know,
Of those who have forgotten
You are not who you think you are?

It was like I was living the words, living the meaning. It was like I was living the painting.

The Man With The Purple Scarf

Be'Nad kept playing told-you-so riffs as the three of us drove back to my place. He knew something becursed would happen and it sure as shit did. Speaking of which, he added, the stench in the warehouse had truly been something awful.

Shannon, Randi and Hillary came over right away. We had to decide on a next step, if there was one. Nick the Five, putting the blame on a basic miscommunication between himself and himself, recapped the broad outlines: he'd gone to Izzy Edwards, planning to con him and make himself look like a conquering hero, but he'd gotten conned instead.

This put Randi in a massive piss-off. She called him a stupid suck-butt son of a bitch who'd clearly made a clean break with reality, and when he begged her not to get angry, she informed him that she wasn't angry. I don't GET angry! I NEVER get angry!

If we had any chance of getting the painting back, we needed more specifics. Initially, Nick the Five was reluctant to detail his humiliation any further, but he was helped in the process by Randi picking him up by the ear and telling him to get on with it.

"What I know is," he bleated, "they were gonna *kill* me. Soon as the hand-off was done tonight, they were coming back and killing me. I heard them arguing about it. Actually, Izzy was against it. Said let's let him live—I heard that. But this other guy, he wanted me done."

"Who was this guy?" I said.

"Don't know. Not one of Izzy's regulars."

"Did you see him?"

"For a minute, maybe. When they were dragging me in."

"Was it H-L Lincoln? Anybody you saw at H-L's?"

"No, nothing like that."

"You know where I'm going, right? Izzy and his partner, Mikey Tamburello, they passed the painting the first time to H-L. It's a possibility he's doing it again."

Nick the Five was certain. "It wasn't H-L. Wasn't that voice. And the guy wasn't dressed like some hallucinogenic medieval freak. Dressed a little weird, you could say that, but not like something out of the circus."

"Dressed a little weird how?"

"Wearing a suit, black business suit, and a scarf around his neck. Like a *priest*. I'm thinking, it's summertime, who wears a scarf?"

"But it wasn't anybody from H-L's?"

"Not this one, no."

"It was a *scarf?*"

The question was Shannon's. She said it like she was shocked to say the word. She said it like the word was taboo.

Nick the Five nodded. "Around his neck, you know?"

"Black suit with a scarf?"

"That was it."

"Was it a *purple* scarf?"

His eyes went wide. "Exactly. Purple. A purple scarf. That's why the priest. The purple made me think of a priest."

Shannon moved closer to him, sniffing prey. "What kind of hair did he have?"

"This guy? Hardly any. Guy was bald except for this little I don't know swatch of shit in the front."

"A patch of hair? Like a triangle of hair right in front?"

"It's like, when he looks in the mirror? Probably sees a full head of hair."

"Son of a bitch. Cole Reynolds. It that isn't Cole Reynolds, nobody is."

"I get the feeling you know him," I said.

"Of course I know him. I've *worked* with him. He's on the Whitmore board. He's on the board of the museum."

The click in my head was so hard it practically gave me whiplash. The Whitmore? It made *some* kind of sense. The museum had been one of the parties negotiating with Slim and Genesis for the sale of the painting.

"A *museum*?" said Randi. "You handed it over to a *museum*? The fuck did you do? How're we gonna get inside a fucking *museum*?"

I don't know what she called it, but Randi sounded pretty close to angry to me.

Nick the Five bowed his head, tried to find some explanation. "Sometimes you do things nobody understands, but *you* do, so you do it," he said. "Sometimes you do things nobody else understands and neither do you, but you do it anyway."

I've heard many definitions of addiction, but for my money, nothing beats that one right there.

CHAPTER 15

THIS IS THE MOST LUNATIC THING I'VE EVER SEEN

A Visionary Who Couldn't See The Future

One thing you can say about Harold Whitmore, he knew what he wanted and he knew he wanted to make everybody else want it too. In Shannon's words, the museum founder was a scrappy, belligerent, pig-headed industrialist—he was usually described as an industrialist because, really, what else do you call a guy who made everything from semiconductors to piston rings to plastic plumbing fixtures? Anyway, there he was, chugging along with his life when he began losing his balance and his concentration and his powers of speech on top of getting these sudden, wincing headaches that often left him flat on his back. Like a lot of people who work under stress, he attributed it to stress and never got off his butt to see a doctor.

By the time he did, the tumor in his brain had spread like an octopus and made itself at home. Inoperable, the doctors said. Chemo and radiation will give you a year to live at most. Whitmore said yes to the treatments and prepared to face the end.

But two months into the ordeal, while he was lying in an outpatient bed with vicious chemicals pumping through his body, he received an unusual visitor. At least he said he did, *swore* he did. He opened his eyes to see an angel standing by his bedside, a shimmering, translucent, wings-and-all woman named Avanaliana who told him not to worry, everything will be all right.

Whitmore wasn't used to getting visits from angels, so he tended to take it seriously. He took it even more seriously when the tumor began to shrink and go into a baffling remission. The symptoms disappeared, the treatment stopped, and the doctors were left with no other explanation except to call it a medical miracle.

Whitmore half agreed. It was a miracle, he believed, but not a medical one. From that point on he turned his considerable passions to spiritual matters, especially to artwork inspired by supernatural intervention. He hung the paintings on the walls of his many factories. He even forced his employees to take art classes so they'd be better motivated to make semiconductors and piston rings and plastic plumbing fixtures. And when he died—massive stroke, the tumor never returned—he left $50 million for his family to build a museum devoted exclusively to art created by holy crazies.

So far so good. I hadn't known all those details before I'd first wandered in The Whitmore Primitive Museum, but I'd known the fundamentals. By the time I'd walked out of the museum, however, I was a carrying a question that was still hanging open. Why had Joy Cheng, the Whitmore's Public Affairs Administrator, been so reluctant to talk to me? Asking her about Robonnet was like asking for her PIN number. Now I was learning why. Shannon was giving us the museum's backstory, stuff you wouldn't find on the Whitmore website, and I was beginning to understand why questions about Robonnet could provoke all kinds of pathological avoidance syndrome.

Two years after its founder's death, The Whitmore Primitive Museum opened in Sea Cliff. Notice the name. *Primitive* Museum. Not *Spiritual* or *Mystical* or anything that would more accurately reflect Harold Whitmore's intentions. That was the first sign. Even in the name you could see that his family wasn't quite down with the old bastard's enthusiasms. In fact, it was plainly embarrassed by them. Paintings by serial killers who'd converted in prison? Or by delusionnaires who'd been abducted by aliens? This was one queer legacy to carry on.

True, the museum was a success. As noted, it had amassed close to 3,000 works of deeply eccentric art. Its endowment had fissioned to $140 million. It housed the largest collection of Robonnets in the world. But the family still saw it as a grotesque novelty shop, and they saw themselves regarded by others in the art market as kooks and cranks, treated with scrutiny and scorn. Outside of its Robonnets, the museum wasn't buying the family any art world cred.

As Whitmore's children grew up and got married and had entitled children of their own, they tried to put more and more distance between themselves and wild Harold's crazy spiritual roots. Board members like Cole Reynolds, who'd married one of the Whitmore daughters, would admit that the old man was *a visionary, absolutely, but a visionary who couldn't see the future*. If they could sweep all that mystical shit under the carpet, the family came to believe, they could make new acquisitions and put the museum on a far more respectable path. Cole, for example, was particularly fond of Neo-New wave, but he was up for anything. *As long as we're promoting outsider art*, he'd say, *we'll always be outsiders.*

A few months ago, the family finally took some tangible steps. They formed an internal advisory group, The Committee on the Current Crisis, to come up with a face-lift plan. Chaired by Cole, The CCC decided the museum would carefully, deliberately sell off the fanatic art and restock its permanent collection with more acceptable, blue-chip inventory. But The CCC quickly discovered that, if they were going to raise oodles of cash, the only things worth serious money were the Robonnets. So Cole hit on the idea of quietly divesting a select number of the prized paintings. He'd arranged deals with a few well-chosen, discreet Robonnet collectors and had already completely two sales when I came barging in the museum, saying I was an investment consultant with a client looking maybe to make some Robonnet buys. That's why Joy Cheng had gone all paranoid.

Shannon had known about the selective offloads and she wasn't bothered by them—the more people who owned Robonnets, the more potential clients for her—but that was all she had in the way of facts. What she was telling us now was on spec. Still, she had no conceptual difficulty seeing Cole Reynolds as a bad guy. How he hooked up with Izzy Edwards she couldn't guess, but if someone like Izzy made an approach, yes, she could see Cole going for it. She wouldn't put it past him—he was desperate enough for respectability to consort with criminals. She could certainly see Cole buying a stolen painting from Izzy Edwards and reselling it to a black-market buyer.

And if the painting was *Sex Death Dream Talk* with say a 30% markup? You're talking a huge infusion of ready cash.

There were two other things Shannon could see. If Cole wanted to hide the painting while he put a sale together, he'd probably keep it at the museum. The place was secure, guarded and had plenty of hidden room. There was a whole warren of archival storage areas on the basement level.

And the other thing? She wasn't terribly surprised to hear that Cole had wanted Nick the Five dead. She didn't have a hard time believing that. Permanently dispatching anyone who could damage him was completely in keeping with Cole's character.

Shannon wasn't alone in her opinion. As soon as I called Genesis and relayed our Cole Reynolds suspicions, she went rabid-rat angry and there wasn't even the tiniest element of disbelief holding her back. She was so upset she put in a conference call to Slim. He sounded frail from the recent hospitalization but that didn't stop him from cussing out Cole. Again, no shock, no it can't be. Slim called him a motherfucking two-faced charlatan and he and Genesis both agreed that nobody could cut integrity corners like Cole. *He's supposed to be this fountain of wisdom and savvy*, she said, *but he's three coins short.*

Okay, they didn't like him, but how much did they know? Were they aware, for instance, that Cole had been selling off some of their father's canvases? Suddenly their voices dropped a few volume levels and became much less precise. Same thing when I asked about how Cole had acted during the *Sex Death*

Dream Talk negotiations. Their answers were so vague you could hear them evaporate as they hit the air.

Genesis tried to recapture some ground by telling me to do whatever it took to get inside the museum. *Spend what you need—we'll bake in the costs.* Still, I couldn't get what they *hadn't* said out of my ears. If I'd been trying to convince myself that these two had nothing to hide, I'd have to say I'd gotten exactly zero help from them.

A Day At The Museum

Strangely, it felt *good* to be David Branigan again, VP of Sheridan Financial Services. Maybe it felt good to be *anybody*, I don't know. All I knew is I was tired and wired—*twired* I think the technical term is—and I'd put in a call to Joy Cheng. My client, I told her, had revived her interest in Robonnet, so could I get another meeting with your curator, Shannon Kubliak? Joy sure didn't sound thrilled, but she reluctantly agreed. What else can a conscientious Public Affairs Administrator do?

Now maybe it was me, maybe I was seeing it with different eyes, but the museum didn't seem exactly the same. The place still looked like a pure white supermarket crowded with intense art students, tour groups in sensible shoes, Japanese visitors asking directions to the serial killer section. But the security somehow seemed tighter. I saw guards standing everywhere, as animated as hood ornaments, staring at everybody with the hard stares of professional Calvinists. Were there more of them now? Or was I going paranoid? And what about all those wall-mounted cameras? Why did they all seem to be pointing at me?

Or at us? Be'Nad and Nick the Five had come along as my Sheridan Financial associates. They were both wearing suits, both carrying attaché cases stuffed with impressive looking but meaningless financial papers.

We announced ourselves at the info desk in the lobby and waited. Nick the Five was jumpy. A black wig was hiding his orange streaked mop-top, but if we happened to come across Cole Reynolds, would the rug be enough of a disguise?

Be'Nad was a whole other story. I've seen bodies dredged up after weeks underwater in better shape. Despite the purple polka-dotted bow tie he was sporting, he looked puckered and sickly and withdrawn, closed up in himself, and I could tell as soon as he walked in the entrance that he'd taken an immediate dislike to the museum.

He'd stopped eating—that was his problem. Whole way over, he kept telling us that from now on he was never going to eat again. The famous Robonnet curse, he was now convinced, would visit him in the form of poison, and personally he'd rather starve to death than allow himself to succumb to poisoning,

"I've got these words," he said, "they keep materializing in my head. *Do Not Eat. Do Not Eat.*"

Interesting, I thought. Those were the exact words on the bloody bag his mother kept in her freezer, the bag holding his placenta.

We'd been waiting a minute when Shannon, as arranged, came out to meet us in the lobby. I faked introductions to Be'Nad and Nick the Five while she told us she'd just had a talk with Joy Cheng. Her instructions re David Branigan and these Sheridan Financial people: *Do anything you can to discourage the yahoos.*

"Am I dreaming this?" I said, "or is security a couple of notches higher?"

Higher, said Shannon. Definitely higher, and she took us to the entrance of the Heavenly Visitations section, where the UFO art was housed, to show us why.

There were still some board-disapproved paintings on display, big fat close ups of cosmic creatures with round baby-squirrel eyes and reptilian skin. But most of the gallery was taken up by workers who were erecting platforms and metal framing. A bald woman with tortoise shell glasses was at the other end of the space, arguing with a worker. Joy Cheng.

The board was holding a party here in two days, said Shannon. No, check that—not a party, an *event*. That was the preferred terminology—an *event*, a function showcasing installations of new, non-metaphysical kinds of art. Extra security had been brought in for the construction, and they'd probably hire even more for the event. It was a first step in what Shannon had been telling us about, the museum trying to change the spin of its story. The board was hoping the event would begin to attract a new kind of crowd, a new kind of donor.

A pile of coated-stock flyers announcing the affair sat on a counter. The artists who'd be showing that night were listed. Their names meant nothing to me, except one: HIPS (Hidden In Plain Sight), the performance group I'd seen that time at the Milk Studios, when I'd first run into Genesis. I doubt if there's anything about that evening I'll ever forget, and that includes HIPS with their hula hoops and feathered devil masks, putting on some piece of apocalyvia called *The Flat Earth Theory, Part 6* with kazoos, noisemakers and tambourines.

They'd be on hand at the Whitmore, performing a new piece, *UnFounded Foundation*, duration unknown.

Reason enough to stay away.

I watched the work getting done in the gallery. "This isn't necessarily a bad thing," I concluded. "The staff's scrambling, they've got this one thing on their minds. They're distracted. We should make the move before the event, take advantage of the confusion."

Nick the Five had an idea. "How about *during* the party? Even more confusion."

"Maybe too much. We don't know how much security they're bringing in. How many guests they expecting?"

"Few hundred," said Shannon.

"Then it's impossible. We can't control a scene like that. We need to do it before."

"What*ever* we do," Be'Nad said sourly, "we won't be coming in through the front door."

I looked. He was staring at the ceiling as if a variety of unseemly odors were just *streaming* out of the vents. "What're you hearing?"

"Sounded like a Utrecht-40Z. Out of the question."

"How far out?"

"A bitch of a system. It can take 30, 40 good minutes to decode. I can't be standing naked to the world outside for 30 to 40 minutes."

"You won't be. We won't let that happen."

"As for the rest of it..." His eyes searched the ceiling tiles. "The rest of it is, I don't know, there's something strange about it."

"Let's deal with that when it comes. First we make sure the painting's here." I turned to Shannon. "You have the card?"

She took something out of her pocket and palmed it to Be'Nad. It was her Whitmore ID card, which gave her swipe access to the entire museum. Once we'd blended with the crowd, Be'Nad would try to get downstairs and gauge the basement security.

But not now—I caught Joy Cheng sneaking a peek at us. Not now and not here.

"Let's go look at some Robonnets," I said. "Let's try to act like we're supposed to be here."

It Takes One To Know One

It took all of three seconds for the full effect to hit me.
The full Robonnet effect—the pull of all those
tropical textures and sacred colors, the hypnotic draw
of two galleries worth of titles.

I Am Ready To Go With You
Dumaine Street Dream Talk
Eve Told Adam We Must Wait For Our Fate

I took a look at a painting I hadn't much noticed
before, *All Our Dreams Are Really Ghosts.* In the
center, a thousand butterflies were lifting a corpse off
a deathbed. A strip of block-printed words floated
above the wings.

I told you I would tell you
The mystery was announced in the dream:
Our selves are nothing but stories
That we tell ourselves to sleep.

The stuff was just *seeping* into my head. I was
getting a powerful buzz on listening to what the
angels had to say.

I wasn't the only one. Be'Nad was tripping out
as well, only his was a bad trip. He was turning pale
and going limp, like he was caught in some sickening
force field.

It was the paintings, he said—not just one
painting but all Robonnet paintings. He couldn't stand
them. He couldn't stand all this *swamp* mysticism. He
couldn't concentrate around Robonnets, he couldn't

hear anything. All they did was make him think of death—Bobby Hucknail, the kid in the warehouse, Robonnet's own murder. The paintings were inhabited by the souls of the dead and buried population and Be'Nad wasn't liking it one bit.

"As I think I've told you, I have issues with death," he said.

Nick the Five was at a loss to understand. They're just paintings, he pointed out.

Be'Nad couldn't disagree more. They're *not* just paintings. They're *diseases*. They're diseases and parasites and dirty dresser drawers. They're dusty Bibles and leprous cripples and rusting locks on the door. They're Ethiopian mummies and dead mammal eggs and all the ships at sea.

At this point Charles Manson would probably consider him unstable.

He was trying to catch his breath when I saw a bald head and brown-red glasses appear over his shoulder. Joy Cheng had walked into the gallery, checking in on us. Shit. "Be cool *now*."

"Look at the wall," Shannon told us, "and pretend you're paying attention." She turned to the paintings and began a curator spiel. "Much of Robonnet's work," she said, "is deeply informed by his Catholicism. The logic he uses is sacramental and associative, rather than linear and…"

Joy was upon us. "Hello, Mr. Branigan. Good to see you again."

"Where's the restroom?" Be'Nad asked with completely transparent urgency.

"Down that way," said Joy, "and to the right."

"I'm not well. I need to use the bathroom."

"I highly recommend it."

We watched Be'Nad wobble away. He was making a real effort to keep his balance while he walked.

"Will he be all right?"

"He needs to clear his head," I said.

"He's not used to art," Nick the Five explained.

Joy spent a few perfunctory moments in our company, piling on as much corporate bull as she could. Nick the Five was staring around the whole time, looking to see who else might show up. When Joy finally left, I put it to him. "You've got concerns about Cole, why don't you wait outside?"

"I'm here, I'm staying—no need for worry. You wanna worry about somebody, worry about Be'Nad."

"I am."

"There's your person to pity." He made another eye sweep of the gallery. "Was he like this at Bobby's, when the guy started eating the peach?"

"Pretty close." Not a good memory. I glanced at my watch. "Let's take a look."

We found him in one of the cubicles, unconscious, slumped on the toilet, pants up, legs spread, a Handi-Wipe still clutched in his hand. Nick the Five splashed cold water on a wad of paper towels and we pressed them on his face as we tried to carefully shake him awake.

Where was this deadly farce taking us now?

He gradually came to, addled but aware enough to render an opinion. "This is my most unfavorite job. *Ever*."

He said he wasn't sure what happened, but as best he could tell he must've blacked out.

He blacked *out* blacked out? Or more like he fell asleep?

"I don't know which. Sometimes I can't tell anymore if I'm asleep or awake."

We helped Be'Nad out of the stall and over to the sinks. He couldn't even grab fresh paper towels by himself, his coordination was so off. Last thing he remembered, he said, was buckling his belt and reaching for the latch on the door. He'd just finished relieving himself—he apologized for the lingering odor, his diet hadn't been right without the addition of food—and that's when he passed out.

"Take slow breaths," Nick the Five advised. "Tranquilize yourself."

"There's something wrong in this place," said Be'Nad. "Something's filled with the madness colors."

"The paintings, I know," I said.

"The paintings, certainly, but something else." He pushed himself away from the sinks and headed for the bathroom door on legs that barely held him up. "Something I noticed on my way here."

We followed him. Nick the Five nudged my arm and gestured to Be'Nad's cubicle. "Don't ever tell me," he whispered, "his shit don't stink."

Shannon was waiting in the corridor outside and she went to intercept Be'Nad as he stumbled through the door. But he just drifted past her, head slightly raised, zeroing in on the microscopic whispers of the ceiling.

I filled Shannon in on the pass-out while we trailed Be'Nad into the nearest gallery, back to Heavenly Visitations. Prep work for the museum's big event was proceeding apace, but we weren't paying attention to that. Our eyes were on Be'Nad and he didn't look happy. Or, more precisely, he looked
even unhappier than he did before, if such a thing is possible.

Finally he turned to us, much offended. "This is *ridiculous*. They've got a Kyoko X719 operating in here, but they've got a Plexico D-series running by the restrooms. And that's not counting the Ultrecht out front. Who designs such a thing? They've got all these different systems jim-jammed together. It's inelegant. It's *inexcusable.*"

"Is it a problem?" I said.

"A problem?" He regarded me as if I'd lost my mind. "Is it a *problem?*"

And instead of answering he began shaking. His whole body was going—he had a bad case of the all-overs. He began shivering and spaz-walking out of the gallery.

He was the Bobby Fischer of thieves—amazingly gifted, sure, but as crazy as a shithouse weasel.

We now embarked on what was basically a mini-tour of the museum. His hyperhearing tuned way up, Be'Nad led us through the Caribbean section (Tropical Flowers), the 19th Century Americans (Pioneer Trails), the serial killers (Angels of Death), everything but the Robonnet galleries. Too much tragic magic there. By the time we circled back to Heavenly Visitations, he was so disturbed I thought he might start dematerializing in front of us.

"This is the most lunatic thing I've ever seen," he said. "Every part of the building has a different security system. They must've just installed new ones as they went along. They're all different systems and they're all integrated with each other. They're all functioning on different frequencies and they're all linked together. It's *schizophrenic.*"

Right, it takes one to know one.

"What's it mean?" I said.

"What it means is, there's nothing I can do."

"Nothing?"

"Nothing."

"What's *that* mean?"

"It means there's *nothing* I can do! I knock one system out, the rest go with it and every alarm in the place goes off to kingdom come. *That's* what it means. There's nothing I can do."

"Gotta be *something*."

"*Nothing!*" he said. "*Nothing, nothing, nothing!*"

He began hyperventilating, and from the way he was squirming you'd think a Tourette's fit was about to descend on him.

"Be'Nad," I said, "calm down. Okay? Just calm it down. There's a lot at stake here—right?—so just calm down and let's think about—"

"*SHIT!*"

The exclamation was Nick the Five's. It was delivered with deep agitation as he looked past me.

A man and woman had just walked into Heavenly Visitations, another man behind them. The front guy was wearing a suit and tie and had a purple scarf wrapped around his neck. And yes, he had a little triangle of hair on his forehead that probably deluded him into thinking he had a full head of hair.

Cole Reynolds.

The woman was a stiff-shouldered septuagenarian with a powerful head of gray hair. Cole was showing her the installation work, guiding her in for a better view.

Then I caught full sight of the other guy.

Help me, Jesus.

I recognized the slab of a body, the pock-marked face, like a ham with acne. Last time I saw him was on the grounds of the castle, when he'd had H-L Lincoln tied up and stripped down to his wherewithal. He still had the same general expression about him, like a person who'd spent his childhood innocently disemboweling dogs.

The three of them were walking this way. My skin was twitching like someone had just brushed a hand over the back of my neck.

Nick the Five was sputtering. "Fucking Cole's gonna recognize me. He's gonna fucking clue to me."

"Not with the rug on your head," I said. "You're fine with the rug."

"Really?"

I didn't believe it either.

We were standing in front of a fairly hideous painting showing two flabby people of indeterminate sex being probed and examined by a bunch of aliens whose faces bore a remarkable resemblance to pussycats. The whole thing was washed in a pathetic green.

"Look at the painting," I said. "Crowd up on it."

Nick the Five stood right in front of the canvas. Shannon and I formed a shield directly behind him. Be'Nad brought up the rear.

Cole, the woman and the ham-faced gentleman were about 40 feet away.

"Just pretend we belong here," I said. "Who's she?"

"A sponsor," said Shannon. "Good for 100 thou a year. The other one, I've seen him with Cole."

"I've seen him too. He was trying to steal the painting from H-L."

"We're going to *die*," Be'Nad said behind me. "We're all going to *die*!"

"Be'Nad," I said, "shut the fuck up."

"Sorry."

When Cole and his party were 20 feet away Shannon began curating.

"The green tones reach for a kind of archetypal significance, representing renewal, verdant life…"

"Oh shit," Nick the Five whispered. "Oh shit."

"Stay tight, man. Stay tight."

Now we could hear Cole talking. "…been putting this event together for months. We feel it's a way to connect to a wider audience. Sometimes, you know, we're not always connected to the people we think we are, and it's possible that we…"

His voice trailed away.

We kept staring at the canvas, waiting it out. Four seconds went by.

"Okay," I said, "we're gonna step back, mingle for a couple more moments, then go start looking for the painting. Okay? Be'Nad, you up for that? Be'Nad?"

No response.

I turned around.

No Be'Nad.

He was gone. Up and down the gallery, nothing but work crews. He was just gone. He must've flipped and scooted away when Cole's trio was getting closer. That's how he'd stayed so silent.

"I knew it was coming," said Nick the Five. "I knew he'd melt on us."

We searched the other sections, even the Robonnets. I looked in the men's room—nothing. I tried his cell—no answer. It's possible he'd used Shannon's ID card to hide in the basement, but of course since he had the card and we didn't, who knew?

This was turning out to be one of those days.

Nick the Five thought he could've bolted the scene and suggested we check the parking lot. We looked. The car was still there.

"Know what this feels like?" Shannon said as we walked back through the lobby. "I was in college, I tried speed reading *Finnegans Wake*? I'm getting the same effect with this job. I don't know what we're doing anymore. Absolutely no idea."

It was true. Every time we started to get a rhythm going with this job, one of us would trip over the drums.

From Crap To Gravy

My thinking was that while Be'Nad had gotten
scared, once he'd calmed himself he'd come back.
But he didn't. A strong 15 minutes went by with us
roaming through the museum and he never showed.
Nick the Five came up with another thought: Maybe
we should actually look *inside* the car. Knowing
Be'Nad, he could be hunkered down in there,
cringing on the floor and keeping out of sight.

Sounded plausible. Nick the Five and I went to
look while Shannon watched the floor. It was quiet
outside. There were just a few people standing by the
planters far away from the entrance—a group of
nicotine lesbians taking a smoke break.

Nice day. The sky was a clear, fantastic blue. It
was the kind of sky that if you saw it in a painting
you'd say it was too fake.

I was looking at the sky when something tiny
and hard hit me in the head. Wherever it came from, I
didn't see anything when I whirled around. Then
another mini missile bounced near my feet. I looked
at the roof.

As previously noted, the Whitmore is built like
a supermarket. It's one big sprawled out level, with a
flat roof broken only by a tall air vent here and there.
I'm sure the architects who designed the place never
intended to include a skinny, demented-ass black guy
on the roof, but there he was, taking cover behind one

of the air vents and tossing pebbles from the roof in our direction.

"Man is deeply, *deeply* eccentric," Nick the Five said.

We walked back a bit toward the building. I shrugged at Be'Nad—what the fuck? He began going through a series of painful grimaces and wild hand and arm gestures. Obviously he was trying to pantomime a message, but let's face it, whatever his talents, the guy was no Marcel Marceau.

I took out my cell and pointed to it. He did the same with his. I called.

I'm STUCK up here! he said.

"I can see. What happened?"

I took off. I just couldn't stand there with those people coming so close. I ran off. I thought for sure...

"It's okay, we got through it."

Then I got lost. I found a staircase and went downstairs, then I found another staircase and tried to get back up, but I ended up here instead and the door locked behind me and I can't get back in.

"How long you been up there?"

I don't know. Ten minutes is possible.

"Be'Nad, a question? Why didn't you call? And why didn't you answer?"

Because God would punish me if I'd used the cell.

"Sorry?"

God would punish me. God's fire is everywhere, waiting to avenge.

"So you couldn't call?"

No.

"But now you can *get* a call?"

Out here, yes. Out in the open, incoming calls are fine, yes, I believe they are.

As long as there are rules.

We moved closer to the building.

"You still have the card?"

Yes.

"Okay, toss it to me, carefully. We'll come up and get you out."

Be'Nad produced the little plastic rectangle and gave it a gentle Frisbee wrist flick. And as the card began softly tumbling and floating down, he says, *Oh, Quinn? I found the painting. I found the room.*

Nothing about this job is easy, not one damn thing. This job and easy don't exist in the same cosmos.

We went back inside, picked Shannon up and found a fast opportunity to sneak off the floor. The service areas of the museum were all-white, bare-bones concrete, designed as all these places are to look like an industrial mausoleum. It took us maybe three minutes of swiping the card at doors to find a staircase leading up.

Be'Nad's little stay on the roof hadn't done much to relax him. He looked like he'd left today and gotten back yesterday. He assured us that he was fine—*somehow* he'd survived—but he wanted to get home and wash his hands. "I'm running low on Handi-Wipes. My hands have been everywhere. God knows *what* I've been touching."

"First," I said, "we retrace your steps."

The basement was a low-ceilinged cluster of unmarked doors and hallways that twisted and turned for fucking ever. All you could hear was the endless buzz of the building's generators.

This was not a simple layout by any means. Yet Be'Nad could remember the exact path he'd taken, even though he'd been in a dead panic while taking it. He'd headed east down one corridor for about 200 feet, he said, went through the third door closest to the end, gone south for 75 feet, went east again, then west, then kept angling to the north in the last corridor before he'd stumbled on the room with the painting. And not only did he know where he'd gone, he remembered where the security cameras were located and where their blind spots were. Man might be a March-hare freak, but he was a pro.

What he'd found was a small, empty storage room, about as well lit as a cave. It held just one lone painting leaning against the opposite wall, and even in that lousy light you could see what it was. You could see every butterfly in every jungle in the world suddenly taking flight. You could see the stained glass colors and the blood-thick paint. Even from the doorway you could hear the ancient (macumba) cries. You could hear a voice asking, are you dreaming what I'm dreaming?

The painting had been tacked to a crappy, scrap-wood frame to keep it stretched. Nick the Five's insulated tube sat on the floor next to it.

"They just left the painting here?" said Nick the Five, not really able to believe it. "Anybody with a card can just walk in?"

Not so. Be'nad pointed to the two black boxes mounted on each of the side walls. "Laser protected. There's a whole matrix of beams running across the floor."

Nick the Five stared at the invisible light. "Can you freeze it?"

"Of course. The problem, once again, is that it's integrated into another alarm system..." He stopped, studying the airwaves. "Another one of those Plexico-D series, that's what they've got down here. Which leaves us with the same problem. If this Plexico goes down, everything else goes down."

Nick the Five couldn't believe frustration could be so complicated. "It's like something they'd show at the movie theater."

"I'm sorry," said Be'Nad, "but I can't help. Everything is linked together. Everything is..." He backed out of the doorway and into the hall, cocking his head like he was trying to locate a speaker. "Okay, wait. Just wait." He closed his eyes. "Just wait a minute."

"*What?*" said Nick the Five.

"I don't know." Be'Nad's eyes opened slowly, carefully. "Maybe I'm hearing things. It's possible—I wouldn't put it past myself. I might be hearing things. Or I might *not* be hearing things, but maybe this Plexico isn't connected to anything else."

"What're you saying?" I said. "It's *not* hooked in?"

"I thought it was, but now I can't..." He shook his head. "No. It's not connected. It's operating on its own."

"What you're saying, just to be clear. You think you can disable this thing and nothing else will go off?"

"There's nothing here." He looked up at the ceiling. "It's not serial wired like it is upstairs. There's nothing here."

"Well *shit!*" said Nick the Five, pleasantly enthused. "We got a *shot!*"

And so we did. Just like that, the whole thing turned from crap to gravy.

We were on—this was a go.

But we still couldn't break in through the front—Be'Nad reminded us about that. Strenuously.

That hadn't changed. The upstairs situation hadn't changed.

So I said, well, do we have to break in? Can't we just *walk* in through the front? We'll come back as Sheridan Financial advisers, slip down here and find someplace to hide until the place closes down.

Shannon thought this was very do-able. There were a lot of spaces down here, she believed, that were very low priority. They used them to store cleaning supplies, stuff like that. No alarms needed. In fact, taking a walk, we found an ample size closet just down the hall. It held electrical supplies, replacement bulbs, and had plenty of room for us to wait.

We were getting closer.

"What I'll have to do," said Be'Nad, sounding his thoughts, "I'll have to find the smallest processor I can. I'll have to find an ultrasonic processor that I can conceal on my person."

"Can you do that?" I said.

"I've got tomorrow, right? Most of tomorrow? I can find something, I'm sure I can. Just one thing. I have to wash my hands. I *really* have to wash my hands."

"Fine," said Nick the Five. "But we are *not* going back to that bathroom."

That Which Is Past Is Neither Secret Nor Dead

I woke up in what I thought was pretty decent shape. The morning felt like a drug high kicking in— everything your eye fell on looked bright and hopeful and brand smacking new. A good start, I figured, to the last day. My plan was to just let loose and take it easy until we met in the afternoon and set out for the museum. Let this be a day of rest.

Didn't happen.

9:20 am

Randi called, up in flames. I'd filled her in yesterday about what had happened at the Whitmore, located in what she kept calling Nasser County, like it was a province of Egypt. She had no problem with what had transpired. But Nick the shitloaf Five had just called her, she said, and he'd given her a slightly different version, one that awarded all of the blame and none of the credit to his supposed rival Be'Nad.

According to Randi, Nick the Five had no confidence in Be'Nad's sanity anymore, none whatsoever. Give Be'Nad a competency hearing right now and Nick the Five was pretty sure he was going away. All of which may be true to one degree or another, Randi conceded, but where does some fucktocious scumbag like Nick the Five get off badmouthing Be'Nad? That's what she wanted to know. However off the wall and around the bend Be'Nad might be, least he never tried to *steal* the painting for himself.

If there was one thing Randi couldn't stand, she said, it was people who maligned their colleagues. They're moaners and they're whiners and they're not to be trusted as a group, which is why she was calling me. She was warning me about her ex, warning me to watch out for him, because Nick the Five was every inch a moaner and a whiner with a dick so small he had to pull his pants all the way down to piss.

"You really hate him that much?"

I don't hate him, she said. *It's not hate. It's dislike. It's like total dislike.*

I didn't know what Randi was planning to do with the Robonnet money, but opening a Hallmark franchise probably wasn't at the top of the list.

9:45 am

Nick the Five called, posing a question: Why was Randi still part of the crew? Did we really *need* her? It had occurred to him yesterday, he said, while we were at the Whitmore, that the services of an electronic eavesdropper were no longer required, and unless we just wanted her around as a ballbusting distraction with a marked ability to drive us all batshit, why didn't we just include her out?

I remembered the night Shannon and I had gone to see Genesis and Shannon began reciting her you-won't-choose-me monologue. I remembered what Genesis did.

No, I told him, not a chance we were gonna cut Randi loose. Did we really want her roaming the streets with attitude, looking to fuck us over? The closer we kept her around, the less chance of her going off and talking about the job.

You know why she's still with us? he said. *You know why she's sticking, because you KNOW why. She wants to get into Be'Nad's pants is what it is.*

"Nick…"

She wants some humpity-hippity action out of this. She wants to get him to dip his wick.

His wick—these people were fucking crazy. No, check that. These people were already fucking crazy and they were getting fucking *crazier*.

It was just like being at work. Endless streams of complaints, conflicts, threats, resentments, hysterical accusations and insurmountable personnel problems. Different toilets, same crap.

10:30 am

Genesis was still angry about Cole Reynolds. She told me so when she called and she continued telling me when I drove out and met her in her library. She was still angry about what he'd done, and still vague about whatever pre-theft negotiations she'd had with him. When I tried to—I thought—subtly probe for a few answers, she switched the topic to tonight. What exactly were we planning to do? About what time would we make the delivery?

The central air on the big house seemed to be working fine against the hot July day, but her face was covered with a layer of light, delicate sweat. I didn't even notice it until she kissed me and began telling me—as she took me by the hand into the bedroom—about West African legends. Among certain tribes, she said, hunters believed that if they dreamed they'd slept with a goddess, they'd find good luck the next day.

This was no dream. When she dropped her caftan, her nipples were already swelling with blood flow. And what am I thinking about? I'm thinking, I'm sleeping with two women—what the fuck do I think I'm doing?

I knew this guy once who was going out on a serious basis with two women at the same time. This was a state of affairs that had been going on for months, at least half a year, and like Nick the Five the guy was able to keep juggling his balls because neither woman knew about the other. So when Valentine's Day was rolling around of course he want down to Hallmark and bought two cards, filled them out with appropriate terms of endearment and dropped them in the mail. His one mistake: putting the wrong cards in the wrong envelopes.

By February 15, he was alone.

Genesis was on the satin sheets, arcing her back as my tongue slid down her belly button and over the green and gold tattoo of a macaw, just like that first night we made love here, and as the flesh below her navel began to darken with heat, my phone went off.

I saw Be'Nad's number.

Okay, this was important.

She understood.

Good news. He had the processor he needed. It was perfect for the Plexico-D series and just the right size. *It fits right in my pocket.*

"Well that's great, that's just great. I knew you could do it, so…" Genesis was waiting beneath me. "…so I'll see you in a few, and we'll…"

My mother wants a word.

Mrs. Harrison said she wasn't at all happy with the way Be'Nad was eating, or more to the point not eating. She'd tried to stuff his face with all manner of sustenance but he wouldn't take a thing. *I even tried to pour him a glass of milk and he's telling me milk disgusts him. Did you ever? It DISGUSTS him.*

I could hear Be'Nad yelling *MOTHER* in the background.

I promised Mrs. Harrison I'd keep an eye on him and assured her that, things being what they were, Be'Nad's diet would probably go back to normal after tonight.

She put him back on. I suggested he not worry about anything, including food, and just get some rest for the remainder of the day. He was against the idea.

I always try not to sleep too much, he said. *If I sleep too much, my dreams stay with me. Too much sleep, I'll remember my dreams.*

Noon

One person I *didn't* expect to hear from today was Kumiko Davis. So I guess it was entirely in keeping with the way the day was going that she'd phone as I was driving back to the city. She'd been meaning to call, she said. No big thing, but while she was researching Bobby Hucknail's obit, she'd come across a coincidental connection between him and the Robonnet family. Did I know about it? An incident at the Whitmore Primitive Museum?

I didn't know, but I was interested.

About a year and a half ago, Kumiko said, the Whitmore had held an onsite party catered by Appellation, the well-received restaurant on Varick

Street, which largely accounted for Bobby's presence on the premises. In any case, toward the end of the evening, some sort of altercation had broken out between Slim and Genesis Robonnet and their father. Kumiko found a mention of it at *ouruppercrust*, a gossipy website devoted to commenting on art society events like the museum's party. While the food was praised, the night itself was described as a large bore, redeemed only by a head-swerving shouting match between Isaiah Robonnet and his two children. The cause was unknown, but the volume attained was near supersonic, and it ended only when the three participants left the museum in a passionate huff.

Bobby had nothing to do with the fight, Kumiko said—when she was searching his name he'd simply shown up as one of the guests. But didn't I think it was randomly bizarre that he was there? Especially since Robonnet was murdered three nights later? Again, no big deal, just one of those things she thought I might find curious.

As always, Kumiko's instincts were impeccable.

1:10 pm

I couldn't believe how fast the day was disappearing but at least I was home now, I could grab a break, look for a pause in this twisty Hindu epic. Only one thing was keeping me from a prolonged moment of peace. It was hard to get what Kumiko told me out of my head. The family fight at the Whitmore tied in too closely to the clues Shannon had found in the painting.

And naturally, since I was thinking about Shannon, Shannon called. Such was the perverse magic of the day.

She sounded flat out fucking *awful*. She sounded like she'd spent all morning splitting into pieces, and what I was hearing now was the left over shards.

She had to come over right away, she said. She had to see me, had to show me something. *All the doors are open now*, she said. *The doors just fell open.*

I didn't like what I saw when she walked in *my* door. Right off I didn't like the look in her eyes. It was the kind of empty, unfillable pain you see in anorexic eyes.

The painting was already up on her laptop when she set it on the table. She was going to point to the shadow in the upper left-hand corner again—I knew that. She'd discovered something else near that strange dark patch where the comet's rainbow tail suddenly vanished.

But no. She directed my eyes instead to the bottom edge of the canvas, to a cluster of miniature figures. Bending in, I could see that they were some kind of Amazonian priestesses, all carrying astrolabes and compasses and other stargazing instruments. Except for one. One of the women, conspicuously, was holding a bloody sacrificial knife.

"I've found it," Shannon said, hoarse and stressed. "Look at the text. I've found it."

The words running next to the women were so miniscule she had to zoom the view to make them readable.

That which is past is neither secret nor dead.
The trooth of this has been proven
14,877,309,116 tymes.
Eddingstone points to this 14:367
The 30 pieces of silver are weighed and counted,

The Unholy Inquisitor is named.
Eddingstone is the Kompass that points the way.
14:367 Exzeterra.
"I don't know what this means," I said. "What's Eddingstone?"

"I tracked it down. Arthur Eddingstone. A U.S. Congressman in the last part of the 19th Century. Also a self-styled scholar of voodoo. I traced it back." She took a battered old book out of her handbag. *The Systems and Spirits of The Vodun*, by Arthur Eddingstone. "He published this in 1895."

I'm thinking, she's lost it. She's interpreting the painting like a kid building Legos bricks, snapping in any piece of plastic that seems to fit.

But then she opened the book. 14:367. Chapter 14, page 367. The top of the page showed an ancient black-and-white engraving, like a Medieval woodcut, depicting a beautiful woman with a body draped in parrot-like feathers. *The Winged Succubus* was its title.

I wouldn't vouch for the accuracy of Eddingstone's text, but he described this supposed Vodun spirit as *a goddess daemon who seduces men through her allurements. Because she is a supreme dissembler, able to sift shapes at will, the seeker is advised to peer beneath her mask. She is known to torment men in their dreams, even after death. Her eyes are a glacial blue; her protector is the cold fruitless moon. Her humours are concealment and falsity. Her aspect is betrayal; her colors are green and gold.*

"It's Genesis," she said. "Her father is mapping us to her. Can you see it? Blue eyes, seduction, concealment, betrayal, 30 pieces of silver, the blood on the knife. It's beyond question. It's beyond dispute."

I didn't say a thing. I didn't say anything about the fight at the Whitmore, or about the tattoo on Genesis' body. A macaw, a bird with parrot-like feathers. Its colors green and gold.

I couldn't carry this clue any further. Not now, not today.

>>>>>>

My silence didn't go over so well. I paced a little, no problem putting a worried look on my face. She stayed by the laptop, watching me. Just watching me.

"You agree?" she finally said.

"I'm not sure."

"Not sure? It's *her*."

"I don't know what it is."

"What you mean is, you won't admit it."

"I don't know."

"You don't *know*?"

"I don't know."

"How can you not know?"

"Because I don't."

She stabbed the power button on the laptop and shut it down, watching as the screen went to black. Then she looked at me again, staring hard. For five long-count seconds she stared like that. She was staring at me like she was trying to guess the weight of my eyeballs.

"Have you thought about what we talked about?"

she said.

"Talked about what?"

"About what happens. What happens after this. You and me."

"I haven't thought about it, no."

"I didn't think so."

"I've been busy with a couple other things."

"Don't bother with it. I know the answer. You won't choose me."

She's playing that riff again. Her *other* cataclysmic obsession.

"What the hell does that mean?"

"It means whatever you do," she said, "it won't include me."

"And you're sure about that?"

"I know. I don't get chosen."

"What're you, a fucking *contestant*?"

She slapped the laptop closed and shoved the Vodun book back in her bag. "I'm tired," she said. "I'm leaving."

"You keep saying people won't choose you. I heard you say it...almost the first time I met you. Tell me what it means."

"I'm going home."

But she didn't move. She didn't speak and she didn't move.

The silence went on so long it became louder than any word could be.

"Tell me," I said.

This time the silence lasted long enough to become a third person in the room.

I thought she was about to crack in half. I thought she was about to crack and splinter right there.

Or I was.

"My father," she said.

Do It Right Now Or
All Three Of you Die

She was 10 years old when her father broke into the house. Her folks had been separated—lots of fighting, order of protection, the whole yard. One night she was sitting down for dinner in the kitchen with her mother and her little brother, he was 6 at the time. They heard this crash like somebody's smashing through the front door. They run into the living room, her father's standing there with a gun in his hand. His eyes were crazy, by which she meant he was always angry-crazy, but now his eyes were completely calm and focused. That's what was so crazy about them.

Her mother started yelling at him and he was yelling back—Shannon didn't know what they were fighting about. She didn't understand. Then her mother tells him in no uncertain terms to get the hell out and he lifts the gun and fires four times into the living room wall. She remembered—four times. She could remember the smell of the gunfire.

Her father was wearing a blue denim shirt— she'd given it to him for Christmas. Her father was wearing the blue denim shirt and it was a cool summer evening and Shannon was standing in the living room of the house she'd grown up in, but none of it sccmcd familiar anymore. Her father had her mother by the hair and had the gun pressed up against her face. Shannon started crying and then her brother started crying, copycatting her.

She had no idea how much time had gone by before she realized there were police outside. *Lot* of police. All out in the front yard and the street, surrounding the house. Turned out the neighbors called 911 when they heard the four shots. The police were yelling at her father with bullhorns and he was yelling at them and he made her, her mother and brother get down on the floor, they had to lay face down on the floor.

Her mother was begging him—don't hurt us, don't kill us, I think I'm having a heart attack, don't kill us. He told her to shut the fuck up and she said at least let the kids go. Don't let them get hurt. At least let them go.

Then he turns around and looks at her, he's still got those crazy eyes. He's been yelling but he still had those crazy-calm eyes. He looks at her and says, I need one of them here. That's all I need—one. But you, I don't need. Take one of them and get the hell out.

Her mother screamed at him so hard all the police bullhorns went off. What's going on in there? What're you *doing*? Her mother was screaming at him and telling him you can't *do* that. They're your *children*—let them both go.

He just stood there calm. No. Take one of them or they both die. And do it right now or all three of you die.

Her mother got up. She was cursing at him in a voice Shannon had never heard before. She got up and said well which one am I supposed to take? He said you choose. He was always leaving things to her.

Then Shannon's little brother got up. He ran over to his mother, crying and grabbing on to her. He was crying that he was scared and didn't want to die. Shannon stayed on the floor. She didn't want to die either, but she didn't get up. Why? As she remembered it, she didn't want to give in to her father. She refused to give in.

Meanwhile her mother was telling her father I won't do this—don't make me do this. He father pointed the gun in her eyes and said do it now or I'll kill you.

So her mother looked at the little boy clinging to her and she looked at Shannon. The woman broke into hysterical crying, really torrential crying. Shannon never forgot what her face looked like right then. Then her mother grabbed the boy and went for the door. Her father was shouting to the cops—two are coming out. Her mother ran out the door with her brother and that was that. She never looked back. She didn't choose Shannon.

"You helped her," I said. "You helped her make a terrible choice. You made it a little easier for her."

She was sullen, eyes down. "She would've made the same choice anyway."

"Because your brother was just 6."

"Because I'm unchooseable."

"Don't say shit like that."

"Too late."

God help us. "Tell me what happened."

She waited, still standing by the table, the laptop. "My father got weird. *Weirder*. He got very animated when we were alone, almost like giddy. He kept pacing back and forth in the living room, he kept saying it's just us, it's just us, it's just the two of us. Like it was a *good* thing, like we were going to

Disney World.

"He kept walking back and forth, getting more
manic, not paying attention to what he was doing. At
one point he walked right in front of the living room
window. I heard something happen, I didn't know
what it was, but I saw him grab at his chest. I saw
glass all over the floor, blood all over his shirt, blood
staining his blue denim shirt. I saw him fall down,
and right away, as soon as he hit the floor, I saw
blood flooding all around him.

"It was very strange. Watching him fall was
very strange. It was like watching it over and over
again at the same time. It was like watching it on a
loop while it was happening."

She just stood there. She wouldn't finish it. She
wouldn't put a period at the end of the sentence.

"Was that it?"

"They pronounced him dead at the scene. I
wasn't there by then. They'd taken me away. They'd
taken me to the hospital, made sure I was all right."

"Then they turned you over to your mother?"

"Yes."

"What did she say?"

"About?"

About?

"About taking your brother instead of you."

"Nothing. We never talked about it. To this day,
we've never talked about it."

I couldn't breathe.

I moved closer, brushed my hand through her
hair and held her head. She was all tightened up,
holding it in.

"You can cry," I said. "It's all right."

She pushed my hand away. "I won't. I have a
million reasons to cry, but I won't." She picked up

her laptop and headed for the door. "Think you know me better now?"

"A little."

"You don't. You don't know me. You don't know shit about me."

The Sound Came Crashing Out Of My Heart

Two hours had gone by since we'd heard the magic words—*Attention, please, may I have your attention. The museum is about to close.* The taped voice sounded friendly but firm as it echoed through the ground floor and filtered down to our storage closet. We'd been waiting since then, killing time while cleaning crews dusted and mopped and security guards took their first sleepwalk-steps into the night shift. Another hour it would be totally dark outside and we could put this into play.

Things were looking good, very promising. Our get-out plan was all set. We'd found a fire exit not far away that led up into the parking lot. Yes, the door's alarm was linked with the other security systems and as soon as we opened it the whole shebang would go off. No way around that, said Be'Nad. But what we'd do, we'd run along the bushes and trees that lined the parking lot, getting lost in their shadows while the guards came downstairs and checked the doors. By the time they realized what was afoot, we'd be out of the lot and headed for the car we'd parked at the remote end of a nearby residential street. As far as get-outs go, it was pretty damn nice.

The waiting, though, that was hard. I was dragging some major ass after a while. I'd never gotten any rest after Shannon left—her story had bothered me way too much. Plus I had to deal with sitting still here for hours, shifting position to keep from stiffening up. Huddling in that closet, I was thinking, was a lot like being in solitary. Except I was with Be'Nad and Nick the Five.

Be'Nad couldn't stop wondering about his health. He really thought it might be advisable to get a whole battery of blood tests. Only one thing was stopping him. "Do you think it's possible," he whispered, "to hire a personal phlebotomist?"

Yes, I thought about Be'Nad as the time slogged by. Could I count on him not to go nutso? Could I trust him? And what about Nick the Five? Was he gonna hold up? And Randi? Genesis? How about Shannon and her heart-blowing story? How much could I trust anyone?

"You could stop washing your hair," Nick the Five suggested.

"Why would I want to do that?" said Be'Nad.

"It's what you call a folk remedy, for closing the evil eye. You don't wash your hair for a month. My grandmother used to talk about it."

"I'll take it under advisement."

It was getting claustrophobic in here. Butterflies were eating my stomach alive. The air seeping into the closet was mechanically cold, yet the three of us were sweating like Okies.

Nine o'clock. Thank you, Jesus. Time to gut it up and get this thing going. *Sex Death* words:

I will chart a map on the darkness,
A map that will lead you to the unseen lands.

Twenty seconds of white concrete corridors and we were at the door. Be'Nad pulled out Shannon's ID card and did some mad rubbing with a Handi-Wipe before he swiped the door. The painting was still there—I could see its screaming trees even in the low utility light. A forbidden treasure just 25 away, separated from us by a no man's land of invisible beams.

Be'Nad's new ultrasound processor was about the size of a thick wallet. It wasn't as powerful as the one he'd used at Bobby's place or at the warehouse, but it could deliver enough juice to cripple the lasers. He hunched over it, made some adjustments, listened, checked the meter, listened some more, straightened up.

"We ready?" I said.

He nodded, searching the room with his eyes. "We're ready."

Now there are certain ways of saying *we're ready* that can mean anything but. Make a few changes in tone and pitch and you can suggest that, in fact, the opposite is true. Which is what Be'Nad was doing now.

"What's the matter?"

He was still staring into the room. "I don't know. I'm not sure. I thought this was a free-standing system. Now I'm not sure."

I looked at Nick the Five. He looked at me. Be'Nad wasn't looking at either one of us.

It was a little unnerving.

"You're not sure?"

"It didn't sound wired-in yesterday. Though at first, if you remember, at first it did. Now I'm not sure. I just can't *concentrate* on it."

"This is the *ass!*" said Nick the Five. "You told us it *wasn't.*"

"I know."

That's all Be'Nad had to say. He went back to listening, straining at it like he was trying to decipher a message.

We stood there with no idea about what should come next.

"Be'Nad," said Nick the Five, "I don't want to step on your fucking tootsies, but you can't leave it hanging like this."

"Is it my fault?" said Be'Nad.

"Yes it's your fault! Who the fuck's fault do you *think* it is?"

"Easy," I said. "Let's show some patience here."

"Patience?" said Nick the Five. "Quinn, I know patience is a virtue, but who's got the fucking time for it?"

"I'm just trying to avoid a mishap," said Be'Nad.

"You're just trying to run *away* from this."

"That's not what I said."

"I know, but that's what you *meant*, you bug-eyed fuck. Quinn, what're we gonna do about this?"

"To be honest," I said, "we might think about scrapping this for now."

"We are *not* scrapping this thing," said Nick the Five. "We're *standing* here. We are *not* just walking away."

He meant it. I knew that because a second later he'd pulled a gun and was pointing it straight at Be'Nad. It was a Detonics CombatMaster, I believe, and he was holding it inches away from Be'Nad's head.

"You fuck this up with your blowjobby excuses," he said, "I'll blow those fucking ears to kingdom come."

Be'Nad didn't care for this. He looked like he was staring into all the darkness of all the universe and he was muttering, "I'm dead, I'm dead."

My mouth had gone instantly dry.

"You stay calm," I said.

"Oh I'm calm," Nick the Five insisted. "I'm completely calm. I'm just putting the facts in front of him in a clear and objective light."

"Why're you even carrying that thing?"

"After what happened to me? You *serious*? I'm gonna let myself get tied to a post again, pissing in my own pants?"

"I can't work like this," said Be'Nad.

"No," said Nick the Five, "problem is, you can't work *period*. You're losing your nerve. That's the nut of it—you're losing your fucking *nerve*."

"Nick," I said.

"No, it's *true*! It's true and he fucking *knows* it. He knows what his job is, what he has to do, and he won't *do* it! And you know why? Cause of his *personal* aesthetics. That's what it is, his personal fucking *aesthetics*!" He lowered the gun two inches to make his point. "Everything has to be just fucking *SO* with him!"

I put the Glock right up against his neck. "Take three deep breaths."

"Quinn, I'm just trying to get this done."

"This is a bad way to do it. This is a very bad decision making process. Breathe and hand it to me."

This is what I hate about stag nights.

Nick the Five did breathe—though it was more of a deep, surrendering sigh—and gave the butt of the Detonics to me. "Everybody thinks I'm a fuck-up. But *he's* the weak link."

I slipped his gun in my waist and put the Glock away. "You're pretty much of a sick fuck."

"Maybe I am."

"It's nothing to be proud of."

"He might be right." Be'Nad said it quietly, his voice soft and confessional. "He might have a point. Maybe I *am* losing my nerve." He was gazing at his

processor like it held all the mysteries of a moon rock. "I know I don't feel any confidence in myself anymore, I know that. Maybe that's what this is
all about."

"Just take your time," I said.

"Maybe taking time is just losing nerve," he said. "Maybe the system isn't connected after all."

"It can't be maybe. Are you totally *sure* it's not connected?"

"I'm fairly certain I'm totally sure." He slowly, carefully put his finger on the release button. There was no rush about it. "Maybe even a notch more than fairly certain."

What happened next happened so fast I *still* haven't thought about it.

The sound of all those alarms felt like it came crashing out of my heart, exploding along the walls of my arteries. The sound bounced off every possible surface, off walls and floors and ceilings, and it was bouncing so hard you'd swear it actually shifted the shape of the walls and floors and ceilings.

Time to be somewhere else.

We headed for that fire exit—which suddenly didn't seem all that nearby. We were Cadillacking through a world of chaos and confusion and we'd reached the point where anything could go wrong. If the earth opened under our feet I wouldn't be surprised

"It's all the generators down here," Be'Nad shouted as we ran. "I couldn't hear. I couldn't hear over the whine."

"Doesn't make any difference now," Nick the Five replied.

"I'm only saying."

"Don't say it. Don't say another fucking word."

The alarms were so loud I was hallucinating inside the noise. I thought I could hear myself being addressed over the speakers upstairs. *Okay, Quinn, you can get off now.* earth opened under our feet I wouldn't be surprised.

The night sky was a halfshell of clouds reaching from the horizon to the moon. We scrambled up the exit stairs and got it into gear, running along the shadow line of trees and bushes that bordered the parking lot. We were sticking to the original plan— only we didn't have the painting and we were way behind schedule.

Still we had a shot. Halfway there I thought we could make it to the car without soiling our butts. Then I heard Be'Nad's breathing behind me. We were all breathing fast and shallow, but his suddenly turned stutter-gun rapid. I stopped. He'd stopped too, caught in a hyperventilation fit.

Nick the Five stopped. "C'mon, B, keep it together."

Be'Nad's chest was fluttering in and out like a plastic sheet in a hurricane. "This…is…a little…overwhelm—"

Then his eyes slot-machined in his sockets, his legs gave out and he did a faceplant in the parking lot.

We could hear guards shouting now back by the fire exit. We meaning me and Nick the Five, since Be'Nad was comatose. We could hear their questions, their walkie-chatter. They'd spot us in like 15 seconds.

"Fuck we gonna do?"

"Drag him in the bushes," I said. "Drag him deep and stay with him. Hide yourself in there."

"You?"

"I'll draw them off, try to pull 'em away."

Nick the Five just looked at me. "You're gonna bait yourself? Kind of a fucky idea, isn't it?"

"Got anything better?"

"Best of luck to you."

I handed him my wallet with my ID, just in case. "When everything's clear, and when he comes to, get to the car. I'll call when I'm clear." I gave him my gun and his. "Just don't shoot Be'Nad. Promise?"

I'd gotten to the end of the lot when the guards made it up the stairs. I let them get a look at me, hesitating for a moment like I didn't know which way to go. Then, as they started yelling and moving, I took off into the street.

The first house I saw was maybe 100 yards away. It had an open yard, nice acre of grass bordering a long stretch of woods. I hit the property with shouts and running steps behind me.

A hummingbird's heart pumps 1,400 times a minutes.

I had that beat.

The woods beyond the house were denser and deeper than I thought, and the darkness didn't help. I stumbled, tripped, rolled and crawled at least three times each during the first quarter mile. I could hear feet snapping twigs and crashing through the brush, but they began to fade after a while. Somewhere in the distance police sirens flared for a few moments, then they died away too.

I wish I'd looked at my watch when I took off. I had no idea how long my nature trip had lasted so far. Maybe 15, 20 minutes? That was my guess, though it could've been five minutes. It could've been an hour.

Time was turning liquid out here. Wandering through these woods was like wandering through the painting.

I heard the black words that are spoken everywhere,

But always in disguise.

But I hadn't heard any trailing noises in a while—that much I knew. Exactly how long that while was I couldn't say, but it seemed like long enough. Going by the moon, I made a 90-degree turn and started walking that way. Where it might lead I didn't know and didn't much care as long as it wasn't the way I came and as long as it was out of here. The darkness was getting to me. The darkness and the moonlight and the adrenaline. Every time I turned my head, I'd think I'd see hundreds of leaves drifting down like snowflakes in the corner of my eye.

Then it stopped. The leaf-fall stopped because all of a sudden the woods were thinning out. There was clear dark space ahead. It was a street. Few house lights in the darkness. No sidewalks, no streetlights. Just a quiet residential street.

Silence. Safety.

I moved out on the road pavement, took two or three steps. Out of nowhere a light appeared before me, a bar of light just floating in the air in front of me. A horizontal bar of moving white light suspended five feet off the ground.

Then headlights blared on and I could see what it was. A cop car. A voice announced itself from the mounted speakers. *Stay where you are. Right there. Don't move. Just stay right where you are.*

And this time the voice I was hearing was no hallucination

>>>>>>

Busted

I hate this job. I loathe it, I detest it. I can't even put how much I hate it into words, except to say that I despise it, I abhor it, I dislike it, mislike it, tear it up and spit it out, stomp on it till its guts bleed, burn it in hell and haul its miserable ashes to the ends of the fucking earth *hate* it. Only once before in my life have I managed to land my ass in jail and that was because I'd shot a guy to death in a drunken, methed-up, blood-rage stupor. I *deserved* to be in jail for that. But since that time I've committed various and much more minor infractions of the law and I've never ended up in police custody. Until now. Until fucking now. I think that says something about this job. I think it's a testament to the general karmic fuckupedness of this job.

The cop car? The two cops inside? They'd been on patrol and they'd responded to the alarm going off at the Whitmore. After hearing about what happened, they decided to park here and wait for the asshole who disappeared to come waltzing out of the woods. Maybe they'd get lucky.

They did.

They patted me down and cuffed my hands behind me with plastic twisties and tossed me in the back. I never said a thing. I just sat there as we drove, feeling the world getting smaller. That's what happens with depression. The boundaries of the world start to shrink, start to tighten up until—what a coincidence—they match the exact shape of the skin around your head.

The car went south, headed for Manhasset. We crossed Northern Boulevard, the Miracle Mile, home to Barneys and Gucci and Tiffany. The cops pulled into a building on Community Drive. I knew it from my P.I. days. The Sixth Precinct. I was hustled inside, feeling that I'd finally reached a destination three stops past desperate.

The squad room was a mess of Ikea desks piled with mounds of paperwork—the consequence, no doubt, of a computer system that had aged out decades ago. The walls were painted with some kind of industrial color, either gray or a former green, I couldn't tell.

I couldn't do this again. I couldn't spend any appreciable amount of my life again in a place with this kind of sick-shit paint on the walls.

In a room off to the side I was told to drop trow and was given what to my mind was a way overlong examination of my anal cavity. Then it was up with the pants and out to the squad room, where I was taken to the desk of the detective who was gonna question me.

His name was Steve Lupski, and if you can imagine a lizard with a smile, then you've got a good idea of what his face looked like. Lupski had his own personal form of bullshit rigmarole, which consisted of him reading through random files, frowning once in a while as he read, pursing his lips and then grunting through his nose like he'd discovered something with true meaning. He'd do this several times during the interrogation.

First he wanted to know what I was doing wandering around in the woods. Credit where credit's due, this was a fair question. But since I didn't have anything close to a good answer for it, I didn't try to make one up. In fact, I didn't give Lupski much of anything. I pretty much maintained a dumb and puzzled expression throughout, like the idea that setting off a museum alarm in Nassau County during the evening hours could be a crime was news to me.

"So what were you doing trying to break in?" he said. "What were you looking for?"

He asked the same questions, or variations thereof, I don't know how many times. Each time was a tiny cause for celebration. It meant they thought I'd tried to get *in* through the fire door. It meant they didn't know I'd *started* from inside the museum.

Another piece of good news: Lupski never asked me about anybody else. He never mentioned two other guys, two accomplices. A safe assumption: Be'Nad and Nick the Five had gotten away.

But that was it as far as glad tidings went. All other signs pointed to me going back behind the fence. Take my lack of ID. Lupski kept speculating that I'd conveniently ditched my wallet in the woods, but he'd always add that it didn't matter. Once we were done talking they'd take my prints and run them through the system. He was sure they'd get a match.

So was I. Getting-fucked time was about to begin.

It was my own fault. No denying it—the whole thing was my fault. I never should've taken this stupid fucking job. I never should've stepped into this venomous shitstream. Maybe Be'Nad for all his madness was right. Maybe this job carried some kind of curse, some kind of prohibitive cosmic payback.

I didn't know. All I knew was that panic was squeezing my chest and the stars outside were about to explode with their own heat.

It had been a quiet night in the squad room. The only perps being questioned were me and some guy with a bow tie who'd been carted away soon after I sat down. But 20 minutes into my conversation with Lupski, or 20 minutes into his monologue, the place suddenly got very busy. A group of seven screaming, fighting woman lurched en masse into the room, escorted by four beleaguered cops. These were some high class reprobates. I spotted some Prada, some Armani, and I don't even *know* designers. What happened was, one of the stores on Miracle Mile—I couldn't catch which one—was holding a huge sale and two of the women had started arguing over a deeply discounted handbag. The battle was soon joined by their respective friends, though from where I was sitting I couldn't tell which was which.

But the combat was still most definitely going on. The women were all yelling at the same time, trying to scratch and kick each other. A detective who seemed to be in charge ordered the women separated and made it clear that he wanted their statements taken ASAP. Get 'em the fuck *out* of here.

"Later for you," Lupski said, yanking me out of my chair and making room for one of the shoppers. I'd have to wait for this to get straightened out, he explained. I'd have to wait for them to do my prints, and I'd have to wait for them to transfer me to Mineola for booking. "Looks like a long night," he said as he took me around a corner, undid my cuffs and tossed me in a holding cell.

At this point, I think, the reports would be divided. Some would say my situation was bad. Others would say my situation was very bad.

>>>>>>

The holding cell was a 15'x20' piece of the universe painted in that same nauseous gray/green/whatever color as the squad room, only here the paint was flaking in patches to show the royal blue primer underneath. Clash wasn't the word for it.

There was nothing in the cell but metal benches bolted to each of the three walls. I took the one on my right. Across from me was the guy with the bow tie I'd seen before. A thick, round face with thick, round eyeglasses, blitzed eyes and a fatty groin, a bow tie with green polka dots and a blazer with tragic stripes of green and white. He looked like a commodities trader on a bender.

Whoever he was, it took him a while to notice he had company. He seemed to spot a vague shape on the other side of the cell, and then, after much foggy blinking, he realized he wasn't alone.

"I never would've thought." Those were his opening slurred words.

"Never would've thought what?"

"I never would've thought it would come to this. Here."

"Tell me about it."

"How, you know? *How*?"

"Exactly."

"What it is, I think, I think this must be huge. I think this must be *quite* huge."

I nodded. "It's a big huge."

"A *big* huge?"

"It's either a wee tam or a big huge. This is a big huge."

"Probably something to that."

Pause. He took a breather, apparently pondering a number of existential themes at the same time. Then he squinted heavily at me.

"I'm drunk," he announced.

"I see."

"Are you drunk?"

"No."

"Why not?"

Good question. "I used to be."

"When?"

"Long time."

"But not now?"

"No."

"I think there's something wrong with me."

"Maybe. Maybe not."

"They took me to the restroom when I got here. A number two. Only it wasn't a number two. It was all this yellow liquid. I'm shitting this yellow liquid. I think I'm shitting piss."

"Better than pissing shit."

"Well that's a good point. You know what, that's a very good point." Bow Tie leaned back on the bench, rested his head against the wall. "I'm going to suspend all further remarks at this point."

Good. I needed to be left alone. I needed some quality brooding time. Cause not only was I stuck in this shithole and in all likelihood destined to be stuck in an even worse one for some time to come, but my shot at a million? It was fuck-broke *gone.* I immediately thought about my daughter. How was I gonna pay for her education now? What school costs today, what would it cost in a decade?

I wanted to throw up.

Two or three minutes of regret and remorse had gone by when I got the impression that my fellow holdee was feeling a bit neglected. What brought me to this conclusion was me looking up and noticing that Bow Tie had left his side of the cell and was now standing over me and giving me a swift kick in the shin.

Yes, it hurt. "Fuck is your problem?"

"I just need to ask you for one thing," he said. "Please don't fuck with me. That's all I'm asking. Just please don't fuck with me."

"I'm not fucking with you."

He kicked me again. "What did I say? I said please don't fuck with me!"

"Zen out, man."

"I never would've thought it would come to this, you fucking with me."

"I don't know what you're talking about."

"You don't? Well, I *do*."

He went to deliver another kick. He was getting to be a real nuisance. I caught his incoming foot with my legs, locked my ankles around his calf and jerked my knees.

I was thinking a little visit with the hard floor would straighten him out. But no. Almost as soon as he landed he was getting back on his feet, and I have to say he was surprisingly quick and graceful for a flabby drunk.

"You're about to get an ass-smacking," he said just before making a mad lurch at me.

All I did was throw an elbow into his belly as he came in. He bent over, gasped for air and hit the floor right away. There was no stumbling hesitation-fall. He just went plop down.

Which is about what I expected. What I didn't expect was that he'd curl up in a fetal ball and go completely spastic. His arms started twitching and flailing and he was letting out loud yelps in a hysterical and uncontrollable rhythm.

I got up and checked on him, thinking Jesus, what have I done now? His eyes were open but he looked out of it. He was having a guaranteed fit.

>>>>>>

Now you can't make noise like that without attracting attention in almost any squadroom. I heard footsteps and took a seat on the other side of the cell.

One of the detectives appeared at the bars. "Is he all right?"

Are you kidding me?

"I don't think so."

"What's wrong with him?"

"I don't know. He was sitting there, all of a sudden he's on the floor, writhing around."

The detective appraised him again. "It just happened?"

"Just happened."

"He might need an ambulance."

"He might."

"Could be the DT's, something like that."

"Could be."

"I guess I should call."

"Probably."

Or maybe not. About 10 seconds after the detective left, Bow Tie's arms stopped jerking. His yelps simmered down to moans, then to nothing. He sat up.

"Take it easy," I said. "Help is coming."

He looked over at me, then, with much effort—most of it negotiating the delicate requirements of balance—made it to his feet.

"Maybe you should stay down," I suggested, "stay calm."

Bow Tie apparently disagreed. A second later he was coming at me in a full bore growling charge, bull's-head down and arms out like horns.

Enough with this shit.

I got up and met him with one roundhouse right. It was a clean shot, delivered with full arm extension and pretty decent follow-through.

His body actually seemed to float for a couple of seconds. I had a quick feeling that, under the right circumstances, it could stay in the air forever, except it smashed into the wall and crash landed on the bench below. And then didn't move. He was unconscious.

I was thinking shit, *now* what've I done? Then I wasn't. Then I was thinking something else entirely, taking a thought from somewhere deep in the backbrain. I was thinking that whatever was going to happen in the next few seconds was going to mean everything.

I went close to the bars. Underneath the women still fighting in the squadroom, I could hear the detective on the phone, calling for medical assistance—we've got a situation at the Sixth.

I went back to my cellmate, worked his arms out of his blazer, then took off his glasses and bow tie. The latter, fortunately, was a clip-on. After a little maneuvering, I had him stretched out on the bench with his face to the wall and his arms tucked under his head. I draped my jacket over his shoulders, using the collar to cover a good part of his face. It looked for all the world like he was catching up on his beauty sleep.

Besides being ugly, his blazer was a bad fit on me, but tough shit. No problem with the clip-on tie. His glasses? They blurred my vision when I put them on, but they were gonna have to do.

I got on the floor and went extremely fetal, really trying to bury my face inside the blazer. When I heard steps coming back, I started letting out little gasps of pain and thrashing my arms around like I was in the middle of a grandstand conniption.

"It'll be a couple of minutes," I heard the detective say, yelling it over to me like he expected an answer. "Just hang in there."

He left. I stopped. Bow Tie remained in dreamland. Ten minutes later I heard a commotion, lots of voices and footsteps. I went back into my act. The bars slid open. I couldn't see much through those myopic glasses, but I could make out a gurney wheeling in, a pair of EMTs kneeling and asking me questions. I cut down a bit on the arm motion—I didn't want to be strapped down like a mummy—but I kept the moans and groans going. Good enough. The EMTs slipped a backboard under me and hoisted me on the gurney. Goodbye holding cell.

But here's the squadroom. I couldn't tell if my dear friend Det. Steve Lupski was looking, but just in case, I threw an arm over my face like I was gutting out some real agony. A minute later we were outside, ambulance light pushing bursts of white into the night air. One of the EMTs got inside with me. So did a uniformed cop. The doors slammed. We took off, the sirens screaming out of the exact middle of my head.

We Have A Winner

Okay, I was gone. I was out of jail. But now what? How do I get out of this? I'm stuck in an ambulance going who knows where with a cop by my side. Now the fuck what?

The EMT started hooking me up to monitors. "He trouble?" he asked the cop. "He need cuffs?"

"Just a DUI," said the cop.

I focused on the back window as the EMT took my vitals, trying to see which road we were taking, which direction we were going in. Nothing. Everything through these glasses was a Robonnet blur.

"His numbers are looking okay," the EMT said, "but his pulse rate is through the roof."

Really? Could that be because my ass was about to fall off from panic? I could've told him about the pulse. He didn't need a set of electrodes for that. My heart was going so fast and hard I could feel every beat shuddering along the length of my spine.

Can't lose it. I can't lose it now. I needed to pray. I hadn't prayed in a long time and I needed to pray myself into getting calm. Sometimes I think of God as gravity. God is what keeps things from falling apart. I needed to surrender myself to that force. I needed to do a centering prayer—repeat a phrase with rhythmic breathing. But what should I say? I couldn't come up with the right words. And when I tried to breathe my lungs felt like they were so filled to capacity there was no room for any more air.

The ambulance pulled to a stop. We were at a hospital but I couldn't even guess which one. I had no sense of how long we'd been traveling. Everything I saw was melted light.

Automatic doors opened. There was movement, voices, people, cries, the yellow halo of artificial light. We were in an ER, that much I knew.

The cop stayed next to me. Apparently, wherever we were, he hadn't been there in a while. People kept saying hello to him, long time, how you been. They were yapping away. Me, I was just incidental. Nobody said a thing about me, except to tell the cop things're backed up, it'll be a few minutes. Thank God I was faking it.

Nobody paying attention to me, though, really didn't help. I still felt as conspicuous as a turd in a church aisle. I was aware of every square inch of my body, every pore, every microscopic cell of flesh. If they'd wheeled me in here naked with a bow tied to my dick I couldn't have felt more self-conscious.

And I think I had a good reason for it. What was I facing? Attempted break-in at the museum. Attempted escape from jail. Attempted impersonation. Probably even attempted theft of medical services. This was one heavy load.

Okay, don't give in to the panic. Deal with it. Turn it the fuck over to God. I closed my eyes. I really goddamn needed to pray. But the only things that were coming to me were Robonnet words.

I have known this in another time.
I have found this on 12047 maps.
Do you remember who you are?

The fucking painting. Fucking Shannon and her fucking 12047 clues. I'm trying to clear my head and all I get is

The name that can be named
Is not the true name.

Somebody in the room was talking to the cop. Had he heard about Dawn Mustafah? That she hit the lottery? Won 13 mill? The cop freaked—no, he hadn't heard. Holy shit, the other guy said, you didn't hear *how* she won?

Obviously the cop hadn't heard, but I could hear him move away from me, move closer to the other guy. I opened my eyes.

What happened was, Dawn Mustafah always played the same numbers. Played the same set for years and never missed a Wednesday or a Saturday drawing. Last week she buys her ticket, somehow the clerk gives her the wrong one. Somebody else's ticket was still in the machine, something like that. Dawn doesn't notice until that night—she blows a gasket. The numbers are nothing like her old tried and true. She's fucked. But then she's watching Eyewitness News, *those* are the numbers that come up. The *wrong* numbers are the *winning* numbers. Thirteen million all hers, half after taxes.

The cop was floored. Dawn Mustafah that works here? Who else? Only problem now is, does she take the lifetime payments or the lump sum? The cop had definite opinions on that. Lump sum, he said. Take the lump and put it to work.

I took my glasses off like I was rubbing my eyes.

The cop was talking to a male nurse. They were 25, maybe 30 feet away.

"You want like 25% in bonds," the cop was saying. "Twenty-five to 30. Something like 20% in the S&P 500 Index. Diversification is the key."

I sat up. The cop kept on talking—he wasn't paying attention to me. "International's a little risky right now, but small cap blends are worth looking at."

My balance was a little off as I got down from the gurney. I took a step. Nothing from the cop. He was too caught up in discussing the Asian markets. Couple more steps—test moves. I had the glasses off, looking at the exit, thinking I can't get away with this. But four or five steps later I'm thinking I might get away with this. I'm just somebody walking through a busy, crowded ER. Please God keep me calm and maybe I might get away with this. I kept moving, nobody looking at me. It was like invisible magic. And as the doors parted in front of me I'm thinking I *am* getting away with this shit.

A summer fog had settled over wherever this place was—fat fog silvered by moonlight, traffic sounds in the distance. I had no idea where I was or where I was going, but it didn't matter. I was streeting it—I'd been saved. Yes, I was wearing a green polka dot bow tie, but I was otherwise unscathed. I'd been most definitely saved.

Though saved for what?

The fog was almost mirage thick even as I was passing through it, and whether it was that or eye strain aftereffect from the glasses, I seemed to be seeing images float in front of me. Vaporous images of levitating bodies and nuns giving birth. Hubble patterns and burning skies. Tropical vines and New Orleans trumpets and feathered devil masks.

Wait. Feathered devil masks? That wasn't from the painting.

That's when I knew. That's when I knew what I had to do.

The fog was thinning out. I saw a dumpster ahead of me—no illusion. I ditched the blazer, the glasses and the bow tie inside and kept walking toward the traffic.

Now I knew what I had to do.

CHAPTER 16

HOW TO HULA HOOP

A Dream Facilitator

Carl Jung once said that you can't change anything unless you accept it. Guy was right. If all the alarm systems in the Whitmore were interconnected, why fight it? Accept the fact and deal with it. And if the museum was holding a party—sorry, *event*—tonight, well, maybe Nick the Five had been right after all. Maybe we should just accept the reality and use it to our advantage.

And how would we manage to infiltrate the event without getting recognized? Simple. All it took was a trip to a Target, a dancewear store and a costume shop, where we bought, respectively, hula hoops, black leotards and feathered devil masks. Be'Nad, Nick the Five, Randi and I would go in disguised as members of HIPS (Hidden In Plain Sight), the performance group scheduled to put on a show tonight.

Admittedly, the approach posed certain drawbacks. Be'Nad wasn't thrilled about wearing a devil mask, but at this point he was willing to do almost anything to get this job over with. And Hillary's red and white carry bag clashed brutally with the HIPS uniform. But what the hell? We were artists now—we could break a few boundaries.

The plan: Once we got inside and scoped out the landscape, Be'Nad would disable the alarm in one of the ground floor galleries. This would set off every other security system in the building and create some large scale confusion, and as the guards rushed to the breeched area, we'd run downstairs, make our grab, leave by the basement fire exit and go straight to Genesis'.

Payday was upon us.

For which Nick the Five was taking full credit. Doing it during the party, he kept telling us on the way to the museum, had been his idea from the go. "Sometimes I'm sending myself mixed messages, I know that, but not this time. This time I had it nailed."

True, the notion that we were following one of his suggestions made us all uneasy, but that was one more thing we had to accept.

We met Shannon at one of the service doors on the side and she let us in. She looked nervous, pinched. The event, she said, wasn't going well. Maybe we should call it off for tonight. The problem was the crowd. They weren't taking to Cole Reynolds' new vision for the museum. She'd talked to a few of the patrons and donors and they were all saying the same thing: We liked the old, eccentric, spiritual based artwork. This other stuff we can get in other places. Why would we come to the Whitmore for it?

Shannon reminded us that we'd been counting on a happy, easily distracted audience. This wasn't it. Cole was going to try to win them over with a speech, but so far the amount of enthusiasm in the room was about the size of Mother Teresa's lingerie bill.

Well, we were already here, I said, and we're all dressed up. Let's take a look. Maybe we can get an ugly mood to work just as well.

Shannon split off from us as we slipped to the edge of the Heavenly Visitations gallery. Drinks of many colors were being served to hundreds of unsettled and grumpy guests who seemed communally lost in dull shock. A DJ was playing genteel house music, and occasionally two or three of the attendees were able to rouse themselves and snap their fingers. A concerned Cole Reynolds was standing in one part of the gallery, sweating into his purple scarf. His beef-fed bodyguard, the one from the castle, was right next to him. Joy Cheng's bald head bobbed in another part of the crowd. A couple dozen hula-hooped devils—our fellow HIPS members—were massed by the gallery entrance, waiting to go on. Guards were scattered everywhere.

The installations, of course, were completed. What I could see:

•Maybe 500 feet of glass tubing twisting and turning at every possible angle and pumped through with some kind of amber liquid that looked like Turkish moonshine.

•An artist chained to a 12-foot-high lock.

•Mannequins submerged in the green suspension of a tank filled with lime jello.

•Thousands of bicycle parts welded into one gigantic 20-foot-long bike.

•The biggest piece looked like some sort of utopian lollipop fantasy—hundreds of translucent glass bricks in bright Pantone pastels stacked to spell out a massive, six-foot-high version of the word WORLD.

And none of this was working any magic on the crowd. So what did it mean? Could we still get away with our plan? I thought so. Our strategy depended on people panicking and fleeing the museum. Hell, these people were *already* primed to stomp out.

I was talking this over with Be'Nad, Nick the Five and Randi when a young woman with the bitter sneer of a 60-year-old approached. She identified herself as a reporter from the *ouruppercrust* website.

"What's with the dog?" she asked.

I followed her eyes to Hillary's conspicuous candy-cane beach bag. "What about the dog?"

"I've never seen HIPS use an animal in the act before."

I explained that we never stopped experimenting, never stopped looking for something new. My costume, I felt, made the bullshit come easier. I was just getting into the necessity of ever-constant innovation when I caught Joy Cheng on the other side of the gallery. She was regarding us with a major load of suspicion. Because we weren't standing with the other HIPS folk? Because we were talking to a reporter? Either way, she was giving us a look that can only be called queer.

The reporter asked how we felt about the Whitmore's change of direction. "People are saying the event's not worth the price of admission."

"I thought it was free."

"Exactly."

I started to say we didn't comment on institutional philosophies when I saw Joy on the move. The striped suit, the tortoiseshell glasses—she was heading for us.

"It's not our policy to pass judgment," I said, wondering where the hell in here we could hide ourselves.

Then Joy stopped. Right in the middle of the crowd she stopped and switched her attention to the DJ's platform. Cole Reynolds was climbing the steps with an assist from his bodyguard, getting ready to address the grumbling throng. The music went to a quick fade and out. Cole patted his swatch of frontal hair in place, smiled like a sick swan and leaned into the microphone.

I've always thought of myself, he said, *as a dream facilitator.*

And that's exactly when I stopped listening. I heard him say something about the many months he, the board and the CCC had spent preparing for tonight, but I was talking to Be'Nad, Nick the Five and Randi about our next move. Which part of the museum should we hit? Despite his grave misgivings about the paintings, Be'Nad was voting for the Robonnet galleries. They held the most valuable goods, he said. The guards would do a thorough check when the Robonnet alarms went off, buying us some extra time.

It's a celebration of transience, Cole was saying, *and, in the same breath, a commemoration of permanence.*

His line of BS was worse than mine.

I found Shannon's eye in the crowd, gave her the look: We're on the way—be ready.

No one in the audience paid much attention to us as we threaded our way out. Most people were staring at Cole, trying to decipher him when he explained that the WORLD sculpture over there, for instance, the thing with all the pasteled glass, was *an example of extrovertive semi-absurdism, one that combined an ancient form—the brick—with advanced borosilicate technology.*

His voice died away as we left Heavenly Visitations and tootled down the corridor. That was the good news. The other kind of news? We wouldn't have the Robonnet galleries all to ourselves. Two fixed-faced guards were standing at the entrance with their hands clasped behind their backs, giving us the *yes?* eye. Shit. We said we were looking for the restroom. Directions were given and we were sent on our way.

So much for Robonnet. Would've made the best target, but no matter. There were other galleries for us to work with. Tropical Flowers, maybe. Or Pioneer Trails. Or Angels of Death.

No. No. No. Each section had at least one uniform on duty with a Whitmore-issue walkie-talkie. Even the lobby was out—three guards were on hand to let late arrivals in and show departees out.

Kind of a paradox, I know—the place was too secure to set off an alarm.

As we were herded back to Heavenly Visitations, we realized we had to get at least one of the gallery guards out of position. We needed a diversion. We needed to improvise something.

Back at the party, it was obvious that even the merciful end of Cole's speech had done nothing to soften up the crowd. An epidemic of misery had broken out in every part of the room. Cole and his bodyguard were standing off to the side as the HIPS troupe assembled in front of the DJ's platform. I saw Shannon nearby. Her expression was easy to read: *What's wrong now?*

No time to formulate a non-verbal answer because Joy Cheng was also staring at us again, and her thoughts were just as easy to understand: *Why aren't they joining the other HIPS flexors? Why are they still off by themselves?* These didn't seem to be idle questions, since a moment later Joy was heading toward one of the local security guards.

If she hadn't made us yet, she was about to.

Shit on a pastel brick. What choice did we have? We pushed through the audience and huddled at one end of the devil-masked squad.

One of the HIPSters announced that the following was a tribute to the performance artist Allen Kaprow, titled *UnFounded Foundation*, and then they launched right into it. We were suddenly sideswiped by a wail of voices, half singing and half shouting some sermonic blarney about violence, injustice and infectious diseases.

Anger shimmers in the skies
Over the compost heap of history
As we cry below
For the faith of our fathers,
The myths of our mothers

Like the Milk Studios production, this was accompanied by a full orchestra of kazoos, tambourines and tin drums and above all by the hula hoops in synchronized swing.

I did okay keeping up with them—I'd retained my childhood skills. And Randi was doing fine—holding Hillary wasn't slowing her down at all. Be'Nad, though, Be'Nad was a bad hula hooper. Not physically gifted to begin with, he was conspicuously awful at this, dropping the hoop, letting it clatter on the platform and just moving in general like he had a pantsload.

The HIPS members kept looking over at him. Fortunately, you can't gauge expressions through masks, but I still thought there was a good chance he'd get us busted.

What he was trying to do was move his hips in a circle—a common mistake. You're better putting one foot forward and shifting your weight back and forth from one leg to the other. Much easier that way. It's less of a rotating motion than a rocking or pumping one, like Nick the Five was doing.

In fact, Nick was in his element. He was putting his whole heart into his hula hooping, not to mention his ass. The way he did it was more like sex than geometry. He was putting on quite the exhibition, and at one point, just after Be'Nad dropped his hoop one more time, Nick the Five moved directly in front of him. Whether this was to shield him or show him up, I don't know, but Nick was really getting into it, snaking his body, swaying his head.

Swaying his head *hard*.

The masks we'd bought at the costume shop were held on by rubber bands and clasps. They seemed tight enough for normal use, but for overenthusiastic gyrations maybe they were too loose. In any case, as Nick the Five was rocking his head forward in one particularly energetic swerve, his mask flew off and went sailing into the audience.

He stopped in mid-wave, realizing he'd just exposed his face.

Randi stopped too, pretty pissed. "You fucking pinhole brain." She said. "You can't control yourself?"

Titters came from a few people in the crowd. They thought it was part of the HIPS patter.

One person who didn't laugh was Cole Reynolds. He saw the familiar face, the distinctive orange streak in Nick's black hair, and he looked as if the goddess of shock had kissed him in a dream and filled every path in his lungs with staggering surprise.

He broke for the platform with a speed that was almost silent-film funny. Nick the Five reacted to the sudden movement with less than perfect composure. He jumped out of the hula hoop and hit the ground running. But Cole was sprinting fast—too fast even for his bodyguard to follow—and he caught up with Nick in front of the WORLD sculpture, throwing a flying tackle and slamming him to the ground.

The punching, grappling and fumbling started right away, Cole and Nick the Five swiping and kicking at each other until one of their arms or legs or whatever struck the WORLD sculpture. Specifically, the L of the WORLD sculpture. The pastel tower tottered for a second like a skyscraper resisting an earthquake, then it gave out and toppled over, sending a couple hundred glass bricks crashing down.

Meanwhile, the HIPS group went on performing. They could stick to a script no matter what.

By now Cole's bodyguard had snapped to and was coming to his boss' aid. He arrived at the WORLD sculpture—or WORD—as Cole and Nick the Five were still swarming all over each other on the floor. The bodyguard got his meaty hands around Nick's neck and started dragging him off.

It was turning out to be one of those nights.

I ran up, grabbed the bodyguard's tie from behind and yanked him around, pretty much replaying the scene from the castle. Only this time, instead of trying to put 10 years of pain in one punch, I hit him in the head with one of the bricks I'd picked off the ground. A moment later, with absolutely no training or preparation, the bodyguard had become the most unconscious glass-covered man in Sea Cliff, N.Y.

Cole and Nick the Five were on their feet now. I don't know what happened since I looked last, but Cole had snatched a brick from the top of the W and was raising it over his head, ready to shatter it on Nick's porous skull. But before he could lower his arms Nick shot a leg straight into his stomach. Cole staggered, the brick held in front of him, and stumbled a few feet into the crowd, coming to a stop in front of one of the guests. She was the stiff-shouldered, gray-haired sponsor I'd seen him with the other day. She looked at him with high confusion, then looked at the brick he seemed to be offering her.

The whole room went silent. All singing and hula hooping had ceased.

The woman accepted the chunk of glass—it was a bright, technologically shimmering pink—and hesitated, not sure what to do with it. Then she let out a howling giggle like a cartoon hyena and smashed the brick to the floor.

You could hear the lungs, a whole roomful of sucked in breaths. And you could see what happened next—a slurry band of guests darting for the sculpture, picking up bricks and hurling them to the ground.

They all understood. This was part of the act. This was what you were *supposed* to do. Cole had called the sculpture extrovertish semi-absurdism. Is this what he meant? Well all right. This was *fun*. This was *art*!

In moments the gallery had turned chaotic enough to look just like rush hour in Cairo. The guards ran to the sculpture to stop the wanton brick tossing, but it's impossible to fend off a crowd that's finally found an outlet for a long night of frustration. They attacked the sculpture like it was slated for demolition, tearing into it with crap-happy delirium.

I pulled Nick the Five to a safer part of the gallery. Be'Nad, Randi and Shannon met up with us. Randi was still angry.

"Look what you've done," she said to Nick. "You couldn't leave Be'Nad alone? You have to half-ass your way through everything?"

Nick was trying to mount a manful comeback when we noticed the other guards from the other galleries pouring into Heavenly Visitations. Including the two guards from the Robonnet galleries.

It finally hit home. We were looking for a diversion? The diversion had come to us.

The tapestry we faced was all raucous confusion. I saw Cole's bodyguard getting to his dazed feet, saw Cole himself fighting off marauding guests. Didn't help. The crowd was going after those bricks like they wanted the night to last forever.

>>>>>>

No one saw us as we snuck off to the Robonnets. Be'Nad made only a 3.4 second adjustment to his pocket processor—a world speed record for obsessive-compulsives—before letting the ultrasonic waves rip loose. The result, a tsunami of sound set off by every interlocked alarm system in the museum, felt like thunder in the chest.

A full-panic riot was on by the time we got back to the party. Sheets of screaming people were scrambling for the exits, leaving behind a field of broken glass and selected puddles of vomit. Guards were splitting off from the crowd and, alerted by their walkie-talkies, were running for the Robonnet galleries. We went to the door leading downstairs and swiped the lock. Finally something on this job was going right—through little fault of our own.

Be'Nad took us through the basement maze of dim-lit, low-ceilinged concrete, everything shaking with the seismic shock of the alarms. I felt like I was running in a dream. I was moving with that same kind of nerve-charged freedom.

We were just about deaf when we got to the storage room and Be'Nad went to swipe the door open. Still, we could all hear the head-shattering boom that exploded somewhere in the corridor. Either a big-caliber gun had just gone off or someone had just dropped a dumpster right behind us.

We turned around. Okay, a *human* dumpster. A pock-marked, ham-faced dumpster. The bodyguard had followed us downstairs. I couldn't see the make of his gun in the bad light but it looked to be as large as it sounded.

"You move away from that door," he shouted over the alarms. "Everybody."

We moved.

"Take off the masks."

Be'Nad, Randi and I complied.

The bodyguard paid particular attention to me. He gave me one of those long and possibly drugged-up looks—unbroken focus but with no emotion in the eyes. "You. I remember you."

"One of those faces," I said. It felt like my lungs were filled with water.

"It's over down here," he said. "We're going upstairs now."

We were so close. Too much for Randi.

"You cunt-faced bucket of scum," she yelled. "Go fuck yourself."

"Your objection is noted," said the bodyguard. "Now move."

"We're not going fucking anywhere!"

The guy, evidently, was in no mood to debate, because he reached out and—again, with no expression, with as much feeling as he'd show taking off his jacket—he grabbed Shannon, twisted her around against his chest and put the big gun to her head.

She never gets chosen? Goodbye to all that.

"Enough talk," he said. "Everybody upstairs."

He was pressing the weapon into her head, just like her father had done to her mother.

It was so hot down here I thought the air would catch on fire.

"*Now*," he said. "Back upstairs."

Then, for a moment, he showed emotion—a look of surprise, followed by a wince and a sharp scream. Hillary was on the floor, biting into the steak of his calf. The Maltese had jumped out of her bag and was staging an all out assault on his leg. Whatever crimes he'd committed against the departed—probably more than a few—he was being punished for them now.

The bodyguard shoved Shannon away and went for the dog. I shot a foot in his crotch, jammed a thumb in his eye and felt his whole face go flat as I landed a flush punch. Not a bad effort. Within three, four seconds he was on the floor and in the land of nod.

We opened the door. The painting was there, waiting on the other side of the room, a kaleidoscopic canvas that opened into an abyss of stars. We waded through the crisscrossing lasers like kids romping through the surf. With the alarms all going off, no need to hold back now.

Nick the Five lifted the painting off the wall. I stood behind him, my eyes automatically going to that strange dark corner on the upper left side, where the comet's clotted tail disappeared into shadow.

"Wait," I said. "Wait a second."

There *was* no shadow.

I'd always wondered why the paint suddenly lapsed into blackness on the digital copy, but I couldn't ask that question here because there was no black patch on the original. Instead, the comet's tail scattered around a single image and a small set of words.

"Wait," I said, moving closer.

I'd seen the image before—an iconic angel in amber and red, drawn with no perspective in one Byzantine dimension. The tattoo on Slim's right hand.

"Quinn," said Nick the Five, "we don't have time. Police'll be here."

"Wait." I bent to read the words.

I can smell the tongues and skulls,
The dried frankincense, the rotted myrrh.
I can hear the closing of the final age,
The Kali Yuga, when the gods will no longer appear.
I can see that my own son will end my life,
My own son will put the blade in my heart.

The words rushed through my brain. I could hear Nick and the others yelling at me but the only thing I was conscious of was the words roaring and splitting to pieces inside my head.

We didn't need to bust any codes to figure this one out.

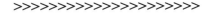

CHAPTER 17

MY FACE WILL BE BATHED IN MY OWN BLOOD

I Can Hear His Cries

She was waiting for us in the library, blue caftan, jade and aquamarine necklace, hands on her hips like a queen ordering a beheading. Her security guys brought us all up and left us there, Be'Nad, Randi and Nick the Five gaping at the room's birch and leather, all Park Avenue wide. Genesis glanced at Hillary in the bag but didn't question it, just shrugged and asked us to help ourselves if we wished. One of the tables had been cleared of catalogues and laid out with fruit and veggies, water and juices. No one took her offer. Business first.

Nick opened his cylindrical container and carefully removed the canvas, then looked for a spot to roll it out. Genesis suggested taping it to the flat screen on the wall, the monitor where I'd first seen the digital copy of the painting. Nick spread it out, one corner at a time. It was all there—the fire-blood symbols, the angels and corpses, the nuns and newborns, the words.

I have told you, I have promised,
I will secretly tell this story
716194552945
I recognized the face in the darkness,
I will secretly speak the name.

It was as incredible to me as it'd ever been, like it was painted with the substance of the brain, but I couldn't get into it this time. Its other version, its digital analog, kept clawing at me.

Genesis moved from side to side in front of the painting, leaning in for closer inspection, nodding to herself. The room smelled of oranges and apples and the clear night through the windows was as wide as forever.

I kept looking at the words.

I heard the black words that are spoken everywhere,
But always in disguise.

The examination went on for a heavy minute, Genesis pausing, staring, moving on to another area of the painting. Finally she turned to us and made her pronouncement. "I see nothing wrong."

It was intended, clearly, as the final curtain, a signal that the deal was complete. I looked at Shannon. She looked at me.

"We should talk about something," I said.

Genesis seemed puzzled by my words, puzzled even more when she realized my *we* included Shannon.

"Next door," she said.

We stepped inside the New Orleans bordello she called her bedroom.

Do you think I could not heer
The echo of the words
In the fatal rooms and liquid chambers
Of the Secret Pyramids.

"I assume this is about the money," she said. "No need to worry. The checks are downstairs, they're all made out."

"It's not the money," I said. "It's about the site. The official Robonnet site."

"The site." No hesitation in her reply, though her voice, I noticed, was a trace deeper now.

"Who runs it?"

"My brother."

"He puts all the digital copies up?"

"Yes."

"Including *Sex Death Dream Talk*?"

She nodded. "All of them."

"Did you know his copy isn't exactly the same as the original?"

She just stared at me. Not once did she look at Shannon, never, just at me.

"How so?"

"There's a shadow on the site copy. If he's in charge, then I guess he's the one who dropped it in."

"A shadow."

"Small dark patch, upper left corner. It's weird because it doesn't seem to go with the rest of the painting."

"No?"

"No. But what it does do, it hides an image of an angel and a pretty interesting piece of text."

She turned away from me and looked out one of the bedroom windows. You could hear the world breathing outside.

A few moments later her eyes came back to me. Somehow, there seemed to be slightly less flesh on her face now. She looked as if she could feel the future putting its hand on her face.

"You should probably talk to him," she said. "My brother."

"Not you?"

"It's his responsibility."

"You have nothing to say?"

"You should talk to him. He'll probably answer the questions."

"You think?"

She took a breath. "He's not well. His heart. He doesn't have a long time. I think he'll want to talk to someone."

She eased herself over to the wall and leaned against it.

"I'm sorry," I said.

"It's time," she said. "I know it's time. I love my brother. But I loved my father more."

I thought about driving with Slim, him talking about his father's house, gradually slipping into the subject of his father's murder. I remembered saying it was a terrible way to die, and Slim agreeing with me. *I've replayed it so many times in my head*, he said, then quickly added, *the police report of it.*

She glanced at Shannon, just for a moment, then brought her eyes back to me. If it was possible to weep without tears, this is what it would look like.

"Do you remember what people said that night?" she asked. "The people who lived near that park? They said the screams were like demon howls, like something that hadn't come from anything on earth."

"I remember."

"It's a strange thing, but sometimes, when I look at the painting, I can hear those screams in there. I can hear his cries in the paint."

The Souls in Tor-ment
At the Southern Gate of hell
Number 900,413,777,262
And there is no release for them.
They suffer fever and sleep
But they will never be released.

She moved herself away from the wall and stood upright. "I think it's possible," she said. "I think it's completely possible to hear his voice. He believed angels' voices told him what to paint. I believe I can hear his voice in what he painted."

I could hear a voice too—a cry, a shout. We all could. But not from paint or heaven or hell. From the library.

Look At What You've Done

Looking back on things, maybe I never should've told Nick the Five about Be'Nad's peculiar peach problem. Maybe I never should've mentioned how the peach-eating bodyguard in Bobby Hucknail's kitchen had sent Be'Nad into a monumental bone-shaking meltdown, or how Be'Nad's mother had told me her son suffered a lifelong aversion to the fuzzy fruit.

But I did tell him, which explained why Be'Nad was going limp with hyperventilated hysteria when we ran in and looking like somebody needed to foam the runway for his crash landing. Nick the Five had grabbed one of the peaches from the snack table and, staring at Be'Nad with straightjacket eyes, was dangling it in front of him like a live grenade.

"Look at him now!" he was shouting to Randi. "Look what he looks like."

Be'Nad, in the meantime, was trembling and yelling *put it down* while Hillary barked herself into a fury. Randi didn't translate because she was too busy telling Nick at full-scream volume that he was a squiggle-dicked jerkoff with birdshit for brains.

God knows exactly how it started, but Randi must've said something because Nick was saying he was tired of her shitting all over him and if she thought Be'Nad was such hot shit well what did she think of him in his current quivering condition?

Randi replied that he was a blistering asshole and that she'd known jellyfish with more perception. Be'Nad, eyes on the peach, wrapped his hands around his head like he was trying to squeeze the words out of his ears.

"What's going on here?" Genesis demanded to know. "What are they *doing*?"

I stepped toward Nick the Five. "This so fucking ridiculous. Put that down."

He ignored me.

"*Do* something!" Be'Nad pleaded. "I *know* these people—I've read the literature."

"I want this stopped," said Genesis. Clearly an order. "Stop it right *now*."

Capital idea.

"Nick," I said, "put it down. Put the fucking peach down." I couldn't believe I was saying this.

"I can't," he said. "It's her. She's a sad, bitter *bitch*. She's sad and angry and sad and bitter and a *bitch*."

"*Listen* to yourself," Randi screamed at him. "You're a fucking *illiterate*."

"What does *that* mean?" he yelled back.

"Ex*act*ly!"

When he tossed the fruit, it wasn't at her or Be'Nad. It squished against one of the bookshelves, leaving a pulpy mess on what looked like volumes devoted to Fra Angelico, Egyptian amulets and the art of the Savannah Empires. Randi shrieked. Genesis made a strange held-tight noise at the back of her throat. "What have you done?" That was all she could say. "What have you *done*?"

I turned in her direction. The only part of her body that was moving was the artery on the side of her neck. It was jumping like a downed wire in an electrical storm.

But at least the peach threat had passed. The crisis was over.

Or maybe not, because Genesis' eyes suddenly zoomed scary wide and Randi was calling somebody *a stupid slice of shitloaf* and all the nerves in the room were lighting up like phosphorous.

I swung back to Nick. He had his gun out, the one from last night. The Detonics. He had it pointed at Be'Nad.

"Come *on*," I said. "What're you doing?"

"Don't start up with me, Quinn."

"Start?"

"Don't try to fool me again."

"I'm not. I'm trying to talk to you."

"Yeah well talking's how it starts."

I took one step toward him. The gun moved on me.

"Why're you doing this *now*?"

"You don't see? The job's over now. We're done. So what am I gonna think about? I got nothing to fill my mind. I got nothing to take me away from my own shit."

He saw movement from Be'Nad and switched the gun to him. No attack—Be'Nad had gone malted-pale and was just trying to steady himself and keep from passing out.

The whole room was pulsing with dry sick-flashes. It was like the house had ingested some really bad speed.

"Nick," I said, "you know, we're all crazy, it's just a matter you learn to live with it."

The gun arced back to me. "It's not just crazy. It's nothing. It's looking at yourself and seeing nothing. Remember what I told you about looking in the mirror? I don't see anything. All I see is the sky full of nothing. I can't help it. I can't help what I see."

"Nick," said Randi, "put it down." She said it softly. No shouting, no threat of a curse. "Not like this. Please."

He wasn't angry when he looked back at her. He lowered his head a quarter inch and looked at her with begging eyes. It felt like he was about to ask her a question.

I thought she'd lulled him. I thought she'd brought him back down.

I was wrong.

He swung his arm to Be'Nad and pulled the trigger twice. But in the picosecond just before the first shot thunder-cracked, Be'Nad's brain decided this was too much tension to tolerate. His legs gave out, his body folded and with his face looking like a red snapper with ptomaine poisoning, he fell into a breathless, dead-weight faint. Both bullets passed right over his head and shattered glass somewhere behind him.

I didn't know what Nick hit because I went to reach for the gun and accidentally body slammed him so hard we both went to the floor. We rolled and thrashed for a moment or two, me clawing at his arm, when I heard raw human noises above the gunfire-ringing in my head. Randi and Shannon. Randi screaming like she'd been screaming for all time, Shannon yelling *look what you've done—look what you've goddamn done.*

I raised my head. The bullets hadn't broken one of the windows in the room. No, what I'd heard shatter was the glass of the monitor mounted on the wall. Two distinct bullet holes, one just a half inch away from the other, had been torn into the painting.

Nick was twisting away from me. I tried to get a grip but he was stronger and adrenaline-drunk and he out-muscled me. He staggered to his feet and took aim at the unconscious Be'Nad. But something else got his attention. He stopped.

Shannon had a gun on him. A small gun, .25 caliber Raven, the one she'd pulled on me at the castle. Why was she carrying that tonight? What had she been planning to do? You think you know people.

"You've ruined it," she said to Nick. "You've *destroyed* it. You've shot it all to *shit*!"

As she went to squeeze the trigger, Randi, screaming now like she was screaming in her sleep, grabbed her arm and shoved it away from Nick.

The Raven was an automatic, meaning that if you hold the trigger down—the way Shannon was holding hers—you're going to set off a bursting spray of bullets.

Not all of Shannon's rounds struck the painting, but most did. They landed with glass-smashing thuds, no ricochet, burying themselves in the monitor after knifing through the canvas. By the time the gun was empty, every part of the painting was ripped and shredded. It looked like a bedsheet in a tornado.

One thing about houses on the North Shore of Long Island: No matter how big they are, it's hard to fire guns inside without attracting the attention of the security staff. The dark-suited gargantuas came in ready for action, shifting their weapons back and forth in robotic, stiff-armed sweeps.

Shannon began to cry. Actually, she began to sob—it was that wet and uncontrollable.

No tears from Genesis, though. No nothing from her. She never moved. You could find igneous rock with more animation. She just stood there staring at what was left of the painting. Her turquoise eyes were duller now, more metallic, as if they'd been washed with acid.

The smoke from the gunfire was settling in layers under the high ceiling. Something similar was happening to us. Now that the circus thrills were over, the reality of the damage was setting in. The full extent of the consequences was becoming clear. There were fucks-ups and there were fuck-ups, but this was the fuck-up of all fuck-ups.

Security relieved Nick the Five of his Detonics, Shannon of her Raven. One guard began shaking Be'Nad back to life. Genesis, still not saying anything, began to move toward the painting, brushing against the tables she passed like she was seriously stoned. She walked like someone negotiating a cloudbank.

Her staffers watched her while they held their weapons on us. They were looking for direction.

"Ms. Robonnet?" one of them called. "What do you want done?"

Genesis regarded him with a perplexed, out-of-it expression. She seemed surprised to see that she wasn't alone. She seemed to be wondering why the library was filled with people.

She turned away without answering.

The guard tried again. "Ms. Robonnet? What should we do with them?'

"Get them out of here," she said, not even looking at us, keeping her eyes on the ruins of the painting. There was no anger in her voice, no despair, no emotion. Her voice was beyond all that.

She stepped closer to the painting, bending down and picking up a piece of tattered canvas that had fallen off the frame.

"All of them," she said. "Get them all out of here." No emotion, no tears. If she was crying, then it was all inside. The tears were only falling in her blood.

The Proclamation Has
Been Written In Hell

It's not everyday you can say you lost a million in the space of a few seconds. And I don't mean a paper million. I'm not talking about investments and holdings and points and yields that can vanish in one quick slipknot-turn of the market. I'm talking about cash. I'm talking about losing a million actual, bird-in-hand, aces-high, the real mazuma dollars in less than a fucking minute.

Gone. Over. Too late now. What's dung is dung. Still, there was something to salvage out of this misadventure. If not money, then an answer.

I called my cop friend, DeMarcus Boyd. Told him I had something on the murder of Isaiah Robonnet a year and a half ago. DeMarcus to be honest was not overly impressed by the theory of hidden codes in *Sex Death Dream Talk.* He thought it highly unlikely that Robonnet had experienced a legitimate premonitory vision and had used numbers, misspellings, repeated words and images to point to the identity of his killer.

But he *was* interested in the shadow on the website. Nothing theoretical about that. Slim Robonnet had deliberately overlaid a shadow on the digital copy of the painting. And DeMarcus was intrigued by what Genesis had said about the darkened area: Go talk to my brother. Considering the state of his health, he'll probably have something to say.

And what really kicked it in for DeMarcus were the words concealed beneath the shadow. *My own son will put the blade in my heart.* Yeah, he conceded, that did sound rather compelling. It was certainly worth a talk. Certainly worth a call to his new contacts with the New Orleans police.

They picked Slim up that afternoon at his gallery on Toulouse Street. Genesis had been right about his willingness to talk—she'd inherited at least part of her father's predictive power. Slim's doctors, he told the cops, had given him only a few months before his heart gave out forever. It's too late now to keep quiet, he said. Just too late, no matter how you look at it.

The magnet at the center of the murder, he admitted, was the Whitmore Museum. Slim had wanted to strike a deal with one of its board members, Cole Reynolds. The Robonnet family had made good money from the museum's attentions; his sister had forged good relations with the board. A year and a half earlier, Slim decided to reach an agreement of exclusivity with the Whitmore. Every new Robonnet would first be displayed at the museum and offered for sale by the museum. In exchange, the family would receive a much more generous cut of the sale price than they were getting from their other dealers. Genesis supported the deal, but the idea was all Slim's, one he'd set up in good faith with his board buddy Cole Reynolds. As much profit as the family had made before, they were about to traipse down the path to truly phenomenal wealth.

That greed is like fire.
The more it is fed
The hungrier it gets.

All the agreement needed was their father's approval. They presented it to him three days before his death, during a party at the Whitmore. Isaiah wasn't going for it—not at all. He didn't want to hurt the other dealers, he'd argued, and he surely didn't want any deal with Cole Reynolds. He didn't like Cole, found him shystery and loathsome and several thousand miles beneath all trust. When Slim started talking about the additional money they'd earn, Isaiah accused both children of turning against him and stomped out of the museum like walking thunder.

The betrayer will seek to punish
The proclamation has been written in hell.

His father's assessment of Cole, Slim said, turned out to be dead on. Only recently—just the other day—Slim and his sister learned that Cole had been quietly selling off the museum's Robonnets to finance a rebirth of the Whitmore. Cole had been deceiving the family, secretly liquidating the museum's Robonnet assets and cheating the children out of their percentage, all to pay for some mad crack-pipe vision of the future.

But that was now. Back to then. Isaiah refused to speak to either his son or daughter after they left the Whitmore party. Wouldn't give them a word, not even a primal grunt. Instead he shut himself away in a room in Genesis' house and began painting for the next 72 hours straight. Never stopped. No eating, no sleeping, no calls of nature beyond what he was hearing in his head. Slim said it was scary—they'd never seen their father work like that.

The result was *Sex Death Dream Talk*, a title unlike any of his others, a painting—a dark

denunciation, a prophecy of meta-frenzied violence—
unlike any of his others. The canvas, Slim said, had
frightened the hell out of him and his sister.

Then Isaiah said he wanted to talk to Slim about
the proposed deal. The time had come to talk. But not
here. We'll have the talk somewhere else. Get in the
car and drive.

So they drove, Slim shitting in his pants. They
drove through Nassau County and into Suffolk, Isaiah
never saying a word. Finally, at a spot four miles off
the Northern State, they passed a place called
Dominicus Park. Here, Isaiah said. Stop here. This is
where it will happen.

They got out and walked. The park close to
midnight was empty and black. They could barely see
the dirt paths, the ground. Still, his father seemed to
have some sense of where to go, even though Slim
believed he'd never been here before. He led them
into a grove of trees, a dense wall of cypresses and
pines that blocked off anything from view.

I recognized the face in the darkness
I will secretly speak the name

Isaiah bent down and examined the soil, felt the
roots with his hands. He nodded, stood up. It will
happen here, he said. *I've replayed it so many times in*
my head. Then he turned to his son, full face to face.
Are you armed? He said.

Slim showed him the knife. He'd it snatched
from the kitchen as they were leaving the house.
He was afraid of his father, thinking after seeing his
behavior, after seeing the contents of the painting,
that he'd completely lost his mind. So yes, as a
precaution, he'd brought the knife.

I recognized the one who will sacrifice me,
Like a flower that grows from the souls of
the dead.

His father came at him, screaming at him, telling him no matter what promises had been made he'd never take part in any agreement made by fools like him. His father was screaming words at him, then not words, howls, shrieks, blood-riven cries as Slim realized he was stabbing him with the knife. He'd been so angry and afraid of the big man—bigger than Slim, more powerful—that he'd been stabbing him in the chest, not knowing it, not planning it, carried by the pure momentum of hypnotic rage and fear, and the only things he could hear now were scorched-throat animal screams that vibrated in his heart and echoed through the black sky.

I looked into the darkness,
I saw my body covered in blood.
This will come to pass.
My blood will flow everywhere,
My face will be bathed in my own blood.

Slim's formal confession was filed at 9 p.m., signed with his legal name, Leviticus Robonnet. By 11 that night DeMarcus had called and told me what happened. I didn't expect to feel so sad about it, especially since I'd set the arrest in motion. But there it was, a deep-chested sorrow for Slim, for his sister, for Isaiah Robonnet and his lost painting.

Strangest of all, most unexpected of all, I was sad to realize that Shannon's readings of the clues had all struck home. The signifiers of disaster, the anti-money themes, the orbits of suspicion narrowing to a dealer or collector, than to the children, then to one of the children—almost every call she'd made turned out to be true.

The Storey is everywhere
Hidden only to those
Who do not see

All those codes had led to the end. Joshua nearing Gericho, the Aztec Calendar, the Sign of the Four, the first atomic test, the temple of Essaglia, where Maduk tore open Tiamat's chest with a lightning bolt, the day Cortes landed in Mexico, 14:367, the men bearing knives at Jesus' trial. They'd all played their part, all taken us closer to the sad totality, the sad result.

The Dead aren't coming back.
They don't want to.

Fracture Lines

I went to bed around midnight and scissor-kicked through four hours of bad sleep, truly rotten sleep. The phone took me out of it. I vaguely recognized the voice—one of Genesis' security people. Calling at 4:04 a.m. Ms. Robonnet, he informed me in a hitman-cum-social-secretary tone, wants to see you at the house.

When?

She wants to see you with Shannon Kubliak. She expects you both within the hour.

The July sky was wide and clear when we pulled into the old Colonial's semi-circular driveway. Neither of us had done much talking and neither could guess why we'd been summoned. What kind of revenge was she planning to lay on us? Our feet clicked over the cobblestones as we walked to the door. Birds were crying in the dark predawn blue.

Genesis was a sleepless wreck, her eyes lost in some desert-vision daze. She answered the door herself, dressed in the same caftan she was wearing the night before. So much of her weight had worn away in the last 24 hours you could almost see the atoms vibrating in her body's molecules.

Her voice was calm, though, pitchless, muted by a crazy serenity. She asked us in, thanked us (???) for coming, stood with us in the tall foyer of black marble and white spider lilies. She sounded like she'd spent

days in ascetic contemplation, praying for everything
and for nothing.

"Sorry about your brother," I said.

She didn't react. Nothing disturbed the hush of
the foyer.

"You know about your brother?"

"Yes," she said, "I know. Of course I know. I
know all about it."

She reached inside the bag she was holding, a
satchel of black Russian corrected-grain leather.

"I wanted to do this myself," she said. "In
person."

Out came a handful of envelopes. Each
contained a cashier's check, each amount first issued
from the account of the family's private 501C3
foundation. There was a check for Shannon and a
check for me, both making full payments, with
watermarks, security threads and color-shifting inks,
as originally promised. There were also checks for
Be'Nad Harrison, Nick Manetto and Randi Gutierrez.
And yeah, one for my expenses. *All* my expenses.

We'd destroyed the painting, shot it up like a
paper bull's eye at a gun range, and she was paying
us off? I didn't ask why. I didn't want to break the
mad spell. I just tried to hide my smacked-in-the-head
shock.

"Our business is finished," Genesis said, "but
there's something I want you to see. I want to show it
to you." She waited. "Both of you."

Shannon exhaled hard through her nose. She
pushed the air out with so much force you could
actually hear that the jets of breath streaming from her
nostrils each had a different timbre.

"If we're finished," she said, "I'd prefer to go."

"Feel free," said Genesis. "But I think you'll
find this interesting."

"What is it?" I said.

"You'll have to come see. It won't take long." There was a slight, half-traced smile on Genesis' face but her voice was still monotonously calm. Her words sounded like they were floating on a black ocean somewhere in the universe.

"I'm leaving," said Shannon. She glanced at me, then reached for the door. "We're done here."

I watched her walk out and I didn't know what to do.

Genesis turned away. "If you decide to look, I'll be waiting. Upstairs. In the library."

A wiccan dawn was breaking in the east, a pink-orange sky spreading out forever. This was one serious sunrise.

Shannon had crossed the upper loop of the driveway. She wasn't facing the house, moving instead toward the gigantic Satsuki azaleas bordering the street. I'd never realized it before, all my trips here, but those bushes were so thick and high they blocked any view of the house from the road.

She stopped when I caught up with her, a dream-lost look in her eyes.

"Where're you going?"

"Home. I need sleep."

"You don't want me to drive you?"

"I can call a cab." She held her envelope up. "I can afford it."

"It's a little extreme you can't wait."

"I'm done with her. I'm leaving." Her eyes arrowed straight into mine. "Are you coming?"

"She said it wouldn't take long."

"*Now.* I'm leaving *now.*"

A cloud of exhaustion was setting on my eyes and I couldn't stare through it.

She watched, then gave me a small but utterly defiant shoulder shrug. "You know what you're doing, right? You're choosing her."

"What, over *you*?"

"Just like I said."

Enough. Enough with all these self-fulfilling prophesies.

"It's your feet doing the walking," I said. "It's your *choice*."

She didn't move. She didn't storm off in denial or anger. She just stood there staring at me. You could draw a perfect, undeviating line between her eyes and mine.

She didn't move, but she didn't say anything either. Not a word. Me neither. No words. At least a couple moments went by. I guess that made it official: There was nothing left to say.

Now there was movement. She took a step toward the street. "Maybe some other time," she said. "You just never know, do you?"

And that was it. I watched her walking toward the bushes, walking away from me in the soft downfall of morning light.

There's a Japanese phrase, *mono no aware*. It means sad awareness, a quiet acceptance that all things in the world must pass, and a wordless pain when they do. A fading sound, a falling flower, a bluenote bending deep in the heart.

A pinpoint of white light was still visible in the western sky. A leftover planet. Venus maybe? I didn't know, but it made me remember something: I was still alive.

>>>>>>

The door had been left open. No alarm went off as I walked back in. The keypad hadn't been set. The motion detectors detected nothing.

I passed through the foyer, came to the great room. Bronze, alabaster, an acre of oriental carpets. No guards. None of the security staff was around.

Up the grand staircase, up the familiar steps of Carrara marble. Heading for what? Was this smart? I could feel my stomach shrinking by two inches, prepping for fear. But my legs kept moving. The bottom half of my body clearly wanted to get to the top. I gave into it, let myself be carried to the second floor.

Genesis was bent over one of the library tables, the same one where she'd served food the night before. Where Nick the Five grabbed the goddamn peach. The table was still cleared off, only now it held what looked like an enormous jigsaw puzzle.

I came closer. It *was* a kind of puzzle. The shreds of the painting had been spread out on the surface and fitted back together. The images—the nuns and lepers, the corpses and coffins, the beggars and angels—the words, everything was back in place, but separated by the spidering fracture lines of the torn canvas.

"I haven't slept since it happened," she said, not looking at me, only at the slashed remains. "I've been up all this time, trying to restore what was. I failed, of course. I can't restore it. But I've done something else instead. I've reinvented it."

Reinvented? All I saw were the bullet holes and the tension rips. I felt like an arson investigator poring over what's left of a firebombed building.

"I know what I'm going to do," she said. "I'm going to stretch a new piece of canvas, and I'm going to attach these pieces to it. Just the way they are, just the way you see them. It'll be beautiful, even more beautiful than the original. It will be so beautiful I can't even say.

She was long-gone crazy. The sun from one of the windows caught her head with a yellow halo. She was even crazier than she'd been before. The thing was a worthless ruin—what was she talking about? But even as I stood there thinking this, I could see, yes, there was a kind of weird, broken beauty to it. There was a kind of visual logic to the fragments, a kind of sacramental order. You could look at the rips and tears as new textures, new dimensions, marking not where the pieces separated but where they joined. You could look at them as borders, boundaries, as serpentinely beautiful as the outlines of rivers on maps, or the cortextual ridges on a cross section of the brain.

"I think what happened," she said, "what happened was almost an act of purification. What happened was something that had to happen—the painting had to pass through a crucible. Something had to cleanse what was here, had to clarify it, so that things that couldn't be seen before could be seen now."

Sometimes if you smash a piece of pottery and can glue it back together, what you have is more interesting than what you started with. The cracks, the running veins, create a webbed beauty that didn't exist before. Something like that had happened here. Putting pieces of the canvas together had broken down the substance of the paint itself, converting it into waves and particles of pentacost light.

"Remember what I said about his cries?" She still wasn't looking at me, only at the table's collage. "I could hear his death cries in the paint?"

"Of course."

"They're even stronger now, clearer. It's like the gashes are letting more of his voice through."

Her voice: no sorrow, no ecstasy, stripped down, matter of fact. Just telling the naked truth.

I didn't say anything. All I remember was standing there, taking slow, deep breaths, intensely, hypnotically conscious.

The painting was so beautiful I thought the middle of my chest would split open.

Time went by, who knows how long. Neither of us spoke. Another official marker: Nothing left to say.

Even as I was leaving, her head never moved.

The steps of the stairs were buzzing under my feet. It was like the marble had been embedded with pebbles of radioactive quartz.

I'd never felt so alive in my life.

The painting had shaken me again. The painting, the new form of it, was touching me with the power of revelation. It was whispering to me, trying to tell me something, a forgotten message, like the echo in a face, a song, a sky. The painting was murmuring something about the way the mystery of God moves and flows, but the meaning was buried too far below the surface for thought to think it.

What was your name before you were born?

Outside. Shannon was gone. The planet was gone. Nothing but early morning summer. On a day like this they started building the first city, the 12 gates to the city.

Everything signified. The trees, the bushes, the light—everything carried weight, like letters from an unknown alphabet, like words that had never been spoken.

I wanted to laugh. I wanted to break out laughing, laughing like a kid at the world, laughing at myself, laughing because I just realized I was realizing.

The painting was trying to give me something, tell me a secret that was right here, in this breath I'm breathing right now, but it would take me a while to understand it. It would take some time to find out exactly what it meant.

###

Who The Hell Wrote This?

I worked as an Executive Editor at *Entertainment Weekly* for 11 years and (in two separate stints) at *People* magazine and people.com for 12 years. I often speak to young journalists and try to use myself as an example for inspiration—a guy who spent time in jail, rehab and a psych ward and somehow become a successful editor at Time Inc. and managed to stay sane and alive. I've tried to reflect those experiences in this book.

I owe much of my survival to my wife, Laurie. We've been married 41 years. And we still live together! In Garden City, N.Y.

Feel free to contact me.
Facebook: http://on.fb.me/l02cd4
Twitter: http://bit.ly/ii7Kn1
Many thanks,
Richard Sanders

Other Quinn McShane Books
[All available at Amazon, Kindle, iPad, Barnes & Noble and Smashwords.com]

The Dead Have A Thousand Dreams
The lit-crit take: A genre-bending, character-driven thriller, centering on themes of prophecy, mortality and salvation.

The pure plot pitch: He was told he had exactly eight days to live. By a blind psychic photographer. Okay, Wooly Cornell was plenty crazy—not to mention a huge asshole—but he asked me to help him. So I did. And as the countdown to his death started and I found myself facing threats, shootouts, a mysterious scarred woman and weird predictions that somehow managed to come true, I could only come to one conclusion: Fate is one strange thing to fight.

For a quick taste, please go to: http://bit.ly/oQ43KK

Tell No Lie, We Watched Her Die
The lit-crit take: A genre-bending, character-driven thriller, centering on themes of celebrity, addiction and survival.

The pure plot pitch: The sex tape of a famous actress suddenly turns up on the internet, showing her on the last night of her life. The full version is being offered for sale, and the reason for its high price goes way beyond celeb voyeurism. The video also contains a

clue to who killed her. That's why everyone is--
literally--dying to see it.

For a quick taste, please go to: http://bit.ly/orJgQu

The Lower Manhattan
Book of The Dead

The lit-crit take: A genre-bending, character-driven
thriller, centering on themes of redemption,
responsibility and spiritual freedom.

The pure plot pitch: Just before he dies in a
downtown hospital, a doctor passes along the half-
formula for a powerful new hallucinogenic drug. Find
the other half, and you've got a

miracle drug—one that can save lives, save the world,
and make a lot of money. Which, of course, makes it
worth
killing for.

For a quick taste, please go to: http://bit.ly/pjE5Sy

The Seventh Compass Point Of Death

The lit-crit take: A character-driven thriller, centering
on the themes of terrorism, understanding and hope.

The pure plot pitch: Here's bad day: Guy sets out to
rob a bank but ends up pulling a carjacking, and when

he's arrested a body is found in the trunk. The victim is a Sunni community leader, and why was he killed? Who killed him? The search for answers takes me into a homegrown Islamic terror underground, into plots, counterplots, deceptions and love affairs, all leading to an attack on a major NYC landmark.

For a quick taste, please go to: http://bit.ly/pjE5Sy

Dead Line

The lit-crit take: A genre-bending, character-driven, word-burning thriller about memory, identity and making peace with the past.

The pure plot pitch: Sure, we all know about arrogant, self-centered media executives. But how about one who served time as a teen for murdering her sister? And who suddenly believes she's possessed by the spirit of Indira Gandhi? And now, at the height of her power, a secret from her past is threatening to destroy her empire, while someone from that past is trying **to** take her life. Stop the damn presses!

For a quick taste, please go to: http://bit.ly/kHVjSl

Dead Heat

The Lit-Crit Take: A genre-bending, character-driven, word-burning literary thriller about politics, love and the haunting pain of memory.

The Pure Plot Pitch: I didn't know—or care—much about the tight race for governor of New York until someone took a shot at one of the candidates and killed his wife instead. The main suspect, it turns out, was an anti-government crazy (and a devoted quilter—yes, you heard that right) who once did time with me. So suddenly I'm trying to track him down, getting sucked into the panicky heart of a closely fought election campaign, into an affair with a troubled political operative, and into the dangerously surreal world of people who prefer casting their vote with a sniper's bullet.

For a quick taste, please go to 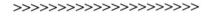 http://bit.ly/nVXk6Y

>>>>>>>>>>>>>>>>>>>>>>

Made in the USA
Monee, IL
02 October 2024

67040297R00240